SINGLE STEPS

An M Todd Gallowglas Sampler

*In these pages many mysteries are hinted at.
What if you come to understand one of them?*

*Words let water flow from an unseen, infinite ocean
Come into this place as energy for the dying and even the dead.*

*Bored onlookers, but with such light I our eyes!
As we read this book, the jewel-lights intensify.*

- Rumi

Thanks for being an awesome fan girl!!

M. Todd Gallowglas

Table of Contents

M. Todd Gallowglas

4

THE GOBLIN KING IS DEAD
For David Bowie

All across the world, children went to bed a little easier. Most were satisfied with just one story. They didn't ask for another glass of water or plead for "Five more minutes...two more minutes... One more minute..." You see, children knew something their parents didn't, because children were still in touch with the magic of the world, they still listened to the whispers that crawled up from the deep shadows and danced upon the fluttering of the crispest winds.

Children had heard the call during recess, walking home from school, taking care of their chores, and while avoiding doing their homework. Normally, not every child hears every secret that bubbles up from the Hidden World, but something like this...they all hear, one way or another.

And so, the children of the world played a little harder, their food tasted a little better, and bed time was not at all terrifying. Every aspect of their young lives brightened, though not at the cry of, "The Goblin King is dead!"

Rather...

Because they had not heard the cry that normally followed...

"Long live the king!"

For the Goblin King had two sons and a daughter, and each of his offspring refused to take the throne, not because they didn't want it, but because their father was so great a king, so feared, that each believed they could never live up to his legacy, could never steal away as many human children as he had.

Then, the morning after the Goblin King had died, his daughter went to his sons and said, "What if we leave the throne vacant for a time, and have a contest to see which one of us should take it."

"What kind of contest?" both of her brothers asked at the same time.

"The contest lasts for a year and a day," she replied. "After that, whoever stole the most human children takes the throne. That should ratchet up their fear."

5

Both of her brothers grinned their wild grins, showing off twin rows of nasty teeth. That plan was just the thing to terrify the children into truly fearing the change in leadership within the Goblin Kingdom.

That night, bedtimes became harder as children wanted two more stories, yet another glass of water, and, "Fifteen more minutes...fifteen more minutes...five more minutes." All through the day, they heard a new cry bubbling up from the Hidden World, something they had never heard before. "We are coming for you. We...are...coming..."

TEARS OF RAGE
Part One:
First Chosen

For Robin
Without her, there wouldn't be a Julianna.

Acknowledgements

I would like to thank the following people for their continuous support in this journey I started on when I was a little boy and first realized I wanted to tell stories through the written word: My dad for getting me the very first fantasy novel, and then getting me even more despite the fact I don't think he understood the obsession. My mom, for giving me permission to dream as big as I wanted. Damon Stone, for dreaming big with me and also helping to keep me from getting lost in those dreams. Aunt Penny, for getting it and calling me on my crap. Jim Czajkowski and Dave Meek, for believing that I had it in me. Steve Moore, Pat "Snipe" Ruele, and Trey Cromwell for letting me play in the cool kids' club. Bill Watters and Marti Miernik for giving me a venue to build the best fan base a storyteller could hope to have. Steven Erikson, who taught me how far I could push the envelope of fantasy fiction. Matthew Clark Davidson and Alice La Plante, the two teachers who demanded more of my story-telling than anyone else, before or since; I've tried to live up to your expectations. Ashlin Ferguson, for keeping me from going out in public with my fly down. Ed Litfin, for the awesome cover.

Finally, Robert and Mathew, for being the coolest kids in the world.

SINGLE STEPS

Dramatis Personæ

The Komati

Julianna Taraen – A duchess celebrating her twenty-first birthday.
Alyxandros Vivaen – A count. Julianna's uncle.
Maerie Vivaen – A countess. Wife of Alyxandros. Julianna's aunt on her father's side.
Khellan Dubhan – A baron, suitor to Julianna
Ingram Dashette – A viscount, friend of Khellan.
Jansyn Collaen – A baronet, friend of Khellan.
Sophya Mandak – Julianna's friend.
Perrine Raelle – Julianna's friend.
Sylvie Raelle – Perinne's little sister.
Bryce Anssi – A drunk

Kingdom of the Sun

Octavio Salvatore – Kingdom Governor of Koma
Dante Salvatore – Octavio's younger brother
Hardin Thorinson – Adept of Old Uncle Night.
Carmine D'Mario – Half-blood noble both of the House Floraen and of Komati blood.
Nicco D'Mario – Carmine's younger brother
Luciano Salvatore – House Floraen Inquisitor
Santo Salvatore – House Floraen Inquisitor
Roark – Adept of Old Uncle Night

Commoners

Raenard – A Komati soldier
Maerik – A Komati soldier
Saeryn – A Komati soldier
Theordon Barristis – Man at arms to Alyxandros Vivaen
Colette – Julianna's maid
Faelin vara'Traejyn – a bastard wanderer
Jorgen – A Kingdom soldier

Celestials, Infernals, and Others

Grandfather Shadow – Known also as Galad'Ysoysa. A Greater God.
Yrgaeshkil – The Mother of Daemyns, Goddess of Lies.
Kahddria – Goddess of Wind
Skaethak – Goddess of Winter
Innaya – An Aengyl

Kaeldyr the Gray – a Saent of Grandfather Shadow
Nae'Toran'borlahisth – A Daemyn
Razka – A Stormseeker
The King of Order
The Lords of Judgment
Maxian
Kavala

PROLOGUE

Why do people consider being touched by divine powers to be a blessing? – Talmoinan the White

She will come to the world when man and Daemyn fight together against the heavens. Born of wolf's cunning and man's wit, she will be blessed thrice by seven, seven by thrice. Once those blessings are spent, her anguish will give truth to what she forgot. – Attributed to the Blind Prophet

M. Todd Gallowglas

ONE

Blessed by Once

In the moments before Julianna's birth, Kaeldyr flew on wings of shadow toward the one chance to save his god. His flight through the spirit world was a calculated balance of speed and stealth. He had only remained undetected this long by traveling in hidden corners of the World Between Worlds; however, he would have to interact with the mortal realm soon. Once that happened, his intentions could no longer remain hidden. Then the celestial powers would intervene.

Even though it was the middle of the night when Kaeldyr arrived at the manor house, everyone in the household was wide awake. Servants scurried through the hallways. The lady of the house was with child, and her labor pains had started earlier that day. Even the barrier between worlds barely muffled the noise as her cries echoed through the halls. In the physical realm she must have been deafening.

Entering the birthing room, Kaeldyr looked down upon the lady. The sheets clung to her sweat-soaked body. Her eyes, deep gray like a storm rolling in from an angry sea, blinked through the tears. A midwife sat next to the lady's head. She whispered to the lady in a calming voice and dabbed the lady's forehead with a wet cloth. Another midwife sat at the far end of the bed, swaddling clothes ready. Surrounding each of the midwives, Kaeldyr saw a nimbus of light, shifting and multicolored, revealing the strength and age of their souls. Despite the physical age of their current lives, both possessed relatively young souls. The oldest of them had only been reborn five times. The light of the lady's soul was different, as her kind only had one life. Where the midwives' souls were rainbows of bright, vibrant colors, the lady's soul was shades of blue, gray, and white.

Looking past the flaring emotions of the lady and the two midwives, Kaeldyr saw the reason he'd come: a fourth soul in the room, the lady's unborn child, a soul who had never seen life. The baby's soul was nearly pure white, with edges of blue and gray. This unborn child, unscarred by the cycle of life, death, and rebirth, possessed nearly infinite potential and possibility. As it was with souls born into the world for the first time, this child would possess a strength of spirit unknown by all but a few. No matter what path these children took, their lives almost always changed the world.

This child was going to free Kaeldyr's god, Grandfather Shadow.

Pushing his finger through the woman's abdomen, Kaeldyr touched the unborn soul. In all his centuries as a celestial being, Kaeldyr had never done such a thing. Touching this soul was like tasting sweetened fruit tea, smelling a rose, and listening to a mother's lullaby – all through his fingers. As he probed the soul, he felt like it – no, not it, *she*; this was definitely a girl – she examined him in return. The sweetness that Kaeldyr felt turned slightly salty, though not enough to be unpleasant. She seemed to be asking, *What are you?*

He smiled, drew on his faith, and whispered in Grandfather Shadow's divine language, speaking a miracle. Written words formed in the air as Kaeldyr spoke, the letters appearing in the spider-web scrawl of Grandfather Shadow's alphabet. The words hung in the air for a moment, then floated down and settled into the unborn girl's soul. Even with all the divine powers Grandfather Shadow had bestowed upon him as Saent Kaeldyr the Gray, Kaeldyr chose to use the power of miracle, a power available only to humans. Within moments, all but the faintest shred of his faith belonged to the girl. His faith would lie buried deep in the folds of the girl's dreams, waiting for her moment of greatest need. When that moment came, she would release Grandfather Shadow from his imprisonment.

"Stop!" shouted a voice behind him.

"*Mina suoda, Thanya'taen,*" Kaeldyr spoke the miracle and summoned the ancient sword to his free hand.

The sword was long and thin, forged of a metal that mortals had come to call Faerii steel. The hilt was bound in black leather and silver wire. It was long enough to be used with two hands, but the blade was thin and light enough that the wielder could fight one-handed if he chose. Runes in Grandfather Shadow's divine language had been etched into the lower half of the blade, declaring the weapon's name.

Thanya'taen. Tears of Rage.

Kaeldyr turned.

Three Aengyls stood facing him, appearing mostly human but for their feathered wings, taloned feet, and bird-like heads. The closest Aengyl had the head of a great horned owl. Two with the heads of eagles flanked it. They regarded him with eyes that glowed pure white. Each held a sword of shining light.

"Saent Kaeldyr," said the owl-headed Aengyl, "the King of Order commands you to step aside."

"No."

A moment later, Stormseekers in wolf form and Stormcrows in avian form surrounded him, growling and cawing their defiance. These Faerii creatures bound to Grandfather Shadow formed a wall between Kaeldyr and the Aengyls.

So long as the girl was unborn, her soul could be sent into the Dark Realm of the Godless Dead to be cast outside the cycle of life, death, and rebirth. Her body would be stillborn, and Kaeldyr's faith would evaporate, sacrificed for nothing. Kaeldyr had to hold them until the child was born. After that, the ancient treaty between the King of Order, the Lords of Judgment, and the Princes of Chaos would protect the girl.

"You have one chance to avoid punishment," the owl said. "Stand aside."

"No."

The Aengyls raised their swords. Kaeldyr smiled and tightened his grip on *Thanya'taen*. He had been waiting for this moment since the Battle of Ykthae Wood.

"Attack," he said.

The Stormcrows flew in first, lightning sparkling along their talons. They did not damage the Aengyls, but they weren't meant to. They were only a distraction. After the tempest of talons, wings, and feathers, the Stormseekers followed, snapping at the Aengyl's arms, legs, and wings.

In the midst of that assault, Kaeldyr dove to his right and lunged forward. He brought his sword up, severing an eagle-headed Aengyl's sword arm. White light shone from the amputated limb. A screech pierced through the spirit world, and Kaeldyr knew he wouldn't get in another lucky shot.

Ducking under a cut from the owl-headed Aengyl, Kaeldyr spun, blocked a second cut aimed at his head, and lashed out with a counter. His blade nearly sliced into the Aengyl's neck. At the last moment, the Aengyl's wing flapped up, blocking Kaeldyr's blow. Sword and wing met, producing a shower of feathers.

The Stormseekers darted in and out of the third Aengyl's sword range, keeping him from joining the fight against Kaeldyr.

The one-armed Aengyl rushed in under Kaeldyr's guard and grappled him around the hips. Not bothering to try and free himself, Kaeldyr parried the owl's attacks. He didn't need to win. He only needed to last a few more moments.

The eagle grappling with him plunged its beak into Kaeldyr's side. He screamed as pain burned through him. The owl took advantage of that opening and thrust its sword at Kaeldyr's head.

Another sword – a black blade that pulsed with a cold sickness – came out of nowhere and parried the Aengyl's blow. Something pulled away the Aengyl on Kaeldyr's waist. A Daemyn stood next to him, sword of black flames dancing in its hand. It smiled and beckoned to the Aengyls.

Kaeldyr recognized the newcomer. Leathery wings rose from its back, and ram's horns sprouted from behind its bat-like ears. Its short name was Nae'Toran. Kaeldyr had fought the creature several times in the Second War of the Gods, finally defeating and humiliating him at the Battle of Ykthae Wood. Nae'Toran launched himself at the Aengyls, and Kaeldyr followed; there was no time to question the Daemyn's presence now. With this creature's help, there was a greater chance to see the girl born.

Kaeldyr, the Stormseekers, Stormcrows, and the Daemyn fought hard against the Aengyls, but their numbers kept dwindling.

When more than half the wolves and crows were down, a voice came from the physical world, "It's a girl."

A moment later, the baby cried for the first time.

Now that the mortal world was affected, the King of Order could not change it.

"Name her Julianna," the mother gasped, "after Saent Julian the Courageous."

Kaeldyr hoped Julianna grew up to have more in common with Saent Julian than just a name. The girl would need all of Julian's bravery, and more.

"You failed," Kaeldyr said.

As Kaeldyr felt himself being pulled from the spirit world back into the celestial realms, he threw *Thanya'taen* away. He could not let anyone who was not a follower of Grandfather Shadow come to possess that weapon. Nae'Toran scrambled for it, but a large Stormcrow, larger than an eagle, snatched the weapon and flew down a path into the deep spirit, where the Daemyn couldn't follow.

"You have broken the celestial decree of the Ykthae Accord!" came a chorus of voices. The Lords of Judgment spoke as one. They were the Incarnates who maintained a balance of power between the King of Order, Princes of Chaos, and the Queen of Passion.

"I did," Kaeldyr said.

"You will be punished!"

"I am ready."

First they removed his word – *the Gray* – that Grandfather Shadow had blessed him with so many centuries ago. They ripped it from him without ceremony or trial. Without it, he was no longer a Saent, just a mortal husk in the celestial realms. His body aged to the state it had been in when he died: old, frail, and broken. It didn't matter, because then they shredded his body to nothing in the span of a heartbeat. He would have screamed, but he no longer had lungs or throat. Kaeldyr felt something caress his soul, the only piece of him that remained. It was Nae'Toran.

"They have given you to me as a warning to others who might follow in your footsteps." The Daemyn's smile held no warmth. "Your punishment is being my plaything until I am done with you, then your soul can rot away wherever I decide to drop it."

Then Kaeldyr, Grandfather Shadow's first high priest, named at the moment of his first death, Saent Kaeldyr the Gray, was removed completely from the cycle of life, death, and rebirth – exiled to the Dark Realm of the Godless Dead.

TWO

The spirit world was quiet. The lady's labor cries had ended with the birth of her daughter. The battle between the Saents, Aengyls, and Daemyns had chased away any spirits that might have taken residence here. In this silence, Yrgaeshkil, wife of Old Uncle Night and mother of all Daemyns, lowered the Lie that hid her from the sight of men and Eldar, those beings that mortals called gods. This evening, she wore the form of one of her children, even though she despised it. She had a bat's head with deer's horns, and she wrapped her leathery wings about her shoulders like a cloak.

Nae'Toran bowed before her.

"It is done, Mother," her son said. "Soon you will be able to take your rightful place among the celestial hierarchy."

Yrgaeshkil was a Lesser Eldar, with command over but a single dominion, the dominion of Lies; however, she wanted more. No, she *needed* more. The desire for it burned in her the way she imagined that mortals desired sex and strong drink. She had instigated two wars that had raged throughout all the realms in her quest to command more Dominions and achieve a place among the Greater Eldar.

At the very end of the Second War, Yrgaeshkil had finally gained a second dominion, and then promptly lost it again. This had been the greatest stroke of luck any being, celestial, infernal, or mortal had ever received. Shortly after Yrgaeshkil had lost her second dominion, the King of Order had imprisoned the five Greater Eldar. Had she maintained control of that second dominion, she would have been imprisoned too. Several of the other Lesser Eldar had argued that Yrgaeshkil should be imprisoned as well, but the King of Order could only abide by the letter of his decree, no matter what the spirit of that decree was.

"How long will you wait before forcing the child to use Kaeldyr's gift?" Nae'Toran asked.

"Seven years should be sufficient."

"Seven years? Why so long?"

Yrgaeshkil shook her head. Even with all his centuries of existence, her son still had not learned patience.

"Seven is a number sacred to Grandfather Shadow, and since Kaeldyr's faith is attuned to that god, it seems appropriate. The girl will need to grow old enough to learn about Grandfather Shadow. I've waited nearly a thousand years for circumstances to be this perfect. I can wait a little while longer."

Yrgaeshkil peered between the worlds as the lady nursed her daughter, her little Julianna. The pure, near-white of the girl's soul shone between the worlds, declaring her strength to any creature who knew what to look for. Yes, this Julianna was going to change everything.

THREE

Blessed by Twice

The night before her seventh birthday, Julianna woke up. It wasn't the slow waking that came naturally in the morning, with the sunlight peeking through the curtains. This was a quick waking in the middle of the night, the kind of waking that came when the nightmares grew too much for her to bear, when those eyes wouldn't stop staring at her from within the darkness of her mind's eye. However, this time, the nightmares hadn't come, and those eyes had been absent from her mind more and more.

Her room was dark. Moonlight shone through the small space between her curtains making a ghostly line of white in the middle of her black floor.

She heard voices downstairs. Did Mother and Father have guests? She didn't recall a formal supper being planned, and while her parents' friends would occasionally surprise them with an evening visit, it would be unusual for them to stay this late.

Perhaps Mother and Father were speaking to Julianna's nurse, preparing her for the next day when the nurse's services would no longer be needed. Julianna smiled at the thought of that conversation. After tomorrow, Julianna would never have to suffer her nurse – who she always thought of as *that woman* – again.

Footsteps echoed throughout the house, and Julianna thought she heard the fourth step of the main stairs creak. It had been like that for years, and both Mother and Father refused to get it fixed. The stair creaked again, and again. Someone said something. Julianna couldn't understand the words, but the tone sounded like Father speaking to one of his followers who had disobeyed him.

A gunshot sounded. Julianna tensed so much that her heart seemed to stop. Her breath came in quick in-and-out blasts through clenched teeth. This wasn't the first time someone attacked the house, and it wouldn't be the last – Father and Mother had many enemies throughout the Kingdom – but this was the first time anyone had ever fired a gun in the manor.

Firearms were illegal; possessing one was a capital offense in the Kingdom of the Sun. The estate had never been as quiet as it was in the few moments that followed that gunshot. Another gunshot sounded, and fighting broke the silence. Julianna's heart sped up as if it needed to catch those beats it had lost in the silence. She gripped her blankets and pulled the covers over her head.

The door opened. She held her breath and tightened every part of her body to be perfectly still. The door closed. She bit her lip to keep quiet.

"Julianna?" Mother's voice whispered from the other side of the blanket.

Julianna leapt from her bed. "Mother? I heard gunshots. Are they in the house?"

"Help me with the sheets," Mother said.

Together they stripped the bed. All the while fighting continued in other parts of the house. Steel clashed. Gunshots rang out. Mother made a long rope out of the sheets, tied one end to the foot of Julianna's wardrobe, and tossed the other end out the window. Julianna took a step toward the window, but Mother grabbed her and pushed her under the bed. A moment later, Mother joined her amongst the dust, forgotten toys, and spiders.

"Take this, Julianna," Mother said. "It will protect you against anything less than a god."

Mother pushed something into Julianna's hands. She looked down. It was one of Father's knives. The blade was nearly as long as her arm and twice as wide as her thumb. It had a single word etched into the blade in the language of the god Mother and Father worshipped.

Kostota.

"Listen to me, Julianna," Mother whispered. Mother only used Julianna's proper name when she was angry or very serious. Any other time, Julianna was *Little Duchess*. "If they find us, I want you to fight. Fight like the forty-nine Morigahnti at the Battle of Ykthae Wood. Fight to make your father proud. Fight hard enough to make them kill you." Mother shook Julianna's shoulders. "Do you understand me? Do not let them take you while you live."

Julianna nodded and gripped her weapon. "I understand."

"Now quiet," Mother said.

Julianna buried her face in Mother's shoulder.

They waited. Julianna couldn't tell how long. She tried to track the time by counting her heartbeats but lost count well before one hundred.

Eventually, the sounds of fighting diminished. Julianna tried to crawl out from under the bed. Mother grabbed her and pulled her tighter. Footsteps echoed on the upper floor. They came closer and closer. The door opened and light spilled in. People came into Julianna's room. She couldn't help but glance at their feet. She saw between six and eight pairs of legs.

"They're gone."

"Check the wardrobe."

Both voices belonged to men.

Feet moved across the floor. She heard her wardrobe doors open, and her favorite outfits started to fall on the floor.

"Adept," another voice said. "The sheets aren't long enough to reach to the ground safely."

They would check under the bed next, Julianna knew it. Her breath quickened as she imagined what horrors these men intended. Julianna squirmed out of Mother's grasp and slid out from under the foot of her bed. There hadn't been any feet there, and the men wouldn't be able to see her crouched low. Julianna decided the dumbwaiter was their only chance. Mother could fit inside of it if she squeezed.

A hand closed on Julianna's shoulder and yanked her back. She shifted her grip on the knife like Father had shown her. She jabbed backward with the blade, and the air in front of her shimmered with motes of silver light. A wolf appeared from out of that light and leapt over Julianna's head. Julianna didn't have to look back when she heard a gurgled cry to know the wolf had clasped its jaws onto the man's throat.

Julianna scrambled for her escape. Another hand grabbed her, this time by her hair. The strong grip nearly pulled her off her feet.

Julianna gritted her teeth and sucked in a deep breath that cooled her mouth. She reached out for the dumbwaiter with her mind, she thought about being there a few moments ago. There was a flash of silver light, and then Julianna was next to the dumbwaiter.

She scrambled inside. Looking back, she saw a figure in black hardened-leather armor with an oversized skull for the helmet. The Brotherhood of the Night. Father's most hated enemies, and servants of the God of Death, Old Uncle Night. The terrifying figure held onto her past self, but paused when he saw her double appear at the dumbwaiter. Julianna watched herself sink the knife into her attacker's leg. Then a wolf appeared in a shower of light and ripped out the attacker's throat.

Flashes of light appeared throughout the room, and the she-wolf seemed to be everywhere at once. Then three more Nightbrothers ran into the room carrying staves made of some silver metal. They struck the staves together, and a brilliant light shone in the room. It was so bright Julianna had to look away.

When she looked back, the she-wolf was gone, and the men in black armor held Mother pinned to the floor. Mother tried to move, tried to shift through the world as Julianna had done. A nimbus of silvery light formed around her, but the three staves came together, the room filled with light again, and Mother remained trapped. Julianna started out of the dumbwaiter.

"No!" Mother screamed. "Run! Find your father."

Julianna pulled on the rope inside the waiter as hard as she could.

"Let her go," the man said. "She won't go far. Besides, it's the husband we want. Get her clothes off and he'll find us."

Laughter echoed behind those skull masks.

Julianna knew she could call for help. Something from deep in that place where she remembered her dreams hours or days later told her she had someone who would help her. She wanted to speak the words, but couldn't. She could only ask once, and the help had to be for her and only for her.

Instead, she locked eyes with the one who looked like the leader, the only one without a white skull masking his face.

"My father's god is going to eat your soul!" Julianna yelled as she hurried downward.

FOUR

Yrgaeshkil wanted to scream. She paced back and forth in the darkness of a copse of trees watching the battle raging around the manor house. Morigahnti, the followers of Grandfather Shadow, fought against the Brotherhood of the Night. Even though the Brotherhood warriors outnumbered the Morigahnti more than three to one, the battle was going against the Brotherhood. They did not have the advantage of firearms, and only one in six or so of the Brotherhood could channel divine power as miracles, whereas nearly half of the Morigahnti could.

She wanted to kill someone. No. She specifically wanted to kill the scarred-faced man standing next to her. But she couldn't. Kavala was a necessary component of too many of her schemes. Even if she didn't need him, Yrgaeshkil wasn't sure she could contain her power in her current mood. Getting noticed wandering around the physical realm was the last thing she wanted.

Somehow, Julianna had managed to escape the initial attack. The girl had gotten out of the building, and her grandfather had spirited her away to who knew where or even when. It couldn't be too far. The girl's human blood would make shifting her over too great a distance impossible, but a Stormseeker could still travel beyond reach very quickly in a series of rapid, short jumps.

The only consolation to this failure was the Morigahnti corpses that littered the ground outside the manor; unfortunately, this was countered by an even greater number of her husband's followers. While Yrgaeshkil didn't actually care about these mortals in the greater scheme, she needed them for the time being as she built her own powerbase.

Yrgaeshkil turned to the man known as Kavala. "You promised me it would happen."

Even though the left side of his face was a mangled mass of cuts and scars, she could see the boredom in the way his gaze would not quite meet hers and how his shoulders rocked slightly back and forth.

"It should have," he replied, looking past her to the house. "I cannot control the men if they attack the wrong person, especially from out here. I recall wanting to lead the attack myself."

"It matters not," Yrgaeshkil snarled through her teeth. "In seven years, I will ensure that she calls him forth."

FIVE

Blessed by Thrice

Julianna should have been celebrating her fourteenth birthday. She should have been treated to one of the finest meals of her life, danced with handsome and powerful young lords, and been introduced to all the other nobles of House Kolmonen and their allies. These thoughts plagued her – should-haves and could-haves dancing about her in feverish visions.

A fire burned in the hearth of Julianna's bedroom, but its heat could not compare to the fever that burned inside of her. She lay wrapped in thick down blankets to help protect her from the chill of an early winter. Sometimes in Koma, the autumn storms came in midsummer, which brought winter early. Having snow storms in summer was rare, but not unheard of. This early winter had also brought sickness.

Julianna slid her hand under the pillow and gripped the hilt of her mother's dagger. Even though it had been under her pillow for days, the hilt was still cool to the touch. It was the only thing Julianna possessed that had belonged to either of her parents. Sometimes, late at night, she would stare at the weapon by candlelight and try and decipher the single word etched into either side of the blade, *Kostota*. She felt as though there had been a time when she had known what that word meant, but like so many things from before the fire killed her parents, she couldn't seem to remember, no matter how hard she tried.

Faces swam above her bed: Mother with her piercing gray eyes, Father with the scar that ran down his face, and her cousins. Her cousins were gone, just like her parents. The fever had not addled Julianna so much that she could not hear a death bell ring twice in the last week. The first time it rang, it sounded twenty-three times for Marcus's age. The second time, two days later, it rang sixteen times for Raechel.

Nobody had told Julianna about their deaths. She knew because no one mentioned Marcus or Raechel in her presence. Once, Julianna had asked after her cousins. "Just worry about resting," was the reply, "everything will be fine."

The bells would ring for her next, unless some miracle saved her. At the thought of a miracle, all the faces vanished. A pair of dark eyes replaced them. She didn't remember much before she came to live with her aunt and uncle, but she felt that those eyes had always been with her, just like the words that swam in the back of her mind, words that she could speak and receive aid. She didn't know what form the aid would take, and she'd never wanted to ask for it, because for some reason, she felt that she could only call for that help once.

Well, she was about to die. If she was ever going to satisfy her curiosity, she would have to take that offer of help now. She licked her lips. She hadn't spoken a word in days. Just as she began to form the first syllable, the door opened. The light from the hall hurt Julianna's eyes. She let go of the knife to shield her eyes.

Two people entered. She recognized Uncle Alyx's short and wiry silhouette. As usual when he was at home, Uncle Alyx wore his hair down and the graying strands fell around his shoulders. The other man was more than a head taller than Uncle Alyx. Even in the dim light from the hall, Julianna saw that he wore tan leathers and furs like the wild Dosahan to the west.

The stranger came right up to Julianna's bed and leaned over her.

"I'm glad that you were able to come," Uncle Alyx said. "This sickness has taken so many already."

"I'm sorry I couldn't be here in time to help Marcus and Raechel." The man's voice sounded familiar.

"The fault is mine for not thinking of you sooner," Uncle Alyx said. "I was too lost in my own grief."

"Your family was dying around you," the other man said. "I understand how that can cloud your thinking." The other man looked Julianna over. "She is bad, but it's not too late. Julianna, you have to drink this."

The man slid his hand under the pillow. He lifted her head, and the room swam in Julianna's vision. Something touched her lips, a cup or bowl of some kind. She sniffed at it. It smelled like spoiled beer mixed with seaweed. Her stomach tightened. She clamped her lips shut between her teeth and tried to turn her head away.

"Colette," the man said. "Hold her head."

Colette had been Raechel's maid.

A pair of small, cool hands grasped each side of Julianna's head. There was not much strength in them, but in her sickened state Julianna could not free herself. Another hand, this one rough and calloused, covered her nose. Again, the vessel containing the nauseating concoction came to her lips and pushed its way between them. The liquid scalded her tongue. She tried to spit it out, but another calloused hand covered her mouth. She could swallow or choke. She swallowed.

The rough hands released her, and she gasped for breath.

"She must drink a mouthful of this every five hours," the man said. "Then she will live."

"Yes, my lord," Colette replied.

There was a flutter of wind in Julianna's room, and then the man was gone.

"Watch over her, Colette," Uncle Alyx said.

"Yes, my lord," Colette replied with a curtsy.

Once Uncle Alyx left the room, Colette sat on the edge of the bed. Julianna heard soft splashes next to the bed. A moment later, a damp cloth touched her brow.

"Don't worry, my lady," Colette's soft voice said. "I'll take care of you."

"Julianna." Julianna's voice came out in a whisper through her dry throat.

"Excuse me, my lady?"

Julianna swallowed. It didn't help much. "When we're alone together," she took a breath, "call me Julianna."

"Yes, my..." Colette paused, as if speaking a noble's proper name was a blasphemy she dared not risk. "Julianna." After a moment, she spoke again, "Julianna," this time with more courage. "We'll see you though this, Julianna."

SIX

Yrgaeshkil stepped to the side, fleeing the room where Julianna had again failed to call for aid in what should have been her most desperate moment. The Goddess of Lies appeared in her husband's throne room and collapsed into the throne of bones and dried human flesh. She had fled in fear, but not the fear that something ill might befall her. Yrgaeshkil fled because she feared that she might kill Julianna. Yrgaeshkil needed the girl alive if she ever hoped to gain more dominions. This plan would not likely work a second time.

There was a commotion in the throne room. Yrgaeshkil looked up.

Daemyns scurried this way and that, heading for the tunnels that led out of the throne room. Well, it wouldn't be as satisfying as killing the girl, but it might help her mood a bit. She let out a howl full of such fury that it shredded several of the slower creatures. She looked at the mangled, bloody remains and sighed. It hadn't helped.

"I take it that the sickness failed, Mother," Nae'Toran asked. He had wisely remained next to the throne, out of her direct sight.

"Yes," Yrgaeshkil said.

The illness had been a calculated risk – much riskier than any other part of her plan had been. She had drawn on her husband's power over the dominion of Sickness. If she'd used even a breath more of it, the King of Order might have accused her of usurping the dominion and imprisoned her for becoming a Greater Eldar.

"What am I going to do?" Her wailing voice echoed throughout the throne room.

"Might I make a suggestion, Mother?" Nae'Toran asked.

"Speak."

Nae'Toran told her his plan.

"Yes. Yes, of course. You are the only one who has managed to get anything right in this scheme. In seven years, I will send you to finish what you started. But do not fail me."

"Never, Mother," Nae'Toran said. "I am no flawed mortal. She will speak the words. And you will know your heart's desire at long last."

CELEBRATION OF BIRTH

The moment the greater gods were imprisoned was the first moment mankind commanded its own destiny. – Talmoinan the White

Grandfather Shadow would rather have you defiant and full of cunning rather than meek and obedient in your faith. Let the other followers have their mindless drones who worship any words a priest gives to them. The other gods wish to be considered great by their followers. Grandfather Shadow wishes to be considered for his followers' greatness. – Kaeldyr, the first Lord Morigahn

M. Todd Gallowglas

ONE

Julianna sat at breakfast on the morning of her twenty-first birthday, the traditional day of Komati adulthood, and just as with the sickness when she was fourteen, the gods threatened to take this day from her as well – unless, of course, Julianna defied the gods. And why shouldn't she? It was her life, her memories of a day she would carry until she died.

Julianna leaned forward, clutched both hands to her stomach, and made a gagging sound. At the other end of the table, Aunt Maerie nibbled on carefully cut bits of pastries while Uncle Alyxandros sipped at his tea and read a letter. Breakfast had been a simple affair, consisting of porridge, fruits, and tea. They had to save room for all the food at the introduction supper when Julianna would officially meet Duke Martyn Collaen, a boorish oaf of a man who had expressed interest in a political marriage between Julianna and himself.

"What better way to enter into the adult world," Aunt Maerie had said, "than to accept the hand of one of the wealthiest and most powerful men in Koma."

The thought of being courted by Duke Martyn, a man nearly twice Julianna's twenty-one years, made her stomach churn. She gripped the table with her right hand, and groaned, "Gods and goddesses."

Aunt Maerie's fork stopped halfway between the plate and her mouth. She set the fork down without as much as a *clink* on the plate and folded her hands together. Her lips formed a thin line as her face tightened so that Julianna could see every one of the worry lines in the old woman's face – lines that Aunt Maerie claimed came from watching over Julianna. Uncle Alyxandros looked up from his letter. His gaze met Julianna's, and she thought she saw the left corner of his mouth creep up a bit. As always, she could gain no insight from his deep brown eyes.

"Julianna." Aunt Maerie stared straight ahead and her lips barely moved. She spoke in the same, almost singsong tone she used when her undersized dogs wouldn't perform their tricks properly for guests. "I won't tolerate that language at—"

"Maerie," Uncle Alyxandros said.

"Alyx, do not attempt to defend her—"

Uncle Alyxandros cleared his throat, cutting off Aunt Maerie's protests. She opened her mouth, but he waved his letter toward Julianna. The instant she had Aunt Maerie's attention, Julianna took her hand from the table and covered her mouth.

"Permission to be excused?" Julianna said between quick breaths. "Please?"

The crow's feet at Aunt Maerie's eyes softened and her lips relaxed. "By all means, dear."

A brief twinge of guilt twisted into a knot a few inches behind Julianna's naval. Aunt Maerie had spent a considerable amount of time arranging this dinner with Duke Martyn. Many other high ranking men from other noble families would also be there – on the chance that Duke Martyn did not take a fancy to Julianna. Then Julianna recalled a party not even two months ago. Duke Martyn's hand seemed unable to resist pinching the breasts and bottom of every girl, and even a few of the boys, who served him that night.

"Thank you." The words came out in a quick whisper as Julianna bolted from the table.

In her haste, she knocked her chair over. The crash startled one of the new servant girls, who dropped a tea set. Shards of white porcelain and hot tea sloshed across the floor as the girl danced away from the shattered tea pot and cups. Julianna gave neither the accident nor the gaping-mouthed servant any attention as she fled the room. Her maid followed behind her.

Just as Julianna had planned, one of the downstairs maids waited right outside the door. Just like the girl who had dropped the tea pot, this maid had only recently come to the estate in the past few months. Aunt Maerie hadn't had time to burn their faces into her memory yet, which made them perfect for helping Julianna avoid Martyn Collaen. The maid stood with a bowl of watery gruel that also contained just a bit of bile from inside a lamb's stomach.

"Are you sure, my lady?" the girl asked.

"Do it," Julianna said. The illusion of sickness had to be perfect.

The maid dumped the noxious mixture on Julianna's sitting dress and the floor in front of her. As the mixture soaked into the fabric, the girl squeaked and fled.

Julianna made vomiting noises. She had spent many parties, balls, and dinners listening to men vomit up their excess liquor. Sometimes, she'd even sought out opportunities to listen to this activity in order to imitate those noises. One never knew when one might need to invent an excuse not to attend an outing or an appointment. The maid shoved the bowl into a nearby plant just as Aunt Maerie followed Julianna out of the breakfast room.

Behind Julianna, Colette and Aunt Maerie came out of the sitting room.

"Aunt Maerie," Julianna said in her weakest voice. She gestured at the mess all over the front of her dress.

Aunt Maerie brought her hand up to cover her nose. She looked about, up and down the hall. "You! Girl!"

The maid who had helped Julianna hadn't quite gotten around the far corner. She squeaked even louder as she stopped and turned around. Julianna felt that she might actually vomit. Had Aunt Maerie seen?

Aunt Maerie waved at the mess on the floor. "Run to the kitchens, get some hot water, and clean this up."

The girl curtsied and hurried off. Julianna took a breath, not realizing she'd been holding it.

"Oh, Julianna," Aunt Maerie said, taking in the sight of Julianna. "Your favorite dress."

It wasn't Julianna's favorite. She hated the vile thing, though she had worn it more frequently than any other in the past month. Aunt Maerie had urged Julianna to add variety to her wardrobe, claiming that the dress did nothing to enhance Julianna's complexion or her beautiful eyes. Julianna had countered by reminding Aunt Maerie that no one besides her, Uncle Alyxandros, and the servants ever saw Julianna in the dress, so it didn't matter how unflattering it was.

Julianna made several gagging noises as if she were going to vomit again, and then started off toward her room. After five paces, she clutched at her stomach and leaned on the wall. She wanted to hear any words her aunt and her maid might exchange.

"After her, Colette," Aunt Maerie said. "Your mistress needs you."

"Shall she be needing me to bring her breakfast?" Colette asked.

Don't overdo it, Julianna thought, though she could see the image of Colette's slightly faraway look as the maid spoke with Countess Maerie Vivaen. Colette was a more practiced deceiver than most of the high ranking lords and ladies that frequented court. Most servants were. It was a requirement of their position.

"Can't you see she's ill," Aunt Maerie asked. "She needs washing and a bed, not food. See that she gets them."

Colette dropped into a curtsy. "Yes, Excellency."

Julianna thanked all the lesser gods and goddesses at once. Half of her ruses and deceptions would never have succeeded if Colette did not play the part of the simpleminded maid so well.

A moment later, Julianna felt Colette's soft but firm grip on her arm. Together, they headed toward Julianna's suite, stopping every ten to fifteen paces for Julianna to feign another attack of her unsettled stomach.

Once they rounded the first corner, their pace quickened. They hurried past servants who were packing the multitude of paintings, tapestries, and stone busts that populated the walls and corners of her aunt and uncle's summer home.

Summerrain, a small estate of forty-nine rooms, had been in Aunt Maerie's family for over a dozen generations. It harkened back to a time when barbaric men still tried to unseat each other from horseback using lances and other weapons without the least bit of finesse. Aunt Maerie had done her best to disguise the inner antiquity of the estate by having the floors carpeted and the walls covered by as much art as she could. One of the servants' houses had been converted into an artist's house. Throughout the late spring and summer, Julianna had been forced to sit for a painter or a sculptor at least once a week. Aunt Maerie seemed to believe that Summerrain's halls could only be brightened by cramming them with as many renditions of Julianna and Uncle Alyxandros as possible.

When Julianna reached her rooms, she attempted to wriggle her way out of the sitting dress. Normally, this would not have been a challenging task, but she had an appointment, and every moment from her departure from the breakfast table to leaving the estate had been painstakingly planned. In the practice sessions at taking this dress off in a hurry, Julianna had forgotten to account for the vile concoction that soiled it. Her schedule only included time to quickly wash her body, but not her hair.

"Mistress," Colette said. "You're taking too long."

"I know that," Julianna snapped.

She stopped her wrestling match with the dress and went over to the bride's chest at the foot of her bed. It had belonged to her mother, and unlike many of the bride's chests young ladies used these days, this one was made to come apart. Each side, the top, and both bottoms – there was a false bottom about seven inches above the true bottom – were made of forty-nine interlocking pieces of carved ivory.

Young ladies used these chests to store anything they felt they might need for their wedding. When a man wished to marry a girl, he would ask her to gift him with her bride's chest. She was honor bound to grant him that gift. However, she was not required to give him the chest intact. If a lady disassembled the chest before giving it to a man, he had seven days to reconstruct it. If he did, she was honor bound to marry him. If the man truly repulsed the girl, she could always keep one piece from each surface so that finishing the chest became impossible. When he returned the uncompleted chest, she could then choose to reveal the seven missing pieces or not. That was the first challenge a Komati man must pass in his quest to win a bride.

Julianna opened the chest. "Colette, get the knife."

A knife lay hidden deep in the chest just above the secret compartment.

Colette thrust her hands into the chest, drew out the knife, and handed it to Julianna. From tip to pommel, the weapon was just a hair longer than Julianna's forearm. For the most part, it was a nondescript weapon. The hilt was a dark brown wood that nearly matched the dark brown of the leather sheath. The blade had a blood groove the length of Julianna's middle finger on one side. Aside from that, and the reddish tint of the blade, the weapon's only distinctive feature was a single word etched into the blade opposite the blood groove.

Kostota.

Julianna didn't know what the word meant, but every time she looked at it, she felt that she should know. She'd once shown it to Uncle Alyxandros, and he had quietly suggested that she might want to keep the knife hidden away, or better yet, dispose of it entirely. Julianna could not do that. It was one of two things she'd received from her mother. The other was her eyes. Her deep, piercing gray eyes were extremely rare in girls born of Komati blood, and they were nearly nonexistent in girls from other lands. It was the first of Julianna's features that most men complimented, and in doing so, they earned the first coin of Julianna's contempt. Complimenting her eyes was far too easy.

The knife sliced through the material of the dress, and in a moment, Julianna was free without any damage done to her hair. She tossed the dress into the chamber pot.

"Burn that horrid thing," she told Colette.

"Of course, Julianna," Colette replied. Then she pinched her nose with one hand as she balanced a tray holding a bowl of water, soap, and a washing cloth in the other. "But I know how much you loved it. I'll fetch the seamstress to commission a new one that is exactly the same."

Colette had perfected her imitation of Aunt Maerie's nasal tone.

"Oh, but Aunty," Julianna said in a tone of exaggerated innocence. "I couldn't possibly wear a counterfeit of the original, no matter how perfect. It just wouldn't do."

They both laughed and then composed themselves. They had only a minute or two before Aunt Maerie came to check on Julianna. Julianna slid the knife back into its sheath as Colette began to untie the strings of Julianna's morning corset. The door opened sooner than expected. Julianna dropped her knife, kicked it under her bed, and hurried to the window.

As planned, just outside the window, there was a splash of the same concoction that Colette had spilled over Julianna's dress. From the acidic smell wafting up from that mess, it hadn't been but a few moments since one of the other conspiring servants had spilled it there. The stable boy must have been waiting for the sound of their voices. Julianna couldn't suppress a small smile.

"Oh, you poor thing," Aunt Maerie said from behind Julianna. She still spoke in that condescending tone. Julianna's smile faded, and she clenched and unclenched her fists several times to keep from turning around and strangling her aunt. "Duke Martyn will be so disappointed."

Julianna turned around. "I can go." She kept one hand on her stomach and the other near her mouth. "Give me a few moments to recover."

"And allow you to embarrass me, your uncle, and yourself by rushing from the feast table, or worse, vomiting all over the high table at the main course?"

Julianna noticed where Aunt Maerie had placed herself in that list. Whenever she spoke of more than one person, Aunt Maerie always listed them in order of their importance. Oddly enough, Aunt Maerie usually named herself first.

"You will stay," Aunt Maerie continued. "Your Uncle and I will still attend and make our apologies to His Grace, *Duke* Martyn Collaen, Lord of Storm's Landing and Autumnwind. Did I mention that he has a seat on the Komati's advisory council to Governor Salvatore?"

"Yes, Aunt." *Only about forty-nine times.*

"*And,* did you also…"

Julianna stopped listening to Aunt Maerie's praise of Duke Martyn. She waved Colette to get the water and soap.

Gods and goddesses, Julianna thought. *Please let her leave.*

Instead of leaving, Aunt Maerie sat on the edge of Julianna's bed, and her foot came down on Julianna's knife. The weapon clattered against the stone floor.

"What's that?" Aunt Maerie asked and leaned forward.

Julianna stared at Colette. If Aunt Maerie found the knife, Julianna might not only lose today's activities; she might well lose the knife.

"Night below us," Julianna groaned and went to the window.

"Julianna!" Aunt Maerie cried. There was only so much profanity that she would forgive, even considering Julianna's illness.

With her back shielding her, Julianna shoved her finger into her throat. She gagged, but nothing else happened. With Aunt Maerie this close, Julianna couldn't trust her imitations. She needed to truly vomit. She wiggled her finger around, tickling her throat until her sides tightened and the porridge she had eaten spilled onto window sill and the ground outside. Julianna had never expected to go to this much trouble for a man.

"With all due respect, Your Excellency," Colette said in a demur tone. "I must ask you to leave so that I may attend my mistress."

Aunt Maerie sputtered. Julianna stayed leaning out the window, envisioning Colette gently leading the Countess of Summerrain to the door. The door closed.

Julianna stood up. Colette turned over a small sandglass that counted two minutes. As the sand poured from the top of the glass into the bottom, Julianna shifted from foot to foot. It would be so much easier to just jump forward a few minutes, but she might need the power to help her get out of Summerrain unnoticed. While she bounced up and down next to the window, watching the sand move in agonizing slowness, Colette turned down the blankets on the bed in case Aunt Maerie returned to check on them. That rarely occurred, but it had happened often enough to warrant caution.

At last, the final sands slid into the bottom of the glass. Julianna crossed the space between her and the glass in two long strides. She tipped the glass over and spread her arms. She and Colette had practiced changing from one outfit to the other twice a day for the last fortnight. By the time the top of the glass was empty again, Julianna was in her favorite burgundy velvet and black silk riding dress. Every time she looked at it, Julianna thanked the gods that Uncle Alyx could deny her nothing. All she had to do was tilt her head down, hunch her shoulders up, and give him a faint half-smile. It had worked ever since she'd recovered from her sickness when she was fourteen.

Once the dress was on, Julianna turned the sandglass a third and final time. Colette attacked Julianna's hair with brush, comb and hairpins – long, needle-like things that many men called "maiden's defenders." Julianna's dark hair was so long and thick that she needed between four and six, depending on the style of the braid. That morning, just to ensure the intricate braid remained intact throughout the day, Colette used seven. By the time the glass had emptied again, two curling ringlets fell across each of Julianna's ears, framing her face perfectly; the rest of her hair had been woven into a dozen braids that were pulled back into a bun and cascaded down her back.

Dressed and groomed, all Julianna had to do now was navigate the halls of Summerrain and get to the stables without being discovered by her aunt and uncle. Normally, this might be a challenge, but Julianna had arranged the work schedules so that all the servants who loved her more than they did the count or countess were on duty at this time. They were prepared to delay Uncle Alyx or Aunt Maerie with any number of questions or minor emergencies that could not wait.

Julianna opened the door. Uncle Alex leaned on the wall opposite her room, reading his letter. He glanced up through his spectacles. Julianna shut the door, grabbed Colette, and shifted backward in time a few moments.

"Wet cloth," Julianna said as she jumped into the bed and pulled the blankets up to her chin.

Colette gathered a bowl and cloth from the table, wet the cloth, and spread it over Julianna's head to hide her hair.

A moment later, a knock sounded on Julianna's door.

"Come in." Julianna tried her best to sound fatigued.

Uncle Alyx came in, still wearing his spectacles. He looked around the room, scanning, and finally fixed his attention on Julianna. He walked over to her bed and yanked the covers off her. He stared at her over the rims of his spectacles. Colette shrank to the other side of the room.

"Not exactly what I would consider clothes for recovering from an illness," Uncle Alyx said at last. He pulled the cloth off her head, looked at her hair, and shook his head. "It seems as though you have an appointment."

Julianna sat up. Uncle Alyx offered his hand and helped her out of the bed.

"Please Uncle Alyx," she said. "Don't make me go. This is my last chance to have a real seven birthday. My friends have planned a picnic."

He fixed her with his most disapproving stare, the one where his cheeks tensed so much it made it look like his lips were pursing to kiss something. "You know your aunt will be furious when she finds out."

To counter the disapproving stare, Julianna hunched up her shoulders, and gave him her best smile. "She doesn't have to find out."

Uncle Alyx shook his head. "There are times when your aunt may be flighty and obtuse, but she is not stupid. She *will* find out, and she *will* suspect I've had some hand in this. We'll both suffer for it greatly."

"Please, Uncle Alyx."

"Will there be any young gentlemen at this picnic?"

Julianna chewed the inside of her right cheek. "Yes."

"Anyone I know?"

Julianna ground her right toe into the carpet. "Khellan Dubhan and perhaps a few of his friends."

"*Baron* Khellan Dubhan?"

Julianna nodded. Even the mention of Khellan's name caused her ears to warm and her stomach to churn a bit.

Uncle Alex crossed his arms, sucked in a deep breath, and let it out in a long sigh.

"Well, it is apparent that I cannot keep you from being rash and impulsive, but I know viscount Dubhan and his son. Fortunately, they are both rational, level-headed men. You may go."

Julianna threw her arms around Uncle Alyx and kissed him on the forehead and both cheeks. He sighed and rolled his eyes. She'd done that ever since she was thirteen and taller than he, and he'd always pretended that he didn't like it but she knew differently. Uncle Alyx did not allow anyone do something to him that he didn't like.

Julianna gestured for Colette to follow, and they fled the room, heading toward the stables.

"If your aunt asks," Uncle Alyx called after them, "I will deny knowing anything about this."

"I'm a grown woman," Julianna cried back. "She can't treat me like a child anymore."

Uncle Alyx's laughter trailed after the two young ladies. Julianna knew better. Aunt Maerie treated everyone like a child, everyone but important people at court who outranked her in the order of precedence. Well, now that *Duchess* Julianna Taraen was an adult in her own right, she did outrank *Countess* Maerie Vivaen. Once Julianna returned from her outing, she would have a conversation with Countess Vivaen on who was and was not worthy to marry a certain duchess of House Kolmonen.

With the exception of Uncle Alyx's surprise visit, the plan to get from her rooms to the stables worked perfectly, just as they had planned it. Julianna waved her hand in frustration at the servants who curtsied and bowed to her as she and Colette rushed by. Normally, Julianna wouldn't have dismissed this show of respect in such a flippant manner, but Uncle Alyx had disrupted her timetable by several minutes. While she could have gotten them back, Julianna didn't want to risk tiring herself out before even getting to the picnic. So they hurried, not quite at a jog, but close to it.

When she and Colette reached the stables, Julianna stopped short.

"What are you doing?" Julianna demanded.

The serving boy and two of the stable hands were passing around a bottle. It was a bottle of fine Aernacht whiskey. It had been Julianna's gift to the boy for his assistance.

At the sound of her voice, all three snapped to the perfect attentive stance all who served the nobility learned to master early in their careers of service. The servant boy tried his best to hide the bottle behind his back. Unfortunately, they had already consumed enough whiskey that maintaining that rigid posture proved impossible. Each of them swayed slightly side to side, and none of them could meet her gaze, finding anything to look at besides where Julianna stood.

"Do you think that just because the nobles of this house are away that you can spit in the face of your duty?"

"No, my lady," the three of them said together.

"Excuse me?"

Julianna walked to stand a single pace from them. Gods and goddesses, she needed to get on her horse and get on the road, but she could not let this pass. The three of them stiffened even more.

"No, Your Grace."

"Better."

Julianna fixed her attention on the young man she'd given the bottle as a gift. He glanced up at her for a moment, but looked away almost immediately. She imagined what it must be like for him, with her eyes, the ones noble men were so quick to compliment, focused on him. His feet shuffled for just a moment, and then he caught himself, standing stiff again. They remained like that, a pace away from each other, Julianna looking down at him, him looking down at his feet. Moments ticked away to over a minute.

At last he said, "Forgive me, Your Grace. I will not spoil your generosity ever again."

"Accepted," Julianna replied and moved away from him. "To your duties. You can get as drunk as you want when your time is your own."

The boy bowed deeply, all trace of drunkenness gone from his movements.

Julianna turned to the two stable hands. "Our horses had better be prepared."

"Yes, Your Grace," they said in unison, and started for the stable doors. "They are just outside, Your Grace."

"Stop," Julianna said.

The stable hands froze midstep. They faced Julianna and resumed the attentive servant stance.

"You are drunk. You will *not* handle my horse while you are drunk. See the stable master. Tell him I relieve you of your duty for today. You can double your post tomorrow."

They bowed, shuffling off toward the stairs that led to the stable master's apartment. "Yes, Your Grace. Thank you, Your Grace."

She watched them walk up the steps. Once they knocked on the door, Julianna allowed a satisfied smile to break the cool mask of her displeasure. She couldn't remain angry with them. Not today, when Khellan was waiting to meet her and her friends to give her a true seven birthday celebration.

Two horses waited outside, tacked and saddled, just as the stable hands had said. When they came into sight of the horses, Colette handed Julianna a green apple. Julianna's horse, Vendyr, liked all apples, but he liked pure green apples the best. It was the only kind he would eat completely, without spilling some chewed-up mulch onto the giver's palm.

"Vendyr," Julianna said, and smiled when her horse's ears perked up, one black and one white.

All the horses at the Summerrain estate were of the Saifreni from Heidenmarch, a protectorate on the southern coast of the Kingdom of the Sun, all of them pure black with lush manes and tails. Well, at least all the horses ridden and seen by Countess Maerie Vivaen and her guests. The working breeds were in another stable entirely. Julianna's gelding was the only exception, and how the countess hated that blemish on her perfect collection. Vendyr was a rare -blood of Saifreni and Nibara, a breed from the Lands of Endless Summer across the southern sea. This mixed breeding gave him a white star on his forehead, one white ear, white socks above his hooves, and white patches on his neck and rump. This breeding also gave him strength, speed, and almost tireless endurance, thus his name. Vendyr was the name of an ancient Komati hero who had outrun the Goddess of Wind, the only mortal to ever have done so.

Now, even though his ears perked and he did the slightest dance of curiosity, Vendyr did not turn to face Julianna. She'd taken too long. Vendyr hated waiting once he was tacked and saddled. She let out a sigh and rolled her eyes at everything that had thrown off her carefully planned schedule.

While her plans did not depend on Vendyr being good this morning, he certainly could make the day harder to enjoy. Normally, Julianna would not placate him. She would endure whatever nasty little games he decided to play with her in revenge for whatever little thing she had done to slight him. Today, she didn't have time to struggle for dominance, and she suspected her horse knew it. The only question was: would he behave himself for the rest of the day if she placated him now, or spend the rest of the day testing her every step of the way. Well, there was only one way to determine that.

Just short of stomping her feet, Julianna walked right up to Vendyr's face. She offered him the apple with one hand and scratched behind his ear with the other. Vendyr whickered as he sniffed the fruit. He took one tentative nibble. Less than a heartbeat later, his lips pulled the fruit from her palm. As he chewed, Vendyr shifted his hindquarters, offering his flank to Julianna so she could mount.

Colette snickered.

Julianna leaned to her left so she could see her maid sitting on her own horse, Onyx, a pure black Saifreni. Well, Onyx wasn't exactly Colette's horse. A simple lady's maid could not possibly afford a horse in the first place, much less the upkeep. However, pretenses and appearances must be maintained at all times, so when they went riding, Colette got to ride Julianna's other horse, Onyx. In reality, Colette and Onyx had just as strong a relationship as Julianna and Vendyr.

"Really?" Julianna asked. "You find humor in this?"

Without bothering to hide her smile, Colette replied, "Of course not, Your Grace. A lady's maid is well aware of her station, and knows to keep her personal emotions reigned in at all times."

"Bah."

Julianna turned back to Vendyr. She hadn't fallen for this trick in a handful of years, but that didn't stop Vendyr from continuing to play the game: *I'll just look like I'm a happy horse, and I'll let my mistress try to mount me, and when she's halfway up, I'll move; won't that be funny to see her in her pretty dress sprawled in the dust.*

"Look, you," Julianna said, stroking Vendyr under his chin. It was his favorite spot. His lips quivered ever so slightly. "Today is not the day for this. Please, will you be good?"

Julianna knew that Vendyr couldn't understand her words, or at least most of them, but she knew he understood the tone of her voice. And after seven years, they had formed a strong bond, almost as strong as the bond Julianna had with Colette. The only trouble was that Vendyr did not recognize the order of precedence nor respect Julianna's title in any way. No horse did, no matter how much the nobility wished it otherwise. Julianna's familiarity with Vendyr served to remind her that, in many ways, the order of precedence was an illusionary construct.

As she had hoped, the tone of her words seemed to soothe Vendyr. He lowered his head and licked his lips, a sign of submission.

"Thank you," Julianna said, rubbing her hands gently over his face.

A few moments later, she sat in her saddle, waiting to see if Vendyr was going to test her in some way. He turned his head slightly to the left to look at her, lowered his head, and licked his lips again. Good. Finally something was going right this morning.

"Ready?" Julianna asked Colette.

"I was on my horse and ready minutes ago," Colette replied. Then with a wry smile, she added, "Your Grace."

Julianna blinked at her maid three times, sighed, and blinked three more times. Without any further response, Julianna kicked her heels gently into Vendyr's flanks and started off down the long drive that led to the road outside of the Summerrain Estate. By the time she reached that road, Colette rode next to her. They each urged their horses into a canter in order to make up for lost time. True, her friends would wait. After all, it was Julianna's day, but she didn't need to keep them waiting overly long.

As she left the hard task of escaping Summerrain and the last few moments of Aunt Maerie's dominance over her life behind, Julianna drew in a deep breath. She loved the dusty scent the drying leaves gave the autumn air. Now, barring intervention from some divine or infernal power, this was going to be the greatest day of Julianna's life.

TWO

Just as she had seven, fourteen, and twenty-one years ago, Yrgaeshkil stood and watched events unfold. This time she observed from a window on Summerrain's fifth floor. Few people even realized the room was here. She'd protected it through well-placed lies at corners and intersections all across the fifth floor so that even if someone managed to remember that this room existed they wouldn't be able to reach it unless they knew how to navigate the one true path of travel she'd left open.

Thankfully, she didn't have to wear the form of her detestable children, the one her husband had created for her. Today she was young, her body aged to about twenty-five years, sculpted to the height of male desire, full breasts, ample hips. Long, dark hair hung freely down her back. She reveled in the moment, as much as she could with so much weight on the outcome of the day.

Julianna rode away, down the long gravel drive that stretched from the front of the manor to the gate. Two flower gardens – each a twin of the other down to every single flower – sat on each side of the drive. This meticulous interest in the perfection of both gardens was one of several Lies Yrgaeshkil had placed on Maerie Vivaen within moments of Julianna joining this household after the debacle fourteen years ago.

"That was close," Kavala said.

Again, the scarred-faced man stood next to Yrgaeshkil. She hated how much she needed him. At least, for now. When the time came, she would rid the world of the nuisance of his presence.

"What was?" Yrgaeshkil asked without turning to him.

The door to the room opened and Alyxandros Vivaen entered as Kavala spoke.

"Julianna actually managing to escape to attend this picnic with her friends. It seems only a matter of luck that she was able to bypass her aunt's wishes."

"Luck had nothing to do with it," Alyxandros said, as he joined them by the window. "This morning has been carefully orchestrated down to the last moment. Julianna is a capable young woman, clever, and good at commanding the loyalty of those under her, but she is not perfect. I had to step in and aid her a bit. After all, this is our last chance, isn't it?"

Yrgaeshkil noticed that the mortal did not bow or show any deference as he approached.

She turned to Alyxandros, and the mortal did not have the decency to look away. There was once a time when all creatures knew their place in the order of celestial precedence. Most still did, all save for these humans. Well, the time was coming when she would remind them of their place.

"She will continue to have birthdays by seven," Kavala said.

"But they won't be this birthday," Alyxandros replied. "This is the first birthday by seven Julianna has had since the blessing by thrice has been fulfilled. It must be today, or we will have to start again, and it probably won't be with a follower of Grandfather Shadow."

"Alyxandros." Yrgaeshkil turned the fullness of her gaze on him. E-ven though she detested herself for it, she allowed her face to blur, putting a bit of her husband's preferred form into her features, specifically, twin goat eyes. "If this fails, you will not be able to hide from me, not in any corner of any realm."

"Why do you threaten me?" Alyxandros asked. "My part is done."

Yrgaeshkil wanted to slap this smug mortal so hard his neck would spin around on his shoulders. She turned back to the window. She could still see Julianna and her servant far down the road leading away from the estate. If Yrgaeshkil didn't turn away from Alyxandros, she might well kill him and cast his soul down into the Dark Realm of the Godless Dead for her children to play with for all time.

"Don't look at me like that, goddess," Alyxandros said. "Julianna is headed for the picnic. I have sent messages to those that needed information. I have affected today's events as much as is in my power. If this plan fails now, the fault lies with Nae'Toran and the Brotherhood of the Night."

THREE

The greatest, tallest, oldest oak tree in Koma stood on a hill known as Kaeldyr's Rest, which rose from the earth where the borders of three e-states met: Summerrain, Dawn's Breath, owned by the Dubhan family, and The Shadows Crossing, owned by Mandak. This is where Julianna and her friends gathered to celebrate her birthday by seven.

For every generation since well before the lands of Koma fell to the Kingdom of the Sun, the young lords and ladies of all three families had gathered under this tree. In each generation they believed they met here in secret. And, as with each generation before them, they grew to inherit the positions, lands, and responsibilities of their parents, aunts, and uncles. When they began to raise children of their own, these once-young lords and ladies began to learn the skill of selective memory loss concerning this giant oak. Alas, most of the attendants at Julianna's celebration would not have the opportunity to learn this skill, for the young duchess was no longer blessed thrice by seven or seven by thrice, and these her friends would suffer for the loss of that blessing.

Fallow fields stretched to the horizons to the east and south. A stream ran past the bottom of the hill, going from northeast to southwest. A mill, long unused, stood on the banks of the stream at the exact place apple orchards stretched west. Amongst all this, the hill rose into the sky, and at the hill's summit, the oak rose higher still, like an emperor lording over the surrounding land. This tree had been planted in honor of, and marked the burial cairn of, the first high priest of Grandfather Shadow, the first Emperor of the Seven Mountains, and the first Komati ever to be granted a word and raised to Saenthood by any god. This small bit of knowledge had been stamped out of common awareness by the Kingdom of the Sun in the last one hundred forty years they had ruled over the Komati, as they had stamped out much of the knowledge of who the Komati had been in times past; but small details, like knowing this place was named Kaeldyr's Rest, could not be forgotten.

As the sun set on the evening of Julianna's twenty-first birthday, a fire burned approximately thirty-five paces from the tree. It was the place where fires always burned when people gathered at this tree. That night, blankets had been spread out on the ground near the fire, along with baskets of food and dishes. Bottles of wine, ale, and Aernacht whiskey lay scattered across the blankets. The celebrants had been there most of the day, eating, talking, and dreaming of what their lives would be like when they inherited their various birthrights.

As the daylight faded, they separated into small groups and pairs, believing, as young men and women whether noble or common do, in the illusion that night and darkness gives privacy. They believed in that secrecy with almost the same unwavering conviction as they believed in their own immortality.

A little way down the hill, toward the direction of the mill, another two blankets were spread out for the servants. They ate as well, only they had just started as they had been serving their patrons earlier. Unlike those higher on the hill, the servants did not converse much and did not drink at all. Drinking addled the mind, and gatherings like this were when servants needed all their wits about them, for who knew what tasty bit of gossip they might pick up to share in the servant's quarters later, or perhaps even a secret or two to sell to a rival family.

And so sunset darkened into night, the fire crackled, the nobles paired off to further personal and familial agendas, and the servants watched the games unfold.

FOUR

Khellan leaned against the giant oak. The warmth of wine surrounded his head and stomach in a soft embrace, not drunk, not even really tipsy, just…warm – the perfect bit of warm for this time of day at this time of year.

He had always loved this place, and he loved it even more now that he knew its secret history. It was always best at this time of day, when it was not really day and not really night either, the border between both places, when everything in the entire world became shrouded in the shadows of mystery. He stood away from the others, looking at the Duchess Julianna Taraen of House Kolmonen. Julianna and her friend Sophya

Mandak stood by the fire, speaking in whispers. Every now and then, Julianna would glance over at him, and even in this growing darkness, Khellan could see her eyes clearly as if it were noon. Those eyes were the silvery-gray of Tsaitsu steel and seemed to pierce everything Julianna looked at.

She seemed to like him, or at least, she hadn't seemed repulsed by his scar. Their conversations had never been unpleasant. Khellan had had enough women blanch away from his face in the last year to know when a woman grew uncomfortable with the sight of his face. The closest Julianna had come to that was a startled blinking of surprise the first time she'd seen him after Grandfather Shadow had marked him with the scar. If anything, the scar had increased Julianna's interest in him. Well, maybe it had. On the other side of the coin, she just might be taking pity on a poor, disfigured freak of a man.

"I know what you're thinking," Jansyn Collaen said, coming up behind him.

Khellan didn't jump. He'd heard the footsteps crunching in the twigs.

Jansyn continued, "You've been thinking it since the Mandaks' midsummer ball."

"And how would you know what I'm thinking?" Khellan asked.

"Let's see. Well, first, you're here pining away for her, admiring from afar, as you always do, and second, your mouth breaks out into that stupid, lopsided, asinine grin every time anyone mentions the name, Duchess Julianna Taraen." Jansyn leaned forward and spoke almost directly into Khellan's ear as he elongated Julianna's name, stressing her title.

Khellan's mouth betrayed him, the edges curving upward, making him feel, and no doubt look, like an idiot. Julianna just happened to look over at him at that moment. She smiled politely, or perhaps it was pityingly, and she and Sophya put their heads even closer together, whispering furiously.

Khellan elbowed Jansyn in the side. That helped him rein in his betraying mouth.

"I love you like my own brother," Jansyn said. "And at one point I would have wished the very best of luck to you in this. Not only is she among the most beautiful women in all Komati precedence, she's higher than you have any right to dare for. But you're not just some ambitious lordling now. How many men who have borne your scar have ever died old, in a bed?"

Khellan glanced over to the blankets, but not to Julianna. His gaze flitted over to where Carmine and Nicco flirted with Perrine and Sylvie.

The half-bloods might be cousins on their mother's side to Sophya, but their father was a High Blood of House D'Mario of the Kingdom of the Sun. While they were friends and had grown up together, that friendship might not last long if certain secrets were revealed. Carmine, especially, was an ambitious man, and friendship was the first casualty of such men. Khellan doubted the rest of his friends realized this about Carmine, and Khellan understood that he might not be giving his friend due credit because Carmine's loyalty hadn't actually been tested yet, but Khellan didn't have the luxury of thinking as just himself anymore. Not since receiving the scar.

Both Carmine and Nicco seemed to be focused entirely of the ladies. Perrine, the older sister, seemed to be enjoying the attention, but Sylvie rolled her eyes every time Nicco spoke. That didn't matter. Khellan just wanted to make sure their attention was focused on anything besides Jansyn and this conversation.

"Only one Lord Morigahn has ever died of old age," Khellan responded. They currently stood on that man's burial ground.

"One." Jansyn placed his hand on Khellan's shoulder and gave a squeeze. "Of all the men over all the centuries that Grandfather Shadow has blessed with the mark, he only deemed the first of them worthy to be surrounded by friends and family when the end came. I think you destined for great things, but Kaeldyr the Gray you are not. The only future you can give her is a widow's blacks."

"I know all that," Khellan said, "and I know my duty and responsibility as a Komati lord and the Lord Morigahn."

"Just remember that every marriage involving the Lord Morigahn has ended poorly, at best."

Khellan looked at his friend. Pity showed in Jansyn's half smile and the way he couldn't quite meet Khellan's eyes. Khellan laughed. It was an honest laugh from just below his navel.

Jansyn blinked in surprise and stepped back. He cocked his head to the side and pursed his lips. "I'm trying to figure out why you're laughing. I don't recall saying anything amusing."

"I'm just embracing my role as Grandfather Shadow's high priest," Khellan said. "This evening I am opening myself to the duality of Knowledge and Illusion. Between the discrepancy of my station in comparison to hers and that she does not follow the old ways in the least, I know, deep in my heart, I know that she and I cannot be together, especially if your grandfather is correct and we will fight for our freedom within my lifetime. However, I am allowing myself the illusion that tonight Duchess Julianna Taraen and Baron Khellan Dubhan might know love in a world without precedence or the conflict between our people and our conquerors."

Jansyn laughed as well. "Whatever helps to ease your conscience, *Morigahn'uljas.*" Jansyn spoke the ancient form of Khellan's title with mock subservience. "Look. Here comes an opportunity to further your delusion. Oh, my apologies. I meant illusion."

Khellan looked back to where Julianna and Sophya were talking. Ingram, Khellan's best friend and Sophya's betrothed, was with the two ladies. He said something that made Julianna look away and sigh while Sophya hid a twittering laugh behind her hand. Thank all the gods and goddesses Julianna had never made a sound like that. Ingram offered his fiancé his hand. She took it, and he led her away from Julianna.

Julianna stood there for a moment, looking around, until her gaze fell on Khellan. She smiled and he felt his ears warming.

"Good luck," Jansyn said.

Khellan looked at his friend. "What do you mean?" But the insufferable man was walking away.

Khellan looked back at Julianna. She was walking toward him. The very edges of her mouth curved upward in a mysterious smile, or perhaps it was slightly mocking. She seemed to fancy him in return, but he'd never pressed the issue, going so far as to keep his flirting within very safe boundaries. He swallowed, mouth suddenly dry. Facing the challenges of the Lord Morigahn was easier than this. Still, if he was going to live in the world of Illusions tonight, perhaps he should cast off caution and embrace the boldness that the other Morigahnti would expect of him in the coming months and years.

FIVE

Sophya sat on the blanket furthest from the fire with Ingram Dashette's head in her lap. As they were actually betrothed, they could have a bit more privacy than the others. Well, as much privacy as they could get surrounded by friends and with that gaggle of servants watching from down the hill. To help give the illusion they were alone, Sophya had taken the pins out of her blond hair so that it could fall down, shielding them from the others as she looked into his green eyes, played with his hair, and pretended to believe all the lies he whispered up to her. She didn't mind the lies. She was one of the lucky few who actually loved the man her parents had chosen for her.

"Khellan is doomed," Sophya said, interrupting Ingram.

His eyes shifted away from her for the briefest moment. When he looked back at her, she saw an intensity in him that she'd never witnessed before. His face had grown hard, like a man preparing himself for a battle.

"What do you mean?" Ingram asked, though it seemed almost like a demand.

"Nothing serious," she replied. "Rest easy, my love. I just meant that Julianna is ready to give him her heart. She wants to marry him, and to be damned with precedence or standing or alliances. He might not be prepared for all that will come with that sudden, and unexpected, rise in station."

Ingram let out a long, slow breath, laughing softly at the end of it. The hardness seemed to leave him with that laugh, almost as if it had never been. She'd never seen this side of him, something that she would definitely have to learn about before they were married, but this was neither the time nor place to do so.

"I'm sure Khellan will be fine if that comes to pass," Ingram said. "He has cunning, wit, and bravery enough for any three princes."

"It still might not be enough to handle her, but it will be fun to watch."

Sophya pushed part of her hair out of the way. She could see Khellan leaning against the trunk of the great oak and Julianna standing near him, rocking slightly on her feet, swishing her riding dress back and forth.

"Oh no."

"What?" Ingram asked. He was also looking toward Julianna and Khellan.

"She's getting impatient or bored," Sophya said. "That's a dangerous place for her to go. She causes her aunt, the Countess Vivaen, so much trouble because the countess lets Julianna get bored. Unfortunately, Julianna drags both Perrine and me into trouble with her."

"Oh really?" Ingram asked, looking up at her. "And what kind of trouble does the Duchess Taraen get you into?"

Sophya smiled down at her fiancé and stroked his hair. "Nothing you need to worry about." He opened his mouth to protest or argue, but she placed her finger to his lips. "No. You will not get me to reveal this. They are Julianna's secrets mostly. Besides, what fun would it be to learn all of your wife's mysteries before the wedding?"

She leaned down and kissed him. When she lifted her head again, he was smiling with his eyes still closed. That was the easiest way to stop an argument with him. It might not work forever, but by the time it stopped working, they would be so far into their lives that they would only be fighting about serious things. ·

Sophya pushed a bit of her hair out of the way so she could watch Khellan and Julianna again. Her hair had fallen closed when she had kissed Ingram.

"This is interesting."

"What?"

"Look."

While Sophya and Ingram had been distracted from their friends by Ingram's curiosity, Julianna and Khellan had moved a bit. Now they each stood partially concealed by the oak. Julianna was on the south side of the massive tree trunk, Khellan on the north. The interesting thing was that their heads, Julianna's and Khellan's were completely hidden behind the oak. That wasn't too scandalous, as they couldn't possibly be doing anything from that far apart, but it did indicate a strong desire for secrecy.

"Well," Ingram said, "I am very interested to see how this little game plays out."

"Indeed," Sophya said, stroking his hair.

SIX

Jansyn walked over to where Raenard stood by the fire. Of all those present, save for the servants down the hill, Raenard was the only one among them who had not been gently born. In other words, he was common. That didn't matter overly much because Raenard was greater than any of these others.

"What do you make of all this?" Jansyn asked.

Raenard turned his head from side to side, making a slow sweep of the hill and everyone on it, ensuring that everyone else was occupied with their own conversations or otherwise distracted. Still, when he answered, Raenard kept his voice low. "I think the Lord Morigahn is a fool to be chasing this soft little duchess. I can't imagine how he was raised to be the first of us when it is so obvious that his faith and dedication to our god and order are matters of convenience. He should be busy planning to cast off the shackles that the Kingdom of the Sun has chained to the Komati people." Raenard glared over at where Carmine and Nicco D'Mario flirted with Perrine and Sylvie Raelle. "Starting with those two."

"Bah," Jansyn said. "Carmine and Nicco are harmless, and they are more Komati than not."

"You don't listen to them, then," Jansyn said. "It may appear that those two only have an interest in relieving those young ladies of their virtue, but there is much more to them than they present on the surface. Carmine is especially watchful. I wonder as to his presence here."

"He and Nicco are cousins of Sophya Mandak," Jansyn replied. "They are spending the summer with her family. She would have caused offense if she hadn't invited them."

Raenard snorted. "We should be taking every opportunity possible to give the High Blood offense. But I could go on and on without stopping about the idiocy of this particular outing."

"We've been given a great honor in protecting the Lord Morigahn," Jansyn said. "Especially one of common blood."

Raenard turned to face Jansyn and stepped forward so their noses were almost touching. His words came slow and quiet, yet the edge of anger in them was obvious. "My blood stopped being common the moment I completed weaving my *Galad'fana* and joined the ranks of faithful Morigahnti."

Jansyn tried to hold the commoner's gaze. He could not. After a few heartbeats Jansyn stepped back and looked away. This seemed to satisfy Raenard. He nodded and tugged at the scarf around his neck. "You would do well to remember that I've worn this longer than any of you."

They all wore the deep gray cloth that made them Morigahnti, though in different places so as not to be quite so obvious about it. Khellan also wore his like a scarf, which was all right, because it could be taken that Raenard was just attempting to emulate the nobleman's fashion. Ingram wore his as a sash around his waist. Bryce Anssi, who had already drunk himself to sleep on the other side of the fire, had his wrapped around his leg and hidden in his boot. Jansyn kept his wrapped around his arm.

As Jansyn thought about the cloth he'd spent the better part of his fourteenth year weaving, Grandfather Shadow's dominions whispered to him. No. *Whispered* wasn't the correct word. The tickling in the back of his mind was quiet but didn't come close to being actual words. The touch of them, the sound of them, and the desire they caused in him, urging him to speak them into existence, to pass through his lips as spoken language, as miracles, was a seduction unlike any other thing he'd ever known.

"I remember," Jansyn said. "And so do the others. This play that we are above you is only for the benefit of those around us who are not Morigahnti."

"Is it?"

Jansyn held his tongue. Nothing good could come of continuing down that path. There was a rift growing in the Morigahnti, between those born noble and those born common. He looked around at his fellow noble Morigahnti and sighed.

"Exactly," Raenard said, as if Jansyn's silence was all the confirmation he needed.

Deciding further discussion with the disgruntled commoner would only cause more problems than it would solve, Jansyn moved a bit away and picked up a bottle of wine. He didn't drink; he only desired it as means of escaping without causing too much offense.

Yes, the Morigahnti should work toward casting off the yoke of the Kingdom of the Sun, but there were so many wounds they needed to heal in their own ranks before they could even dream of defeating the Kingdom.

The sound of skin slapping skin echoed across the hilltop. It had come from up by the oak.

Jansyn spun around, ready to defend the Lord Morigahn.

"Julianna wait," Khellan said.

Julianna stormed toward the blankets and the fire. Khellan rubbed the side of his face and worked his jaw back and forth. Well, it didn't take too much work to guess what had happened. Perhaps this soft duchess did not fancy Khellan nearly as much as he had hoped.

"Someone fetch a pair of swords," Julianna said.

SEVEN

Julianna stared down the blade of her rapier at Baron Khellan Dubhan. The arrogant young lord had stolen a kiss without as much as a by-your-leave, never mind that she'd been secretly wanting that kiss for some time. She concentrated on keeping her left hand from touching her mouth, the small bit of wine made this more difficult than she had expected. His lips had been soft, strong, and inviting, and despite the way his smile made her forget to breathe, he would pay for his presumptuousness. She'd made other men bleed for less, but she hadn't welcomed any of their advances.

Khellan stood on the other side of the firelight, rapier held casually at his side. They'd built the fire up for them to see well enough for this duel. The heat of the blaze washed over Julianna as she continued to steady herself.

Khellan appeared disinterested, as if this was some chore that he'd rather finish so that he could move on to more interesting activities. She could just imagine what those interesting activities might be. The right side of his mouth curved upwards, causing his almost-healed scar, running from hairline to chin, to quiver. He'd worn that same smirk just before he had *pretended* to trip – he swore it was an *accident* – and caused their lips to meet. Whatever Khellan claimed, his brown eyes danced with mischief.

Just as her cousin Marcus had taught her, Julianna eliminated all distractions from her mind: her friends and the servants twittering and gasping about the impropriety of ladies dueling, Khellan's friends encouraging Julianna, likely because Khellan's defeat would provide them with months of ridicule, and most especially the wine swimming in her head. The smaller things went next: the aroma of roasting game hens from the picnic, the sound of horses whinnying at the bottom of the hill, and her ringlets, which the wind seemed determined to keep blowing into her face. The hair styling she felt had been so perfect before leaving Summerain became an annoyance she could not afford. She blew a ringlet aside, and this time the wind caught it just right and pulled it to the back of her head.

Khellan laughed. "Perhaps Your Grace would like a few moments to groom before we begin."

"His Lordship is too kind." She waved the tip of her rapier at his half-open shirt. He had removed his coat and vest to allow greater freedom of movement, yet had not removed the long gray scarf that always hung about his shoulders. "However, since His Lordship has decided not to properly dress, I'm sure our audience will forgive me a bit of loose hair."

"As you wish." Khellan gave a mocking bow.

Ingram Dashette, Khellan's closest friend, stepped between them. Ingram had also removed his coat, but had retained his vest and cravat. His bright green cravat caught the color of his eyes, which usually viewed the world as if he understood some fundamental jest the rest of the world could not fathom. However, just like any time he was involved in or watching a competition of any kind, those eyes appeared to be weighing and judging everything around him. Ingram could not tolerate injustice in any sort of competition, and so Julianna and Khellan had agreed that he was the one impartial enough to officiate the duel.

"This is only a minor duel," Ingram said. "Shall you honorably hold to first touch, or must I have your blades blunted?"

"You'd better not put a wine cork over the end of my blade," Khellan said, his smile growing. "It might get tipsy, and there's no telling what it might do then."

"I will trust that Baron Dubhan can handle a rapier with more skill than a razor," Julianna replied, "and will not mar my face the way he has his own." This met with a roar of laughter from his friends. "I will, of course, do my best not to give him a matching adornment on the other side of his face."

Ingram rolled his eyes. "Very well. Duchess Julianna Taraen of House Kolmonen, are you prepared?"

"I am." When Julianna spoke those words, her heart calmed. She *was* prepared.

"Baron Khellan Dubhan of House Kutonen, are you prepared?"

Khellan winked at her. "Always and for anything."

Again, another ploy to break her concentration. Again, it failed.

"Then turn toward your seconds," Ingram said, "and wait for my count."

Julianna lowered her blade. She turned away from Khellan to find her second smiling.

"It's likely you've beaten him already," Carmine whispered.

"I know," Julianna whispered in return. "They always underestimate me."

Of the men present, only Carmine and Nicco D'Mario had ever seen Julianna duel. Thus, Carmine knew that Julianna was more than capable of handling herself with a blade. All the ladies had, including the maids, and none of them were going to say anything and ruin the entertainment of watching Khellan's surprise when Julianna bested him. At least, that's what Julianna hoped would happen.

Carmine and his younger brother Nicco were the only men who could stand as Julianna's second without causing offense. True, they were Khellan's friends, but they were also cousins of Julianna's friend, Sophya Mandak. Because of that relation, either of them could have stood as Julianna's second without betraying Khellan's friendship. Carmine had offered, and Julianna had accepted.

"I will count off," Ingram said. "When I am finished, turn and come at your opponent. Be sure to hold off when I cry *yield*...One."

Julianna took in a deep breath, closed her eyes, and ignored everything except Ingram's steady count.

"Two, three..."

While her sword arm rested at her side, Julianna reached her free hand up to where her bosom rose from her dress and corset. In preparing for the picnic, she had had Colette push her breasts up a little more than usual, almost to the point of impropriety. Khellan had been unable to keep his gaze off her for more than a few moments at a time. Then a few moments ago, it had worked too well, when he'd taken liberties that he should not have.

"Four."

Her heart sped up at the memory of his lips on hers. Grinding her teeth, Julianna pushed her excitement aside.

"Five."

Julianna's fingers slipped into her corset between her breasts and caressed the hilt of her mother's knife.

"Six."

Sliding the knife free from its sheath, Julianna twisted her feet in the grass while keeping her hips and shoulders facing away from Khellan. She would need extra speed when she snapped around to face Khellan when Ingram finally called...

"Seven."

Julianna spun and lunged. It was a risk, but Julianna found most men never expected a woman to be so aggressive right from the start. Khellan was no different. He was still turning and barely brought his blade up in time to parry her full-arm extended lunge.

"What are you—?" Khellan sputtered while trying to retreat, but he found he couldn't move.

Julianna's right foot had come down on his, pinning it to the ground. They were so close, their bodies were almost touching. His breath blew against her cheek. Gods and goddesses, it felt good.

Khellan's eyes widened. The knife she held in her left hand rested against his inner thigh. She pushed the tip into him just enough to let him know it was there. His lips moved, trying to form words, but nothing came out.

Julianna leaned closer so that only two fingers separated their lips.

"Do you yield?" she asked.

Her words seemed to bring the life back into him. He smiled and leaned forward. Was he trying to kiss her again? She gave him a little poke with the knife, just as a reminder. Khellan sucked in a pained breath.

"You give me little choice," Khellan whispered through clenched teeth.

"And your apology?"

Khellan sighed. "I'm sorry for kissing you."

She jabbed him with the dagger again.

"What?"

His eyes went wide, as he looked into hers, searching for the answer she wanted. Good. It wouldn't do for him to have figured out everything about her already. Men needed a bit of mystery.

"I don't want you to be sorry for kissing me."

"Then what do you want me to apologize for?"

"For being so stupid to think you needed to steal what I would have given willingly."

Khellan's face tightened, and he gave her a look as if he were trying to solve a puzzle. He held that face for a few moments, then his eyes widened and he grinned.

Julianna kissed him. Let him know what it felt like to be taken by surprise. Khellan's astonishment was short-lived. Soon, he returned the kiss with an eagerness that bordered on hunger.

Julianna and Khellan dropped their swords and wrapped their arms around each other. However, she kept her knife, on the chance Khellan attempted too many liberties. Their friends called out many colorful jests and suggestions, but Julianna ignored them and melted into Khellan's arms. Damn propriety and family obligations. Now that she was a woman in her own right, she planned to live as she wished, even if that meant ignoring the rules and mores her aunt seemed intent on lacing her into tighter than a corset. Julianna wanted to marry this man. A man who kissed like this deserved to be a duke, even if it was only through marriage.

Julianna had no idea of how long she'd been exploring Khellan's lips with her own when one of the other girls said, maybe Sylvie, "Somebody's coming."

The faint sound of hoofbeats tickled Julianna's ears as she and Khellan ended their kiss. In the last light of dusk, Julianna saw riders coming from the south. They were still far away and rode as a chaotic mob, not the organized way nobles with their house guards would ride. She couldn't tell how many, but it was at least twenty, maybe more than thirty.

"Are they bandits?" Sophya asked, her quivering voice naming one of Julianna's fears.

"I don't think so," Carmine said. "What about you Khellan?"

Julianna glanced at Carmine. His tone had been too even, without a hint of concern. She glanced to Nicco. Carmine's younger brother wore the slightest smirk of satisfaction on his lips.

The hoofbeats pounded louder. Julianna looked back to the riders. They were close enough for her to make the count between thirty and fifty. She could just make out their black leather armor as well as the stark white skulls they wore as helmets. Her breath caught in her throat. These men were worse than bandits. The riders were the Brotherhood of the Night, followers of Old Uncle Night.

MOMENT OF GREATEST NEED

We must prepare for the greater gods' return. That event will likely spark off a Third War of the Gods. I fear it will be worse than the first two combined. We cannot allow either Grandfather Shadow or Old Uncle Night to be the first freed. To prevent this, we should endeavor to set the Morigahnti and the Brotherhood of the Night against each other. To this task, we must dedicate ourselves. To this end, we must not fail. — GrandMaster Myrs Byltaen to the Taekuri Council.

M. Todd Gallowglas

ONE

Khellan kicked his sword into his hand. He wanted to flee, to run to his horse and ride away as if Old Uncle Night were whispering in his ear. In all honesty, the god of death might very well be doing that. He took a brief moment to try and count the Nightbrothers riding toward them. Between the darkness of night and their numbers, it proved an impossible task, but he suspected around fifty of them.

Grandfather Shadow, Khellan prayed, *give me the strength to fight this battle.*

His logical mind knew that Grandfather Shadow was trapped somewhere, had been for centuries or more, and couldn't really help him. Khellan also knew that faith and religion itself was not rational, and he needed to be rational if he was going to live through this. He and his friends *could* live through this, at least he hoped most of them would.

"The mill!" Khellan yelled. "Everyone to the mill. We can make a stand there!"

His stomach revolted with the realization that he wasn't going to be able to save them all. He choked the bile down as he fled to the horses. Part of being the Lord Morigahn was about knowing that some of his people were going to die and that he was sometimes going to have to choose between good people living and good people dying. He just never imagined that he was going to have to start making those choices so soon.

"Ingram! Jansyn!" Khellan yelled. "Get down to the servants. Get them moving toward the mill and be prepared to hold that line. Raenard, you've the most experience out of all of us! Hold them here for seventy heartbeats, and then retreat to the mill if you can!

"Carmine and Nicco, try and get the ladies to safety."

"My brother and I are not your servants, Khellan," Carmine said. "We'll stay and fight."

"We should flee together," Julianna said.

Khellan felt a hand on his shoulder. He glanced back at her. Her skin had gone white. He wanted to give her a rational explanation, but there was no time. The Nightbrothers had already closed half the distance.

"Go, Julianna." Khellan jerked away from her. "Now!"

She blinked and looked as if he'd slapped her. She nodded and started down the hill.

Good. Better to have her hate him and live, than love him and get them both killed by staying.

"What about Bryce?" Ingram asked, as he and Jansyn headed down the hill toward the servants and horses

Khellan kicked Bryce in the shoulder. Bryce muttered something and vomited.

"He's in the Grandfather's hands now," Khellan answered, then looked at Raenard. Khellan knew exactly how Raenard and many other Morigahnti felt about him. "Hold them. Here. Seventy heartbeats." This command would most likely kill him.

Raenard nodded and turned to face the oncoming riders.

Khellan headed down the slope at a full run.

TWO

The ground shook with the power of the oncoming horses. Julianna spared Khellan a final glance before heading toward Perrine and Sylvie. Ingram gripped Sophya's wrist and was pulling her down the hill behind him, so she was at least headed in the right direction. The other two girls had run to the oak and huddled at the base of its trunk, as if it would protect them.

"Get up, damn you!" Julianna screamed over the thunder of hoofbeats, and inwardly sent up a prayer to Sister Wind to give them all speed. "To the horses!"

The goddess must have heard her. Sylvie stood and pulled on Perrine's arm. Perrine ignored it as she clutched the oak tree, seemingly paralyzed by fear. Tears threatened to well into Julianna's eyes, and a cold knot formed in her stomach when she realized that she would have to leave some behind. There was no time to hesitate; anyone who showed the slightest indecision would be a liability for the rest.

"Leave her!" Julianna yelled, barely hearing her words above the charging horses. "Sylvie, you only have time to save yourself!"

Sylvie looked from Julianna to Perrine. Tears rolled down Sylvie's face, but she nodded. They fled down the hill, leaving Perrine. At one point, Sylvie stumbled. Julianna almost stopped to help the girl but steeled herself against that. Anyone who didn't get to safety would be overrun, so Julianna followed close behind Sylvie.

Someone shouted up near the oak tree. Julianna couldn't understand the strange words, but his voice seemed enhanced by something. His voice sounded much like an Adept of a Greater God when the Adept spoke a miracle. She'd seen it happen twice. If an Adept of Old Uncle Night led the Nightbrothers, then perhaps Julianna should kill Colette now, and spare the maid the terror of possibly being captured. Julianna might have a chance at ransom, but surely Colette would be used as a brood mother.

The voice stopped speaking, and for the briefest moment the world seemed to hold its breath. The only sound came from the pounding hoofbeats. Then a wind rushed past Julianna, strong enough to force her back a step. She struggled against it. A moment later, Sylvie fell forward, sprawling to the ground. Then the wind vanished, and without the resist-ance, Julianna stumbled to her hands and knees. The ground scraped her palms, and the impact jarred her elbows and shoulders.

Unable to resist, Julianna looked back the way she'd come. The wind seemed to grow in strength as it went, flattening the grass and picking up dirt, twigs, and leaves; she could see them all swirling and spinning in the moonlight. When the wind reached the tree, it seemed to split around Raenard and the tree, leaving them unharmed. The Nightbrothers – the front line of them had just crested the hill – did not fare so well. Horses reeled in the force of that gale and men flew into the air.

Blinking her surprise, Julianna turned and scrambled to Sylvie to help the younger girl get to her feet.

With power like that to help them, perhaps this wasn't as hopeless as she'd first imagined.

"What happened?" Sylvie asked when Julianna lifted her by the shoulders.

"A miracle, I think. Best not to waste it."

The two girls got to their feet and dashed down the hill again.

Khellan was right. Getting to the mill was likely the only hope they had to survive, especially if somehow they had the power of miracle. Julianna would worry about the questions about the crime of it later. Uncle Alyx knew where she'd gone, and as it got later and later he would event-ually come looking. Julianna could only pray to Sister Wind to allow them to live that long, but could she even hope for the lesser goddess to with-stand the zeal of all these followers of one of the Greater Gods?

All these thoughts surged through Julianna's mind as she raced down the hill. Halfway to the servants, Sylvie sped past her. Julianna offered a quick prayer of thanks that the girl had not fallen when she had stumbled.

Several of the servants had fled, but most stood around, wide-eyed, mouths agape, waiting to be told what to do. Why were so many nobles a-fraid to allow their servants to think?

Of the horses, Khellan's brick-colored gelding, a True Bred, Car-mine's black Saifreni, and Vendyr were the only animals that remained e-ven close to calm. Two horses had pulled free of the stakes tethering them to the ground, and they were galloping away. The others were stomping and pulling at their tethers. Khellan, Ingram, Carmine, and Nicco were yelling at the servants and trying to get some of the horses under control.

Julianna grabbed Colette.

"We'll both ride Vendyr!" Julianna shouted.

Colette nodded, and after a few steps hiked up her skirts, which helped her get her feet underneath her, and kept pace with Julianna.

When they reached Vendyr, Colette cupped her hands together and helped hoist Julianna onto the horse's back. Colette untied the tether and handed it to Julianna. Julianna gripped Vendyr's flanks with her legs and pulled Colette up behind her. It would be tricky without a saddle, especially at the speed they'd require, but better to fall running than to just wait for the Nightbrothers to overtake them.

Julianna wheeled Vendyr around toward the mill. Up the hill, she saw Perrine just starting to flee as the Brotherhood of the Night came over the top of the rise. Raenard was lost underneath their numbers. She watched with her throat tight and stomach clenching into knots as their horses trampled Bryce into the ground. Perrine vanished with a scream a few moments later.

To Julianna's left, Carmine was pulling Sylvie into the saddle behind him. Nicco was already riding toward the mill, trailing behind Jansyn, who was riding double with Ingram. Khellan rode over to Julianna.

"We can't save them," Khellan said. "We can only hope to save ourselves."

Julianna nodded and drove her heels into Vendyr's flanks. They raced toward the mill.

THREE

The door slammed shut behind Khellan as he followed Julianna and her servant into the mill. Jansyn slammed the bar into place.

The mill was lit by several lanterns which had been hooded earlier to keep secret the Morigahnti hiding inside. Khellan never went anywhere alone anymore, not since becoming the Lord Morigahn.

The situation inside was worse than he'd hoped but not as bad as he'd feared. Carmine and Nicco stood shoulder to shoulder in the far corner, swords drawn. Four of Khellan's followers who had been hiding in the mill held weapons pointed at Carmine and Nicco, two of which were firearms. Maerik held a two-shot pistol, which looked huge against his tiny frame, but he was the best shot Khellan had ever seen. Off to the side, Saeryn held a scattergun at her hip. From her angle, she could catch both Carmine and Nicco in the same blast.

Sylvie and the few servants who had managed to make it down here were huddled together in the far corner.

"What is the meaning of this, Baron Dubhan?" Nicco demanded. "Are you also a traitor to the Sun Throne?"

Khellan sighed. Well, now he knew where Carmine's loyalties truly lay. Even still, Khellan had so wanted the mutual threat of the Brotherhood of the Knight to overcome that ingrained animosity.

"Ingram, keep an eye on the Nightbrothers," Khellan said, then he turned his attention to Carmine. "Put your weapons down. Maerik. Saeryn. You should both have your firearms pointed at the Nightbrothers, not at my friends."

Maerik and Saeryn glanced at each other. Khellan offered a silent prayer, hoping that they wouldn't force him to order them to stand down. After a moment, they went to stand at a window. The other two Morigahnti, whom Khellan didn't know, lowered their swords. Khellan stepped between them.

"Carmine. Nicco. Can we please talk about politics and who is betraying who once we live through the night?"

Nicco opened his mouth, but Ingram cut him off.

"They're at the servants," Ingram said. "They've stopped."

"They'll be killing the servants, Carmine," Khellan said. "Building strength to attack. We can kill the two of you now, leaving us without two able-bodied fighters when they get here, or we can fight together, and some of us might live. If we don't, then the gods can sort it out with us when we meet them."

"But you're Morigahnti," Carmine said.

Next to Khellan, Julianna gasped. He'd hoped that if she ever found out, that it would be under much different circumstances. Ah, well. He'd actually hoped Carmine and Nicco never found out, either. He liked them and didn't want to have to kill them, but he'd have to if either of them survived. Yet another unpleasant choice he'd make as the Lord Morigahn.

"Yes," Ingram said. "And so is your uncle."

Both of the D'Mario brothers blinked in surprise at that. The tips of their swords lowered, just a bit, but it meant they might be ready to shift their thinking.

"Is this true?" Carmine asked.

Khellan let nothing in his face betray Ingram's lie. "You'll never know if you force us to kill you."

Carmine and Nicco leaned toward each other and spoke in whispers. Nicco shook his head once. Carmine sighed, punched his younger brother in the shoulder, and pointed toward the hill. Nicco nodded. They both lowered their swords.

"Fine," Carmine said. "We'll revisit this discussion if we survive."

"Good," Khellan said, relieved. He didn't want to risk a fight in here, there was a chance that they might hurt or kill one of the Morigahnti before they fell. "Now, what do you know of the Brotherhood of the Night."

"Probably less than you," Carmine said. "You Morigahnti have been fighting them since before time was an idea. Nicco and I aren't high enough in Precedence to really concern ourselves with them, especially being half-bloods."

"They're coming," Maerik said, and fired his pistol. The *boom* of the gunshot echoed in the room, and acrid smoke crashed into Khellan's nose.

"See you after?" he asked Carmine.

"Indeed," Carmine said.

With that, Khellan went to the door and stood on one side. Ingram stood at the other, ready to slide the bar up and pull the door open. In a brief moment of eye contact, Khellan and Ingram shared all the joys and pains they had lived through as friends for nearly two decades. They also recognized that they were likely going to die.

FOUR

Carmine glanced at Nicco. They shared a sigh of relief. This last minute change in their plans had almost turned out very, very bad. They hadn't expected other Morigahnti to be waiting in the mill, and surviving that surprise had been a masterful display of guile. Well, no, Carmine knew deep down that luck was the only factor. Now that the tension lifted, Carmine and Nicco shared a smile and an almost imperceptible nod. The left side of Nicco's mouth curved slightly upward. Carmine bit his tongue to keep from smiling. If any of the Morigahnti suspected any sort of betrayal, they'd kill Carmine and Nicco without a second thought.

They had traveled a long and risky journey to make it to this moment, and at last he and Nicco would be able to prove their worth.

FIVE

Julianna crept to the window next to the woman with the strange gun. While Julianna had never seen a firearm, she'd heard stories. This one had to be a scattergun, longer than a pistol, but not as long as a rifle. Its wide barrel supposedly fired a mass of smaller pellets. The woman had the weapon braced on the windowsill with the hammer pulled back, the wick glowing ominously, waiting for the riders to get closer.

The woman, who was perhaps a few years older than Julianna, looked down. "You should—"

"Save your breath," Julianna said. "If you die, make sure you reload first."

The woman gave Julianna a grim smile and nodded.

"Morigahnti," Khellan said. "Veil."

All his friends, Ingram, Jansyn, and the ones that had been waiting in the mill, all took dark gray cloths and wrapped them around their heads, so that only their eyes were showing. Morigahnti. The ancient warrior heroes of Komati legends. Julianna pushed the thought out of her mind. She could try to comprehend that later, after she survived. If she survived.

The hoofbeats shook the mill. It was an old structure. Bits of stone and mortar shook loose. The riders came charging as one thunderous shadow in the moonlight. Julianna wondered why they were still charging. A cavalry charge didn't seem like it would do well against a solid building like this mill.

"Now," Khellan yelled.

Ingram moved the bar and pulled the door open. Khellan stepped through the opening.

"*Galad'thanya kuiva an eva ruth!*"

As he spoke the final word, Khellan brought his hands together. When his hands struck, thunder roared, the ground shook so hard Julianna nearly lost her footing, and some wave of force pushed outward from Khellan like a gale and pulled up leaves and dirt in its wake as it hurtled toward the Brotherhood of the Night.

The force hit the riders. The first row flew into the air and back into the second rank. Horses screamed in fear and pain. Few, if any, of those animals would ride away. Most of the men fared no better; however, some rose and drew curved short swords.

At that point, the riders who had not been caught in what Khellan had just done – a miracle, it had to be a miracle, a miracle from one of the five greater gods – dismounted and spread out. Behind those men, Julianna saw smaller groups of shadows approaching. These groups, four or five, stood taller than the men now afoot, and Julianna could barely make out black horses and black hooded cloaks in the moonlight.

"Attack!"

Screaming, the Nightbrothers who had recovered charged. Khellan stood his ground in the doorway. Here and there among the oncoming charge – Julianna could now clearly see their pale skull helmets – some of the Nightbrothers stopped and aimed crossbows at Khellan. Julianna almost shouted a warning, but Jansyn spoke first.

"*Vaejaro'tuletti suojo tass talo!*"

A wind grew and spun around the mill just as the Nightbrothers loosed their bolts. The wind knocked the bolts off course just enough so that Khellan need not fear being hit. How was it possible for her friends to have this kind of power? Why would any of the greater gods grant a Komati the power to speak miracles?

Yelling and screaming, the Nightbrothers came on, a mass of black-bodied, white-faced madmen. Khellan stepped back into the mill.

Gunfire rang out at the window. Julianna looked out the window to see Nightbrothers pitch forward, their leather armor offering little defense against the scattergun. She'd heard about the devastating weapons in whispers, but never thought to see one of those weapons stop three men short.

Khellan started to yell, "*Galad kranu—*" but his words ended in a wet cough.

Julianna looked to him. He was on one knee, blood bubbling up in his mouth. Carmine and Nicco had thrust their swords into his back.

"No!" Julianna shrieked as she reached for the past, grasping at it as if she were drowning.

She only needed a few moments, half a minute would be enough. She willed herself to that time when Khellan was still unharmed and opening his mouth to speak. When she was perhaps four paces from Carmine and Nicco, just as they turned toward Khellan, Julianna slowed, as if the air had become partially solid. Julianna fought against it, struggled to keep moving, but just as she reached the D'Mario brothers, the world held her trapped in place. Very shortly after she had begun to experiment with this strange ability, Julianna learned that some things could not be changed.

Julianna fought to move faster, even though she knew the effort was futile. She watched, helpless, as Carmine and Nicco stabbed Khellan from behind. Khellan coughed up blood again, and dropped to his knee.

Two Nightbrothers rushed in the door. Ingram killed one with a quick thrust of his blade. The second jumped at him, and they both sprawled to the floor. More Nightbrothers came in. With that breach in their defense, it was only a matter of time before they were overrun. But that didn't mean Julianna couldn't make one of the D'Mario brothers bleed.

Changing her intent, Julianna fixed her eyes on Nicco. Hoping and praying, Julianna reached for the moment just after the brothers had a-ttacked Khellan. She moved as though everything around her was stuck in molasses. As she stepped up behind Nicco, Julianna drew her mother's knife out of her corset.

Letting herself fall back into time with everyone else, Julianna grabbed a fistful of Nicco's hair with her free hand, yanked his head backward, and slammed her knife into his neck up to the hilt. A dark fountain of blood gushed out of the wound. Nicco's eyes and mouth opened wide in shock-ed surprise, and his sword clattered to the floor. Julianna yanked on Nicco and twisted her body so that she faced Carmine.

When the first bit of that bloody spray hit Carmine, he batted at it with his free hand, as if he was batting at an annoying fly. Then looking at his hand, his eyes and mouth opened in an expression almost exactly like Nicco's. Carmine turned, and with grim satisfaction, Julianna imagined him taking in the sight of Nicco clawing at the wound, the light fading from his younger brother's eyes.

Carmine howled.

In one fluid motion, Julianna pulled her blade free, let go of Nicco, and flipped the knife so that she held the blade between her thumb and first two fingers. Nicco slumped to the floor as she sent the knife flying at Carmine. He dodged easily, but Julianna had only intended the attack as a distraction. She used that moment to kick Nicco's rapier into her hand.

Carmine recovered from her ruse. His eyes burned with fury and hatred. Good, but that wasn't enough. Carmine needed to die knowing that he would never avenge his younger brother.

Julianna prepared to attack Carmine, every trick her cousin Marcus had ever taught her fixed in her mind, when Carmine yelled, "Don't kill her! We need her alive."

Julianna tried to leap aside but wasn't fast enough to avoid the blow that struck the side of her head. She dropped to her knees and fought against the darkness at the edge of her vision.

Blinking, she willed herself to stand and keep fighting. Someone grabbed her. She struggled, but another blow struck the back of her head. The shouting and ringing of sword on sword slowly faded. Despite her efforts to remain conscious, the dim light from the lanterns and candles that filled the mill faded.

SIX

The scattergun kicked in Saeryn's hands. The three Nightbrothers heading toward her window screamed and their armor tore open. She inwardly thanked them for wearing the obsolete armor. Her brother was a blacksmith, and so she used his metal shavings as ammunition only because it was better against the Brotherhood's armor.

Saeryn stepped away from the window. She ground her teeth together and drew on the dominions of Shadows, Storms, and Illusions through the cloth wrapped around her head. She took a deep breath and formed the words of the miracle in her mind, visualizing what she wished from the blessing of Grandfather Shadow. Once she had the miracle firmly in mind, Saeryn spoke.

"*Varjo ja tuli kierre ja sielha tahlha!*"

Fatigue washed over Saeryn as a cyclone of wind and semi-solid shadows erupted in the window next to her. A Nightbrother had been climbing through. The miracle caught him, already precariously balanced, and spun him around. His head struck the wall, knocking his skull-faced helmet askew on his head. Saeryn couldn't see his eyes, but she imagined them rolling up into his head as the whirlwind flung him to the floor at her feet.

Wasting no time, Saeryn drew the knife from her left boot and thrust it into the sliver of space between the helmet and shoulder. She didn't have to imagine the gurgle that came with his dying breaths.

"May your god embrace you," Saeryn said.

She left the knife in his throat; it would help contain the blood. The last thing she needed was to worry about slipping in a pool of blood while defending her post.

The miracle wouldn't last long, so Saeryn reloaded the scattergun as quickly as she could. She'd never taken to the sword well, nor the precision shooting of the pistols and long guns, nor had she the strength for speaking miracles over and over, but she was a scrapper. She'd been in no less than five skirmishes with Kingdom forces, and each time she'd survived on pure tenacity, earning her way onto the Lord Morigahn's honor guard.

When she had the weapon reloaded, Saeryn released the miracle and got ready to repel even more Nightbrothers. One was already trying to climb through the window. Their eyes met. Well, she looked into the gaping black circles of his helmet. He froze momentarily. Shooting him would be a wasted shoot. She spun her weapon and slammed the butt of the gun into his throat. His neck made a satisfying *crunch*. He dropped his sword, and his hands beat on the window sill. Saeryn pulled her gun back and pummeled the Nightbrother's head twice. The white leather crumpled with the second blow, and the man dropped. He started falling backward, but Saeryn grabbed his shoulder and pulled him back inside so that he slumped across the window sill, making it that much harder for others to climb in.

Four more Nightbrothers stood behind him, waiting their turn to follow their comrade. Saeryn fired. The scattergun roared. The Nightbrothers screamed and dropped. Bodies piling up outside the window would make footing more challenging. At this rate, the Morigahnti might survive long enough for help to arrive.

Saeryn was just about to pull back, to wait for the Nightbrothers to try coming through the window one by one, so she could kill them one by one, when a hand reached out and grabbed her wrist. The grip was a vice on her, stronger than anything she'd ever known.

She pulled back at first, but that only lasted about three or four heartbeats. Then the desire washed over her, spreading up her arm to her heart, her mind, and her loins. Oh, how she wanted that touch to spread over her, caressing her everywhere and forever.

"Come to me," a man said, stepping into view.

His eyes glowed. Saeryn's mind screamed to fight. Rationally, she knew this to be a Daemyn, and death would be the best she could hope for by going to him. She closed her eyes, reaching for any strength Grandfather Shadow could grant her. But Grandfather Shadow was so far away and had never actually spoken to her. This wonderful creature, with this touch that could never be anything but the purest bliss, was here and now. Her body needed that touch, so she did not resist.

"Yes," she replied and climbed awkwardly over the body slumped across the window sill.

SEVEN

Khellan looked down, staring dumbly at the two blades protruding from his chest. The blood seeping from those wounds had ruined his shirt and pants. He gasped for breath, and it was like trying to breathe under water. He would have screamed as the two swords slid out of him, but he didn't have the air.

He dropped to his knees, closed his eyes, tightened his stomach, and forced himself to cough. Bloody phlegm splattered onto the dirt in front of him. That allowed him enough air to force even more of the stuff out of his throat so that he could draw in enough breath to speak. He drew in a deep, watery breath, almost choked, but fought past it. With his chest near to bursting, Khellan struggled for the words he would need to keep fighting. He remembered a story about Saent Kaeldyr that one of the older Morigahnti had told at the last gathering.

Looking up, Khellan focused his attention on the first Nightbrother he saw. He drew on the Dominion of Balance, and spoke, "*Suoda var hano mina vama.*"

One of the Nightbrothers rushing into the mill doubled over as he took Khellan's wounds. Some of the other gods allowed for true healing. Grandfather Shadow did not, but injuries and health could be shared and transferred.

The change was immediate. Khellan's pain was gone, and he could breathe again. His muscles tightened with the ache that came from exhausttion, and he wanted nothing more than to lie down and sleep. But he couldn't. He had to keep fighting.

Some instinct made Khellan roll forward and let the momentum of the roll bring him to his feet. He came up next to Ingram in time to parry an attack aimed at the back of his friend's head.

Khellan pointed at the Nightbrother and drew on Shadows and Vengeance. "*Tuska!*"

A blast of dark energy flew from Khellan's outstretched finger and hit the Nightbrother's sword hand. The hand flowered outward in a blossom of bright crimson.

The veil around Khellan's head tingled with the Dominion of Storms as Ingram spoke, "*Mina kehia turvata!*" He emphasized the miracle by making a sweeping gesture with his rapier. At Ingram's command, a wind with more force than a hurricane caught two Nightbrother, lifted them off their feet, and slammed them into the far wall with a sickening crunch of bones.

Khellan ducked under an attack and picked up a short sword in his free hand. He felt defiled using the weapon of an enemy, but he could regain his principles once he survived. For now, he needed to recall Grandfather Shadow's Sixth Law: *Morigahnti are born to fight and conquer.* He parried an attack with the short sword and counterattacked by thrusting his rapier into an opening in the armpit of the armor. Khellan twisted the rapier, and blood gushed out of the artery leading from the Nightbrother's heart to his arm.

Three of the Morigahnti were still up: Khellan, Ingram, and Jansyn. The others were dead, though they had made the Nightbrothers pay dearly for their deaths. Corpses littered the floor, making footing risky.

"Fight to the rear," Khellan yelled.

If they had any hope of surviving, they had to get out of the mill and hope some of the horses might still be there.

He turned to see two Nightbrothers supporting Julianna's unconscious, perhaps dead, body between them. No, not dead, Khellan could see her trying to waken. Carmine D'Mario held a dagger at her throat. The weapon had a long and thin blade, sharp on both edges – an old Morigahnti style weapon. The blade was slick with blood. Nicco lay close to them; his head lay in a growing pool of his own blood.

"Stop!" Carmine yelled. "Nightbrothers, I command you to stop."

The Nightbrothers stood down and stepped out of reach of Khellan, Jansyn, and Ingram.

"Throw down your arms and *Galad'fana*," Carmine said, "or she dies."

To emphasize this point, one of the Nightbrothers holding Julianna pulled her head back, exposing her neck. Carmine placed the blade against Julianna's skin.

Khellan's arms shook and his lips pulled away from his clenched teeth in a feral snarl. His chest heaved, though he didn't know whether it was in rage or exhaustion. Had he been a normal man, without the power of miracles, Khellan might have complied with Carmine's demand. Instead, Khellan dropped the short sword in his left hand and raised three fingers.

"*Tuska!*"

Three dark bolts flew out. Two struck the Nightbrothers. They pitched backward, faces evaporating into red mist. The third bolt flew at Carmine.

Someone stepped between Khellan and Carmine, and the bolt struck this interloper's outstretched hand. Instead of exploding, the hand seemed to absorb the blast of dark energy. Khellan looked this man in the eyes, eyes which glowed yellow-green.

Khellan's shoulders slumped. He and his friends had no way to fight the power of a Daemyn. Khellan dropped his sword and unwrapped the *Galad'fana* from his head, not that it mattered. Daemyns and such otherworldly creatures were immune to the power of miracles. Behind him, Khellan heard Jansyn's and Ingram's swords clatter to the floor.

"Outside," Carmine said.

Khellan led the way, hoping that somehow he might be able to ransom for his life and the life of his two friends. He prayed to Grandfather Shadow that some semblance of the agreement remained intact, at least enough for some bargaining power.

Outside, the Brotherhood of the Night surrounded the mill. Their pale skull masks seemed to glow slightly in the moonlight. Even trapped as he was in this situation, Khellan couldn't help but think they all looked idiotically out of place, wearing the same antiquated armor that they had centuries ago, when men hacked at each other with broadswords and axes. He supposed they would still frighten peasants, and perhaps the traditionalists of the Kingdom of the Sun, but Khellan noticed all the openings and gaps in their armor, perfect for a rapier thrust.

The crowd of men parted, and four riders came forward. These men caused Khellan even more concern. They wore the long, black mantles of Adepts of Old Uncle Night. Khellan scanned for the other two, the Adepts he couldn't see. With an attack this size, there should be six Night Adepts to correspond with Old Uncle Night's sacred number.

"Adept Carmine," one of the Adepts said. "Where is Adept Nicco?"

"The Uncle has embraced him," Carmine answered.

"And we will soon follow," the Adepts and Nightbrothers replied in unison.

Khellan glared at Carmine. Carmine returned the gaze with the tiniest smirk, as if to say, *now we know each other's secret*.

One of the Adepts nudged his horse forward. He was tall and had light-colored hair pulled back away from his face. While he wasn't what people might consider truly attractive, he carried himself in a way that drew the eye.

"Lord Morigahn," the Adept said, looking down on Khellan, "I bring greetings from the First Adept of Old Uncle Night. He regrets to inform you that the agreement between our two religions is dissolved."

Khellan slowly swept his gaze over the dead Nightbrothers and to where other Nightbrothers carried the bodies out of the mill, Morigahnti and Nightbrother alike, taking the corpses up the hill. Sylvie, Sophya, and Julianna's maid came next, bound with hands behind them. The three young women were placed in a line next to Saeryn.

"I'd noticed," Khellan replied. "The Morigahnti will not allow this attack to go unanswered."

The Adept shrugged and turned toward the Daemyn. "This is the only one we need to fulfill our bargain?" The Adept waved absently at Khellan.

"Yes," the Daemyn replied.

"Excellent," the Adept said. "Feed the other two to the hounds."

Khellan tensed to fight. Better to die fighting than to submit himself and his friends to the whims of the Brotherhood of the Night. Before he could move, Khellan felt someone step just behind him.

Khellan also heard a chorus of deep, rumbling growls behind him. He glanced back to see four creatures that had once been dogs being led from behind the mill. Their muscles rippled under their skin, as if the Daemyns inside were trying to rip free into the physical realm. Orange eyes that burned like embers in a fire stared at Ingram and Jansyn.

"Don't," the Daemyn said, low and quiet. "Fight, and the hounds will consume your soul, taking you out of the cycle of life, death, and rebirth. Submit, and you will know life again."

The Nightbrothers who held those foul creatures released them.

Khellan turned away and tried to ignore his friends' screams. He failed.

EIGHT

As soon as the Brotherhood of the Night attacked, Theordon Barristis, Morigahnti and man at arms to the Count Alyxandros Vivaen, had fled the mill. Theordon nearly killed his horse racing to reach the Summerrain manor house. As he galloped down the gravel drive toward the manor, Theordon thanked the gods and goddesses when he saw the count standing on the porch.

Thoerdon pulled on the reins and his horse slid to a halt a few paces from the steps. He half-leapt, half-fell out of the saddle, scrambled up the stairs, and managed as much of a bow as he could in his panic.

"My lord," Theordon said between gasps. "The Nightbrothers are attacking Julianna and her friends."

Theordon didn't like the smile Count Alyxandros gave him when he said, "I know."

"Then, my lord, we must go and save her."

"No."

That reply surprised Theordon so much that his jaw worked itself up and down. He didn't know whether or not to protest or to berate his master.

Theordon started, "But—?" His master thrust a knife under his chin.

A warmth spread down the front of him, wetting his shirt and waistcoat. He suddenly felt very sleepy.

"Julianna does not need to be rescued by us," Alyxandros said. "She can call for greater aid than any forty-nine mortals can give her."

NINE

A slap stung Julianna's cheek. The bitter taste of blood filled her mouth, and she forced her eyes open. Carmine stood one arm's reach away.

Julianna dropped her head into her hands and shook her shoulders as if she were weeping. Peeking out through her fingers she saw him glaring at her. She reached back, pulled two of the hairpins from her bun, and lunged for him. Carmine spun away from one, and before Julianna could strike with the second, two pairs of strong arms grabbed her. She fought against them, but could not break from their grip.

After a few moments of struggle, Julianna relaxed, hoping the men holding her would relax as well. They did not, so she took stock of her situation. To Julianna's right, Colette, Sophya, Sylvie, and some of the female servants were bound, gagged, and stripped down to their undergarments. Khellan's friends lay in a pile to her left, each one drenched in blood. Perrine's body lay with them, limbs bent in awkward angles from being trampled. Four hideous dog-like things sniffed at the bodies. One of the creatures tore a chunk out of Ingram's thigh and began to chew noisily.

Choking back tears and bile, Julianna closed her eyes.

Another slap caught her across the cheek.

Her eyes snapped open. Carmine replied to her glare with a smug smile. "Before I leave, I wanted you to know there are so many things worse than death."

Carmine grabbed her chin and turned her so that she looked around the oak, past where Khellan's friends lay.

Khellan sat on his horse, hands bound behind his back, blood soaking his shirt and pants. One end of the scarf he always wore was tied around his neck, the other to one of the lower branches. His eyes opened and he looked at Julianna. Even though she realized what they had planned, she couldn't bring herself to look away.

Carmine said, "Now."

One of the Nightbrothers slapped the horse's flank. The animal bolted. Khellan swung into open air, body convulsing. Tears streamed down Julianna's cheeks as she watched until Khellan's body stilled.

"Good-bye, Julianna." Carmine slapped her again. This time she did not feel it.

Carmine walked over to where a large group of the Nightbrothers sat on horses, mounted his horse, and started away, taking about a third of the Brothers with him. Two of the girls were tied together on the back of one of those horses, but through the tears, Julianna couldn't tell which two. Those strange dogs followed after.

Someone pushed Julianna into line with the remaining women: Sophya, the girl with the scattergun at the window, and two servants. Julianna closed her eyes and let her mind wander to other places and happier times: dancing with Khellan, practicing swordplay with her cousin, riding Vendyr fast enough to catch the wind.

Footsteps crunching in the late summer grass, walking up and down the line of women.

"This is a fine looking group you've gathered for me." The voice sounded familiar.

"Thank you," a second voice said. "I always do my best to please you."

"And you say they are all virgins?" the first voice asked.

"Of course," said the second. "All save for that one at the end. Carmine D'Mario told me he'd had the pleasure of deflowering her two months ago, though it appears his seed did not plant."

"Well enough. I think I'll..." The footsteps paused in front of Julianna. "Well, well. What have we here? I may have missed you the night your mother died, but not today."

Julianna's head snapped up at the mention of her mother.

Two men stood before her. One she recognized and one she didn't.

The familiar one wore the black mantle of an Adept of Old Uncle Night.

"I know you," Julianna said.

"Yes," the man said.

She had seen him once, fourteen years ago, and yet had somehow forgotten him completely until this moment. He was older now, his face wrinkled with age, but now that she remembered, she recognized him from when the Brotherhood of the Night had attacked and killed her family. He'd held one of the silver rods that had helped to trap her mother long enough for them to kill her. Until that moment, Julianna hadn't remembered that her mother even possessed the talent of jumping through time. There were so many things about her life before the fire that Julianna couldn't remember.

"You don't know me," the second man said, stepping in front of Julianna. "But I've been waiting to see you again."

He was naked, and his excitement and arousal were obvious, but his eyes were what caught her attention. His eyes glowed with a soft, yellow-green light. It was a Daemyn, an evil creature from the Dark Realm of the Godless Dead. The Brotherhood of the Night often summoned Daemyns to fill human women with their seed, creating half-breed children in order to sew chaos on the mortal realm.

"I will accept this one as the full payment," the Daemyn said. "You can do with the other girls what you wish."

Men cheered. The women screamed as the Brotherhood of the Night dragged them away. She heard horses riding away and cries of anguish fading into the distance.

Julianna fought against the arms holding her. Death would be a sweet release compared to this Daemyn spilling its seed into her and the horror of birthing its child. Two more men grabbed hold of her. No matter how she struggled, Julianna could not overcome the four men as they forced her to the ground. Once they pinned her down, the creature ripped at her clothes.

"I could make you enjoy this," it said, and lowered its full weight on top of her. "To want this more than you've wanted anything in all the world. More than that pretty lordling with his handsome scar." Its hot flesh made her feel as if thousands of ants were crawling across her skin. "But I'd rather have you struggle, to have you fight me, knowing that it doesn't matter. You will bear my child."

Julianna did fight him. She kicked and pulled against the men holding her down. The Daemyn was right; she could only resist so long. Eventually the Daemyn would breech her maidenhead. Tears streamed out of her eyes, and her thrashing transformed into convulsing sobs. After a few moments, even her sobs lost their power and became little more than twitches. How could any god have damned her to this horrible fate?

"That's right. You have no hope."

She lay back, closed her eyes and wished she could die. Her despair woke something she'd only been aware of deep in the night after waking from a nightmare. Those eyes that looked at her from the depths of her dreams appeared in the darkness. Strange words rang in her mind. She didn't comprehend the words, but she knew speaking them would bring help.

Julianna's eyes snapped open. She glared defiance at the Daemyn, and spoke the words waiting to escape her for twenty-one years.

"*Mina sasta.*"

Writing appeared in the air above her mouth. The script was complex, the letters resembling a spider web. Memories came flooding back into her, too many memories for her to sort through, but they were all from before the night of her seventh birthday. She remembered Mother and Father raising her to worship and love Grandfather Shadow, no matter what Kingdom laws dictated.

"You should flee," the Daemyn said. "All of you, before she can speak again."

"I think not," the Night Adept said. "We have a bargain. Do not try to trick me. I know the games your kind play."

"I only wish to be able to bargain with you again," the Daemyn replied.

Julianna glanced at the Adept. His eyes flicked back and forth between Julianna and the Daemyn. She also remembered the promise she had made that man fourteen years earlier, nearly fourteen years to the moment.

Father and Mother had taught her to keep her promises, so Julianna spoke more words, words that had been waiting in her soul since the moment of her birth.

"*Galad'Ysoysa! Mina sasta!*"

Again, words appeared above her in that same spidery writing. This time the words were bigger and glowed pale and gray in the night. Something hidden in the deep dark recesses of her heart emerged from the same place where the words had come from. A weight she had carried for her entire life lifted from her. The world seemed to shift sideways in a dizzying lurch. Julianna's head spun as if she had stood up too quickly.

"Too late," the Daemyn said, though it sounded more amused than afraid. "She's freed him."

"You there! Adept!" Julianna called.

The Night Adept who had helped kill her mother turned from the words fading from the air and looked at Julianna. She smiled.

"I told you, my father's god is going to eat your soul."

GRANDFATHER SHADOW

They will come again, the greater gods. This event begs one question: Will it be too late for man, or too early for the gods? – Attributed to the Blind Prophet

Grandfather Shadow has the smallest army in the Eternal War, but his children are the most feared. We quietly assist the followers of All Father Sun and Old Uncle Night to destroy each other, sometimes with a few carefully placed whispers, sometimes with a sudden ambush on the battlefield. As always, once our part is done, the children of Shadow return to hiding where we wait to strike again. – Introduction to The Tome of Shadows, by Kaeldyr the Gray

M. Todd Gallowglas

ONE

Few things ever surprised Grandfather Shadow.

He wasn't surprised when the Brotherhood of the Night killed Khellan. Men who took up the Lord Morigahn's title rarely died of old age. With Khellan's death, Grandfather Shadow should have returned to the Temple of Shadows. There he would await a man worthy enough to pass through the trials and earn the honor of becoming the next Lord Morigahn and be bound into that man's mind until he died as well. So it had been for the last thousand years since the King of Order had locked the greater gods away from this world.

However, Grandfather Shadow found himself overlooking the scene he'd just left. The stench of blood hung in the air. For a thousand years he had known only two senses: sight and sound. And, even those had been dimmed by his imprisonment. Not only had the world of scent returned to him, but he could feel again also, like the cloth cutting into his neck and the blood soaking his back.

Grandfather Shadow smiled. The reawakening of these sensations meant he was free.

Free.

How many times had that word filled his thoughts over the last millennium? At last, one of his followers possessed enough faith and spoke the words that freed him from languishing in the prison imposed by the King of Order. The words still echoed in his mind.

"Galad'Ysoysa! Mina sasta!"

Kicking his legs, Grandfather Shadow managed to get turned around. A crowd of the Brotherhood stood around four men pinning a woman to the ground. She was Duchess Julianna Taraen. Her clothes had been cut to shreds. Khellan had loved her. From watching her through the eyes of several Lords Morigahn, Grandfather Shadow knew Julianna was a mortal worthy of admiration.

Two men stood at Julianna's feet, arguing. One drew Grandfather Shadow's attention more than the other. Instead of a soul, Grandfather Shadow saw the swirling, chaotic essence of a Daemyn riding inside a dead husk.

The Daemyn looked up at Grandfather Shadow, and its eyes grew wide. It waved the other man to silence, faced the god directly, and gave a deep bow. "When this wench spoke your name, I thought I smelled change on the wind. I just didn't realize how much. Congratulations on your freedom."

"Do not play false pleasantries on me." Grandfather Shadow's voice boomed despite the cloth constricting his throat.

"Forgive me, Great One." The Daemyn prostrated itself before Grandfather Shadow. "Is there anything I can offer that will convince you to spare my existence?"

This show of cowardice was so typical of its kind. Daemyns were arrogant and cruel when they dealt from a position of strength, but resorted to false subservience whenever they had lost the upper hand.

"Doubtful, but it might be entertaining. Try."

The man who had been arguing with the Daemyn pushed his way past the creature, dragging Julianna by her hair. She struggled, until he put a knife to her throat. This calmed her, but the burning hatred remained in her eyes. The knife was an old Morigahnti weapon, long and thin, favored as a last resort weapon because it could be easily hidden in a sleeve or boot. Odd that this one had the reddish blade of Faerii steal.

The man wore the black mantle of a priest of Old Uncle Night. The mantle hung open. He was naked underneath, the weapon between his legs stood ready. It was likely that all of these men would have a turn at her once the Daemyn had planted its seed. Grandfather Shadow detected pieces of bone woven into the fabric of the man's mantle. These bones had been blessed to channel the divine energy of Old Uncle Night, making the priest an Adept, able to effect change in the world by speaking miracles through Old Uncle Night's divine language.

Grandfather Shadow ignored the Adept and looked at Julianna. At twenty-one years old, she was barely a woman by Komati tradition. Her long brown hair was pulled into the Adept's fist, and her gray eyes looked up, pleading for help. Tears of hatred and rage rolled down her cheeks. Words written in his holy language of *Galad'laman* hung in the air above her head. How had she managed to speak a miracle of true faith?

Peering into her spirit, Grandfather Shadow could not find any faith that would have freed him.

"Lord Morigahn, we underestimated your faith, and that of your woman," the Adept said, drawing Grandfather Shadow's attention. "But will it save you from a blade through your heart?"

The Adept raised the dagger, preparing to strike Grandfather Shadow in the chest.

Julianna howled.

She twisted her head and sank her teeth into the Adept's naked thigh. He shrieked, dropped his dagger, and backhanded her across the face. She tore a chunk of flesh out of his leg as she sprawled to the ground. Once free, she snatched up his weapon. Leaping at her rapist, Julianna buried the blade deep in his side. Before anyone could react, she spun around and stabbed another man in the eye.

The Nightbrothers recovered from their shock and rushed Julianna. She slashed at them, but there were too many and the weapon too small to dissuade their thirst for vengeance.

Grandfather Shadow refused to allow them to harm his rescuer. With the smallest effort of will, he brought the Nightbrothers' shadows to life and commanded the shadows to flay their owners' skin from muscle and bone. Blood spilled on the ground, forming small ponds and streams. Agonized screams hit Grandfather Shadow's ears. The sound offended him, so he solidified the shadows in their mouths, gagging them.

As the Brothers died quietly, Grandfather Shadow turned back to the Daemyn.

"Nae'Toran'borlahisth, isn't it?"

"Yes, Great One," the Daemyn replied.

Upon speaking the Daemyn's name, full and true, the creature's subservience became a bit more honest.

"Have you thought of anything that might convince me to allow your worthless existence to continue? Keep in mind, I remember all the ill you have done my followers over the centuries."

"I can offer you two things," the Daemyn said. "If you agree to do me no harm until the sun rises again, I will tell you how this mortal called you from your prison, and I will never raise my hand against any true Morigahnti so long as you remain the Grandfather of Shadows."

"I accept," Grandfather Shadow said.

"Excellent," the Daemyn said, getting to its feet. "By ancient tradition the pact is made, binding our agreement."

Its subservient demeanor had vanished. The bargain had been struck far too easily. Well, it was too late for looking back. The bargain had been set, and could not be renegotiated.

"Tell me how this girl freed me," Grandfather Shadow commanded.

The Daemyn smiled, and its eyes glowed a deeper green. "Your first and most beloved follower, Saent Kaeldyr the Gray, placed his faith into this girl's soul the moment before her birth. To what end, I did not know until this moment. He was punished and cast into the Realm of the Godless Dead."

"Kaeldyr is gone?" Grandfather Shadow asked.

"Oh no." The Daemyn's eyes sparkled. "I still keep him as a play toy."

"Be gone before I decide to ignore our bargain," Grandfather Shadow snapped.

"You wouldn't break your word for fear of being placed back in your prison."

"I wouldn't?"

The Daemyn fled from the physical realm, and the body it had possessed crumbled to dust.

Standing alone, Grandfather Shadow regarded Julianna.

TWO

Julianna vomited as the Nightbrothers died. When nothing remained in her stomach, her sides ached as if she'd been beaten. She still felt polluted by the Daemyn's touch and wanted nothing more than to roll into a ball until the feeling subsided. In that moment, she vowed never to show weakness again.

She lifted her head to find the thing inside Khellan's body looking at her. She still held the knife in her hand, her mother's knife, keeping the blade between them as she struggled to her feet. Fighting dizziness that came from standing so quickly, she edged a few steps to her left. From there she could dive into a roll and come up with a sword in her hand. It was one of the Nightbrother's short swords, which she could not use as well as a rapier, but it was better than nothing.

"I will not harm you." The thing spoke with Khellan's voice, but not with his charm.

"Who are you, really?" Julianna demanded. Having a rational discussion with Khellan *after* she'd watched him die seemed dull compared to everything else she'd just witnessed.

"I am Khellan. I am a priest of a god forbidden by Kingdom law. My god granted me one final blessing to save you before I ascend to the celestial realms."

"Liar." Khellan's eyes danced with mischief. "Who are you?"

Khellan – even though Julianna knew it wasn't her love, she couldn't think of him in any other way – returned her questions with silence. His eyes bore into hers. She shifted under the weight of his gaze.

"Shadows lie to their enemies, not to each other," Khellan-who-was-not-Khellan said. "You are correct. You deserve more of an answer than that, if for no other reason than for your part in this. The man you loved was the Lord Morigahn."

"You're a madman," Julianna said. "The Lord Morigahn is a legend."

She also knew that her own words were false. Memories long forgotten reminded her that her own father had been the Lord Morigahn before the Brotherhood of the Night had killed him. She was now repeating the lies the Kingdom spread to all Komati children in order to keep them good little subjects of the realm.

"I promised you the truth, and then you doubt me when I give it? I suppose showing you will be easier than trying to convince you."

In less than a heartbeat, faster than Julianna could react, Khellan was suddenly in front of her. He put his hand on her wrist and lowered her knife. His touch was gentle as a shadow's caress on a hot day, but behind it she felt the power and strength of a storm.

"Look into my eyes." Khellan's voice carried the weight of ages. Julianna obeyed. "I am Galad'Ysoysa, Grandfather Shadow, the true god of your people. Khellan was the Lord Morigahn. The Brotherhood of the Night killed him for this, just as they killed your mother."

"My mother?" Julianna's heart and stomach twisted together. "I remember."

"Yes. Both your parents followed the old ways of Koma. They worshipped me despite the laws of the Kingdom of the Sun. The Brotherhood executed your mother. However, it could have just as easily been Inquisitors of House Floraen. Ever since the Kingdom of the Sun conquered Koma, thousands of innocents have been killed merely for following the traditions I gave to your people long before the four Great Houses joined to form their Kingdom.

"But it doesn't have to be this way. Koma can be free. If you take Khellan's place and serve me as the Lord Morigahn, I will teach you to speak with the power of storms, to pierce the secrets of the world, and act as the hand of vengeance."

"Vengeance?"

She remembered that Vengeance was one of Grandfather Shadow's seven dominions. She glanced down at the knife in her hand and the word she saw there, covered in the drying blood of a betrayer. *Kostota*. Revenge. But in *Galad'laman* it had so many subtleties based on context. That was the trick with what little she recalled of Grandfather Shadow's language – so many of the words relied on context for definition.

Julianna looked around. Death surrounded her: the skinned bodies of the Brotherhood of the night, Perrine and her twisted limbs, and Khellan's friends, slaughtered just for daring to follow the traditions of their people. She recalled Carmine and Nicco stabbing Khellan from behind, herself as she took Nicco's life, remembered the feel of his blood washing over her hands as the light faded from his eyes. How good that had felt.

Grandfather Shadow came and placed his hands on her shoulders. She felt the raw power in his grip. It didn't hurt, but she had no doubt that he could crush her shoulders into pulp if that had been his desire. The god turned her so that she looked at Nicco. She looked at her hands, still covered with Nicco's blood and remembered the satisfaction she felt at ending his life.

"Serve me," Grandfather Shadow whispered into her ear, "and I will give you the power of revenge over any who have wronged you."

"Anyone?"

"Anyone," Grandfather Shadow replied. "I will lead you to seek vengeance for yourself, your friends, Khellan, and your mother."

"My mother? How is that possible?"

"I control many Dominions, second in number only to All Father Sun. None of your enemies shall escape you. Not even Carmine D'Mario."

More than anything else, Julianna wanted to kill Carmine D'Mario, but she knew she could not do it on her own. He was Kingdom High Blood, trafficked with Daemyns, and seemed to hold a position of some authority in the Brotherhood of the Night. To truly hunt him, she would need power comparable to that. Julianna yearned to see Carmine lying on his back, staring at the sky with the same blank expression as Nicco. Once she finished with that task, then she could seek out the men who had killed her mother.

In that moment, Julianna believed the truth of who Grandfather Shadow was.

Julianna faced Grandfather Shadow. "I accept."

"Excellent."

THREE

Grandfather Shadow passed a hand over Julianna's eyes and put her in that place halfway between the sleeping and waking worlds. He took the knife from Julianna's hand and examined it. The blade was made of Faerii steel, a rare weapon indeed.

"Where did you get this?" Grand Father Shadow asked.

Julianna took in a deep breath, and answered in a long, sleepy-sounding tone, "It was my mother's. I've had it since she died."

Excellent. Marking someone as the Lord Morigahn was always best with a weapon of deep personal significance. This weapon would do just nicely.

He placed the blade of Julianna's knife into the fire.

Being Faerii steel, it would take the weapon a long time to heat enough for Grandfather Shadow's needs.

Giving the weapon time to heat, Grandfather Shadow sent his perceptions across the world, searching for those who still had faith in him. At one time, everyone in this land had followed him and many could command miracles. Now, only a pitiful few of the Komati truly believed. Without the Greater Gods to direct human faith, it seemed that faith itself had become tainted. Mortal man had turned religion into something to fear and mourn when it should exalt their lives. Even at the worst of times, when besieged on all sides by the followers of all the other gods, the Komati had found joy in their relationship with Grandfather Shadow. Now even the faithful lived in fear of discovery by this Kingdom of the Sun, as it was called now.

So it seemed that he must again save his people. He looked at Julianna. Was she the proper choice to lead the Morigahnti to greatness again? Perhaps. The similarities between her and Kaeldyr were not lost on him. Many centuries before, a young man looking for help had accidentally discovered Grandfather Shadow. Julianna, needing help, had also called out to him. Both then and now, the Komati people needed Grandfather Shadow to guide them from underneath the yoke of oppression.

Grandfather recognized something in Julianna, a spark he hadn't seen since the day Kaeldyr had stumbled into that cave. Maybe it was a product of having Kaeldyr's faith bottled up inside her, but Grandfather Shadow didn't think so. Kaeldyr had been searching for something to latch onto and dove into the faith of Grandfather Shadow without looking back. Julianna would be different. She had once believed, as much as a child could believe, but had forgotten. Also, Grandfather Shadow saw something in this young woman he hadn't seen in any of his previous followers.

Julianna Taraen would be the first Lord Morigahn truly marked by the hand of Grandfather Shadow free of his prison in a thousand years. But first, she would need certain things, things that had been long forgotten by those who followed him.

Well, the blade would take time to heat. He could use that time to fetch those things Julianna would need to reunite the Morigahnti and the Komati people.

FOUR

Yrgaeshkil waited a few minutes after Grandfather Shadow left before she partially dropped the Lie that she'd used to conceal herself in the mill – except she maintained it for that scrying cauldron that someone was using to watching from some distance away. The goddess had been there most of the afternoon and all of the night, watching and waiting. She'd observed Alyxandros's servant running off, the fight between her husband's followers and the Morigahnti, and the events that had freed Grandfather Shadow from his prison. At last she could raise herself to her rightful station, though caution was still warranted.

As she walked out of the mill, Kavala stood there leaning against the outer wall.

"It went well?" he asked.

If she could have, Yrgaeshkil would have flayed the mortal's mind with Lie after Lie until nothing remained of him but a sniveling creature that could retain no sense of Truth at all. Unfortunately, no divine or infernal power could touch the man.

"Even better than I had hoped," Yrgaeshkil replied. "Grandfather Shadow has personally named a Lord Morigahn, and if my sources are correct, he will soon place a Saent in the world. Compared to that, what can the King of Order do to me for simply claiming what is rightfully mine by marriage?"

"Been playing with Stormseekers again?" Kavala asked.

Yrgaeshkil fingered the wolf-skin mantle she wore about her shoulders.

"The rest aren't going to be pleased by that."

She shrugged in response. "Considering that many of my children find them a delicacy, I hardly think one torture and murder will make things significantly worse."

"I suppose you're right," Kavala said. "As for the here and now, it seems the previous failures to draw the God of Shadows forth were not really failures at all." Kavala's voice held a smug tone that Yrgaeshkil did not like.

"Yes," Yrgaeshkil replied. "And, as the mortals say, it has taught me that patience is a worthy virtue. I will wait and watch for my proper time to strike. I'm sure that Grandfather Shadow will not be able to contain himself, especially considering that he is currently the only Greater Eldar free in any realm. He won't be able to resist meddling with his precious little Komati."

"Well, then," Kavala said. "I'm pleased that everything is working, if not according to the original schedule, at least to your benefit. If you will excuse me, I've been away from court almost long enough to be missed. Nae'Toran, always a pleasure."

As he spoke the words, Nae'Toran materialized in his true form, horns, bat's head, wings, and all. Yrgaeshkil turned away from Kavala before he vanished. She didn't understand how his strange powers worked without some form of divine blessing, but she did know that it churned something inside her as if she were a mortal creature with mortal frailties.

"What would you have me do now, Mother?" Nae'Toran asked.

To that, the Mother of Daemyns smiled. "Avail yourself to any Adept of Night that calls to you or wishes to bargain with a Daemyn. Sow chaos wherever you can, especially amongst the Morigahnti and Adepts of House Kaesiak."

"As you wish, Mother."

Nae'Toran vanished, and Yrgaeshkil walked up the hill to the multitude of corpses lying sprawled about the oak. Two of those corpses held particular interest for her – the two Morigahnti killed by the Daemyn hounds. She knelt down next to them and touched the one with pretty green eyes on the cheek. With his soul gone, not just ascended to the celestial realms but devoured by the Daemyn hounds and sent to the Realm of Godless Dead, his skin felt like moist leather. The Goddess of Lies took hold of the Morigahnti's chin and turned his face this way and that, memorizing his features. His soul would be wearing this same face in her husband's realm, and she wanted to find him. She meant to question his soul quite thoroughly about the current state of the Morigahnti, and she meant to take full advantage of his friendship with the most recent Lord Morigahn.

Yrgaeshkil looked over at Julianna and considered killing the girl, or better, giving her to Nae'Toran as a plaything. He could place her soul right next to Kaeldyr's. But no. That would not do. Grandfather Shadow would return soon, and if Yrgaeshkil guessed anything about the knife currently heating in the fire, she knew what that was about. If the God of Vengeance returned and found his new favorite pet missing, his wrath would be terrible. She would not risk that so soon.

The wind picked up. It carried a hint of divine power, a touch of heat and light that made her skin crawl. Yrgaeshkil cocked her head to the side and reached outward with her divine senses. Close by, she felt the blazing white power of All Father Sun – not enough to actually be the god, but enough for it to be one or more divine foci dedicated to the God of Truth and Light.

For a moment, she considered leaving, not in flight but out of caution. After a moment, she changed her mind, went to the oak, leaned against it, and wrapped herself in a Lie.

FIVE

Grandfather Shadow stepped back into the physical realm. Being in his proper body felt far better than being trapped in Khellan's corpse. He closed his eyes and took a deep breath, not because he needed to, but rather because he wanted to revel in any sensation he could.

The air was chilly without being cold, the kind of autumn air where a man could be comfortable in just a coat or a light cloak. The air smelled of pine and earth. The dull ever-constant roar of the wind through the pine needles was like a symphony to his ears. How he missed that sound. It had been too slight a sound to really perceive while trapped in the multitudes of Lords Morigahn over the centuries.

Opening his eyes, Grandfather Shadow exhaled.

A large wolf, larger than any natural animal could claim to be, sat on its haunches regarding the Greater Eldar. The beast was mostly black. White and gray peppered the wolf's muzzle, paws, ears, flanks, and tail. It had been completely black at one point in its life, but neither Grandfather Shadow, nor any other creature, save for another of the wolf's kind, could tell its age or where in its life it happened to be.

Lords and Princes, Grandfather Shadow had missed this one. Unfortunately, he also knew that the wolf and all his kind had turned away from him after the Battle of Kyrtigaen Pass. Grandfather Shadow had to tread carefully, or things might be very bad for Julianna.

"You knew I'd be here?" Grandfather Shadow asked.

The wolf nodded.

"You know what I want."

The wolf nodded.

"And knowing you, it's some where or when I cannot reach."

Again, a nod.

"Will you give it to me?"

The wolf just looked at him. Grandfather Shadow knew better than to try and wait out this particular wolf.

"Razka, please," Grandfather Shadow said. "I could not have done anything at Kyrtigaen pass. I wanted to. Think of how it was for me, trapped in the mind of an idiot that never should have been named Lord Morigahn, never mind how he ever managed to survive the trial."

When the wolf did not react, Grandfather Shadow decided that a bit of waiting wouldn't hurt. As it was, he'd waited a thousand years; he could wait a little while longer.

For a long time the wolf and the god regarded each other. Each moment took them closer to the moment the knife would reach the perfect heat. Also, there was no guarantee that someone or something with malicious intent wouldn't come along and find Julianna helpless. Sloppy. He'd been so sloppy and careless. He could have hidden her in Illusion, or made it so anyone arriving there could have no Knowledge of her presence.

"Unlike some others," Grandfather Shadow said, "I do not have all the time in existence. I have to return to the new Lord Morigahn soon, or she may be discovered."

The wolf's ear twitched, and its head cocked to the side.

"Oh, yes," Grandfather Shadow said. "I've decided to name a woman. Perhaps you know her, Duchess Julianna Taraen of House Kolmonen."

The wolf growled at him, deep and menacing.

"Spare me, Razka," Grandfather Shadow said. "You may be bitter. You may be angry, and yes, I told you this in order to manipulate you into doing what I want. I don't have time to stroke your pride or nurse your old wounds. Julianna waits in a half-sleep for me to return. I will mark her, and set her upon the Lord Morigahn's path. It's your choice if she walks that path fully armed."

The wolf vanished in a ripple of localized lightning. A small clap of thunder echoed a moment later. That could be either good or bad. Either way, Grandfather Shadow didn't want to wait any longer. If Razka had decided to help, Julianna would get what she needed when Razka decided it was time.

When he returned to the fire, Grandfather Shadow found the knife blade glowing red. Picking up the knife, he examined the blade. It was too sharp, so he picked up a rock and ran it across the knife's edge seven times, dulling the blade. Grandfather Shadow returned to Julianna and released her from the half-sleep. She looked from his eyes to the glowing blade. She tried to back away, but Grandfather Shadow grabbed her.

"This is going to hurt." He would never lie to her again.

Julianna screamed as the knife cut down her face. She struggled, but the god was too strong. As the blade bit deeper and deeper into her flesh, the god spoke words in that strange tongue, and Julianna felt the knife pass through her physical form and into her spirit. A bond formed between her and Grandfather Shadow, and the heated blade became a bridge between them. He leaned in close to her and whispered in her ear. His voice carried the words, but she received the god's information from where the knife penetrated her soul.

All the knowledge and secrets of the Lord Morigahn swam in Julianna's head, though not all of it came from Grandfather Shadow. There were some fragments of memories that came from her own childhood that she had only remembered in her deepest dreams. She had learned much of *Galad'laman* as a child, and then she had forgotten. She tried to make some sense of it all, but there was too much. Each time she pulled something to the front of her mind, all the rest would crowd around it, as if seeking Julianna's attention.

"The pain will fade faster than you think," Grandfather Shadow said. "In time, you will grow accustomed to both the knowledge and the scar. Now, gather the Morigahnti, find the heir to the seven mountains, and reclaim Koma's once great empire."

Grandfather Shadow finished marking Julianna, took Khellan's *Galad'fana*, and wrapped the gray cloth around her head. He would have preferred her to have the same holy cloth that he had given to Kaeldyr so many centuries before, but that would have to wait until Razka decided it was time for her to have it.

He had given the Lord Morigahn everything she needed to lead the Morigahnti. Everything, except a guardian.

Looking out through every shadow in the world, Grandfather Shadow found the perfect man to protect Julianna.

Only one problem remained. The man was still alive.

Grandfather Shadow sent lightning crashing down from the sky, and just as the mortal's life ended, the god channeled a small portion of his divinity into the man.

"I name you the Sentinel," Grandfather Shadow said.

Then he moved the man hundreds of miles to the northeast and laid him against a tree in the apple orchard. Best to give the young man a bit of time to acclimate to the sudden change.

Having taken care of everything he could think of for the moment, Grandfather Shadow paused for reflection. The King of Order's prison had been meant to teach the Greater Gods humility. Grandfather Shadow had acted just as he had during the Second War of the Gods. If he wasn't careful, he might wind up back in his prison. Should that happen, Julianna would never survive, much less lead the Komati people back to him.

The world had changed. Grandfather Shadow needed to change with it. Subtlety, something none of the greater gods had ever been adept at, was required. For now, Grandfather Shadow would wait and assist Julianna only when she asked him. Perhaps he might send her a boon when she really needed one. If she was truly all Grandfather Shadow hoped, she wouldn't need his help very often, especially with the Sentinel by her side.

SIX

A cauldron bubbled in a secret chamber in the Governor's Palace of Koma city. Octavio Salvatore, the First Adept of Old Uncle Night, ground his teeth as the mists from the cauldron dissipated. For the most part, Octavio considered himself a man of even temper, but now he fought the urge to reach out and break something. True, there were moments when he doled out punishments terrible in severity, but when that happened, it was out of necessity, not fury.

This disaster could not have come at a worse time. The Brotherhood of the Night was about to seize control of the Kingdom of the Sun, and part of that aim required that the Morigahnti remain quietly in the background. An unauthorized attack on any Morigahnti and the murder of the Lord Morigahn broke all agreements Octavio had made with his few contacts within the Morigahnti.

The doors to the Chapel of Night opened. Dante, Octavio's younger brother by six years, entered, wearing a self-satisfied smirk while his dark eyes glimmered with a secret. He wore these expressions more and more frequently as the years passed. Dante possessed the gift of prophecy and foresight. While any who saw visions and spoke prophesies were sought after by all the Great Houses, it usually took these individuals years to understand their gifts well enough to assess the predictions with any accuracy. This was not so with Dante. Within minutes of speaking a prophecy, he understood with alarming regularity what his gift had told him of the future. In addition, his youth gave him an arrogance that he wore like a garment. Dante only removed that garment in front of the Sun King, the Speaker of the Sun, and occasionally Octavio. This was not one of those times.

"Do you know anything about this?" Octavio gestured at the cauldron.

Dante swaggered over and glanced at the bloody scene revealed in the mist.

"I ordered it," Dante replied as if he were replying to a question about the seating placements at a banquet or the choices of refreshments at a ball.

"What?" Octavio's hands clenched into fists. "Why?" He opened his hands; it was a struggle not to wrap them around Dante's neck. "We had an agreement with them."

Dante traced his finger along the edge of the cauldron. "An agreement we were planning to break as soon as it was convenient for us."

"Yes. But once we secured the throne."

"But it was necessary for us to kill the Lord Morigahn now," Dante replied. "The Morigahnti had no intentions of holding to the agreement either, and I'm surprised that you believed they would. Now they will be in a state of chaos until well after we have secured the Brotherhood's control of the Kingdom."

To emphasize his point, Dante thrust his finger into the water. Ripples disrupted the water and caused the vision within to warp and fade.

Octavio said. "Did your prophecy tell you anything of a new Lord Morigahn being named today?"

Seeing Dante's face break from his usual all-knowing mask was almost worth this development – yes, think of this as a development rather than a disaster. A moment later, Dante's lips shifted from a gaping circle of surprise back to a wide grin.

"Nearly had me there, Octavio," Dante said. "But it will take the Morigahnti months to gather in order to choose a new leader."

"Not anymore. The new Lord Morigahn freed Grandfather Shadow. He named her himself."

Dante's face fell again. "Gods and goddesses." He took a deep breath. "Wait. Did you say *her*?"

"Yes." Octavio waved his hand over the cauldron. The waters smoothed, and Octavio shifted the view to focus in on the woman cuping her hands over her face. "That is the new Lord Morigahn, Duchess Julianna Taraen."

"Taraen. Didn't we—?"

"Yes," Octavio said. "Do you see why this creates an entirely new situation we must deal with on many different levels? It may be as you say, that it will take time for them to organize under her, but I would rather have some idea of what the future will bring. Until you can bring me some good news, I want you to clean the chapel while I—"

"Me? Why not one of the disciples? That's what they're for."

"It's always good to remember where you came from, little brother."

"Then why don't you clean it?" Dante snapped.

"Because I have a Kingdom protectorate to govern," Octavio said. "And I am not the one who possibly ruined years of careful planning."

"I haven't," Dante said, "My speaking clearly—"

Octavio raised his hand. "You did not foresee this new Lord Morigahn, much less Grandfather Shadow coming to personally name her."

Leaving Dante in the Chapel of Night, Octavio pondered how to solve the problems this new Lord Morigahn posed. He wasn't even going to consider the ramifications of Grandfather Shadow himself being freed when none of the other gods had been. It seemed Dante didn't want to either, or it would have come up. It was much easier to focus on mortal dilemmas, leaving the celestial and infernal realms to deal with each other.

The biggest problem with Julianna Taraen was that Octavio could not act directly, or his ties to Old Uncle Night might be discovered. Fortunately, he had many strings to pull and pawns to play, most of which he could deploy through layers and layers of contacts and allies so that it would be nearly impossible to follow the path back to him. And if somebody did begin to deduce the true mastermind behind the events, well, it wouldn't be the first corpse Octavio had left in his wake. Assassination, lies, treachery, and extortion were the weapons of choice in the battle for Zenith of the Throne. All the Houses used these tools. There were only two ways for one House to take the Zenith away from another. One involved a considerable number of political marriages, and the other requireed many deaths. Of course, the Brotherhood of the Night preferred the second.

Just outside the chapel, Octavio saw Kavala, Dante's bodyguard. Kavala leaned against a wall, head down with the hood of his dark cloak pulled down low over his face. He held a pipe in his mouth and puffed on the stem. The hood hid the man's mangled face. Scars of some torture endured long ago marred Kavala so much that seeing his face made Octavio's stomach churn. However, Kavala had been a gift from Old Uncle Night's wife, sent to insure Dante's safety, so Octavio endured Kavala's deformity.

"Good evening, Your Darkness," Kavala said.

At least Dante's dog had manners, which was more than Octavio could say for his younger brother. If nothing else, Kavala knew his place and remained ever respectful of Octavio's status both as a Duke of the Realm and as First Adept of Old Uncle Night.

"I'm sorry to say you may remain there for some time yet," Octavio said.

"I have no pressing engagements, Your Grace," Kavala replied with a bow.

Octavio nodded. He needed to think, and for that, he needed his wife. She would get him to relax, and then he would talk to her. She would sit there and listen, as she always did, and might even interject an idea or two, until some form of plan came to Octavio.

SEVEN

A few moments after Yrgaeshkil felt the scrying from Octavio's cauldron vanish, a small flash of lighting illuminated the air next to Julianna; a clap of thunder roared less than a heartbeat later. A man dressed all in furs and leathers, hair wild and snarled, leaned over Julianna. He watched her trembling and crying for a time, much longer than Yrgaeshkil had ever seen any of his kind remain still.

Yrgaeshkil knew him. She'd known him for a long time. Like with so many Minor Eldar who could not be commanded by their names, she hadn't bothered to remember his.

The man reached down, placed his hand on Julianna's head, and gently stroked her hair.

"I'm sorry," he said.

Then the man stood and faced Yrgaeshkil. "You forgot smell. Don't worry. No one is watching."

Yrgaeshkil dropped the Lie completely.

"I forgot how crafty you people are," the goddess said.

"We are what we are," the man replied. "Just as you, we act and react according to our nature."

"I have no quarrel with you," Yrgaeshkil said.

He snorted a sound halfway between a laugh and a growl. "And I believe you, why? The Mother of Daemyns and Goddess of Lies."

"I would shake off both of those mantles if I could."

"Would you?"

"Indeed."

"Again, I believe you, why?"

Yrgaeshkil shrugged. "What do you want?"

"To warn you," the man said. "You have toyed with her enough. Leave off. If you don't, I will become displeased."

Suddenly, her wolf-skin mantle felt a bit warm and uncomfortable.

"Are you threatening me?" Yrgaeshkil couldn't believe his audacity.

"I am."

She opened her mouth to say something, but words failed her. This lesser being, barely even a Minor Eldar, was threatening her who had given birth to the multitudes of Daemynic species.

"Don't know quite how to take that?" This time he did laugh, an amused chuckle from deep in his belly. "Been a long time, has it? Well, I know that I might not be able to do much to you, myself, but I and my kind can be anywhere we need to in order to know your plans and upset them. You may eventually strike us all down, and you may wear our skins as mantles, or make boots out of them, or whatever suits your whim at the moment. But not before we ensure that every scheme you have for the next thousand years turns against you."

How she wanted to end him, to destroy him utterly and completely, but she couldn't ensure that she'd be fast enough. If he got away, a war between the Stormseekers and Daemyns would erupt across the realms. While the Stormseekers could not hope to win that war, it would be costly indeed, and she could not afford the distraction with Grandfather Shadow roaming free.

"Very well," Yrgaeshkil said. "Do you mind if I watch?"

"Do what you will, so long as you leave her be."

Lightning flashed. Thunder roared. He was gone and appeared again, this time carrying a massive book. It could only be the *Galad'parma*. The man pushed the book underneath Julianna. She wrapped her arms around it as if she were drowning and it could save her. It might very well save her, Yrgaeshkil thought.

He looked at Yrgaeshkil. The lighting and thunder came again, and he was gone and did not return.

Yrgaeshkil leaned against the oak and covered herself with a Lie, this time masking scent as well.

EIGHT

Luciano Salvatore, Adept of All Father Sun and Inquisitor of House Floraen, woke with a start as his prized possession buzzed and chimed him awake. He sat up, rubbing the sleep from his eyes. He and his younger cousin Santo, who was also an Inquisitor, had decided to camp in a copse of trees by a stream rather than avail themselves of the hospitality of the local Komati nobility. Luciano had reports that several of the local families illegally worshiped Grandfather Shadow. Staying at the wrong estate could find them both the surprised recipients of slit throats.

"What is it?" Santo ask.

"Something's happening," Luciano rifled through his pack, which he'd been using as a pillow. After a few moments he found it.

He called the thing The Detector, which most people, at least the few who ever saw it, mistook for a pocket watch. Any similarities The Detector might have to a pocket watch were purely cosmetic. It had hands, but five rather than two. Instead of numbers, the apparatus had five symbols, one for each of the greater gods. In the presence of divine power, the device would chime. The closer the divine power that was being channeled, the louder the chimes rang. If divine power had been channeled in an area but was being channeled no longer, The Detector would vibrate. When Luciano opened the gold and silver device in the presence of divine power, one of the hands would point to that god's symbol – the larger the hand, the stronger the source of divine power. To date, the largest hand had not moved from the blank spot that twelve o'clock normally occupied on normal clocks.

Today was different. The two largest hands, including the one that had never moved, pointed to Grandfather Shadow's symbol. The middle hand pointed to Old Uncle Night.

"Well?" asked his cousin.

"Look for yourself." Luciano handed him The Detector.

"Two hands for one god? Has that ever happened before?"

"No."

Santo handed The Detector back.

"What can it mean?"

"I couldn't even begin to speculate." Luciano continued staring at those two hands pointing at Grandfather Shadow's symbol – especially the one hand that had never moved before. He sighed.

"What's wrong?" Santo asked.

Luciano looked at his cousin, fresh to the Inquisitors, full of zeal, and eager to prove himself worthy of the title. How long ago had it been since Luciano had felt like that? It seemed a lifetime, when in truth, he'd only been an Inquisitor for nine years. Nine years of fighting Morigahnti, and Daemyn worshipers, and those firearm-toting madmen of northern Heidenmarch. He could just imagine Santo's heart beating with excitement at the prospect of discovering the source of this oddity that The Detector had discovered. Every fresh Inquisitor Luciano had ever known, himself included, always wanted to be the one who discovered some terrible new threat to the Kingdom of the Sun. They were all idiots, Luciano included. The ones who grew out of that idiocy were the ones that survived.

"Nothing." Luciano said. "I suppose we'll have to investigate to find out."

Santo's entire face grinned like some child going off to fair for the first time. "Of course we will!"

They broke camp and dressed as quickly as they could.

"Santo," Luciano said, as he helped strap his cousin's breastplate into place. "I need you to listen."

"Of course," Santo said. "I always listen to your wisdom and value your experience."

"No. You are lying." Santo opened his mouth to protest, but Luciano held his hand up to quiet him. Santo had seen the gesture enough times to recognize its meaning. "You're not intentionally lying, but you are lying all the same. I did it as well when I was fresh to the Inquisitors. The most important Truth to know is the Truth within ourselves. When we know that, All Father Sun will bless us as he blesses no other, and the lies of the world cannot take hold of our minds, hearts, or spirits."

"I'm not afraid." Santo said. "I will not fall victim to Old Uncle Night's lies."

"Fear is a part of life," Luciano said, "just as death comes for all men. Each god and goddess has a place in the world, and reality would crumble without their control over the dominion. By not acknowledging our fear, we fall victim to the lies we tell ourselves, and those are the most dangerous lies of all, the hardest lies to see beyond.

"We are also only two. We do not share the Father's full blessing without a third, and so, we must be doubly cautious, especially should we meet an enemy whose numbers coincide with their deity's numbers."

"Yes, Luciano," Santo replied. "I understand."

But the young man didn't. He looked the part of the stoic Inquisitor, sitting stiff and straight in his saddle, but that was only because it was what he was taught, what was expected. Were they riding through a town, Luciano would have assumed the same, authoritative pose. However, out here, on a road far between towns, where the Komati nobility kept their summer estates, most of which would be empty this close to autumn anyway, Luciano didn't bother with the pretense of appearances.

As they rode to investigate this mystery, Luciano quietly prayed for All Father Sun to open Santo's eyes to the Truth within himself.

NINE

Faelin woke with a start. His heart pounded hard in his chest, and his breath came in quick gasps. For a moment he had felt as if he was on fire, but now the pain was gone. It must have been a dream. He forced himself to breathe at a steady pace.

He noticed two things right away. First was that the air was a bit colder than it should have been at dawn. Second, the scent of apples filled the air. More changes to his world came after that. He was leaning against a tree. When he'd gone to sleep, he'd lain out under a tree in a field of tall grass – now he was at the very edge of an orchard.

Faelin suppressed the urge to jump to his feet and draw his rapier. If someone had wanted to kill him, they certainly would have done so. No, it wasn't death that had come for him but some other power.

Rather than jump around in a panic, Faelin got up slowly, stretched, and pulled the small, palm-sized journal out of the secret pocket in his left boot. He flipped through it until he came to the words he wanted. He'd managed to memorize very little of the *fyrmest spaeg geoda*, but he'd made extensive notes of statements he could make and what their uses were. He studied the one he wanted for a few moments, making sure of the pronunciations.

"*Kahhdria ekbilak jyvmirjy,*" Faelin said.

A rush of winds surrounded him, warm and cold buffeted against his skin and whipped at his clothes. A moment later, a beautiful young woman stood a few paces away. She was naked, but a continuous breeze containing dust, leaves, and twigs spun around her, covering the more distracting parts of her body. This morning her hair was a deep platinum-blond with just a hint of the whitish-blue that hung on the horizons at the height of spring.

He hadn't expected her to appear so soon. This sudden arrival meant she must have been close by. However, with Khaddria, that could mean within a few hundred leagues.

"I really hate it when you do that," the goddess of wind said.

"I'm not too fond of being made a pawn in your games again," Faelin replied.

"I'm not…" Kahddria trailed off.

She looked him up and down, floated in a circle around him. Faelin felt like a prize piece of livestock being examined at a country fair.

"What?" Faelin asked.

"You've changed," Kahddria said. "And you aren't even aware of how much you've changed."

"I'm not in the mood for games, goddess," Faelin said, flipping the pages in his journal.

"I'm not playing any games. Well, at least not with you. I'm playing against much bigger players with much higher stakes."

"Tell me," Faelin said.

Kahddria stopped circling when she came back in front of Faelin. She crossed her arms and actually settled her feet on the earth. "You may have that little book and my promise to do you no harm," Kahddria said, "but that's not going to motivate me to betray the secrets of others who frighten me much more than any temporary annoyance you might be. Good morning Faelin vara'Traejyn. It was nice to see you again, even if you interrupted a very important conversation. May your summers and winters be short, springs be mild, and autumn reaping plentiful."

The wind around them started picking up, meaning she was about to depart. Faelin considered forcing her to stay and answer his questions, but after a moment he rejected the thought. The goddess might not be able to hurt him, but that didn't mean she couldn't arrange for life to be very difficult.

"Oh. You'll want to go that way." She gestured toward the east. "Once you get to the stream and mill, I'm sure you'll recognize your surroundings."

With that, she vanished into the wind.

"Damn," Faelin muttered. What had he gotten himself involved in this time?

Well, he saw no reason to put off figuring out what was going on. Faelin packed his camp, which didn't take long, as whoever had moved him here, hadn't bothered to bring anything other than his blanket and pack. His food bag, tied in a tree, and cooking utensils had remained in Heidenmarch. He chuckled to himself as he imagined some passerby walking along the road and finding the remains of the camp. With his journal back in his boot and his pack and bedroll slung across his shoulders, Faelin started walking.

As soon as he came to the mill and saw the towering oak tree at the top of the hill, Faelin recognized Kaeldyr's Rest. Ravens circled the oak.

Faelin drew in a deep breath and let it out very slowly. He'd suspected he'd be in Koma, but had hoped that maybe, just maybe, he'd been drawn to some other place. And of all the places in Koma it could be, it had to be Kaeldyr's Rest. Nothing good could come from climbing that hill. He ran his hands through his hair and looked about, noticing a few crossbow bolts scattered about the ground outside of the mill. Looking closer, he saw the bloodstains in the earth. He hurried to one of the windows, glanced in, and saw pools of blood on the stone floor.

The only people he could imagine fighting a battle here were the Morigahnti. But who would they be fighting against? Faelin supposed it didn't matter. They were either still here, or they weren't. If they were, he'd figure out a way to deal with it. No matter what the gods threw at him, he always managed to scrape through.

Despite the amount of blood spilled, the mill was clear of bodies. He looked up the hill toward the ancient oak tree and the ravens circling in the air.

As he went up the hill, Faelin drew his rapier. He'd considered leaving his pack and bedroll hidden by the mill, but reconsidered. They helped to add credibility to his strange and sudden appearance, and they might be stolen. Replacing his cooking gear would be bad enough.

At the top of the hill, Faelin discovered the remains of a small battle. Dozens of bodies littered the earth around a great oak tree, many of them skinned alive. Panic threatened to overwhelm him, but Faelin forced himself to remain calm. This was not the first time in his life strange things had occurred with seemingly no explanation. He gave a quick prayer, partially for the fallen and partially for luck not to get drawn into a game between deities again. Something told Faelin that only the first part of his prayer would be answered.

Something moved next to him. Faelin jumped away and brought his rapier to bear. A woman in the tattered remains of a lady's riding dress writhed on the ground. The only garment she wore that wasn't in tatters was a dark gray scarf wrapped around her head. It looked almost like a *Galad'fana*, one of the wrappings the Morigahnti wore in their worship of Grandfather Shadow.

Faelin scanned the other bodies in case someone else was feigning death, waiting in ambush for an unsuspecting, kindhearted soul. The remnants of black leather armor lay in tatters around the skinned bodies, except for one, who wore the black robes of an Adept of Old Uncle Night.

Some of the other bodies wore coats cut in the Komati fashion, decorated with House and family colors. But more than that, each one had a long gray cloth wrapped around his neck. Those veils were *Galad'fana*, making the men Morigahnti.

Faelin swatted at the flies buzzing around him and looked beyond the gruesome scene now that he was on top of the hill. He saw horses, many of them saddled, grazing in the fields around hill. Some of them were Saifreni, though most had the look of Standard Blood working horses, probably for the rank and file of the Brotherhood of the Night.

Finding no obvious threats, Faelin sheathed his rapier and glanced at the single survivor of the battle. As he got closer, he saw that the girl actually was wearing a *Galad'fana*. Her pained moans pulled at his heart. Faelin wanted to reach out to her, but he had to know if any miracles or other surprises were lingering about.

"*Aeteowian ic seo wat sodlis ikona,*" Faelin said. That was one phrase he knew by heart.

The ancient first tongue of creation was lost to all but a few scholarly orders. Unlike the divine languages of the greater gods, the *fyrmest spaeg geo-*

da did not have the power to perform miracles. It only revealed the presence of celestial powers or creatures.

The moment Faelin spoke, words appeared written in the air. Some were in the spidery script of Grandfather Shadow's language. Others were the dizzying, sweeping loops of Old Uncle Night's. The *Galad'fana* and the Adept's robe glowed from the small bits of divine power blessed into them. All these images began fading almost immediately, indicating that the words in the air representing recently spoken miracles had all taken effect. There were no surprises waiting.

As these letters faded, Faelin studied them, trying to tell where each had originated. Each miracle had a thin bond with the divine focus that had been used to channel it into existence, and each one connected with one of the *Galad'fana* worn by the Morigahnti. Some of the miracles in Old Uncle Night's language had been spoken by people no longer present.

"Wait a moment," Faelin said to himself.

He should have seen them before, but there were so many other words hanging in the air, that Faelin had missed the few that had no ties to any foci. Those words could have only been spoken from the lips of pure faith, without the use of a divine focus. Nobody in any land had spoken a miracle of pure faith in centuries. The girl had spoken one of those miracles, but whoever had spoken the others was gone. Faelin looked closer. He saw that someone else had spoken through the girl.

Reaching into his boot, he brought out his journal. After a few moments of rifling through the pages, he found what he was looking for. He read the passage several times in his head, mouthing to practice forming the words.

When he felt he had it well enough not to butcher it, Faelin said, "*Audsyna egni hinn hulaetur.*"

Three ghostly forms appeared. One hovered above a pile of dust, the second lay in the same spot as the girl, the third stood in the same place as one of the Komati men. The first had a human's body, leathery wings, and a bat-like head with ram's horns sprouting from behind its ears. The other two ghostly images looked human. However, the one sharing space with the girl had some small aspect of divinity bound to it; that must have been what had spoken the miracle through the girl. The third spectral form caused Faelin to step back. The truth of its origin was well hidden, but ultimately could not hide from the primal power of *fyrmest spaeg geoda*. It was Grandfather Shadow, walking free on the physical realm. Somehow, a soul from the Realm of Shadows had given the girl enough faith to free Grandfather Shadow from his prison.

Faelin chewed on his lip. Grandfather Shadow was free. Were any of the other greater gods? No, he could not think about that. There were too many frightening possibilities down that path, and Faelin had often been accused of having too much imagination for his own good. He returned to the image of Grandfather Shadow. Was that who had put Faelin here? If so, why? The girl was the only thing he could think of.

"Are you hurt?" Faelin asked, kneeling next to her.

She made a sound part way between a scream and a growl and pulled away. As she scurried backwards, the girl slashed at the air between them with a dagger. The movement caused her to drop a large book and the veil to come away from her face.

Faelin read the title and gaped. *Galad'parma.* The Tome of Shadows, Grandfather Shadow's holy book. This volume was larger than any Faelin had ever seen. His heart pounded as pieces began to fall together. No, the gods had not answered his second prayer.

Looking from the book to the girl, Faelin saw a deep gash running down the right side of her face, glowing with divine power. That wound confirmed his fears. Grandfather Shadow had marked this girl as the new Lord Morigahn.

Taking in the rest of the poor girl's face, Faelin recognized her. She'd been sixteen and was growing into a lovely young woman when he saw her last. He hadn't thought about her in years. She would be twenty-one now. Actually, twenty-one as of yesterday. The years had been good to her. Aside from that scar, she possessed more beauty than any three women had rights to.

"Julianna?" he asked. "Is that you?"

Her steel-gray eyes darted back and forth, trying to look everywhere at once, but she kept the dagger leveled between them.

"Julianna," he repeated. "It's Faelin. Don't you remember me?"

Her gaze rested on his face. She nodded slightly. He stepped forward, but she raised the knife. Thin wisps of smoke rose from the blade, as if it had been heated in the fire.

"I want to help you, Julianna. Can you talk to me?"

Her mouth opened, and her head moved forward slightly. Her lips looked as if they were trying to form words, and her eyes rolled up a bit, as if she were trying to gaze into her own mind. She took a deep breath and closed her eyes. When she opened them again, her head and shoulders slumped forward and her eyes fixed on her feet.

"*Ji*," she finally whispered, sounding utterly defeated.

The word was *yes* in *Galad'laman*, the language of Grandfather Shadow. Faelin's father had taught him the forbidden tongue. How could Julianna have learned it?

"I'm going to look around," Faelin said. "Then we're leaving."

Faelin went over to the man closest to Julianna. Turning the body over, Faelin recognized his old friend, Khellan Dubhan. Khellan also bore a scar like the one on Julianna's face, except that Khellan's scar had healed some time ago. In the right pocket of his waistcoat, Khellan had a pocket watch. Such a device was a blatant symbol of hatred for the Kingdom. Though pocket watches were legal, the Kingdom usually kept a close eye on the possessor for fear of what other suspicious or outlawed technology they might own.

Faelin had walked away from any contact with the Morigahnti long ago, vowing to never deal with them again, choosing to follow Grandfather Shadow in his own way instead. He looked at Julianna, alone and half mad. He couldn't leave her to face the journey before her. Deep in his heart, Faelin was Grandfather Shadow's servant. Morigahnti be damned, he would walk this road next to her. Julianna would need someone to protect her, teach her about the Morigahnti, and explain the subtleties of Grandfather Shadow's laws. Faelin didn't know if he was the one to teach her; it had been so long since he'd spoken to a Morigahnti, much less been a part of their rituals, but he couldn't imagine the infighting and politicking having died out in the last few years. He glanced at Khellan's body. No, it had not died out. While Faelin had liked Khellan, and the young lord might have the scar of a Lord Morigahn, he was no *Morigahnti'uljas*, Lord of the Morigahnti. Somehow, someone must have managed to determine a way to cheat the trials.

Well, that was a question and a challenge for another day. For now, he had to get them both as far from this place as possible. With the amount of divine energy that had been flung around, not to mention one of the greater gods having been freed from his prison, Faelin didn't want to guess who or what might arrive to investigate.

He rummaged through the remains of the picnic. He found a basket of pears and apples, the perfect thing for tempting horses. He wouldn't be able to get them too close to the gory scene at the top of the hill, but a little closer and gathered together was better than nothing. With the basket under his left arm, Faelin went hunting horses.

At first, he headed toward a group gathered close to each other in the fields below the hill, but then movement near the apple orchard caught his eye. There, in the shade of the trees, was a familiar black and white animal. The last time Faelin had seen that particular horse, it had barely been old enough to ride, and now it had grown into quite the monster, but those markings hadn't changed enough to make it unrecognizable. He couldn't help but smile. That horse might very well make it possible to get Julianna calm enough to ride from this place. And, if Faelin remembered correctly, he had the perfect bait to trap that prey.

The apples in the basket worked even better than he'd hoped, and Vendyr seemed to remember him. Faelin spent a good ten to fifteen minutes feeding Vendyr and stroking the animal's neck and face, especially around the ears, eyes, and nostrils, gently caressing those areas to build intimacy between him and the horse as Vendyr kept his muzzle in the basket, happily munching on the apples and pears. Faelin shook his head. Even before he'd fled, this horse had been the most food-motivated animal Faelin had ever known. It was good to see that some things, the simple things, did not change.

Once he'd created the beginnings of a relationship with Vendyr, he used the horse to collect others. Horses were natural followers, inclined to group together. Vendyr was a dominant animal. Even at two and three, Faelin recalled the horse challenging older horses. He used Vendyr to gather up four of the other horses, selecting those that were already saddled.

Things became more difficult when Faelin took them closer to the carnage at the top of the hill. The trouble with herd animals was that when one started spooking and the rest of them caught onto it, the feeling spread like a plague, only faster. It took Faelin the better part of an hour to get them even halfway up the hill. He practiced steady breathing techniques to calm himself, but even still, he just wanted to punch the horses. To keep them from wandering off, he'd taken the basket that he'd used to bribe Vendyr, filled it with apples from the orchard, and scattered the fruit on the ground at the point where the horses refused to go any higher.

Finally, his hands raw and muscles sore from fighting with the horses, Faelin had the animals chomping away about halfway up the hill. Faelin prepared Vendyr for riding, taking tack and saddle from a collection gathered at a point partway down the hill. Likely, the servants had been sent here while the lords and ladies enjoyed themselves by the oak. That's how it had been when Faelin had been invited to join them so many years ago. Hoping the scattered apples would help keep the horses from wandering too far, Faelin went back up the hill.

First, Faelin scavenged the camp. He put the Tome of Shadows in his backpack, collected some usable clothes from the Komati lords, and gathered up what food he thought would travel well: bread and cheeses mostly, and some dried fruit. He considered taking the weapons and perhaps selling them along the way, but he wanted as little to do with the Brotherhood of the Night as possible. And someone selling that many weapons would be remembered. He settled on three rapiers, even though he already had one. That gave them two blades apiece. He hoped Julianna had kept up practice with her swordplay. As the Lord Morigahn, she needed to learn to handle a blade better than he remembered she could. The only other thing of value he found was a small purse filled with gold and silver coins. He collected all the *Galad'fana* and stuffed them in his backpack with the *Galad'parma*. Those were not items to be left for any passersby to stumble upon. With that in mind, he stoked the fire back to life, took the mantle from the Adept of Old Uncle Night, and tossed it on the fire. Faint snarls and cries of pain whispered out of the smoke and flames as the cloth burned.

Now the hard part began.

"Julianna," Faelin said softly.

She jerked at the sound of her name, shifting to keep the dagger between them.

"I'm not going to hurt you. I got your horse ready so we can leave this place. Look. There's Vendyr."

When Faelin said Vendyr's name, Julianna stood and looked down the hill. Her eyes brightened a bit.

"Listen carefully," Faelin said to Julianna. "I'm going to help you onto Vendyr. We need to be away from this place as soon as possible."

Julianna nodded. She dropped the dagger and let him help her to her feet. Faelin picked up the dagger and handed it back to her.

"You might need this later," he said.

She took the blade and held it close.

Faelin managed to help her into a coat that covered most of her tattered clothes, and then led her down the hill. Getting her onto Vendyr was easier than he's expected. She almost flew into the saddle.

Faelin mounted and gave one last look at the bodies at the top of the hill. It wrenched at his heart that he could not perform the Ritual of Sending, but he had never learned it. Even the Nightbrothers deserved better than to have their spirits wallowing here. Hopefully someone would come along who would be able to perform the ritual so the souls here had a better chance of ascending to one of the gods' celestial realms rather than being cast down into the Dark Realm of the Godless Dead.

Turning his horse, he led Julianna and the spare mounts away from the sun. His plan was to flee Koma before the Kingdom or the Morigahnti found them. They would stay away for as long as it took for Julianna to learn what it meant to be the Lord Morigahn. Faelin set a brisk pace; they needed to cover ground as fast as possible. If the Brotherhood of the Night found Julianna, death would likely be the least of their worries.

TEN

Luciano and Santo Salvatore reached Kaeldyr's Rest just before noon. They first noticed the air and trees filled with crows or ravens, Luciano could never remember which. He wondered if any happened to be those blasted birds that the Morigahnti associated with. True, the followers of all the gods made pacts with various spirit animals, but the Inquisitors knew the truth, that these creatures were not actually divine in nature, and thus steered as far from them as possible.

As they rode up the hill, their horses trained not to balk at anything, the sickly-sweet hint of rotting flesh hung in the air. Bodies of Komati and Nightbrother, as well as a few horses, littered the ground surrounding a giant oak tree. Both Inquisitors dismounted and withdrew their ruby pendants from underneath their mantles. These chains of office, gold with bright rubies the size of lemons at the center, declared them not only House Floraen Inquisitors but also that they were acting in the official capacity of their office.

After just a few moments, Luciano pieced together the conflict between the Brotherhood of the Night and the Morigahnti. He marveled at how many of the Brotherhood the Morigahnti had managed to kill. He also wondered which side had ultimately won.

"Luciano," Santo said, as he circled the gruesome scene. "I've found a few trails leading off."

Santo was a natural tracker. He understood the comings and goings of men and beasts over terrain in much the way a virtuoso musician could play a song perfectly after hearing it once. Luciano possessed a similar gift, in that he could determine much about the way someone died by examining the corpse and its surroundings, but for some reason he couldn't translate that ability into tracking the way Santo could.

Luciano went over to his cousin.

"A large group went that way," Santo pointed southeast. "And there is a second."

Even Luciano could see the trampled grass and multitude of horse prints now that Santo showed him. Luciano took The Detector and walked about twenty-seven paces in the wake of that trail. The symbol of Old Uncle Night glowed, and the middle hand pointed toward that symbol.

"Where's the other," Luciano asked, as he returned.

Santo took him to the other side of the hill and pointed at something on the ground Luciano couldn't see.

"Just point me in the direction of the path and tell me if it turns," Luciano said.

"There." Santo adjusted Luciano's shoulders so he faced almost due west. "It doesn't turn."

Luciano walked twenty-seven paces along that path. When he stoped, the symbol of Grandfather Shadow – with the first two hands pointing toward it – glowed when he held it out.

"Which do we follow?" Santo asked.

Luciano tilted his head from side to side, as if he were a scale coming into balance. "Both might be pertinent to the security of the realm."

"But two hands?" they said it at the same time.

They gave each other the same sidelong glance, complete with a lopsided smile. Both had become Inquisitors because they wanted to solve mysteries that threatened the Kingdom. There was still so little known about the protectorates and the world beyond the Kingdom's borders. So much of it was hostile, and keen minds had been needed to puzzle these mysteries out.

"We could split up," Santo said. "Toss a coin and see where chance takes us."

Luciano glanced down at The Detector. A third hand shifted toward the symbol of Grandfather Shadow, and it glowed even brighter. He sucked in a quick breath.

"What is it?" Santo asked.

Luciano handed The Detector over.

"Well, that decides it." Santo spoke in a hushed tone as if he were witnessing a miracle spoken by pure faith and not one through a foci. "We have to discover what this means."

"Agreed." Luciano said.

ELEVEN

Yrgaeshkil smiled as the two Inquisitors rode away.

True, she had promised Razka that she would not harm Julianna. Yrgaeshkil believed him and his threats. However, the world was a dangerous place for anyone bearing the title of the Lord Morigahn: the Inquisitors of House Floraen being among the most ruthless and tenacious threats. It was the simplest thing to manipulate the enchanted device to ensure those two Inquisitors followed Julianna. With any luck, the Inquisitors would take Julianna by surprise and kill her. What did it matter if that protector was a Saent when the two Inquisitors were armed with Faerii steel?

HUNTER AND HUNTED

Octavio,

An Inquisitor just left my cell. His smug arrogance filled the room, and he spoke and carried himself as though expecting me to beg for my life. It amazes me how Adepts of the other Houses believe that execution could punish a servant of the God of Death. Do not weep for me, dear cousin, I yearn for Old Uncle Night's embrace.

Do not think that I hold any malice toward you. You made the right choice. It was not the Brotherhood's time, and I applaud your patience. I believe the Brotherhood's time will come, and when it does, I am confident that you will be the Night King. However, be warned: some Brothers will try to lead you down an evil path. Let your ears be deaf to their false words. Old Uncle Night is not an evil god, just as death is not an evil thing. Life and Death are two sides of the same coin. Keep your faith strong, and we will meet again in the Uncle's hall.

Vincenzo Salvatore

> Grandfather, bless me to this sunrise.
> Grandfather, bless me to this sunset.
> Bless, O bless, God of Shadows
> Each hour and stride of my journey.
> > May my summers and winters be short.
> > May my springs be mild,
> > And autumn reaping, plentiful.
>
> Grandfather, bless this pathway on which I go.
> Grandfather, bless the earth beneath my sole.
> Bless, O bless, and give me your strength.
> O God of Shadows, bless my travel and rest.
> > May my summers and winters be short.
> > May my springs be mild,
> > And autumn reaping, plentiful.

ONE

Carmine D'Mario sat watching the Daemyn hounds at the edge of the campsite. He loved how their strong and agile bodies moved. Sleek and black, Daemyn hounds were the ultimate hunters. Some claimed the Draqon breeds were greater hunters, but Carmine disagreed; Draqons were the greatest warriors – a different thing altogether. Daemyn hounds existed for only one purpose, to hunt and kill whatever their summoner sent them after.

Nicco had also loved Daemyn hounds. Just before they had ridden to meet the others for the picnic, Nicco couldn't stop talking about how when the Brotherhood rose to Zenith he would always have a pack ready to devour anyone who displeased him. Now he would have no pack, now or ever, and it was all Carmine's fault. He had predicted every detail of the attack except Julianna. Khellan and the Morigahnti had reacted just the way he expected, and the other girls had transformed into so many hens when the fox comes calling at the coop. Not Julianna. She was a fox in disguise, possessing some reserve of strength. If only the higher ranking Adepts had listened to Carmine's instincts and attacked with the hounds first, Nicco would still be alive.

Trying to ease his spirit, Carmine pictured Nicco now in the Uncle's hall, feasting on the finest food, served by those whose souls had been punished by the Rite of Undoing. Nicco would have the most beautiful women whenever he wanted. If he grew tired of one, Old Uncle Night's servants would find another more to his liking. Even with these comforts, Carmine could not bring himself to feel any joy at his brother's passing. Nicco was gone, and Carmine missed him.

His only joy, though hollow, was in knowing that the vile whore had a Daemyn spawn growing in her belly at this very moment. It wasn't a harsh enough punishment to satisfy Carmine, but it would have to do for now. Once the Brotherhood rose to Zenith, he would find Julianna again. Then she would spend the rest of her life as a brood mare, forever pregnant with Daemyn spawn. Occasionally, Carmine might allow her to believe that her torment had ended, but then he'd return and smash that hope. After a lifetime of suffering at his hand, Carmine might consider that restitution for Nicco's early death.

Taking his eyes away from the hounds, Carmine made sure camp was being set up properly. Even in his heartache, he still had duties to perform. And a true Adept of Old Uncle Night did not show grief at the death of a loved one. Death was a necessary part of the cycle of Life, Death, and Rebirth. All creatures must play out their appointed role, then pass through the cycle again, but understanding that did not still the ache in Carmine's chest.

Four Nightbrothers cared for the horses, brushing down and watering both the riding animals and the draft horses used to pull the wagon carrying the food and gear. Three Brothers staked out a perimeter. Two gathered firewood, while one stood guard over the girls, Sylvie and Colette, who were making dinner. Six erected a large pavilion for Carmine's master. Another four, these also in pairs, busied themselves with pitching the small tents shared by the rest of the Brothers. Normally they would have slept under the open sky, but it looked as though a storm was coming in from the east.

It wasn't compassion that caused Carmine's current teacher, Hardin Thorinson of House Swaenmarch, to order the tents pitched. He didn't want the men using the rain as an excuse for inept performance of their duties. Hardin was a stern taskmaster who required every aspect of life to adhere to his exact specifications. According to Hardin, this attention to every detail, no matter how miniscule, helped maintain that same precision when bargaining with Daemyns. Carmine saw no fault in this logic and followed Hardin's footsteps by putting this philosophy into practice in his own life. Much of the time that meant making sure the rank and file Brothers followed Hardin's orders to the letter. If they failed, the Brothers rarely felt Hardin's wrath. That cold anger always focused on Carmine, and the punishments were far from pleasant.

Turning his mind away from any potential punishments, Carmine looked over at the girls again. Julianna's maid, Colette, had transitioned nicely into a serving girl for the men. However, Countess Sylvie Raelle remained full of the overconfident pride the young nobility of any land seemed to share.

As if she felt Carmine's eyes on her, Sylvie turned to look at him. Her lips began to curl, but she stopped the movement and smoothed her face. Yesterday she'd learned to keep her face and words respectful. The Brothers refused to tolerate her spoiled behavior, and she sported a dark bruise on her left cheek for her attitude.

Sylvie's eyes tightened around the outside edges as she glared at him. The ice-blue of her eyes, so bright that it was still easily seen in the fading light of dusk, looked like the clear sky of winter just after a blizzard. Carmine had seen such a sky once in the northern lands of House Swaenmarch. After he had been trapped indoors for three days, the blizzard finally blew itself out, and Carmine went outside wrapped in furs against the cold. The sky that morning was a crisper blue than he'd ever seen in the southern lands of House Floraen, but it also held defiance stretching from one horizon to the other that said, *You shall never conquer me.* Sylvie's eyes were the same color.

It wasn't the first time he'd received that hateful glare. Several times he'd approached her about becoming his woman. Where Sylvie was not yet a woman by Komati custom, her sixteen years barely made her an adult in the Kingdom of the Sun. And sixteen was not really that far from his own age of twenty-one, the age of majority among the Komati. She was pretty, despite her bruised cheek. Carmine could see the beauty she would become when he closed his eyes and set his imagination adrift. There had been an attraction between them over the past two years. He called attention to that frequently as they rode. He'd argued that they might develop enough passion to lead to marriage. His peculiar station in Kingdom precedence allowed him a freedom in choosing a wife that was unknown to most Kingdom High Blood. Each time he broached the subject, Sylvie fixed him with that scornful glare.

"Carmine!" a voice barked from the other side of the camp.

Master Hardin's call pulled Carmine from his daydreams. It also pulled Sylvie from her defiance, and she returned to work. Their guard, Jorgen, a commoner from House Swaenmarch, should have been paying attention to the girls. However, he stood sharpening a knife. Obviously, that task was far more important than watching the prisoners.

Drawing his rapier, Carmine veered behind Jorgen and gave his backside a quick jab. Yelping, Jorgen spun, murder in his eyes. Finding Carmine gazing back at him, Jorgen's eyes grew wide.

"No dinner for you this night," Carmine said. "And a double watch."

"Yes, Adept." Jorgen bowed. "Thank you."

Carmine sensed the gratitude was genuine. Although strict, he tried to make any punishment fit the offense. This contrasted with Hardin's leadership, who was prone to cruel punishments for the smallest incidents. The Brothers might not like Carmine, but they hated Hardin, and the younger Adept felt he'd earned their respect.

He could live with respect.

He often laughed over the invulnerability that most Adepts felt while wearing their mantles. He had no such delusions. A day was coming when Hardin would push Carmine too far. When the confrontation came, Carmine wanted the Brothers to stand behind him.

Clapping Jorgen on the shoulder, Carmine said, "Don't thank me too loudly. Adept Hardin might hear you. You're not supposed to look relieved by a punishment."

Jorgen nodded. His cheeks sank, but there was nothing hiding the smile in his eyes when he said, "*Thankful?* For no food and little sleep after the hard ride we've had today. I'll be lucky to stay in my saddle tomorrow."

"See that you do," Carmine said, "else wise, you'll be walking the next day."

"Yes, Adept Carmine."

Before turning toward Hardin's pavilion, Carmine looked at Sylvie. She'd been shooting glances at him during the interchange with Jorgen. He smiled. It was his mother's smile, full of warmth and caring. He'd practiced that smile for countless hours in front of a mirror. More than one maiden had lost her resolve, and subsequently her virtue, to that practiced expression. Sylvie's older sister had been one of those maids, and less than a month ago at that.

"I can free you from this," Carmine said, gesturing at the pots, food, and fire.

"At what cost, *Marquis* D'Mario?" Sylvie spoke his title as though it were a profanity.

He knew that she knew what he wanted. She was a countess by birth and spoke frequently of marrying higher, a duke at the very least, perhaps even a prince. Ever since his father's people had conquered hers, the Komati no longer had kings or emperors.

"Only your heart and your love," Carmine replied, refusing to let her goad him.

"You could at least use different words to woo me than you did my sister." Though her tone was the essence of civility, she spoke through clenched teeth. "It's like you have a script for this."

Jorgen snorted a laugh. Carmine turned his head and glared at the Brother, whose face reddened. Clapping Jorgen on the shoulder again, Carmine forced a chuckle.

"Let her scoff. It will only serve to continue her servitude to you and the others. Good evening, Countess Raelle." This last he said with a great bow.

So, Perrine had told Sylvie. That explained much. It would also make it that much sweeter when Sylvie finally gave herself to him. Carmine felt her eyes on his back as he strode toward Hardin's tent. Before he'd taken five steps, Jorgen barked at her to get back to work.

When Carmine approached the pavilion, the Brothers on guard saluted.

The furnishings were not as lavish as a palace, though Hardin did demand a certain level of comfort. The pavilion had a canvas floor covered with fine carpets. There was a table with two chairs, with one table setting waiting for the girls to finish cooking. A bottle of wine was already open with a crystal goblet next to it, half-full. To the right was Hardin's bedroom, containing a bed with a feather mattress. All of the furniture was collapsible and carried in the wagon.

Turning left, Carmine entered the room that Hardin used for his observances to Old Uncle Night.

Hardin stood before a pedestal of silver about two arms high, supporting a circle of the same metal one arm across, with a variety of gems worked into both the circle and stand. Each of those gems shone with an inner light. Multicolored smoke swirled within the circle. The object was an artifact used by the faith Hardin publicly claimed. To those outside the Brotherhood of the Night, Hardin was an Adept of Aunt Moon, goddess of House Swaenmarch.

The Brotherhood were the only ones to realize that the gifts of all the gods were open to those who understood the god's divine language and knew the proper steps of speaking miracles, performing rituals, or creating artifacts. Any Adept from other Houses that discovered this always met with unfortunate accidents, insuring the Brotherhood of the Night were the only ones who knew this secret.

"You took your time," Hardin said.

"One of the Brothers watching the girls was growing lax," Carmine replied. "I took it upon myself to insure that it did not happen again."

Hardin grunted and gave one quick nod of his head. The wisps of gray hair on the sides of his head waved as he made the gesture. Those wisps were the only hair he had. Although Hardin was in his early thirties, he looked ready to leave life behind. He'd traded his youth to a Daemyn. Now he looked as frail as his thinning hair. Carmine had yet to learn what Hardin had received in that bargain.

"I am about to contact the First Adept," Hardin answered. "I thought you might like to be present for the communication."

"Thank you, Master," Carmine said.

"I have already begun the ritual," Hardin said. "We are waiting for the First Adept to grant us an audience."

Of course he had started the ritual. One of Carmine's greatest annoyances about serving Hardin was the other Adept's need to constantly state the obvious, as if he felt Carmine possessed an infantile mind that needed constant coddling.

After a few minutes, Hardin started grumbling under his breath. Carmine couldn't make out most of the words, but then one word came out clearly.

"Octavio." Hardin actually spoke the First Adept's name out loud.

Carmine kept his face still. It was forbidden to speak the First Adept's name while acting as a member the Brotherhood of the Night. If Harden suspected that Carmine had heard him, Carmine could count himself dead within the next day. It wouldn't be murder, but one of the many *accidents* that happened while traveling hard.

The smoke contained within the silver circle gathered, and the First Adept's face took form out of the smoke. His features were muted, but there was no mistaking the weight of his strong gaze. The First Adept looked from Hardin to Carmine. He studied them, looking for something in their eyes, as if he could ferret out their secrets with his gaze alone. There was nothing pleasant in his scrutiny.

"Is something amiss?" Hardin asked.

"Yes," the First Adept said. "Although your mission to kill the Lord Morigahn was not a complete disaster, you and Roark butchered the task."

"First Adept," Hardin said, "we made sure that…"

"Stop." The First Adept's voice snapped like a cracked whip. Hardin flinched as if struck. "You made sure of nothing. Somehow, Julianna Taraen summoned an avatar of Grandfather Shadow to save her. Roark is dead, as are all the Brothers who served him. The avatar marked her as the new Lord Morigahn and summoned a guardian for her. The guardian's name is Faelin vara'Traejyn."

Carmine gasped, both in outrage that Julianna had escaped her fate and at hearing Faelin was still alive.

"I'm as surprised as you are," the First Adept said. "The Kingdom thought all the Traejyn family dead. I will be speaking to several High Blood of my House over this." There was an ominous finality in that remark. "I don't understand how the girl managed to summon an avatar, but it is done. Leaving saved your lives, and that is a blessing. However, your task remains incomplete. Your prey rides hard to the northwest. You still have a chance to catch them. When you do, kill them both."

"First Adept?" Carmine said, keeping his eyes downcast. One did not normally address the First Adept before he acknowledged you.

"Yes, Carmine?"

"I had no knowledge of Julianna's faith," Carmine said.

"I believe you," the First Adept replied. "I know that you lie to me. We serve the God of Lies. However, you wouldn't keep that from either Hardin or me."

"Yes, First Adept." That was half a lie. Carmine wouldn't keep information like that from the First Adept, but he would keep it from Hardin, for the right reasons.

"And I am sorry for Nicco," the First Adept said. "I was very fond of him."

"Thank you, First Adept." Though Carmine felt anything but thanks. Hearing Nicco's name was like drinking poorly aged Aernacht whiskey; it burned from neck to navel.

"Some of our order might tell you that showing any emotion for your loss is a sign of weakness. They would have you believe that the sooner death comes, the better, for that means the Uncle will embrace you. Do not believe these things, Carmine. Death can only be appreciated by celebrating life, and one of the ways to celebrate life is to mourn the passing of those we love. I give you my full leave to shed every tear you must in order to bless your brother's passing. I will mention Nicco tonight when I speak at the service. He will be well remembered."

"Thank you, First Adept," Carmine said, choking back his tears. He refused to cry before Hardin. There was time for tears after he'd gone to bed.

The First Adept's image turned to Hardin. "Catch them and fix this. Do not contact me again until you have done so."

"Yes, First Adept," Hardin said.

The smoke in the circle dissipated, and the first Adept was gone.

Hardin turned to Carmine. "We leave at first light. They have a day and a half on us. I mean to catch them within the week. The last thing we need is for them to join with other Morigahnti."

"Yes, Master." Carmine bowed and left the pavilion.

None of the Brothers would be pleased. They were expecting to return to their homes and families. Even though they were all devout, they had lives outside the Brotherhood. Over the next few days they would all be discussing the lies they would have to tell to explain their delayed return.

Carmine moved through the camp, telling the Brothers of their early departure. They hid their disappointment well. He tried to reassure them, explaining that while Hardin would never consider their feelings, Carmine appreciated their sacrifice and would remember them to the First Adept when the Brotherhood took the Zenith away from House Floraen. While his words were eloquent, his voice sounded hollow even to his own ears. Now that Carmine discovered that he was permitted to mourn, his grief threatened to overwhelm him.

As he passed the girls, Sylvie muttered under her breath. He couldn't make out the words, but understood her condescending tone all too well.

Carmine's lips pulled back in a snarl, and all the muscles in the back of his neck and shoulders tightened. He spun and fixed his gaze on Sylvie. Her sideways smirk dissolved as she took a step away from him. They stood, locked in each other's gaze. Carmine wanted to scream some retort, but his rage took all his words away.

Finally, Sylvie turned away and returned to her work.

Carmine retreated to his tent and managed to keep the tears from flowing until he made it inside. He buried his face in his pillow as the sobs started. Time lost all meaning as he wept in grief for Nicco.

Later, after he regained some semblance of self-control, Carmine rolled over and stared at the ceiling of his tent. Pushing thoughts of Nicco out of his mind, Carmine forced himself back to the present. The First Adept was right. The best way for Carmine to honor Nicco's death was to celebrate life.

At the moment, he needed to discern the First Adept's reasons for pairing him with Hardin Thorinson. The only certainty was that it was not a true master and disciple relationship. The First Adept was Carmine's true master although he frequently sent Carmine to study with other Adepts within the Brotherhood. Sometimes he was convinced that the First Adept sent him to learn what *not* to do as often as what to do.

Thunder roared in the distance, and Carmine rolled onto his side. As sleep overcame him, his thoughts wandered between memories of Nicco and wondering what lessons he was supposed to learn from Hardin.

TWO

Julianna's eyes snapped open. Her breath came in ragged sobs as she tried to push the nightmare aside and ignored the throbbing in her right cheek. She had tried to nap when Faelin had stopped to rest the horses and hunt for food, for all the good that did her.

She should have known better.

Resting was impossible for her. Every time she closed her eyes she saw either Khellan swinging from the tree or the Daemyn's glowing eyes. This time those visions had waited until she was asleep, and in her dreams Julianna dreamt of the Daemyn's eyes looking out of Khellan's face while they both raped her.

As Julianna struggled to drive the nightmare away, the strange language and knowledge Grandfather Shadow had placed in her mind threatened to overwhelm her. She pushed her palms against her head, trying to squeeze the interloping words and visions away. With slow steady breaths, the visions of Khellan and the Daemyn's eyes faded. The words didn't. It was like the morning after a feast or a ball when she woke with the best songs always at the front of her memory. Only she never remembered all of the songs, just enough that they bled together, making an unpleasant jumble of words that refused to go away.

This was far worse.

At least she understood the songs. She could comprehend the words dancing just behind her eyes if she concentrated on them, but that took too much effort. And most of those words told her things she'd rather not know. Some told her how to make a man's shadow skin him alive, how to summon lighting and thunder to devastate her enemies, and other, even more horrid, things.

Rolling to a sitting position, Julianna hugged her arms around her shoulders, trying to warm herself from a chill that had nothing to do with the air around her. The late afternoon was fairly warm, just like it had been yesterday and the day before for her birthday picnic.

Thinking of the others made Julianna shiver. Maybe the dead were the lucky ones. The Brotherhood of the Night had carried off Colette, Sophya, and Perrine's younger sister, Sylvie. Were any of them still alive? If they were, had they been offered over to Daemyns for breeding? She forced the thoughts away. Dwelling on her friends' fate would do nothing but work Julianna into a frenzy of worry and guilt.

Faelin was still gone, presumably to gather food in order to help make what he'd scavenged last longer. Julianna had mixed feelings about his return to her life, and so she'd said nothing to him. However, she couldn't stay silent forever, and that meant dealing with even more harsh truths.

Reaching into the saddlebags, Julianna took an apple and stood. She walked to where Faelin had tethered the horses to graze.

Julianna called out softly, "Vendyr."

Vendyr came away from the other horses.

Julianna waited for Vendyr to approach before offering the apple. If she got too close with the fruit, all the horses might come searching for treats. Once Vendyr discovered the apple, he tickled Julianna's fingers with his lips. Julianna opened her hand and gave the apple over. Vendyr chomped happily, rubbing his nose into Julianna's shoulder as he did. Julianna, in turn, wrapped her arms around Vendyr's muzzle and drew in a deep breath. The musky scent of him filled her nose.

Vendyr finished the apple and started sniffing for another.

"*Minas ankae—*." She had started to say, *I'm sorry. I don't have another apple*, but that strange language pushed its way into her speech. Forcing words that should have been as familiar as breathing through her lips, she said, "What am I going to do, Vendyr?"

Vendyr just kept searching for a second apple. Julianna couldn't help but smile at his tenacity. Even though Vendyr couldn't make these current troubles better, he provided a solace and a strong foundation.

"Julianna?" Faelin said from behind her.

She started a bit. She hadn't heard him approach. Vendyr danced away from her sudden movement.

Julianna turned. Faelin really hadn't changed in five years. He was still dark and handsome, without being pretty or desirable.

"Are you alright?" Faelin asked.

Julianna concentrated, making sure she spoke in her normal language. "Yesterday the man I loved was hung before my eyes, I was nearly raped," she intentionally left out, *by a Daemyn*, "a god rescued me, that same god cut my face with a red-hot knife, I found out that you are alive, and ever since I've been fighting to stay awake to keep the nightmares away. I think I'm doing quite well, considering."

Speaking of those things brought the memories fresh to her mind. Turning away from Faelin, she buried her face into Vendyr's neck and choked back her tears. She had shed enough tears already. Somehow she would find her vengeance, just as she had been promised.

"Don't shut me out, Julianna," Faelin said. "I'm still your friend."

"What do you know of friendship?" She spun on him. "You let us all believe you were dead. We grieved for you."

"*Kostota*," Faelin whispered.

Julianna's grasped her mother's knife tucked into her belt. She recalled some of the memories that came before Grandfather Shadow filled her mind. Her parents had taught her some words in *Galad'laman*. *Kostota* could mean debt, obligation, or revenge. No matter how one viewed *kostota*, it must be repaid, whether for good or for ill.

"I'm sorry for leaving," Faelin said. "It was wrong to let you all think I was dead, but it couldn't be helped. I can only try to make it right now that I'm back."

"You wish to meet your *kostota*?" Julianna asked.

Faelin nodded.

"Why did you come back now? It's awfully convenient that you appeared right when I needed someone most."

Faelin took a deep breath, looked into the sky, and let the breath out. He was keeping something from her, thinking that he was doing her some good, or protecting her in some way, just like when they were younger.

"I am in no mood for secrets, Faelin vara'Traejyn," Julianna said. "I have very little trust for anyone right now."

"Yes, my lady," Faelin said. Then he added, barely above a whisper. "Shadows lie to their enemies, not to each other."

Again, words came unbidden into her mind. *The hunter does not lie down with his prey.* It was Grandfather Shadow's Fifth Law.

Faelin bent to one knee. He drew his sword, put the tip on the ground, and gripped the hilt with both hands.

"I, Faelin vara'Traejyn, natural son of Raelian Tsieskas'Traejyn, swear to serve the Lord Morigahn, Julianna Kolmonen'Taraen, first chosen of Grandfather Shadow with my life's blood and breath. I am a true-blooded child of Koma and shall serve with no expectation of reward, payment, or recompense. I live and die by the will of Grandfather Shadow and the Lord Morigahn."

Julianna's breath quickened, and her hands started trembling. She looked away, first at the horses and then to the sky. How could he mock her like this?

With a deep breath, she stilled herself and looked back at Faelin. He still knelt there, looking expectant. Julianna took two steps, placing herself right in front of Faelin. She looked down at him, and he returned the gaze.

"Why are you doing this?" she demanded.

"You are the Lord Morigahn," Faelin said, "as Khellan was before you. I didn't know to be here. I was traveling through Heidenmarch. When I woke, I found myself near you. Grandfather Shadow sent me to protect you."

Julianna slapped him.

The instant she struck Faelin, pain flared down the right side of her face. She felt the hot blade cutting down her forehead, missing her eye, and continuing down her cheek all the way to her chin. The god had cut her only a day ago, but the pain had faded shortly after and remained gone until now. Her vision blackened, and she dropped to the earth. A pair of cold eyes regarded her in the darkness of her mind.

This behavior ill becomes the Lord Morigahn, a voice sounded in her mind.

As the disapproval sounded in Julianna's mind, the pain stopped. It went away just as it had come, suddenly, without any warning. But even though the physical hurt was gone, the memory remained. She sat up, gasping for breath.

"No," she said, barely louder than a whisper. "I will not do this. I will not be this." She turned her face to the heavens and shouted. "I *cannot* be this!" She dropped her chin to her chest. "Please, find someone else."

You have already agreed and stepped upon the path, the voice said, barely a whisper at the back of her mind. Then, it was gone.

Thunder rumbled in the distance.

"There is no one else," Faelin groaned.

She turned to him. Faelin sat cross-legged, rubbing his face where she'd struck him. Tears rolled down his cheeks. As children, he'd kept his emotions in tight control. His father thought excessive emotions were a weakness, and Faelin spent most of his youth trying to win his father's approval. Faelin's only outlet for his feelings had been the times he and Julianna were alone.

"How do you know?" Julianna asked. "How can you be sure that I am the only one who can do this?"

"You can't pass it on, Julianna. Anyone worthy of the title would not take it from you."

"Why not?"

"You are the first Lord Morigahn marked by Grandfather Shadow in a thousand years. You are his first chosen, his high priest. All of those who are faithful to him will look to you for guidance. Some will even want you to lead a Komati rebellion."

Comprehension hit Julianna like a biting wind. Everything she had been taught about the gods and religion was wrong. More than that came the realization that Grandfather Shadow had marked her for death. It was only a matter of time before the Kingdom discovered her. Then she would be executed for breaking the Kingdom's highest law. Only the

High Blood of the four Great Houses worshiped the greater gods. Anyone within their conquered lands found worshipping above their station was sentenced to the Ritual of Undoing, a public execution ceremony that damned the offender's soul to the Dark Realm of the Godless Dead. Bearing a Daemyn's child would be better than that. Once that horror was over, she would eventually die and pass through the cycle of Life, Death, and Rebirth, forgetting the horrors of this life.

Now she understood Faelin's tears.

He looked at her with concern in his eyes. She remembered that look.

"I don't want to talk about it," Julianna said, as Faelin opened his mouth.

He paused for a moment, and then said, "I understand, but there is something I have to ask you about. Just one thing, and I'll leave it be. If it weren't important, I wouldn't ask."

She drew in a deep breath. The last thing she wanted right now was to think about it in any way, and she thought she knew what he was going to ask her about. It was something that he needed to know, and he deserved an answer no matter how much Julianna wished she could pretend none of it had happened.

"Alright," she said, bracing herself.

"While you were sleeping last night, you muttered something about a betrayer," Faelin said. "Did someone betray you, or perhaps Khellan?"

That was not the question she expected, not the question she had prepared for. Caught by surprise, her breath caught in her throat as the shock and fear returned.

"Yes," she whispered.

"Who?"

"Carmine and Nicco D'Mario." She felt vile and unclean speaking their names.

"Our friends Carmine and Nicco?" Faelin asked.

"They are friends to no one," Julianna snapped. "They worship Old Uncle Night. They're the reason Khellan is dead."

Faelin's face hardened.

Khellan was one of the few Komati nobles who accepted Faelin as a man in his own right, rather than as his father's mistake. Faelin was a bastard, sired by a noble father on a peasant girl. He spent all of his life trying to live down a shame that was no fault of his own.

Carmine, on the other side of the coin, was much like Faelin. He was one of those poor products of a union between the conqueror and the conquered. His father was High Blood of House Floraen, and his mother a Komati noble of the Raelle family. The Raelle family shared the same house as Faelin's family, Traejyn. In some ways, Carmine was an even greater social pariah than Faelin. Faelin was just a bastard. Carmine was a half-breed with no real place in either society.

"*Kostota*," Faelin said. "We will find a way to make them pay."

"We can have *kostota* with Carmine," Julianna replied. "It's too late for Nicco."

"Why?"

Julianna allowed herself a grim smile. "I killed him."

"I had a reason for asking you about betrayal," Faelin said. "Soon, the Morigahnti will come looking for you. The power they give you might be intoxicating, but you must not let it rule you, and you must always keep your guard up around them. Some of them may want to betray you."

"I'm the high priest. Why wouldn't they be loyal to me?"

"Just because someone is a Morigahnti doesn't mean they hold to the old traditions. If the Morigahnti managed to stop their squabbling, they might unite Koma to successfully rebel against the Kingdom. It has almost happened a few times in the past, but has always failed because someone high in the Morigahnti ranks has betrayed the Lord Morigahn. Once, the Lord Morigahn betrayed all Koma. That's how Koma fell to the Kingdom of the Sun."

"Why?"

"Because all men can be corrupted by power. It is much the same with Kingdom Adepts. More and more, being a man or woman of faith in any land becomes more about mortal politics and less about cultivating the small spark of divinity in the human soul."

"Where did you learn all this?" Julianna asked.

"In my five years of traveling," Faelin replied, "I saw the evils of the world firsthand." He turned toward the horses. "We've been here long enough. We can talk more on the move."

They fell silent as they saddled the horses. Even when she hadn't been speaking to Faelin, she'd made it known that she could saddle and tack Vendyr. The familiar process helped calm her. As they mounted and rode, Julianna found herself dwelling on Faelin's words about the Morigahnti. Grandfather Shadow wanted her to lead these people? It seemed that some of them might not be too welcoming. Perhaps Grandfather Shadow enjoyed the irony of her, an unbeliever, leading his army of people who claimed to be believers, yet most of whom were not. Yet, was she really an unbeliever? Mother and Father had believed, before they were killed. Julianna even remembered times where Father had preached to the household. The memories still felt like they belonged to some other person, but at one point, Julianna had been part of a community that remembered the truth.

In the distance, thunder roared, low and angry. The word *ruth* came unbidden into her mind. It was Grandfather Shadow's word for thunder, but it could also mean raw, unbridled power, or even anger and rage. As she thought of the ways various words in *Galad'laman* changed definition depending upon context, each of those phrases struggled with each other for her attention. The knowledge of that language was her power, her *ruth*, only she didn't know how to harness or control it yet.

"Are you—?" Faelin started.

Julianna held up her hand. She closed her eyes and focused. Something in all those various words had pulled at her, something that might have an answer for her. She needed to get those mostly out of the front her mind in order to determine what it was.

"*Kostota?*" That wasn't it. "*Kraestu?*" No. "*Karkota?*" Julianna felt as though she was getting further from what she wanted.

She shook her head.

This was the wrong way to go about it. She could keep thinking of words in *Galad'laman*, and it would take her forever. It was something Faelin had said, or maybe that he'd asked. He'd asked her about something she'd said in her sleep.

"*Kavala,*" Julianna said.

"What?" Faelin asked. "I am—"

"Not you," Julianna said. "*Carmine un aen kavala.* I wouldn't have used 'betrayer' in my sleep. I would have spoken of *kavala*. You speak *Galad'laman*."

Faelin nodded.

"Where did you learn it?"

"My family. We all worshipped Grandfather Shadow. The House Floraen Inquisitors killed them all."

They rode in silence for a time. Julianna suspected Faelin was thinking of his family, as she was thinking of hers, but her memories of that time were still clouded. More of her thoughts were about *Galad'laman*. If Faelin knew the language, perhaps he could tell her how to command its power.

THREE

A wet wind, cold enough to bite straight to the bone, howled in the night. Rain pattered against the wagon. Sylvie shivered, her teeth chattered, and no matter how she tried, she could not stay warm even with her two blankets wrapped around her. At least she and Julianna's maid had been allowed to sleep underneath the wagon, which offered some small protection from the rain and wind. Sylvie glared at the shadowy lump of the maid, also shivering in her two blankets. The girl should have at the very least offered Sylvie one of the blankets; the girl was, after all, only a servant, while Sylvie was a countess. But it seemed proper decorum had been forgotten the moment the two had been taken prisoner by the Brotherhood of the Night.

Deciding the rain had calmed as much as it was ever going to, Sylvie crawled out of her blankets. She tucked them underneath the axel to keep them from blowing into the mud. She shed her overdress and put it next to the blankets.

"What are you doing, my lady?" The maid whispered.

Sylvie fixed the servant with her most practiced look of disdain.

"Your Excellency," Sylvie corrected. "Not that it is any of your concern, but I'm going to make myself a little more comfortable."

"Please, my lady, uh, Your Excellency. Don't do anything to get us punished."

"You are no one to command me," Sylvie said, and crawled out from under the wagon.

The only thing Sylvie's plan might earn her was a little bit of momentary humiliation, but it was time to stop living like a peasant. If that meant sharing a bed with a man she could barely stomach, so be it. She would rather suffer that indignity than spend one more day under the illusion that she and the maid were in any way equal.

Once out from underneath the wagon, the wind bit with an even greater chill, but Sylvie had expected it and steeled herself against it. Like many ladies at court, she had practiced the art of appearing unperturbed in the face of humiliation and great discomfort. She allowed herself to shiver and her teeth to chatter only as much as needed to gain sympathy. The thin material of her chemise rubbed against her hardening nipples. Carmine would like that. Even though she had seen only sixteen winters, she knew what men wanted and what they liked to see. She'd seen her father's friends leering at her alongside their sons.

"What are you about?"

Startled, Sylvie turned around. Jorgen stood not five paces away. His eyes bore into hers for a moment, and then he lowered his gaze. This attention nauseated and excited Sylvie. She pulled her shoulder blades together, helping to enhance her small bosom.

"I'm going to entertain Adept Carmine D'Mario," Sylvie said.

Jorgen sucked in a deep breath through his nose as he chewed on his lower lip. Sylvie saw the war waging in his mind. Adept Harden had commanded the men not to touch Sylvie or Colette. That command might be all well and good while the girls were fully dressed during the light of day, but being alone in the night with a girl in only her small clothes, Jorgen's eyes shone with hungry temptation.

"I'll not have you wandering the camp on my watch," Jorgen said. "Get back under that wagon."

Apparently his good sense won out over his desire.

"I don't think you'll be punished for letting me go to Adept Carmine. In fact, he might even reward you." She covered the distance between then. "And so would I."

Jorgen pulled back a bit. "You would lay with me?"

Sylvie smiled her most flirtatious smile. "Don't be silly. Carmine would punish us both for that. But there are *other* ways for me to pleasure you."

"How?" Jorgen looked suspicious now.

"I have hands." Sylvie leaned toward him, and said in a low, conspireatorial whisper, "and if you're very nice to me, I have a mouth."

In truth, she found the idea vile, and choked down the urge to vomit, but she'd heard her sister talking about it once. It might well be the most disgusting thing in the world, but if it got her out from under the wagon, Sylvie would do it. She might not be very ladylike right now, but once she escaped and told Father everything, he would go directly to the Kingdom Governor, Duke Octavio Salvatore. Then everyone here would die, and whatever she had to do to survive until then would die with them.

Jorgen grinned. "Well then, let's put those hands to better use than cooking."

He took her wrist and led her to a spot where the wagon blocked most of the camp from view. As he pulled at his belt, Sylvie swore she would please Carmine enough tonight that she wouldn't have to endure this again. After tonight, Carmine would take her straight into his bed.

FOUR

It was well into the early hours of the morning when Carmine heard hushed voices outside his tent. Even though the weather had settled, he could not make out the words. Reaching under his pillow, Carmine grabbed the forearm bone of a man long dead. The bone had been hollowed out and was filled with a powder blessed with the divinity of Old Uncle Night. The powder would paralyze any who inhaled it. If some interloper was going to sneak into his tent, Carmine wanted to know who and why before they died

The tent flap opened. A small, shadowed figure crawled through the opening. He was about to blow the powder out when the invader spoke.

"Carmine?" Sylvie asked. "Are you awake?"

Carmine removed the bone from his lips. "What do you want?"

She crawled toward him. In the dim light he saw her hair plastered to her face from the rain, her eyes still holding that hard edge of hate.

"I've been thinking about my situation," she said. "You're right. I don't want to suffer through this any longer."

She kissed him. Her lips were like icicles. The chill of the wind and rain outside clung to her. After a moment, Carmine grew bold and went to deepen the kiss. Sylvie let him put his tongue in her mouth for a moment, and then she sucked on his lower lip. His toes tingled.

When the kiss ended, she pulled her shift over her head and knelt naked before him. With each movement, the hatred in her eyes grew. Carmine smiled, but he could not allow Sylvie to believe charms would win him that easily. She crawled forward and lay down on him.

"Just a moment," Carmine said, rolling out from under her.

"What is it?"

He collected her discarded shift and held it out to her. "You dropped something."

Sylvie's mouth hung open. Carmine could just imagine the torrent of confusion warring in her head.

"But," Sylvie started.

"Go back to bed, Excellency," Carmine said. "I want to be alone."

Sylvie's lower lip quivered. Even in the dark of the tent, Carmine saw her eyes welling with tears. She wriggled back into her shift, a sight Carmine enjoyed very much. Once she was dressed again, Sylvie fled.

The smoldering fire in Carmine's groin screamed at him to call her, to summon her back. Taking her tonight could relieve him in so many ways beyond simply slaking his lust. However, to do so would give her the power, put her in control. If he allowed that, the battle between them would never end. Just as with dealing with Adept Hardin and learning whatever lesson the First Adept intended, Carmine must be patient.

Carmine lay back down and closed his eyes. The vision of Sylvie's body filled his mind, especially her pert breasts. His heartbeat and breath quickened as he used that vision to pleasure himself to sleep.

FIVE

Dawn had come, such as it was with the storm clouds overhead. Julianna and Faelin had been traveling an hour already. The warmth that always preceded the first storm of autumn had gone. The storm had lessened to a steady drizzle and the wind had receded so that the raindrops no longer stung Julianna's face, but her clothes and hair still clung to her skin.

Faelin rode next to her. He'd spent most of their time this morning trying to explain how to focus the power of Grandfather Shadow's divine language through the *Galad'fana* in order to speak miracles. No matter how hard she tried, Julianna couldn't seem to take the words and get them to *do* something.

"What am I doing wrong?" Julianna asked through chattering teeth.

"First, you're not pronouncing the words correctly," Faelin said. "Second, you don't *want* the miracles to happen."

"Yes I do," Julianna retorted. "If I'm going to have this other language filling my mind, I want to be able to do something with it. Grandfather Shadow cursed me with this power. The least he could have done was make it easier to use."

Faelin shook his head and sighed. "You'll never be able to speak miracles as long as you think of them as a curse. You must believe this is a gift."

"How can I think of it as a gift when I didn't want it?"

"Do you remember when Eddryck gave you your first real kiss?" Faelin asked.

"Yes." Julianna's face grew warm.

Eddryck had been Faelin's older half-brother. He had kissed her at a spring ball when she was fourteen. A group of young lords and ladies had gone off to play parlor games. They'd decided to play Wink, a game where the ladies sat in chairs with the gentlemen behind them. One of the chairs was empty, and the gentleman behind that chair would wink at one of the ladies. She would then try to escape her chair and move to that gentleman's chair. When she got to his chair, the lady would give him a chaste kiss on the cheek. When Julianna got to Eddryck's chair and went to kiss his cheek, he turned his head and kissed her lips.

"You didn't know you wanted him to kiss you at the time," Faelin said.

"I was furious," Julianna said. "He embarrassed me so much."

"If I remember rightly, you actually liked it," Faelin replied. "You two spent that whole summer sneaking off together."

Though the memories were embarrassing, Julianna welcomed the warmth that came with her spreading blush.

"You have to think of Grandfather Shadow's blessing like that kiss," Faelin said. "Right now you're angry and confused, but someday you'll see it as something wonderful."

"But if your father had caught us, he wouldn't have killed us," Julianna argued. "The Kingdom will."

Faelin snorted a laugh. "My father might not have, but Eddryck's mother would have skinned you both. Eddryck was promised to Princess Pyrras Collaen."

"Of House Aesin?" Julianna gasped. "That cow would have ruined your brother's life."

"Well, he had hoped to convince Father and his mother that even though you were only a duchess, you would be a more politically advantageous marriage for him, and that Braendyn would be a better match for Pyrras."

Julianna couldn't help but smile. She'd enjoyed the time she'd spent with Eddryck, and not just because of the kissing. He was the first man that made her feel like a woman with his compliments, manners, and by how he treated her as an equal, even though he'd been three years her senior and was a prince of his House. She hadn't found another man that made her feel like that until Khellan. Now both were dead, killed by the Kingdom: Khellan by the Brotherhood of the Night, and Eddryck by House Floraen. Was the Kingdom destined to kill all the men she loved?

She pushed thoughts of both her loves aside. The memories of them only served to distract her, and she had to learn how to speak miracles. Her survival depended on learning to master this skill. If she didn't...well, she couldn't think on that distraction either. She simply must succeed.

As they rode, Julianna kept trying and kept failing.

"Why can't we stop?" Julianna asked. "There are too many distractions, and it's hard to concentrate."

"I hardly think your enemies will give you time to prepare yourself," Faelin replied.

"What I really want is to stop being wet," Julianna said. "If Grandfather Shadow holds dominion over storms, why can't he make it so that the rain doesn't fall on his followers?"

"Perhaps you should ask him for that miracle," Faelin replied.

"Now that *would* be a gift," Julianna said.

She took a deep breath and turned her head to the sky. She felt where the *Galad'fana* touched her head and reached with her mind for the divine power bound into the cloth. Gods and goddesses, she wanted a reprieve from the cold. Julianna's desire melded into the Veil of Shadows, and she grasped the dominion of Storms with her mind. With another deep breath, she made sure she had the words firmly in her mind. She forced her teeth to stop chattering and her lips to stop trembling in the cold. Once Julianna was sure she had complete command of every part of the miracle she wanted, she called to Grandfather Shadow, almost begging.

"Galad'Ysoysa olka hyvae salpa tasti sadela ja kietola ulos herkas mina ja Faelin."

Power surged through her *Galad'fana*. The wind stopped biting her skin, and the rain no longer fell on her.

She had a moment to enjoy this before a wave of exhaustion descended on her. Every muscle seemed to lose some of its strength, and breathing became more difficult. Julianna didn't care. She had spoken a miracle, and Grandfather Shadow had granted it.

She glanced at Faelin. The wind and rain weren't touching him either.

"That was a good miracle," Faelin said, smiling at her.

Julianna returned the smile. Despite the sudden weariness, speaking the miracle had made her feel like she wouldn't be a victim anymore,

more in control of the world around her. The power she'd commanded burned away the last feelings of weakness remaining from the Brotherhood's attack. They would never take her like that again, not when she understood how to bring this power into the world. Wanting even more of that liberating feeling, Julianna sought another target for a second miracle. She saw a small sapling to her right.

Focusing her will through *Galad'laman* and the *Galad'fana*, Julianna drew on the dominions of Shadows and Vengeance, and spoke, "*Tuska.*"

A bolt of dark energy flew from her fingertip. The sapling exploded in a shower of splinters.

Julianna grew even more tired, but she welcomed it. Knowing that she could command the power of Grandfather Shadow filled her with euphoria. Though her body was ready to collapse out of her saddle, she wanted to speak more miracles.

"You have to be careful, Julianna." Faelin's tone carried a hint of reproach. "If you try to do too much too fast, the divine power could burn your body up from the inside out."

"I'll be careful," Julianna replied.

She intended to keep that promise as best she could; she would be as careful as she could. However, she hadn't felt this in control of anything in her life. Now that she understood the process, the phrases and sentencees of *Galad'laman* floating in her mind created a tapestry of miraculous possibilities. Let them come: the Brotherhood of the Night with their foot soldiers in black armor, the House Floraen Inquisitors with their armies of Draqons, and even those traitorous Morigahnti. None of them had the breadth of knowledge that Grandfather Shadow had given her.

Julianna couldn't wait to experiment.

SIX

"Look." Luciano held The Detector out to Santo.

A ball of light and heat, summoned through the divine grace of All Father Sun, floated above them. The glowing orb cast away the gloom of the stormy day and burned the rain to steam above them. Luciano and Santo huddled around The Detector. It had chimed and buzzed, and now Grandfather Shadow's symbol had jumped from a flicker to a steady glow.

"We're getting closer," Santo said. "We should catch up to them by day's end."

"No," Luciano replied. "Not quite, but sometime early tomorrow."

In truth, they could likely overtake whatever was causing three hands to point toward one symbol, if they rode the horses hard and didn't stop to rest. No doubt Santo would leap at that plan, should Luciano give it

voice. However, such a course of action would be foolhardy beyond comprehension. Whatever they faced was outside of the experience of any Inquisitor in memory. Both Luciano and Santo would need to have all their
wits and faculties about them when they confronted whatever they rode
toward.

"We should rest," Luciano said. "Even if only for a few hours."

"And let them get further ahead of us?" Santo's youthful eyes stared
greedily toward the west.

Youthful? Luciano had to suppress an indignant snort.

Santo would likely believe such a scornful display meant for him and
take offense. Truly, the snort was meant for Luciano himself. How much
had nine years as an Inquisitor changed how he looked at the world? Luciano had seen only thirty-nine summers, but he felt ancient next to Santo's thirty-one. Like all Inquisitors, they had each joined the order at thirty
and Luciano had vague memories of being as bright and enthusiastic as
Santo, but that was before nine years of fighting the worst threats to the
Kingdom of the Sun.

"It is likely that our quarry will need to rest at some point also. If they
don't, then we best not face them while exhausted."

"Very well," Santo said, his shoulders slumping a little.

"Don't worry. We'll catch them." Luciano put The Detector in the
pocket sewn into the inside of his sleeve. He sat straight in his saddle and
looked ahead to the west, eyes neither shifting nor blinking. "We are the
beacon that guides the righteous beyond the fear and doubt."

Santo snapped upright and spoke the next line of the benediction.
"We are the light of Truth in the face of bleak tidings."

"We are the hand of the Sun come to purge darkness from the heart."
They both spoke together. "We are the hand of the All Father."

With minds and spirits set to purpose, the two Inquisitors of House
Floraen rode to discover the source of this mystery.

SEVEN

Faelin felt someone behind him. No noise had given the person away,
and the forest didn't sound any different. The raindrops kept falling. The
soft wind continued to blow. Those few birds that enjoyed the rain called
back and forth through the trees. Something tingled just behind his navel,
behind his nose, and at the back of his knees. It was the oddest sensation
Faelin had ever felt, as if all three places on his body were connected to
some never-before-tickled nerve.

At the moment, Faelin was only armed with a crossbow and dagger.
Hunting with a rapier strapped to his side would be impractical. Hoping

the stranger was far enough away for the crossbow to be effective, Faelin spun.

An old man squatted next to a tree, arms propped on his knees. The stranger was dressed in ragged leather and furs, though not in the balanced patterns of the Dosahan to the west, nor did the clothes possess the paint and fringe to commemorate any battles he might have won. His hair and beard were as wild and untamed as his clothing.

For just a moment, Faelin considered loosing the crossbow in his hands, until he saw the man's eyes. Though his hair was dark, the stranger's eyes were the white of fresh fallen snow, and those eyes stared unblinking at Faelin. Even if the quarrel struck true, it would likely prove little more than an annoyance.

"Interesting weaponry you have there." The man's voice came a bit like a growl. "A crossbow and a dirk won't help you much with the people hunting you. What would you have done if I'd been a Daemyn or maybe one of those alchemically-bred Draqon soldiers the Kingdom uses?"

"Crossbow and dirk kill a Draqon just as well as anything else.'

"Perhaps. If you are better than they are." The man sniffed the air. "Something tells me you are not."

Faelin shrugged. "I'd think of something. Though I doubt any of them could sneak up on me as well as you have."

"That is very true," the man said with a chuckle. "But a Daemyn hound could have."

"True enough," Faelin said. "Then I guess I would die."

"At least you have the good sense to know that."

"Once we were like wolves," Faelin said, hoping and dreading that his suspicions of the man were true.

"Our time will come again," the man half-growled in response. "Though I give the greeting as a matter of formality. I hold no belief in it."

"It is my honor to meet you," Faelin said. "I am—"

"I know who you are, Faelin vara'Traejyn. I am Razka. I shared meat and mead with both your father and grandfather before the betrayal at Kyrtigaen Pass."

"My family—"

"I know. I have not come here for vengeance. I bring a warning. As I said, you are being hunted. Once your charge freed Grandfather Shadow, he began tossing around enough divine power for every Adept within a hundred leagues to feel it. You have been gone too long, son of Traejyn, and have forgotten what life holds for the faithful in Kingdom-controlled lands."

Faelin felt the muscles in his face begin to tighten, but he forced them to smooth out. Razka might take any perceived anger or frustration as a challenge, and Faelin chose his battles far more carefully than that. Razka was wrong about one thing: though Faelin had been gone for several years, he would never forget the constant danger to those who worshipped one of the five greater gods in Kingdom lands.

"How much time do I have?" Faelin asked.

"For the Brotherhood of the Night," Razka said, "Half a day at the most. For the House Floraen Inquisitors, a few minutes at best."

Faelin suddenly found it difficult to breathe. "Will you help us?"

"I am helping. Don't ask for more than is offered."

"I meant no offense," Faelin said. "Thank you for what aid you do give. Now excuse me. Julianna and I must put some distance between us and our enemies."

Razka stared Faelin in the eye, looked him up and down, and then nodded.

Faelin turned and raced back to where he had left Julianna.

EIGHT

Carmine could barely hear the sounds of the Brothers breaking camp above the patter of raindrops and wind through the trees. He'd gone a little away from the camp to compose himself before travelling. He hadn't slept well again, having spent the night mourning for Nicco and lusting for an absent Sylvie after rejecting her from his bed again. The hollow pain was still there between his stomach and heart, but not nearly so much since he had decided to fill it with thoughts of finding Julianna and giving her to a Daemyn.

Behind him, footsteps crunched through the leaves and brambles. Whoever it was couldn't be much of a threat if they were moving so clumsily.

"Carmine?" Sylvie said.

Carmine turned. She stood there, wrapped in a cloak, hair matted against her face from the rain. Her blue eyes bore into his with something more than anger.

"You should be about the dishes, your Excellency," Carmine said. "Hardin may have you whipped for shirking your duties."

"Oh, I'm sure there will be no whippings." Sylvie took a step closer to him. "Just as I'm sure I won't be walking, and I won't be sleeping under the wagon anymore."

Sylvie shed her cloak. Aside from her boots, she was naked underneath. Somehow having only those boots on made the sight of her even more arousing. In the full light of day, Carmine lost himself in following the slight curves of her body. A small part of his mind wondered how she had gotten away from the camp and gotten undressed before an alarm was raised, but the rest of him watched dumbly as she came closer and closer. He stiffened a little more with each step she took.

It seemed like it took years for her to travel the distance between them, and when she finally stood before him, she reached for his belt. Her touch reawakened Carmine, and he realized that he was losing control of this. He grabbed at her hands to stop her. She reached up and slapped him, not hard enough to actually hurt him, but enough to stun him for a moment.

"You will not stop me, Marquis D'Mario." Sylvie's voice cracked like a driver's whip. Carmine found himself unable to deny her command any more than a team of horses or oxen could deny the whip that drove them. "There is no Brotherhood here with us. It is just you, a marquis, and me a countess." Her hands undid his belt and loosened his pants while she spoke. "You will obey me. And I command you to stand still."

She pulled his pants around his ankles, and his knees nearly buckled when her mouth became occupied with something other than speaking. He cupped the sides of her head, and maneuvered them a few paces away so that he could lean against a tree. Let her have this illusion that she controlled him while they were alone. He knew where the real power between them lay. Sylvie looked up at him, and the hatred had crept back into her eyes.

Carmine smiled as he leaned back and let her fumble her way through this – now that the initial shock of her brazenness had subsided, it became apparent how awkward this was for her. Yes, he still had the power here. That she hated him so much and still willingly gave herself made it that much sweeter. But she had made her life easier; she would ride the wagon, and she saved herself from the attentions of Hardin's Daemyns.

As he helped guide her through the task of pleasing him, Carmine heard a twig snap. Sylvie had obviously heard it as well, because she attempted to pull her head away from his groin. Carmine moved his right hand to the back of her head to keep her in place and glanced toward where he had heard the sound. Jorgen stood there, watching them. It took the Brother a few moments to realize that he had been noticed. Jorgen's attention had been focused on Sylvie rather than Carmine. When Jorgen's gaze finally drifted upward to meet Carmine's there was no trace of the deference that the Nightbrother usually held when in the presence of an Adept.

"I trust that this is important," Carmine said.

"Yes, Adept."

At the sound of Jorgen's voice, Sylvie tried harder to pull away. Carmine pushed on the back of her head, so much so that she choked a little. She would learn who was the master here.

"The Daemyn hounds have found something," Jorgen said.

"What is it?" Carmine asked.

"You'd best come see," Jorgen replied. "The hounds are in a frenzy."

Carmine released Sylvie's head. "We can continue this in my tent this evening."

Jorgen's lips tightened and he glared at Sylvie. With this look, along with Jorgen's volunteering for the middle watch each night, as well as Sylvie's decline in complaining, Carmine realized that Sylvie must have been granting Jorgen some favors while the rest of the camp was asleep. It made no matter to Carmine. She was his now, and her willingness to please a commoner like Jorgen actually fit perfectly into Carmine's plans for her.

"Take me to the hounds," Carmine said as he pulled up his trousers.

Jorgen spun, and Carmine followed the Brother through the trees.

The Daemyn hounds strained against their tethers, nearly pulling away from the Brothers holding them. In truth, if the hounds had wanted to be free, no human hand could have held them. Only the bargain made between Hardin and the Daemyns who had possessed the hounds kept them under control.

Carmine strode over to the hounds. He scratched one behind the ear. It was strange that the Daemyns seemed to like that while in the dog's body. In their natural form, such a thing would have been demeaning at best.

"What is it, boy?" Carmine asked in a soothing tone. He couldn't call it by name; he didn't know it. Daemyns gave out their names sparingly at best.

"*Zuzak taruzika*," the hound growled. *I smell miracles.*

"Excellent," Carmine replied. "Where?"

"*Tzaasna, gaz tzaasna.*" *Close, very close.*

The creature led Carmine to a sapling that had been blown apart. Looking about, Carmine saw splinters littering the ground around the tree.

"Can you follow this trail?" Carmine asked.

"*Aztu. Gaz mordu.*" *Yes. Very fresh.*

"It's a good day for us lads," Carmine said. "The hounds have their scent."

All around him, the Brothers cheered.

Carmine turned to Jorgen. "Ride and inform Adept Hardin that we have them. I'm taking a few men and one hound so that we don't lose her. He can follow with the others."

As Jorgen ran off, Carmine had to resist the urge to let the Daemyn hounds loose. Daemyn hounds were not known for their discrimination while hunting. Sending them after Julianna would be far too quick a punishment for her. She wouldn't be much use as breeding stock if one of the creatures devoured her soul.

NINE

"That's what we've been chasing?" Santo asked in a whisper. "A girl barely old enough to call herself an adult by Komati custom?"

The girl in question stood with her back to them, her dark hair hung down to her waist in a dark braid. She wore a man's clothes and had a rapier belted at her side. The rain that trickled down on the two Inquisitors – they had released the miracle for sake of stealth – didn't touch her. Shadows cast by the meager fire next to her stretched out and formed a roof over her. She wore one of the Morigahnti scarves – Luciano believed they were called *Galad'jana* – around her head and shoulders.

"She may be more than what she appears," Luciano replied, also whispering.

"But—" Santo started, but Luciano waved him to silence.

The younger man had received many honors. Few men who joined the Inquisitors rarely came to the order without some sort of decoration. Santo was no different, having bravely headed dangerous missions against heathens in nearly every Kingdom protectorate, but he had never served in Koma. Despite Kingdom propaganda, people other than the Adepts of the Great Houses could draw divine power into the world as miracles, using dedicated foci. Every Inquisitor knew this, but only Inquisitors who had fought against the Morigahnti understood that some of those Morigahnti possessed more power than any Adept.

"I want to get the Faerii blades," Luciano whispered.

Santo's gaze shifted between Luciano and the girl. He jerked his head toward her. Luciano replied by slowly turning his head so that he faced back to the horses. Santo's lips parted in a silent snarl, but after a moment, he sighed quietly, and nodded. Together, they retreated back to their horses. Faerii steel was not usually carried while scouting, because some otherworldly creatures, Daemyns not the least of them, could detect the substance if it came close enough.

They reached the horses, and Santo went about collecting the four egg-sized stones placed in a square around the animals. He picked them up in the proper order, first brown, then green, then gray, then white. If anyone had tried to cross the invisible barrier or remove the stones in any other order, they would receive an almost certainly fatal surprise. Sometimes a horse would try to move beyond that barrier, despite all the training that Inquisitor horses received, and die. It was better to have the occasional dead horse than let the tools of the Inquisition fall into the hands of heathens and the unrighteous.

With the barrier down, they went to the horses. Santo slid his hand between the saddle and saddle blanket and produced a thin, yet long-bladed parrying dagger. Luciano pulled his walking cane out of his bedroll. It was an odd thing to carry on a journey through the Koma wilderness, but it concealed a rapier-like blade of Faerii steel.

They looked at each other, nodded, and turned back toward where they'd left the Morigahnti girl.

The girl was there, not ten paces away. She leaned against a tree and stared at them with hard, storm-cloud-gray eyes. She might have been beautiful if not for the fresh scar that cut down the right side of her face. Her right hand held a rapier casually at her side, and her left hand flipped a dagger end over end – a dagger with a blade of Faerii steel. The girl gave him a flirtatious wink. That scar held his attention the most, especially because it was on the right side of her face. Luciano's breath caught in his throat, and his innards churned as if he were once more a twittering disciple at the Academy of the Sun.

"Good morning, High Blood Adept Inquisitors," she said. "How may I serve the Kingdom?"

"Whom do I have the honor of addressing?" Santo asked.

Santo had obviously not studied Komati lore. Why should he have? Luciano had been no different when he had first come here six years ago. He thought that this would be just like any other protectorate. Hard lessons with scars to prove it had taught him otherwise, and he had studied the history and mythology of this land with almost the same fervor that he followed the teachings of All Father Sun. No Komati would mar their face in such a way unless they were mad and wished to be killed or they were...

"I am the Lord Morigahn," the girl replied.

Santo laughed. "Well, Lord Morigahn, if you come peaceably, we may allow you to die with your soul intact."

Luciano cringed.

The girl returned her rapier to its sheath.

"Try to take me, Inquisitor," she said, as she cleaned her fingernails with the dagger, "and my god will eat your soul."

TEN

"Julianna," Faelin said as he burst out of the brush. "We have to—"

Faelin slid to a stop on the wet pine needles. She was gone. He scanned the ground and saw a pair of footprints leading away from the camp. After about thirty or forty paces, Julianna's tracks joined with another pair of footprints.

"Shades!" Faelin swore. "What has she done?"

"*Tuska!*" Julianna yelled up ahead. This was followed by the sound of splintering wood and screaming horses.

"*Seguindus midian aparthan!*" a distinctly male voice boomed. It sounded like the holy tongue of All Father Sun. Light flashed and the sound of flames roared.

Faelin broke into a sprint. Leaves and branches whipped at his face, and underbrush threatened to trip him up as he rushed headlong toward this erupting battle of miracles.

"*Galad mina varjela.*" Julianna's voice croaked the miracle, a miracle that was too strong for her to attempt. She was channeling too much divine energy too quickly and wouldn't last much longer. Faelin was amazed that she could still stand.

Faelin only heard her because he had gotten close enough to make out the figures through the trees. Dozens of shadows stretched toward Julianna, dancing and weaving around her, creating a cylinder that protected her from a man wearing the golden breast plate and scarlet cape of a House Floraen Inquisitor. The Inquisitor struck at the hardened shadows with a rapier and dagger, but could not pierce them.

A second Inquisitor, this one a few years older than the other, walked toward Julianna with a globe of blazing light held in a hand above his head. The closer he got, the more the shadows protecting Julianna faded.

Faelin raised the crossbow, hands clenching the weapon as he thought, *Which one? Which one?* He took aim.

Before he loosed the quarrel, he heard something crashing through the brush off to his right. Faelin turned and saw a handful of men in black leather armor, faces concealed by bone-white skull masks, rushing toward them. Beyond them, a man wearing the mantle of an Adept of Old Uncle Night sat on a horse. Beside him, a huge, hairless dog with luminescent eyes strained on a leather leash.

So much for half a day.

Faelin aimed again, this time at the Night Adept. The Night Adept seemed to notice Faelin's attention and turned to meet his gaze. Now that Faelin had a good view of the Adept's face, he recognized Carmine D'Mario. One side of Carmine's face curved into an amused smirk. At the same time Faelin released the crossbow bolt, Carmine let go of the leash which held the Daemyn hound.

ELEVEN

As soon as he let go of the Daemyn hound, Carmine pitched himself off his horse. Faelin vara'Traejyn had always been more clever than he had any right to be. Carmine didn't want to gamble whether Faelin knew that he could banish the Daemyn within the hound by killing the man who had summoned it. While Hardin had summoned this one, Faelin wouldn't know that. As Carmine toppled from the horse, he heard more than felt something pass within a hand's span of his head. Faelin might be clever, but not clever enough by a few heartbeats, and now the Daemyn hound would ensure that he would never be that clever again.

Carmine hit the ground with a muddy splash. His horse had not been fully trained for combat, and it bolted the moment Carmine fell. Carmine watched his horse run for a total of three heartbeats, then he scampered behind a tree. The Daemyn hound had almost reached Faelin, and Julianna was fighting the two Inquisitors. Carmine could easily support the Nightbrothers and the Daemyn hound from this tactical position rather than put himself in more danger than he needed to.

TWELVE

When Luciano got within ten paces of the Lord Morigahn, the divine light he carried pierced the shadows protecting her enough for Santo's blades to actually penetrate the defense. It wasn't enough for him to make a clean strike, though. The shadows still slowed him so that it appeared that he was practicing his swordplay at half normal speed in order to focus on proper form. The Lord Morigahn easily dodged him, but it forced her to stop speaking miracles – at least for the moment.

Luciano took another step forward. He could tell that she was exhausted. Her gaunt cheeks told him that she shouldn't even be able to stand, much less continue fighting. Another step forward and he saw the crazed feral look her eyes held. Even as she spun away from Santo, those steel eyes met his then glanced over his shoulder.

"Get down," she snarled just as Luciano heard the sound of someone running up behind.

After a moment's calculation and silent prayer to All Father Sun, Luciano dropped.

"*Mina kehia turvata!*" Julianna spoke, and she pushed her hand outward.

A burst of wind flew past Luciano pulling at his clothes and hair. Had he been standing, he had no doubt it would have taken him off his feet or worse. Glancing over his shoulder, he saw a group of Nightbrothers picked up off their feet and flung through the trees as easily as the leaves and twigs the wind carried in its wake. The Lord Morigahn's miracle had only eliminated about half of the Nightbrothers. Six more ran toward them, curved short swords drawn. To his right, a Daemyn hound barreled down on a man who was hurriedly loading a crossbow. This other man was obviously not with the Brotherhood, but had he come as an ally to the Lord Morigahn or had he stumbled into this as an unlucky happenstance?

Luciano had a choice to make. Did he help Santo against the Lord Morigahn, or did he try and work with her to fight the Brotherhood? That was the sanest option. Could he even convince her that their only hope was to work together?

Luciano threw his orb of light at a spot between the man with the crossbow and the Daemyn hound.

He drew on the dominions of Light and Day, and called, "*Lacceo.*"

The orb of light exploded.

THIRTEEN

Julianna screamed as the Inquisitor's blade bit into her left arm just below the shoulder.

Thank you Sister Wind for protecting my sword arm.

The silent prayer came into Julianna's mind by pure habit. Even as she thought the words, she clenched her teeth. A great eruption of pain blinded her as the experience of the knife cutting her face returned in all its agony. The Lord Morigahn could pray to no other gods besides Grandfather Shadow. Breaking every habit that her Koma heritage had instilled in her would be bothersome at best.

Even through the searing pain, Julianna heard someone chuckle above her. "Goodbye, Lord Morigahn." Whoever it was spoke her name with an edge of disdainful sarcasm.

"No, Santo," someone else yelled. "We need her."

Julianna didn't wait to find out whether or not the protest was heeded. She rolled to her left, soaking her clothes on the muddy turf as she scrambled to her hands and knees, and scurried away from the Inquisitors and Nightbrothers as fast as she could — at least she hoped it was away; she couldn't be sure in her blindness and pain. She stopped short when her head collided with something hard. Flashing lights danced in her vision.

FOURTEEN

Faelin saw the orb of light land in a puddle. The water boiled and sizzled from the heat. He'd seen this enough in the battlefields of Heidenmarch and turned around before the Inquisitor called out his miracle. Light blazed all around Faelin, warming him for a moment as he fled the Daemyn hound and headed to where Julianna had run headlong into a tree.

One of the Inquisitors – the younger one – stalked toward Julianna, sword raised to strike.

Faelin sprinted toward them and flung the crossbow as hard as he could. It caught the Inquisitor in the shoulder. He reeled from the blow, and better yet, dropped his sword.

Faelin was on him by the time he recovered. He grabbed a handful of the Inquisitor's cloak with his left hand and a handful of hair in his right. The Inquisitor tried to pull away, but Faelin slammed his knee into the Inquisitor's hip. The Inquisitor gave a grunt of pain as his leg gave out. Faelin let go of the man's hair and brought his elbow down on the soft spot between his skull and neck. The Inquisitor crumpled.

Faelin heard splashing on the ground to his right, and his scalp prickled. He'd learned to heed that sensation ever since the battlefield in Heidenmarch. The one time he hadn't, a pike had pierced his left thigh.

Dropping to his left, Faelin rolled toward Julianna. Something sharp cut into his right shoulder. He grimaced at the pain. He reached out and grabbed hold of what had stabbed, hoping – praying – that it was the Inquisitor's sword. Faelin could never hope to fight the Nightbrothers with just a dirk. His fingers closed around it. It was flat, thin, and sharp. He grasped it with just enough pressure so that it wouldn't slice his palm and fingers to ribbons. He came to his feet, holding a parrying dagger by the blade, barely a hand's length from the hilt.

Its blade had been forged of Faerii steel, but Faelin had no time to marvel over this.

One of the Nightbrothers rushed Faelin, giving him no time to adjust his grip. The Nightbrother lunged. Faelin brought up his left elbow and spun. He avoiding the attack and connected with the Nightbrother's skull helmet. Faelin hadn't intended the blow to hurt, just knock the helm askew in order to distract his enemy for a moment. Faelin completed the spin, using his momentum to help him pierce the leather armor. The knife slid easily into the Nightbrother's neck. Faelin's hand slid up the blade. It felt like fire burned his arm all the way to the shoulder as the blade cut through skin and muscle of his hand and bit into bone.

Ignoring the pain as best he could, Faelin scanned the area as the corpse slid off the blade. A Nightbrother stalked toward Faelin. His eyes flicked from the body of his fallen comrade to Faelin. He seemed less than eager to rush into a fight with someone willing to cripple his hand to defeat a foe. Faelin used that time to shift his newly-acquired sword into his left hand. Another Nightbrother was on his knees next to the Inquisitor Faelin had incapacitated. Blood flowed from a fresh wound on the Inquisitor's neck. All the other Nightbrothers were charging the second Inquisitor.

"No, you fools!" Carmine's voice screamed in the distance. "Let the hound have that one. Get the girl! Get the girl!"

The Nightbrother who had killed the younger Inquisitor stood and joined the one already facing Faelin. Faelin raised his sword. His other arm burned as if he'd thrust it into a blacksmith's fire.

Perhaps he could hold them long enough for Julianna to come to her senses and escape.

FIFTEEN

Luciano wanted to scream.

Why couldn't Santo have listened? The Nightbrothers had done what they always did: they struck while potential allies fought. Luciano could do nothing for Santo now, and the younger Inquisitor's Faerii blade was lost for the moment. If Luciano died here, either the Brotherhood or the Morigahnti would gain The Detector and his Faerii blade. The Inquisition would be unlikely to regain them.

As the Daemyn hound rushed toward him, Luciano grabbed the nine-pointed star pendant that hung from his neck. He could feel All Father Sun's three dominions – Day, Light, and Truth – swirling within it. He closed his eyes and drew on the dominion of Day much more than he'd drawn on any dominion in his life. He didn't know if the miracle would work, but he had to try.

"*Mishrak Amhyr'Shoul, aevidho som vaso mirso aetirumes.*" As the miracle left his lips, exhaustion crushed down on Luciano with such force that he collapsed under its weight.

SIXTEEN

Faelin shifted his left foot, preparing to lunge at the closest Nightbrother. Two more came running up behind the original pair that faced him now. Gods and goddesses, he wished he could read their faces. That would have helped so much in calculating his strategy.

"*Tuska,*" Julianna's voice said from behind Faelin.

A bolt of dark energy flew past his ear. For a moment, Faelin thought he could almost hear a voice whispering *kostota* and *Galad*, the words for vengeance and shadow, the two dominions required for that particular miracle. The bolt hit the front Nightbrother in the helmet. The leather skull mask ripped away from the Brother's head, pulling chunks of bone and flesh, as if some invisible hand was pealing a juicy red fruit.

Julianna stepped into line with Faelin. She raised her rapier straight out from her shoulder, tip pointed directly toward one of the Nightbrother's eyes. She stood on her toes, the perfect position of the second aggressive posture of the House Andres academy of defense.

This gave the Brothers a few moments of pause.

"Are you hurt?" Faelin asked.

"A bit." She smiled. "More my pride than anything else."

Julianna placed her free hand on Faelin's shoulder, and she grabbed a handful of his coat.

"Hold on," Julianna said, and the world shifted around them.

SEVENTEEN

"No!" Carmine screamed when he saw Julianna and Faelin vanish.

Carmine stood and came out from his hiding place. The Night-brothers were regrouping; well, those that were still living or capable of moving.

Out of the corner of his eye, Carmine saw something moving through the trees. His head snapped around. Was that a pair of wolves stalking through the gloom of the mist? That couldn't be anything but bad.

"Orders, Adept Carmine?" one of the Brothers asked.

Carmine barely heard him. His gaze swept through the trees. Wolf sightings were rare, though not unheard of in Koma, and the fighting should have driven any nearby wolves away. But still, wolves did not concern Carmine; the Nightbrothers and the Daemyn hound could handle wolves. A quiet fear whispered throughout the Brotherhood of the Night that not all the Stormseekers had died at the Battle of Kyrtigaen Pass. There were some, the First Adept included, who believed that someday those shape-shifting wolves would return seeking revenge. This would be a very awkward time for the Stormseekers to begin aiding the Morigahnti again – very awkward for him and the remaining seven Brothers.

"I see seven of you still capable of fighting," Carmine said. "I leave it to you gentlemen to fix it so we have a more favorable number."

It didn't take long. The six healthiest turned on the weakest Brother. As they struggled, Carmine considered the possibility that Stormseekers would involve themselves now, *if* he had actually seen them. The Brotherhood had killed two Lords Morigahn since Kyrtigaen Pass, and the Seekers had not interfered.

"Orders now, Adept?" one of the Brothers asked when there were only six of them standing.

"We will return to Adept Hardin," Carmine said. "Julianna has eluded us for now."

He whistled. The Daemyn hound returned. It had been sniffing about the place where the Inquisitor had vanished. Carmine had not been able to hear the Inquisitor's miracle, so he had no idea where that man had vanished to.

Carmine knelt down next to the hound and scratched it behind the ear.

"Find the Lord Morigahn," Carmine said. "Do not harm her, but kill the man with her. Harry the girl until she drops. Give her no time to eat or rest, but do not touch her. I have plans for that one. Kill anything that gets between you and her. Do you understand?"

"*Aztu.*" The hound snorted and dashed off into the trees.

If there were any Stormseekers helping Julianna, the Daemyn hound would likely take their attention away from Carmine and his small band of Nightbrothers. As he turned to go after his horse, an idea formed in Carmine's mind.

"You two," he waved at two Brothers at random, "fetch the Inquisitor's corpse."

They did.

"What of the Inquisitors' horses?" one of the Brothers asked.

Carmine couldn't help but smile. "If you can manage to get in a sad-le and stay there, you are welcome to it."

Inquisitors' horses were notoriously difficult to ride for any who were not trained as an Inquisitor, not to mention the little surprises the Inquisitors left behind. To Carmine's knowledge, that was one of the few secrets that the Brotherhood had not learned about the followers of the other gods.

Carmine found his horse a little ways off. Its head snapped up and ears flicked back and forth as he approached, but the animal did not spook. When he got back into the saddle, he rode toward Hardin and the camp. After the Daemyn hound devoured Faelin's soul, taking Julianna would be so much easier. Then, Her Grace, the Duchess Taraen, would begin to learn the true nature of suffering.

EIGHTEEN

The sensation of being pulled in every direction at once faded, and Faelin fell to his knees. Bile rose in his stomach, and he succeeded in choking most of it down. He spat out the bit of it that managed to come up and got to his feet.

Two Saifreni horses stood black and regal in a clearing not even twenty paces from them. The saddles on them were the high-backed style favored by House Floraen, and even from this distance, Faelin could see the fine craftsmanship that had gone into the tooling of great yellow and red suns all over the saddles.

He turned to Julianna.

She leaned against a tree. Dark, half-moon circles sagged under her eyes.

"We have to go," she said. "They'll be here any minute."

"Who will be?" Faelin asked.

"The Inquisitors."

She pushed off the tree she had been leaning against and stumbled. Faelin grabbed her arm. Her sleeve rubbed against the cuts on his hand, but Faelin pushed the pain aside. He could deal with his injury once they returned to the horses and got underway. He took a step and then realized he had no idea where the animals might be.

"Which way are the horses?" Faelin asked.

Julianna waved in the direction she was facing.

Faelin half-supported, half-dragged Julianna as they raced through the trees. Already his blood soaked into the sleeve of her chemise around his hand.

"Don't go so fast," Julianna said, "or we'll get there too soon."

"Too soon? We can't get there soon enough for my mind."

To emphasize this, Faelin began to move faster.

"No." Julianna grabbed a sapling and pulled herself to a stop, and subsequently out of Faelin's grip.

That sent bolts of pain shooting from his palm up to his shoulder.

Faelin turned toward Julianna, ready with a rebuke, but she continued. "If we keep going at that pace, we'll meet at least one of ourselves back by the horses." She paused for breath. "And be quiet, or we'll hear ourselves."

"What did you do to us?" Faelin dropped his tone.

She leaned on the sapling and took a deep breath. "I took us back before the fight started. We should get back to the camp a few moments after I left, which will give us plenty of time to get a head start on getting away from our enemies. Now give me a hand and don't move too fast. I just need a few moments of rest after all that I've just done."

Faelin offered his hand. Julianna took it. He led her toward the camp in as quick a pace as she could handle without stumbling. He remained silent as they moved through the woods.

They walked in silence, but after a few moments, Faelin couldn't contain himself.

"What were you thinking?" he asked.

"I needed," the words came out between her ragged breaths, as if speaking them took all her concentration, "to practice."

"Practice? This was a battle, not practice."

"Let them come. The Brotherhood. The Inquisitors. Let them all come." Julianna's eyes grew wide and her lips curved upward in an eager smile.

"They did come. Both of them. And they almost killed us. Be thankful the Inquisitors didn't have any Draqons with them, or we would be dead."

"*Aen Morigahnti te kis ulos taetso. Yn'mina Morigahn'uljas. Mina te kis ulos. Mina viholenti raesu ansa mina varjosta yskin.*"

Faelin suppressed the urge to scream. Julianna spoke the same words that Saent Kaethan spoke just before the Battle of Ykthae Wood. *The Morigahnti do not flee from battle. I am the Lord Morigahn. I do not run. My enemies will fall by my faith alone.* That short speech had inspired the few hundred Morigahnti present to fight with such ferocity that, although only forty-nine of those Morigahnti had lived, thousands of their enemies fell for each Morigahnti slain.

That outburst had given Faelin much to consider. From what he knew of Julianna, she should not know much about the Morigahnti – or should she? How much had changed in Koma in the last five years? Had her uncle's family joined the Morigahnti? Khellan had been marked as the Lord Morigahn also. Had Julianna known this? Had she received more from Grandfather Shadow than just the ability to speak *Galad'laman*? Had he also given her at least some portion of the previous Lords Morigahn's memories?

He heard twigs and branches snapping to his left. Faelin watched himself rushing to find Julianna. It was a strange sight, and Faelin couldn't tell if the sudden dizziness he felt was a creation of his own mind, some lingering effect of Julianna's ability, or loss of blood still oozing from his injured hand. Would it get worse if he got closer? He decided he didn't want to know.

"Now," Julianna said, "we can return to the horses."

Faelin decided not to continue their argument. Julianna was still too traumatized by her experiences to listen to any rational discourse. Now was not the time to convince her of the folly of her choices, but rather, they needed to put as much distance between them and the disaster behind.

They returned to where they had left the horses. Vendyr and the other steeds chewed happily on the brush where Faelin had tied them. He silently thanked Grandfather Shadow that he had not planned to camp here for the evening and so the horses were still saddled.

Faelin slid his newly acquired Faerii blade into his belt and helped Julianna into Vendyr's saddle. Then he went to the spare horses and let them go in different directions.

"It may not be much of a distraction," Faelin said. "But it's better than not trying anything at all. It may even throw them off our trail for a bit."

As Faelin stepped into his stirrup, his horse's head jerked straight up. Its ears flattened against its head, and its eyes went wide. Faelin barely flung himself away before the horse bolted into the trees. Had he acted even a heartbeat later, he would likely have been trapped in the stirrup, and the horse would be dragging him for only the gods knew how long.

He didn't have any time to consider this, or what to do about his lack of a horse, when something large and solid slammed into him. Faelin turned as he fell. Hot breath blasted him in the face. It smelled of death and sickness. A great weight pressed down upon him. Faelin struggled to escape, but he only managed to get his left forearm up in time to keep the Daemyn hound from closing its jaws around his throat. His stomach threatened to expel its contents, but Faelin tightened every muscle inside him to keep it under control. He heard himself screaming while at the same time he determined that dying from the infection of the creature's bite was better than having his soul devoured. With his free hand – the hand that had been sliced nearly to ribbons by the Faerii blade – Faelin punched the Daemyn hound repeatedly in the head. It didn't seem to notice, and it didn't try to pull its jaws away from Faelin's arm. It seemed more content to try and chew its way through the bone. It might also succeed, unless Faelin could figure out a way get the creature off him long enough to get the Faerii blade out of his belt.

NINETEEN

Vendyr spun in circles, eyes rolled back and almost completely white with fear. He had tried to bolt, but thankfully, he'd been facing the Daemyn hound when it appeared. The horse had to wheel or else flee directly toward the attacking predator. Exactly as Julianna predicted, Vendyr turned to the left. He'd always been inclined to that direction. Rather than fight to straighten him, Julianna kept a steady pressure on his reins, keeping Vendyr spinning to the left. He fought her, but she kept his neck bent so much that his nose nearly touched his left flank.

As she kept leading Vendyr in those tight circles, Julianna held both reins in her left hand and drew her mother's knife with the right. Mother's words came back from across fourteen years, *Take this, Julianna; it will protect you against anything less than a god.*

After two more turns, Vendyr began to settle. Julianna allowed him to straighten just as they were coming to face away from the Daemyn hound. She leaned forward, tapped both knees into Vendyr's flanks, and held on with every bit of strength she had left. Just as she had trained him, Vendyr kicked out with his hind legs. It was a trick she'd taught him to amuse herself at the expense of overly arrogant lords who attempted to become too familiar with her on long hunting trips.

It felt like both of Vendyr's back hooves connected with the hound. It yipped and whined like a real dog. Julianna turned Vendyr to face the thing.

The hound had already recovered. It was stalking toward Faelin, who had pointed a parrying dagger of the same kind of metal as Mother's dagger at the Daemyn. Faelin was coated in blood, and his left arm looked as if it would need months to heal. Blood also dripped from the hand that held the weapon.

Julianna screamed, "Once we were like wolves!" and kicked Vendyr into a charge.

The hound's gaze, eerie orbs that glowed like a dying ember in a fire, darted between Julianna and Faelin.

In that moment of hesitation, Faelin struck. He lunged more quickly than Julianna would have believed possible had she not seen it. Uncle Alyx had purchased the services of a Floraen Maestro of D'fence for Marcus' twenty-first birthday gift. Even that man who had dedicated his life to the study of refining the science of sword play could not move as fast as Faelin. His speed bordered on Julianna's talent for shifting time and space.

Faelin buried the parrying dagger in the hound's neck up to the hilt. The Daemyn snapped at him, but Faelin leapt to the side, drawing his blade out, creating a gash as long as Julianna's forearm on the creature's flank.

This distracted it long enough for Julianna to strike. She would have never succeeded if it had been a normal-sized dog; it would have been too short. But the Daemyn hound was just large enough for Julianna to stab it in the back of the neck as she rode past. She twisted her knife as she withdrew it from the monster's flesh, creating a gaping hole that spurted brackish, green-gray blood.

The Daemyn hound roared. The sound was like nothing that ever came from a natural animal. It was like a wolf trying to howl with all the ice of winter caught in its throat. Though the sound was cold, it brought back the heat of the sickness that had afflicted Julianna when she had been fourteen.

The hound lunged for Faelin, but its injured leg would not support it. It collapsed. Faelin darted in, giving it another two slashes. This game went on for a few minutes. As the creature slowed, Faelin cut it more and more. Plants died where its blood spilled to the ground.

At last, the creature gave one final howl and collapsed in on itself, becoming an empty husk.

"They will have heard that," Faelin said as he came over to her; Vendyr would not approach the Daemyn hound's corpse. "We must go."

Julianna sheathed her knife, reached down, and helped Faelin onto Vendyr behind her.

"Which direction?" she asked.

"Southeast," Faelin said, pointing

They had been going west since he found her, but Julianna didn't feel like arguing. She was so tired she couldn't think straight. She prayed – to Grandfather Shadow this time – that they found someplace to tend Faelin's wounds before too long, or Julianna was going to be facing the rest of her journey as the Lord Morigahn alone.

TWENTY

Inquisitor Luciano blinked awake. All Father Sun shone into his eyes, blinding him. Luciano groaned as he covered his eyes with his forearm and rolled onto his back. He lay on something damp and spongy. Had he been asleep or unconscious? His head ached and his stomach churned as if he were wine sick. He sat up, pushed his palms into his eyes, and laced his fingers into the hair that hung down past his forehead. Santo was dead, and his Faerii-steel blade was in the hands of the Morigahnti, or at least had been; perhaps the Brotherhood of the Night had claimed possession. Luciano wondered about the Morigahnti. Had they survived the fight as well? He had no doubt that this woman who claimed to be the Lord Morigahn was capable of dealing with a handful of Nightbrothers, even those led by an Adept of Night with them. The question was whether or not she could deal with a Daemyn hound as well.

Luciano got to his feet and took in his surroundings. Bodies of Nightbrothers lay around him, naked now. The Brotherhood cared not for burial rituals. For them, death was the ritual. Flies buzzed in the area, but he saw no maggots eating away at the exposed flesh of their injuries. Santo's body was gone, which troubled Luciano a great deal. Would the Brotherhood of the Night be able to discern secrets from the corpse of an Inquisitor? Such a notion was preposterous. For that, they would need the body's soul, and All Father Sun took the soul of a fallen Inquisitor into His paradise immediately upon death and rewarded the loyal follower by removing him or her from the Cycle of Life, Death, and Rebirth.

Luciano left the scene and made his way back to where he and Santo had first seen the Lord Morigahn. When he arrived, he found the corpse of a Daemyn hound crisscrossed with cuts and punctures. The man who had come to the Lord Morigahn's aid must still have Santo's Faerii-steel blade, though Luciano suspected it was likely that the Lord Morigahn had claimed the weapon for herself.

Luciano brought The Detector out of his pocket. He twisted two of the five knobs at the top. Both hands swiveled to the southeast. Luciano started walking back toward the horses. It would take time to unsaddle, groom, and feed both his horse, Emperor and Santo's horse, Dawn Chaser, but having both of them would cut down on the time between now and when he could reclaim the Faerii-steel blade and bring this Lord Morigahn before the Sun King's justice.

CHOICES

If we mortals are so far beneath the gods, why do they constantly interfere in our affairs?
— Kavala

Kostota na aen paras kostota.
"Revenge is the best revenge"
The First Law of Grandfather Shadow

ONE

In the fading light of dusk, two figures ascended the slopes of Mount Kolmonen. One, dressed in silks of pearl-white and sky-blue that did little to cover her shapely form, floated alongside the other who climbed a narrow trail. The climber wore heavy furs and wools to fight the cold and biting wind. It had taken him two days to reach this high. The floating figure would have saved him the trouble, if he had only asked. But he preferred to make the journey himself and would not accept help from any Eldar.

Human behavior puzzled Kahddria.

The goddess of wind had possessed many other names over the course of human existence, many of those names forgotten, which brought no small amount of sorrow to her heart. She missed some of the more poetic things humans had called her, as well as the grand stories those lost cultures used to tell about her. Now she was known to most in the current human era merely as the lesser goddess, Sister Wind, and most of the stories had grown bland.

"Why do you think that most mortals have simplified the Eldar?" Kahddria asked. "Once there were great mythologies created around us. Now we've become nothing more than a collection of simple stories and superstitions, not counting the Kingdom High Blood. Why do you think that is?"

The human climbing the thin trail below her stopped and looked up at her.

"You have my complete respect, Kahddria," he shouted up into the wind. His voice possessed none of the respect he claimed. "But if we're actually going to converse, would you please come down so that I don't have to crane my neck."

"Of course." Kahddria floated down next to him. "Now, Maxian, give me your suspicions."

"You answered your own question," the man said. "For the last thousand years the Kingdom has conquered and subjugated most of the other lands on this continent. As they stamped out the worship of the Greater Eldar, they also diminished human interest in the Lesser Eldar as well. With their Draqon armies, it's easy for the common man to think that the Kingdom is destined to rule the world. I'd be bitter against the gods if I believed that simplified view of the universe."

"What an intriguing idea," Kahddria said. "Would you share this idea with the others?"

"I don't have to," Maxian replied, and continued his climb. "I've discussed these thoughts with several of the Eldar. Some agree with me, some disagree. I don't really care what any of you believe."

She mulled this over for a moment and opened her mouth to tell him that it did matter, but that wouldn't do any good. Maxian's mind was made up, at least as far as the Eldar were concerned. He wouldn't change his mind about them any more than he would accept her help, no matter how innocently the offer was made. Maxian was one of those rare individuals who had cried out against the Eldar, begging freedom from their intervention in his life, for good or for ill. Due to the Ykthae Accord, any mortal that asked for autonomy from celestial influence would be granted that wish. After that, the mortal couldn't be freed from the influence of just one part of the celestial realms; the mortal had to separate himself from *all* aspects of the realms beyond the physical. However, though Maxian had done just that, it hadn't stopped him from involving himself in celestial politics, which infuriated most of the others because they couldn't do anything to stop him.

"Waiting for you to finish this climb is getting rather tiresome," Kahddria said.

"I never asked you to accompany me. And I never promised to be entertaining."

"Indeed, but you don't have to go out of your way to be so immensely boring."

Maxian shrugged, and continued up the path.

Kahddria left him to his cynicism and flew to a cave near the summit. It grew colder as she approached the cave, colder even than the elevation should dictate. The temperature didn't bother her; she summoned a breeze of warm air from the tip of the southern-most island of Inis O'lean. There were dozens of different kinds of wildflowers growing along that coastline. The scents of those flowers mixed with the salty sea air to create the sweetest aroma of the whole world. She set that wind spinning around her body and separated it from the winds that howled at the summit of Mount Kolmonen.

When she entered the cave, Kahddria saw she wasn't the last to arrive – even taking Maxian into consideration. Two of her fellow Lesser Eldar sat around a table made of skulls. In the normally dark eyes of those skulls, Kahddria thought she saw the hint of eyes pleading for rest. These were souls from the Realm of the Godless Dead. Yrgaeshkil sat in a chair of miscellaneous bones and rotting flesh. She wore a more subdued form at the moment. Her only Daemynic features were the two leathery wings sprouting from her shoulders. Other than that, she looked like a young woman not even thirty years old, dark and beautiful.

Yrgaeshkil possessed power over the dominion of Lies, which she allowed some of her husband's followers to use. She had also enjoyed a great deal of freedom in the thousand years since the Lords of Order had imprisoned her husband. A few days ago, this blatant use of her husband's domain would likely have drawn the King of Order's attentions, but so much had changed since then. It was still a risk, because none of them knew how far they could push the boundaries of the Ykthae Accord.

Next to her was Skaethak, or Sister Winter, as mortals called her. This evening she was an albino waif of a girl, lounging on a couch of snow and ice.

"Is Innaya coming?" Kahddria asked as she floated over to the table.

"I believe so." Skaethak's voice came out as a whispered tinkle, and bits of frost formed in the air with her words.

"I am indeed here," replied a husky voice.

A searing light pierced the cave's gloom, and a tall, voluptuous woman stood at the last vacant spot at the table. Innaya, the Lady of Dawn, All Father Sun's daughter, even went so far as to wear a human head with blond hair and blue eyes and to dress in glowing plate armor from a culture decimated by the Kingdom centuries before.

"Are you ever going to change your appearance?" Skaethak asked. "It's been over three hundred years since those people were killed."

"One of them was my daughter," Innaya said. "I still mourn her."

"I've told you before," Yrgaeshkil words dripped like poison honey, "you may visit her any time you like."

A sword of light appeared in Innaya's hand. "And be powerless in your *husband's* realm? Hardly."

Yrgaeshkil's face tightened with Innaya's slight inflection on the word husband. The Aengyl smiled sweetly, which caused the Daemyn's features to shift into a more bat-like appearance.

Kahddria had to get control of this gathering or they would likely shorten the summit with their squabbling. She didn't really care about the mountain, but devastation of that level would attract attention. There were some of the Eldar that Kahddria didn't want snooping around in this matter.

"Ladies," Kahddria floated between them, "we're not here to bicker. We're here to discuss matters of great importance."

"Let me make a supposition." Skaethak's whispered voice dripped with sarcasm. "One of *them* is free."

"Yes." Kahddria kept her voice even, though she wanted to pull a hot wind from the Lands of Endless Summer to warm the cold bitch. "I'm surprised you didn't feel it, since it was Galad'Ysoysa who was freed."

"Impossible," Skaethak said. "I would know."

"Why is that?" Yrgaeshkil asked. "He is the God of Secrets; perhaps he is keeping this a secret from you. Lords and Princes! Think a bit. If you were suddenly free from a prison after ten centuries, wouldn't you wait and see what the Lesser are up to, not to mention the state of the mortal world?"

"But what proof do we have?" Innaya asked. "Other than her word, of course?"

"I, too, have sensed his presence through my husband's worshipers."

Innaya snorted out a contemptuous laugh. "I know you'll forgive me if I doubt the one of us at this meeting who bears the title, Mother of Lies."

"Calm down, Innaya," Skaethak said. "I agree with you. What other proof do you have, Kahddria?"

Both Innaya and Skaethak fixed Kahddria with demanding stares. She sighed. She'd forgotten how cynical and suspicious the other Eldar were. Like the other elemental Eldar, Kahddria was more straightforward and less prone to deception than the others, especially the seasons.

"Me," came a voice from the cave's entrance.

All four Lesser Eldar turned. Maxian stood in the cave's mouth. How had he gotten here so fast? He should have been at least another hour a-way.

"And why should you know that he has returned when Skaethak does not?" Yrgaeshkil asked. "Considering you have removed yourself from celestial influence, why should we believe or trust you?"

Maxian's mouth curved into a smirk which accentuated the scar that ran down the right side of his face. That old wound seemed to darken. His cold eyes did not reflect the smile.

"I have my sources," Maxian said, "sources that no Eldar can touch."

"And who would be more reliable than one of the Lesser Eldar sworn to Galad'Ysoysa?" Skaethak asked.

Kahddria suppressed a smile. She knew Maxian's secret. Few of the other Eldar did; they could not watch him from afar. Kahddria had taken it upon herself to maintain a close watch on the small handful of people who had done as Maxian. She had cultivated relationships with them, which had taken some doing in certain cases. One never knew when it would be advantageous to know someone completely immune to the powers of the Eldar. Thus far, only one member of that small group of mortals on this continent remained aloof of her advances.

"The Stormseekers," Maxian replied.

"Why would they tell you?" Skaethak demanded. "They haven't been involved in the game since…"

"My wife died," Maxian finished. "A few days ago, Razka informed me that Grandfather Shadow had returned and had marked a new Lord Morigahn with his own hand."

Kahddria watched as the other three considered this. They looked back and forth at each other, then at her, trying to gauge what their next course of action should be.

Yrgaeshkil spoke first. "Who is the lucky man that Galad'Ysoysa has chosen?"

"He didn't choose a man," Maxian replied. "He chose a woman. The Stormseekers didn't give me a name, and I don't care."

"If you don't care," Skaethak said, "why are you telling us this?"

Maxian shrugged.

"There are others who know," Kahddria said. "The First Adept of Old Uncle Night, the Speaker of Lies, this new Lord Morigahn, any Morigahnti bonded to a Stormcrow, and any Morigahnti who will hold still long enough for a Morigahnti bonded to a Stormcrow to tell him that Grandfather Shadow has returned."

"There is one other who might know," Maxian said.

"Who is that?" Innaya said, joining the conversation at last.

"The only other man to shed the mantle of the Lord Morigahn without dying," Maxian replied.

"Why should we care about him knowing?" Yrgaeshkil asked.

"Because," Kahddria replied, "he is currently mentoring the Speaker of Lies, giving him access to the First Adept of Old Uncle Night."

Yrgaeshkil's eyes grew wide. As Kahddria suspected, Yrgaeshkil didn't revel in the thought of her husband gaining his freedom. If Kavala felt enough fear from Galad'Ysoysa's return, he might try to free another of the Greater Eldar.

"Think of what that will mean," Maxian said, "if Old Uncle Night and Grandfather Shadow are the only Greater Eldar free in the world."

"He's right," Skaethak said. "We will have to do something. But what?"

"We will have to bring others into this," Innaya said. "Even if we four worked together, we would be sore pressed to defeat one of the Greater Eldar."

"True," Kahddria said. "Then, let us return in one week's time. Bring at least one of your fellows with you. Eight of us might be enough."

"Wait," Innaya said. "What if one of us thinks to curry favor with Galad'Ysoysa by betraying the others?"

"That would be very foolish indeed," Skaethak said. "The very fact that we are at this meeting and having this discussion might be enough for him to punish us, regardless of whether or not we betray the others. We have just plotted to destroy one of the Greater, something that hasn't been done since the First War. None of them will take kindly to that. It's in our best interest to see this through now."

"Agreed," the other three said.

Without another word Skaethak, Yrgaeshkil, and Innaya vanished.

"That went much better than I hoped," Kahddria said. "There is a fight coming. You would prove a very powerful ally."

"I am done fighting. I will bring you information, and as much as I complain, I do enjoy your company at times. However, I am done with the games the Eldar play with human lives. There is nothing that will bring me back into that never-ending war."

"That's a shame," Kahddria said. "Galad'Ysoysa named Duchess Julianna Taraen of House Kolmonen as his new Lord Morigahn."

Maxian's face went slack. At first his pale green eyes looked far away, not focusing on anything. Then he fixed those eyes on Kahddria. The look of scorn he had given Yrgaeshkil was nothing next to the raw fury Kahddria saw now.

"Damn you, Kahddria."

"I didn't do this," Kahddria said. "I didn't want this. I was content with the five still trapped away."

"Damn you, Kahddria" Maxian whispered. "And damn Grandfather Shadow."

His head sank, chin touching his chest. He stood there, a man defeated.

"I'm sorry," Kahddria said. "But if Grandfather Shadow is keeping himself hidden, you are the girl's only hope to learn what it means to be the Lord Morigahn." Kahddria wondered if she'd broken him. She'd given him something to care about again, something to lose. "I thought you didn't care?"

Maxian looked up. "Now I have to care."

The storm still raged in his eyes, but now he looked stronger, more determined than she'd ever seen any human before. His look frightened Kahddria even more than the thought of Galad'Ysoysa being free. The Greater Eldar had to be careful, as there were consequences for his actions. On the other hand, Maxian had the look of a desperate, cornered animal. He didn't care about consequences. For him, nothing was worse than he'd lived through, and after turning his back on the Eldar, death would only be a release into quiet oblivion.

"I will teach her," he said. "I will teach her things no Lord Morigahn has ever known. The world will shake with her coming, and once she's finished with the world, even the gods will tremble at her name."

TWO

Grandfather Shadow waited for all four Lesser Eldar and Maxian to leave the cave before he entered the World Between Worlds. The moment he left the physical realm, a force stronger than any power the God of Shadows could call upon pulled him into the King of Order's Realm.

Grandfather Shadow had hoped to forestall this moment a while longer – foolish as that notion was.

Every piece of the Realm of Order's clockwork menagerie glowed, destroying any chance for the existence of shadows or darkness. Everything in this realm moved in perfect precision. The gears and pulleys that kept all the worlds moving and working according to each one's natural laws clicked and whirred, creating a soothing harmony.

"GALAD'YSOYSA, YOUR FREEDOM HAS NOT BEEN PROPERLY EARNED," the King of Order's voice boomed from every corner of the realm.

"Your Majesty," Grandfather Shadow said. "The conditions for any of the Greater Eldar to earn freedom were very specific."

"IT WAS NOT THE PURE FAITH OF A MORTAL THAT FREED YOU."

"Begging Your Majesty's indulgence, your decree only specified the words be from a mortal's mouth. You did not specify the faith must be born from that same mortal's heart."

"ONE OF YOUR OWN SAENTS MANIPULATED THE WORDS IN ORDER TO ENSURE YOUR ESCAPE."

"And I'm sure that Your Majesty has punished him accordingly. I hope that you do not seek to blame me for the actions of my Saents while I was unable to control them."

There was a long pause. Grandfather Shadow began to fear he'd gone too far. If so, he'd sent Julianna to her death. Even with Faelin at her side, she could never hope to survive in the world as the Lord Morigahn without her god's aide.

"TAKE CARE, GALAD'YSOYSA, I AM CLOSE TO LOSING PATIENCE WITH YOU."

The gears, pulleys, springs, and cogs grew brighter, and the soft hum of their ceaseless work began to sound a bit more like a growl. Grandfather Shadow was treading on dangerous ground. He calculated quickly. The King of Order was already upset, and the twisting of words and logic that Grandfather Shadow would have to do in order to overcome this would likely upset the Incarnate even more.

"Your majesty is clearly too frustrated to continue this discussion in a rational manner. I request arbitration."

"VERY WELL," the King of Order replied. The suddenness of this compliance gave Grandfather Shadow a moment of pause. "LORDS OF JUDGEMENT, WE REQUIRE YOU."

A moment later, three cloaked figures appeared around Grandfather Shadow. The cloaks were three different colors: white, black, and gray.

The three spoke as one. "We have foreseen your need of us and have been watching events since the first moment that served as the catalyst for this argument. The King of Order brings his grievance. Proceed with your charges and arguments."

"GALAD'YSOYSA IS FREE FROM HIS PUNISHEMENT THROUGH GUILE AND TREACHERY, RATHER THAN PURE HUMAN-BORN FAITH. MORE TO THE POINT, THE ONE WHO FREED HIM IS NOT COMPLETELY HUMAN. I WOULD HAVE HIM PLACED BACK IN HIS PRISON AND THE WORDS OF MY EARLIER DECREE MODIFIED."

"Galad'Ysoysa," the Lords of Judgment spoke, "your counter."

"While I understand His Majesty's irritation, he should have taken more care with his words. For a Greater Eldar to win freedom, a mortal born no fewer than ten generations after you imprisoned us must call for a specific god with words of their own mouth, and those words must be born of pure faith. All those requirements were filled when Julianna called for me."

Laughter filled the Realm of Order. "YOUR OWN WORDS DAMN YOU. JULIANNA TARAEN IS NOT TRULY MORTAL."

Grandfather Shadow felt the unfamiliar sensation of worry creep into his stomach. He hadn't considered that. It might grow into panic if he were some other being, but he'd been manipulating gray areas since the world was new.

"I must politely disagree," Grandfather Shadow said. "She may not be human, but she is certainly mortal. Even with her mother's blood, Julianna will live out her life, perhaps a bit longer than those born about the same time as she, but nonetheless, her life span is finite. I believe that is the very definition of mortality."

"Enough." The Lords of Judgment each held their left hand up. "We understand The King of Order's grievance, and we know that Galad'Ysoysa will attempt to speak circles around any words used in argument against him. We will allow Julianna to determine the outcome of this discussion."

The Lords of Judgment vanished.

"THIS SHOULD BE INTERESTING."

"Indeed," Grandfather Shadow replied.

Without any preamble or word of dismissal, Grandfather Shadow found himself standing in his great hall in the celestial Realm of Shadows.

The chamber was a bit dusty but remained just as he had left it. He walked between twin rows of stone pillars to sit on his throne. Even though this return might be short-lived, Grandfather Shadow stretched out and settled into his rightful place. After a moment, it felt as if he'd never left. He waved his hand, and the Well of Knowledge appeared next to him. Misty water bubbled a bit inside the well.

Grandfather Shadow brushed the water with his fingertips and whispered, "The Lord Morigahn and Saent Faelin the Sentinel."

The water smoothed, flat as any mirror. An image formed. Two riders on a single black and white horse rode through a forest, rain pouring down upon them. The horse slowed and came to a stop a few moments later. Three cloaked figures – black, white, and gray – came out of the trees from different directions.

Grandfather Shadow waved his hand over the well. He could now hear the raindrops pattering on the ground and the wind in the trees.

"Julianna Taraen…"

THREE

Hours after leaving the Nightbrothers and Inquisitors behind, hopefully to kill each other, Julianna guided Vendyr between the trees at a slow walk. Rain came down in a steady drum, and Julianna let it fall on them. No need to give any possible survivors the means to track them.

Vendyr stopped in a small clearing. Julianna was so tired she hadn't realized he'd slowed until all forward movement stopped and the trees no longer wandered past them. She flicked the reins, but Vendyr wouldn't move.

Ahead to the right and left, two cloaked figures, one white and one gray, came out of the trees. She glanced over her shoulder and saw a third, this one wearing a black cloak. The cloaks were voluminous, like folded pavilions in the process of being unfurled in a strong wind.

"Julianna Taraen of House Kolmonen," the gray-cloaked man's voice was deep and full of command, "stand forward for judgment."

Julianna kicked Vendyr's flanks again, wanting him to ride the man down. She grew weary of people threatening her. One day, she would face her enemies without needing to run, but for now, she would have Vendyr trample him. The other two could be eliminated at another time. For some reason, she was sure she would see them both again.

Unfortunately, Vendyr would not move.

Taking a deep breath, Julianna drew on the dominion of Storms through the *Galad'fana*. Faelin's hand covered her mouth before she could speak.

"Don't." The command of Faelin's voice was as firm as his hand over her mouth, though Julianna could sense a bit of desperation in both his grip and tone. "Not with them. Those three stand greater than the gods. I'll explain later. Show deference and respect – but do not grovel."

Faelin slowly released his hand from Julianna's mouth. Then he slid off Vendyr.

"Forgive me, Great Lords of Judgment," Faelin said. "We are unfamiliar with the protocols for your proceedings."

"Speak plainly and honestly," the one in the white cloak said. "That is all we require of your charge, Sentinel."

"Faelin," Julianna asked, "what's going on?"

Faelin looked up at her. "These three are the Lords of Judgment. They preside over disputes within the celestial realms."

Julianna dismounted and faced the gray cloak. She couldn't see a face, just a pair of luminescent violet eyes.

"What do you want with me?" Julianna demanded. Her voice sounded much more confident than she felt, but that was the way of life for nobility. "I have no place among the celestials."

"You speak from ignorance," the black cloak said. "As with many laws, this does not absolve you of the crime."

"Your mother was not in any way human," the white cloak said. "Though her kind has forsaken the celestial realm, the power of their origins did not fade, nor did that choice mean you would not inherit that power to some degree."

"Ironic as it is, in granting upon you the title *Morigahnti'uljas*," gray cloak said, "Galad'Ysoysa has upset the balance of the Ykthae Accord. We are here to right that balance, one way or another."

"And how will you do that?" Julianna asked.

The three Lords of Judgment spoke together. "You stand at the crossroads of destiny. You must choose which path to take."

"What?" Julianna asked. "I thought destiny was fixed in the future, unchangeable. Isn't that why it's called destiny?"

"Not exactly," Faelin said. "Like everything else in creation, destiny is a dynamic force. It's not as if there is one fate for everything in the universe. Chance and freewill are just as powerful. If not, then there would be little point to life. All creatures know this, and that is why everything struggles against the world, because even taking fate into account, freewill and chance might play for or against our favor at any given moment."

Julianna placed her fists on her hips and fixed Faelin with her most practiced stare of authority. "And how is it you know all this, Faelin var-a'Traejyn."

"It's amazing what books you can find in libraries outside of the Kingdom's borders," Faelin replied.

He wasn't telling her everything, but that was fine – for now. She'd ask him about this later.

Taking a deep breath, Julianna faced the gray-cloaked figure.

"What are my choices?"

Again, they spoke as one. "Three paths stretch out before you: your father's, your mother's, and that of mediocrity."

"Why in the name of the five would anyone choose mediocrity?" Julianna asked.

"It is safe," Faelin said. "Well, as safe as life can be for a normal person."

"Will the Brotherhood of the Night and the Inquisitors continue to hunt me?" Julianna asked.

"Those are mortal institutions," the Lords of Judgment said.

"I can't bloody well then choose mediocrity can I?" Julianna said. "I'd be dead within a fortnight." She looked at Faelin. "Which should I choose?"

"The choice must be your own," the Lords of Judgment said.

Julianna closed her eyes. She breathed in and out in the same steady rhythm as she would have as if she were preparing for a duel.

Why couldn't things just be normal? Khellan should be alive. She should be planning a wedding with him that would infuriate her aunt. A-lone in the darkness of her thoughts, Khellan's face smiled at her, eyes amused, handsome despite the scar running down his face. Julianna closed her eyes tighter, trying to hold back the grief as her throat tightened. Now she saw Khellan swinging from his *Galad'fana*, the scar twitching as he died. Soon, she only saw the scar in the darkness. Father had a scar like that too. Father had been the Lord Morigahn, while Mother had been at least partly a wolf and had given Julianna the ability to move backward and forward in time. That ability had saved Julianna time and again; she knew the power and understood how to use it. However, it hadn't helped her save Khellan or any of her other friends, but it had gotten her and Faelin away from the Brotherhood and Inquisitors.

Which path to choose?

Opening her eyes, Julianna drew her mother's dagger, the only thing she possessed from either of her parents. She turned it over and over in her hands, caressing the hilt, running her thumb and fingers over the single word etched on its blade.

Kostota.

She owed a great many people *kostota*. How best could she repay those debts? She couldn't with a life of mediocrity – not that she'd been considering that in the first place. That left Father or Mother? Mother or Father? *Kostota.* In the end, it all came down to that one word. She couldn't imagine any path where that did not lead to balancing her *kostota* with everyone.

Sheathing her dagger, Julianna faced the gray Lord of Judgment and made her choice.

The Lords of Judgment descended on her, cloaks billowing, eyes glowing madly in the gloom brought by the storm.

Being marked as the Lord Morigahn was a scratch compared to the anguish of having the essence of her soul remade.

FOUR

Grandfather Shadow watched from the Well of Knowledge throughout the night. At some point after the first hour, Julianna's voice grew so hoarse that her screams dried to croaks. She reached for Faelin, begging and pleading, but the Saent knew well that he could not help her. Julianna must suffer this alone. Not only would the Lords of Judgment strike Faelin down, this ordeal would teach Julianna to persevere and survive other great trials and suffering later.

The Lords of Judgment moved back from Julianna as dawn brought sunlight piercing through the storm clouds. Her nostrils flared with each ragged breath as she struggled to her feet, lips pressed tight together. After a moment, her knees steadied. She looked from one Lord of Judgment to the next. Her gazed settled on the gray-cloaked one. Julianna took a step forward and spat on him.

Grandfather Shadow laughed, full and deep. The sound filled his hall. He waved a hand over the Well of Knowledge, dismissing the scene. Julianna might not be what other people would call *fine*, and she would not know much of peace, but she would be counted amongst the greatest of those who bore the title of the Lord Morigahn. Yes, Grandfather Shadow had chosen well.

The laughter caught in his throat when he felt a familiar presence in his hall.

"What?" Grandfather Shadow asked. "The Lords of Judgment have made their decree based on Julianna's choice. Leave me be until I actually break the letter of the Ykthae Accord."

"I WILL ALLOW YOU TO RETURN TO YOUR GAMES, FOR NOW," the King of Order said. "HOWEVER, IF YOU DISPLEASE ME OVER MUCH, PERHAPS I'LL SEND YOU THROUGH THE CYCLE OF LIFE, DEATH, AND REBIRTH. HOW MANY OF YOUR ANCIENT ENEMIES WOULD LOVE TO FIND YOU AS A MORTAL?"

And with that, the King of Order was gone.

Grandfather Shadow stretched out on his throne. He was the only Greater Eldar free to roam the world, and that gave him an immense amount of power. For the moment, he could do as he pleased – so long as he didn't violate the King of Order's decrees. Grandfather Shadow understood the difference between bending the law and breaking the law, and he intended to bend as many celestial laws as possible – right up to the snapping point. The law was a lofty pedestal upon which the King of Order sat. If all those laws snapped at once, His Majesty could do nothing but fall. The moment that happened, Galad'Ysoysa would be ready to repay his thousand-year imprisonment.

"*Kostota na aen paras kostota,*" Grandfather Shadow whispered.

The words echoed in the hall, out through the windows, and into every shadow in existence.

Thus ends the first volume of

TEARS OF RAGE

Julianna's adventures continue in volume two

ONCE WE WERE LIKE WOLVES

M. Todd Gallowglas

BACKSTORY EXPOSED

"And we're going live in, five, four, three…" the director completed the countdown in silence by holding up two fingers, then one, then the catchy theme music hit.

Steve Stewart looked into the camera and read from the prompter, "Welcome back to the show. Thanks for waiting through the two opening segments to get to this big moment. Please welcome to the Daily Report, for his first televised interview, the avenging shadow, the bringer of justice, Mister X."

The crowd erupted into cheers and applause unlike anything Steve Stewart had heard in Daily Report history.

Mister X came out from back stage, wearing his gray superhero costume, highlighted with white and black, and with the large black "X" across his chest. His cowl covered most of his face, but just in case, he also wore a mask covering everything but his eyes. But seeing those wouldn't help identify him. He had contacts that made his eyes look completely red.

The crowd grew even louder. Steve Stewart realized they'd made the right call in hiring the extra security.

After a few minutes, the audience finally calmed down to where Steve Stewart could ask his first question.

He and the writing team had gone round and round about the first question. Was the joke too much, too far past the line? Then one of their new interns asked, "What's that you always say, boss? 'If you're worried about crossing the line, it's a line that needs to be crossed. That's what political comedy does.'" And that decided the matter.

"So, Mister X," Steve Stewart said. "Everyone knows your back story. Parents killed by a burglar while you were having a family movie night."

"Yes," Mister X replied in a monotone.

"But what people don't know is that you staged the burglary," Steve Stewart said, and even as he added, "isn't that right?" he knew that he'd hit on the truth.

After years of performing in dimly-lit comedy clubs and dive bars, he'd learned to judge people by their posture, since he couldn't see most of the audience's faces beyond the bright lights. He'd honed that talent to an instinctive level in his years hosting the Daily Report. Mister X shifted, subtly, almost imperceptibly, but enough to tell Steven Stewart that this wasn't a joke. It was the truth. He'd just revealed the deepest darkest secret of one of the most dangerous men on the planet on world-wide television.

Mister X shifted again, and while Steven Stewart's body couldn't react in time to save himself, his mind was more than capable of realizing that with one question, he had inadvertently turned one of the world's greatest superheroes into a villain.

MAGIC AND THE GRISLY MEMORY

More than anything else in all his life, Simon "Wart" O'Bannan wanted to be a magician. Not a rabbit-out-of-a-hat or a card-up-my-sleeve kind of magician. He wanted to be a change-reality-by-strength-of-will-alone kind of magician.

Philosopher's stones.

Greater secrets.

Longevity potions.

A *REAL* magician.

Then, one day, after years of research and following the whispers of rumors, he found a book of magic. Well, he hoped it was a book of magic. Pages of brittle parchment bound in gold and leather, the script a strange variant of Latin. His studies began. More research. More goose chases and false trails. One day, almost by accident, while going over the book and examining the few notes he'd managed to put together from dozens of different sources, Simon managed to get something to *click* in his mind.

A week later, he cast his first spell. A real change-reality-by-strength-of-will-alone kind of spell.

Memories flooded back to him of all the terrible things he'd done across a dozen centuries in pursuit of magic, never caring about the harm his did or the prices he paid, at least, not until a hedge witch managed to get him to gaze into a Mirror of True Seeing. His mind couldn't cope with the forced awareness of what he had become, and so he cast a spell upon himself so that he forgot everything: who he was; what he had done; everything, *including* the magic.

He cast that spell again.

All the memories faded, and his mind stopped screaming in self-loathing.

More than anything else in all his life, Mattias "Wart" O'Connor wanted to be a magician.

ENNIU

Scroll.
Refresh.
No new email.
Scroll.
Refresh.
No new voice mail.
Scroll.
Refresh.
No new text messages.
"I'm sick of being cooped up here. Wanna get out?
"Sure. Where you want to go?"
"Coffee shop first and see from there?"
"Sounds good."
Scroll.
Refresh.
No new email.
Scroll.
Refresh.
No new voice mail.
Scroll.
Refresh.
No new text messages.
"Head home?"
"Yeah. Nothing going on here."
Scroll…
Refresh…

Halloween Jack

and the
Devil's Gate

For Trey, Steve, and Snipe
Thanks for years of encouragement

Acknowledgements

First and foremost, I want to thank Robin, the wonderful lady for believing enough in my dreams to not let me quit even when I felt like throwing in the towel. Alex Jimenez, where ever he is for teaching me the "Jack of the Lantern" story. Marti and Bill for giving me a shot at this whole storytelling thing. All the folks at De Vere's pub in Sacramento; I couldn't ask for a better place to start my professional writing career. The wonderful ladies who work the morning shift at Starbucks in Lincoln, CA for pouring me coffee and dealing with my anguished cries as I finished this manuscript.

And again, Mathew and Robert for giving me the greatest stories I can ever tell.

Prologue

It started with a turnip. True, some stories say it was a gourd, others go with the now traditional pumpkin, but, in truth, that first lantern John the blacksmith carved was out of a turnip. That's when he first became known as Jack of the Lantern. The stories don't all agree on how it was that Jack made the Devil so angry that the Devil wouldn't let Jack into Hell, but the fact remains that all humanity owes Jack a debt, for as time went on and the Devil and his kin became free to roam the world only one night of the year, we carve our turnips, gourds, and pumpkins into lanterns to put outside our doors. We know, that the Devil and his kin know, behind one of those lanterns is a troublemaker of the likes they can do without.

However, deep in the bowels of his dark realm, sitting on his dark throne, the Dark One has not forgotten. While Jack of the Lantern has wandered over the centuries, the Devil and his kin, cunning and crafty one and all, have plotted and schemed their revenge.

SINGLE STEPS

One

Moira O'Neil went about the cottage as she did every Halloween, serving the demons that came through the cottage. While she did, Grandmother checked the demons off the list, one by one, as they returned from their once-a-year excursion into the world of men. Though there were plenty of chairs in the cottage, the demons all stood. With good reason, the demons did not trust the chairs in this house.

One of the demons said something unflattering in Latin to Moira as she plopped a lump of sugar into its tea. It was a tiny little runt of an imp, green and yellow skin, with tiny little horns barely poking out of its forehead, though it did have a long tail that Moira kept having to step around. Just because they were demons didn't mean Grandmother would tolerate her being a poor hostess. Stepping on tails was among the first signs of a poor hostess.

"Oh, right," Moira said, and switched the cup with the demon sitting next to the imp. That was a succubus, with barely enough clothing on to force a man's imagination. "Apologies, Miss Saleesh."

Moira knew the succubus's name because this particular temptress had come out on Halloween every year since Moira could remember.

"Not at all, dear," Saleesh said. "It's been a long night for all of us."

Moira spat in the cup she placed in front of the imp. "Happy now then?"

The imp gave a curt nod and began to sip daintily at his tea.

"Best hurry with your refreshments," Grandmother's deep Irish voice came from over by the door. "Dawn's close, she is. Don't want to be caught behind. Recall what happen last year? Himself will be along any moment to take note of the stragglers."

Most of the demons grumbled in agreement, even the most brazen of them. The man they called The Lantern came just before dawn, on the off chance that one of the demons tried to stay in the human world beyond sunrise.

"Now I'm not normally one to bless anything," Moira heard one of the demons say in a very proper British accent as she handed him a glass of wine, "but I have to say I'm quite pleased with this rise of science and

169

Natural Philosophy. People are forgetting the traditions, and I was able to collect three very impressive souls this year."

"Three?" his companion remarked. "And I thought I was doing quite well with one. Might I accompany you next year? I must know how you do it?"

"But of course. The more we share, the better we're served."

Over the last few years, Moira had heard demons bragging more and more about successes in soul collecting. And they all ascribed it to finding mortals that weren't protecting themselves on Halloween, or as the demons called it, the Darkest Night. Normally, one had to be careful of the things one believed that came from the mouths of demons, as their kind were crafty, cunning, conniving, malicious, malevolent, and most other unpleasant adjectives one might ascribe to them. However, demons were usually truthful with each other over matters of soul collecting. Yes, they were deceitful, but they were also proud and despised being caught in a lie.

As much as Moira wished she could do something about it, she could not. The bargain made by her penultimate grandmother forbade any of the daughters in this line of Jack's blood from interfering with demons on this night so that these daughters could protect humanity the other three hundred sixty-four nights of the year – sixty-five on leap years.

Serving a mug of beer to a hulking monstrosity of all tentacles and claws, Moira felt something brush at the hairs that had come loose from her bun. Faster than anyone might think possible, she pulled a switch out of her apron ties and snapped it across the forearm of a goblin hanging by its tail from the rafters. The sickly looking, greenish-gray creature strung together a slew of insults from at least a dozen languages. Its skin bubbled and burned where the silver crosses imbedded in the switch struck its skin. Other demons, the older ones who had been through the gate many times on the Darkest Night, laughed and howled.

"They knows us better 'n tha'," called a creature that looked human except for the hooves, curling horns, and goat-like eyes. That one was a duke of Hell at least, perhaps even a prince.

Moira curtsied to the demon and went about her serving.

The goblin had been reaching for her locket, which contained a strand of hair from Saint Mary, one of the seven items needed to perform the ritual that kept the Devil's Gate closed the rest of the year. Every year, as the Darkest Night came to a close, some of the demons tried to steal an item or two, but they always failed. Grandmother had taught Moira to mind them well. And as sneaky as they sometimes were, after a while demons became rather predictable. At sixteen, Moira felt that while she didn't know everything about them, she knew enough to expect their tricks.

Moira stifled a yawn as she collected used cups and glasses. She timed each night by her yawns. This was her third this evening. The cottage seemed a bit more crowded this year than normal by her third yawn, and there seemed quite a few demons she didn't recognize. The list of demons who were allowed to roam cycled every couple of years, and it took a lot for demons to get on the list to wander the world on the darkest night. Moira glanced at the great grandfather clock on the far side of the room, the one that showed not the hours of the day, but the balance between night and day. Dawn was almost upon them.

As she cleaned up after the demons, who were definitely *not* leaving as usual when they finished their drinks, Moira made her way over to Grandmother. One look in Grandmother's eyes told Moira that Grandmother had noticed it too.

The clock chimed ten minutes to dawn. Moira glanced at the list in Grandmother's hand. So many demons hadn't checked in yet.

The door opened and six demons came in, imps and goblins all. The last two had tails wrapped around their arms so as not to get them trapped in the door.

"Is it too late for refreshments?" one of them asked.

"Only if you take what you get without complaining," Grandmother said. "You don't have time for special orders at this late hour."

"Thank you kindly," they all said, bobbing their heads.

Moira poured them all tea and spat into the ones she gave the imps.

A minute later, a pair of spiny things came in, and Grandmother told them they were too late and to start making their way to the gate.

At five minutes to dawn, the cottage was more crowded than Moira had ever seen it. It was also hotter than it had ever been before. Her dirty blond hair clung to her face.

"Alrighty then," Grandmother spoke up. "I do not ken what you all think you're waiting on, but best be getting home."

At that moment, the door bust open. A demon with blue skin, with its shoulders up around its ears and twin scorpion stingers twitching behind its back, rushed in. The creature's eyes were wide, and its mouth opened and closed as it tried to form words. Finally its mind seemed to catch up to what it wanted to say.

"He's coming." Those first two words came out barely above a hoarse whisper. Then the scorpion demon spoke louder. "Listen to me! He's almost here! The Lantern is coming!"

Silence crashed down on the cottage like a physical weight. It seemed as if, all at once, every demon in the cottage gave a slow, nervous swallow.

Then the stampede began.

Now, Moira had never seen a stampede, having never been to the American Colonies, but her penultimate grandfather brought her adventure books from all across the world. She loved reading about the American West, and if she were ever going to see anything that ever resembled a stampede, this mass retreat of demons would definitely qualify. Screaming, stamping, and crashing furniture filled the space previously occupied by the silence.

In a moment, silence descended again, this time with a noticeable absence of demons. Moira went to shut the back door before putting on a fresh pot of tea for her penultimate grandfather. Only, the cottage wasn't completely empty. One little imp remained, standing in the middle of the room and facing the front door of the cottage. The creature's head came up to Moira's waist. It had blood red skin, and its eyes glowed like embers in a dying fire. It wore the trousers, waistcoat, and frock coat of a gentleman. One of its horns curled up and back behind its floppy ear, but the other had been broken off only a few inches above the imp's forehead. The stump was rounded, indicating the injury had come some time ago.

"Better get yourself out," Grandmother said, making a shooing motion with her hand. "Things may get bad if you stay."

"Shut it, you old hag," the imp said. "I've got some words for Mr. Jack of the Lantern. It's been a long time coming. I'll speak my mind and be off on my merry way once I'm done."

"Fine," Grandmother replied. "Your funeral."

The imp spat. "No funeral for demons. Much as we could wish it otherwise on occasion, we can't die. But even if we did, where would we go?"

The three of them waited, the silence broken only by the chime of the clock each minute closer to sunrise: three minutes, two minutes, one minute.

The clock gave a massive *GONG* as dawn came. At that moment the door swung open. The imp began to shake, though Moira couldn't tell if it was in anger or terror – perhaps an equal combination of both. A form filled the doorway, not from size, but from the pure potency of his legend. Were they truly in the real world, the man would have only been short and stocky, looking so much like the blacksmith he'd been before he took up the lantern. But the cottage stood in one of the in-between-places where worlds touched and legends and myths took on their own realities, at the border between all places.

Jack of the Lantern stood in the doorway, framed by dawn's light as he always was on the dawn after the Darkest Night. His coat, once fine, now hung mostly ragged which only served to enhance his terrible visage. In his left hand, Jack held a lantern, carved from a turnip this year. The face of it had a sad frown, and Jack had carved what seemed tears under the eyes. The flames of three candles flickered behind that frown and the eyes and tears. This lantern, and all the others he had carved from turnips, gourds, and other plants, was his namesake; this was what the Devil and all of his kin feared; this was the gift Jack had given the world to protect humanity from the goblins, imps, ghouls, and other creatures of the dark realms that were free to roam the world on All Hallow's Eve.

Moira glanced at where the little red imp stood, expecting the thing to have fled once Jack appeared. To her surprise the imp stood his ground.

"I know you," Jack said. "It's been centuries, but I know you."

"And I know you also, blacksmith," the imp said. "How could I forget you? Come to the gates when I was a watching and send me off to tell His Darkness."

"You've grown rather cheeky," Jack replied. "I'm impressed. Most of your kind doesn't want to have anything to do with me."

"That's because you still scare them. You hold no terror for me. Do you have any idea the torments I suffered just for telling His Darkness that you were at the gates? Now it's your turn to learn what centuries of torment feels like, Mr. I-Can-Not-Die."

The imp reached underneath its frock coat and pulled out a strange device about the size of a breadbasket. Steam blew out of several vents here and there, and twin metal bars protruded from the top with tiny lightning bolts arching between them. The imp pulled on a lever and twisted a dial.

The roof above them groaned and creaked. As Jack rushed forward, something pulled the roof off the cottage. Shingles and boards rained down. One struck Jack's leg, and he stumbled. Something struck Moira's shoulder. She cried out and scrambled to the wall, hoping that it might give some protection.

Cackles of laughter rang out from above. Moira looked up. Peering down upon them from the top of the wall were all the demons that she had been serving. Above them, a huge metal form flung the cottage's roof away. The monstrosity looked like a giant metal statue of a demon, except it was moving. Just like with the breadbox device, steam blew from vents and lightning crackled here and there about the thing. Its hand came down, surprisingly fast for something so large, and slammed a cage down around Jack.

The moment he was trapped, the demons invaded the cottage. Even before the first dropped down next to her, Moira had her switch in hand and was lashing out around her. Of all the relics used for the ritual, the one she wore around her neck was the only one that could not be replaced. The others would be difficult, but it could be done. She had to escape with the locket.

A demon screamed as Moira slashed its face with the switch. She didn't try for the door. They'd be waiting for that, but she might have a chance at the window. Thankfully most of the demons seemed more inclined to destroy the cottage and find the other ritual objects than catch and torment Moira. She tried to ignore Grandmother's scream, but Moira's heart beat a bit faster when the cry died out.

The door blew inward. Moira was glad that she hadn't tried that. A smaller version of the metal demon overhead entered the cottage. Moira could see others behind it, marching toward them. How many were there? She wanted to scream, cry, and then maybe scream some more, but the years of her grandmother's teachings would not allow her any thought but escape, even if it looked as if escape were impossible.

"Moira," a voice cried from above. "I give this coat, these boots, and my chair to you freely as a child of my bloodline."

She glanced up. Jack had his arms stretched out of the cage. He held a bundle, and seeing her looking up, he dropped it. As the bundle fell, demons scattered well away from where it might land. Moira ducked, weaved, and switched her way toward the bundle.

Just as she reached it, a hand closed on her shoulder. She slapped the hand with the switch. When the hand released her Moira dropped the switch, grabbed the bundle, and spun around, unfurling Jack's ragged coat. She caught a demon in the face with it. Where the coat touched the demon, the material clung to the creature.

"No! Please no!" came a muffled cry from behind the cloth.

Moira twisted, wrapping the coat around her arm and shoulder. Then dropping, she pulled the demon off its feet. She smiled at the crunching sound it made on impact and grinned at the cry of pain that came after.

"You've my leave to let go of my coat," Moira said.

The coat pulled free of the demon's face, and Moira rolled away from the creature. As she did, she noticed a pair of boots lying where the coat had landed. She scurried over to them before any of the demons saw them and realized what they were. Only the fear of the coat had kept the boots unnoticed for so long.

When Moira reached the boots, she whipped the coat around her, sending demons scrambling away. Then she sat next to the boots, bringing the coat over her, huddling underneath it, leaving no part of herself exposed. She prayed as she removed her shoes and slid Jack's boots on. Her prayers that the demons feared the power of the coat nearly as much as they feared Jack seemed to be answered. She got the boots on, and they hugged her feet, fitting perfectly.

Moira stood, letting the coat hang about her form. Demons surrounded her in a tight circle. They snarled, hissed, and growled at her, but not a single one reached for her.

"Well now," Moira said. "It seems you all weren't as clever as you thought."

A massive grinding of metal groaned behind the cottage, followed by two booming crashes. The gate had come down. After centuries upon centuries of standing and holding back the hordes of darkness, the Devil's Gate was open for any and all of Hell's creatures to roam free, and with Jack of the Lantern trapped in the cage above, no amount of carved lanterns would protect humanity from them. Luckily, men and angels with far more cunning and sense than Moira possessed had foreseen this, and they'd made preparations. Granted, she never imagined that she would be the one who would have to deal with this particular situation.

The next moment, the world seemed a few shades darker, despite the rising sun. Her skin crawled as if something had just walked over her grave. All the demons turned toward the back of the cottage and prostrated themselves. Moira realized that it wasn't walking over her grave, the something was walking toward the moment when it would put her in her grave.

"Jack's chair," she said, and clicked her heels together.

The magic of the boots carried her over the horde, planting her next to a plain wooden chair.

"Stop her, you fools!" The voice boomed over the landscape and inside Moira's head.

The horde leapt up and surged for where she'd been standing a moment before. Lying face down on the floor, they'd not seen her move. That might give her the precious seconds she needed.

Next to her, a demon noticed her and slashed its claws at her face. Moira leaned back and whipped the edge of the coat at it. The fabric barely touched the thing, but it was enough. She gripped the coat hard and pulled harder. The demon, a four-armed thing with sickly green skin and a mouth full of fangs, stumbled forward and fell into the chair.

"You've my leave to let go of the coat," Moira said, and the coat came away from the demon's hand. However, the thing struggled against the chair and couldn't get up.

Moira gripped the back of the chair. She had no idea if her plan would work, if the magic of the boots would carry the chair and the demon or if the demon's weight would pull the chair from her grip. But it was worth trying.

"My jewelry box." She clicked her heels together.

Again, the boots carried Moira into the air. The chair and the demon came with her. As they flew over a crowd of demons tearing through Grandmother's hope chest, Moira leaned down to the struggling demon's ear, or at least where its ear would have been had the thing been human.

"You've my leave to get out of the chair," Moira said.

Freed from the chair's magic, the demon slid off the seat of the chair and crashed into its fellows, taking them to the floor in a tangled mess.

Moira landed next to the fireplace. As she snatched up her jewelry box off the mantle, the back door of the cottage creaked open. Odd that it had never made that ominous sound ever before, but then, the master of all demons had never opened it before. Moira tried to keep from looking, to shut her eyes and think of where to go next.

"Good morning, Miss O'Neil," said a voice of pure sweetness and honey.

She couldn't help it. It was rude not to look at someone when they addressed you in a proper way. For all the years she'd spent with Grandmother, propriety had been one of their defenses against the demons. Now, those good manners served to be her undoing. She looked at the newcomer.

He was handsome, with slick black hair, thin mustache, and a pointed beard. He wore a scarlet tailcoat over a midnight-black waistcoat. His eyes held a mischievous twinkle, and a knowing smirk played across his lips. His appearance was almost enough to make Moira fall in love with him – he looked so perfectly the dashing and handsome male. But as it always was in the stories Jack of the Lantern had told her, where this man's feet should have been were a pair of cloven hooves. Moira kept sight of those hooves as she willed herself to speak.

"The nearest holy ground," Moira said through clenched teeth, and clicked her heels together.

As she flew away from the cottage, the demons, the massive metal thing that held Jack of the Lantern trapped, and the Dark One himself fell away. In the fields beyond the cottage, Moira saw dozens of the smaller metal things, all of them marching on the remains of the cottage as if they were knights assaulting a castle. She didn't know what to make of them, only that the Devil and his kin were free to roam the earth at will, and not one single person would be safe behind a lantern.

* * *

A short time later, Moira landed in front of the church. She burst in and placed the chair just to the left of the door. She closed the door with her foot and turned to head to the secret room in the back, almost tumbling into father McDermott as she did. The stern but kindly old priest grabbed her by the shoulders.

"What's going on?" he asked. In his panic, his brogue slipped in past his normally well-polished accent.

"The Devil's Gate came down," Moira said. "And the Dark One has Jack of the Lantern trapped by some metal creature."

She tried to wriggle out of Father McDermott's grip but couldn't. She saw him trying to let go of her, and then she remembered what she was wearing.

"You've leave to let go of my coat."

176

As she said those words, Father McDermott's hands came away. His face went as slack as his arms as he realized what this meant.

Without speaking further, they rushed to the secret room at the back of the church. The back wall of that room held shelf upon shelf of candles. Normally, these candles always burned bright and never ran out of wax. A name and a location were engraved on each candlestick. These flames represented the descendants of Jack of the Lantern.

One by one, the candles went out. As Moira and Father McDermott watched, the room went from being as bright as noon on a cloudless day to nearly black as midnight. Only three Candles remained: Moira O'Brien: St Matthew's Parish, Daniel McRory: the smithy, and John O'Brian: Boston.

"Lord in Heaven, preserve us," Father McDermott said in a hushed whisper.

"Better yet," Moira said, "preserve John and Daniel. If the demons find either one of them, we're all doomed."

"Well then, we have no time to waste," the Father said. "Did you bring your last coin?"

Two

John O'Brien huddled in the doorway of a bakery, holding a penny in one hand and the last gold coin of his family's fortune in the other. Snow had come early to Boston, and warmth from the ovens seeped through the door. The owner didn't mind folks standing there when the bakery wasn't open, but woe to anyone who tried to stand there during business hours. Her brother was a constable and made sure on a regular basis his sister's business was not suffering due to any sort of lowlife.

John heard a bit of shuffling behind him. He slid the gold coin into his fingerless glove and shoved that into the pocket of his coat. The coat wasn't as fine as it had been, but still the garment served its purpose and was not so worn that people refused him service when he managed to earn a bit of money by doing odd jobs no one else wanted. John was strong, able, and not anywhere near a fool. He should have been able to find work. However, no matter how hard he tried, he couldn't quite get the last of his Irish accent out of his mouth. The instant most *proper* folk heard it, they turned him away.

" 'Elp a poor soul on this cold night?" a voice asked.

John glanced back, mostly at the strangeness of hearing the Cockney accent in Boston.

The beggar was dressed more in rags and tatters than he was in clothes. Didn't have proper shoes, but rather strips of dirty wool wrapped around his feet. Grime and muck clung to his face to the point John wondered if any amount of scrubbing would ever get the face truly clean again.

"Spare somefink for a poor soul to get somefink warm in 'is belly?" the beggar asked.

John suppressed a sigh. Things shouldn't be this bad already. It wasn't even Halloween yet, and it was snowing as if it were close to Christmas. It had been this way every year since the British Empire had closed itself off from the world three years ago.

"Sir," John said, "come stand here, it's warm."

"Oh, fank yous," the beggar said, as he took John's place. "Right kind of yous. God and his angels bless you, young man."

"Just come and get warm," John said.

John wondered how the beggar was alive. He seemed more corpse than man, skin hanging loose on his face and fingers.

John actually sighed this time. He took his penny and placed it in the beggar's hand. The beggar's mouth opened, showing a multitude of missing teeth.

"Take this," John said. "No. Don't say a word." John raised his hand to cut the beggar off. "When the bakery opens, get yourself something warm to put in your belly."

With that, John walked away, leaving the beggar calling thanks behind him. John hoped he'd be able to find work of some kind soon. He hadn't eaten anything but broth and bread at the church in over a week.

As he walked, John tried to think of other warm places. Well, there was always St. Anthony's church, but John didn't want to rely on the church too much. The priests and sisters would never turn John away, he just had his pride. Too many people were asking for handouts, and John preferred to earn his own way in the world.

Halfway down the next block, John decided to try his luck by the docks. Sometimes sailors from several ships would make a fire in the cobbled roads near the docks and trade stories, songs, and drinks. John knew a few stories. His father had been fond of old tales of Ireland and of the early Americas, especially the myths and legends of the native people. Maybe he could get some room by a fire in exchange for a story or two. The season might be especially good for the tale his father used to tell him about Jack of the Lantern. He smiled as he suddenly noticed the few jack o' lanterns he saw here and there, candles flickering behind their carved faces.

Somewhere between two and four blocks later, the back of John's neck tingled. At four-and-a-half blocks, John knew for certain he was being followed. He quickened his pace and fingered the club he kept in a hidden pocket sewn into the inside of his coat. He didn't break into a run or even a jog, but he might as well have. He glanced back. Just as he thought, his pursuers had been surprised by John's increase in speed. They'd become careless in their haste to keep up.

This was where he decided if it was a matter of fight or flight.

He spotted the four of them without any trouble. Four was two too many. Two, he could fight long enough to discourage. Three was pushing it. Four wasn't even worth trying. He'd just wind up making them angry, and the beating would be even worse.

"Now, now, Johnny O'Brien," said a familiar voice. "We saw you give the beggar something. If you did that, then you've got something to spare for us, too."

Thomas was a big lad who led a gang of four other slightly-less-big lads. They'd been giving John trouble for years, even when they had been schoolboys together. And while Thomas was correct – John still did have the last gold coin of his family's treasure – Thomas and his fellows couldn't comprehend that John had no intention of ever spending it. Nor could they comprehend that a person might give their last coin over to a stranger with less fortune for no other reason than it was the decent thing to do.

Since John had only seen four of them, it meant that Paddy had either been left behind or that the other four were driving John toward the meanest, and least bright, of all of them. John turned on his toe and ran to the other side of the street. He might not be as big or strong as the members of Thomas's little mob of miscreants, but John was no weakling. Most of the work he could find as an Irishman involved heavy labor, the kind few others wanted. He also had practice outrunning gangs like this.

"Don't make it harder on yourself than you need to, Johnny Boy," Thomas called after him. "Just give it over, and we'll be off on our merry one way and you can go t'other."

John reached the other side of the street and scrambled up a fence between two buildings. He stopped at the top and looked back. Sure enough, Paddy was running from the direction John had just been heading.

"Sod off!" John called back.

Thomas and the others were not known for being clever or quick witted. They were even less so when angry. John had used taunts and teasing to great effect in escaping these five ruffians many times before. They hadn't ever seemed to catch on to it, and John would keep exploiting this weakness until they did.

Thomas called back something unflattering about John's mother as John dropped down the other side of the fence. John didn't much care. He'd never allowed people's words to affect him.

John found himself in an alley that had been converted to a storage area. Stacks of boxes lined both sides of the alley. John pursed his lips and he squinted with his right eye. In the space of a single breath, a plan formed. He had enough of a lead. Between the darkness in the alley and his pursuers' lack of imagination, the plan should work.

He ran to the other end of the alley, pushed some snow off the fence there, and then backtracked, making sure to walk backward through his own footprints. When he got back to where he'd climbed over, John squeezed in between two stacks of boxes. He clenched his teeth together to keep them from chattering.

The moment after John squeezed all the way back, he heard crunches in the snow where someone landed. Two more followed.

"He's gone to the other end," Thomas said.

A fourth person landed this side of the fence. Footsteps crunched toward the far end of the alley. A fifth person dropped down.

"Hurry up, you daft fool," one of them called from the other end of the alley.

The fifth person over the fence, likely Paddy, grunted something and started after his friends.

John remained huddled, shivering, keeping his teeth from shattering. He had to be sure they had actually fallen for his trick.

He counted to fifty before he crawled back out.

"There he is," one of them said from the far end. "Told you asking that man was smart."

John was up and over the fence even before he could waste time being scared or worrying about his plan failing. He landed and would have been off at a dead run, except someone was standing in his way.

John blinked several times to make sure he was actually seeing what he thought he was seeing. It wasn't a person at all.

The thing in front of him could only be a demon, like the ones from the stories his father had told him before he'd died. Despite its fine clothes, the thing was sorely out of place with its red skin and single horn that curled back behind its ear. It held a device that vented steam and arched lighting between two metal rods.

"It's a pleasure to make your acquaintance, John O'Brien," the thing said in a whiny and grating voice. "It took us quite a while to find you. We're still learning our way around this new continent."

The imp – it had to be an imp, in the stories imps were the little red ones – did some things to the device, and the lightning arched faster between the two rods. Behind him, on the other side of the fence, John heard the *psshh* of escaping air and what sounded like gears grinding.

"Ummm," John said, still trying to wrap his mind around the idea that the stories might be true.

The crack and snap of wood joined the other sounds. Then came a deluge of prayers: "Saints in heaven preserve us," "Mary, mother of god," and, "Though I walk through the valley of darkness."

"It seems your friends are getting acquainted with my Steam Soldiers." The imp winked at John. "Nothing personal, Jack my boy. You just happened to be born into the wrong family."

Thoughts raced through John's mind. The top two were that he hated being called Jack and that the imp's strange device couldn't be good. As the imp kept flicking switches and turning dials, the noises behind John got louder and more frequent. That could not be good.

"You got my name right the first time," John said, and pulled his club out of its secret pocket. The oak club was sixteen inches long and an inch and a half thick. John held it firmly with his thumb and first two fingers.

The imp flicked more switches and dials, and John heard several terrified and pained screams behind him along with a giant crash of shattering wood. He didn't look, but did suspect, that noise was the fence coming down.

John rushed forward and snapped the club at the device three times. One of the dials came off at the first snap. With the second, one of the e-lectrodes bent at an awkward angle and sparks buzzed away from the thing, fading into the night. The third strike never landed. By that time, the imp had caught on and spun out of the way.

In its haste to protect the device, the imp turned its back on John. John couldn't help but grin. He shifted his grip on the club, gripping it firmly with all five fingers. He pulled the club back behind his shoulder, and falling to one knee as he struck, John put all his body behind the blow to the imp's knee.

Now, John didn't know if the length of wood would actually hurt a demon, but he had to try. Just like with Thomas's ruffians, the demon and whatever was coming up behind him wasn't going to get John without as much effort as John could force them to make.

The club met the imp's knee with the expected resistance and the same crunch of bones and *pop* of cartilage that John was used to. John didn't like fighting. Fighting was the last resort, because in most situations he got a little banged up at the very least. Unless, that is, he caught his opponent completely off guard like this and got away before they could get up.

The imp writhed on the ground holding his leg and whimpering in pain. John spared a glance over his shoulder. Massive metallic men that looked like someone had turned a dozen locomotives into suits of armor stood over Thomas and his ruffians. The gang lay in much the same state as the imp, on the ground, groaning in pain. The armored things that stood over them had electrodes protruding from their joints, and those e-lectrodes buzzed and popped the same way the imp's device had after John had hit it.

John supposed those would be the Steam Soldiers.

Without a second thought, John took two steps and grabbed the device. The imp still had enough wherewithal to keep a tight grip.

"No," the imp said.

"Ah," John replied. "Yes."

John pulled harder, but the imp would not let go.

"Fine." John nearly snarled the word in his frustration.

John shifted the grip on his club to two fingers again. He snapped the club twice: first to the imp's nose and then to the wrist below the hand holding the controller. The imp's fingers opened. John snatched the box and considered for a moment what to do with it.

He almost took the thing with him. Then he thought better of it. It wasn't too heavy, but it would get heavier and heavier as he ran. Also, he might be able to hide, and then these things might go away. If he took the device that controlled the armored things, whoever owned these Steam Soldiers would definitely come after him and they wouldn't stop until they got it back.

"This seems to be pretty important," John said, waving the steaming and buzzing controller above the whimpering imp. "Have fun getting it."

With that, John lobbed it up onto the roof of a building on the other side of the street, turned, and started running. He got maybe ten steps before he heard cackling laughter above and behind him.

John skidded to a stop in the snow. There was another one on the roof. Probably lots of other ones. That would figure. It was that kind of night.

He looked back over his shoulder. Sure enough, he saw an odd-shaped shadow holding a thing that flashed and popped. Moments later, other odd-shaped shadows appeared on that rooftop and the other rooftops overlooking the street.

The Steam Soldiers started moving again, coming toward John. One pointed an arm at John. The wrist erupted in steam and fire, and the thing's hand flew at John. It missed him by less than a foot. Instead of his head, arm, or shoulder, the metal hand closed around a pole supporting the porch of a haberdasher shop. Wood groaned and splintered under the grip.

Then John noticed the chain strung between the metal arm and the metal hand.

He didn't wait to see the pole come flying away from the building.

He ran headlong into the night. He heard steam venting, electricity popping, and heavy footsteps stomping behind him. Oh, and crashing wood and shattering glass.

As he zigzagged down the street, two thoughts occupied John's mind. First, where could he hide? Second, what terrible thing had he done to warrant this? Thomas and his gang was one thing, but demons and armored soldiers controlled by some steam and electric box? This would be laughable were he not living it. So instead of laughing, he ran.

After two blocks, he grabbed a street lamp and used that to spin to the right without losing any of his speed. Normally, a series of quick turns would be the surest way to confuse, confound, and otherwise conceal himself from pursuit. However, that was all contingent upon his pursuers actually being human. John was halfway down the block and very certain he could get to the other end and out of sight, when two of those Steam Soldiers came crashing through a storefront not ten paces back.

With nothing readily available to help him alter his course, John slid a bit in the snow and then dashed toward the alley on the opposite side of the street. He really didn't want to go into some place that confined, but better that than possibly having one of those things burst out of a building right next to him.

And so the chase went on for longer than John could recall. He wove through alleys and side streets so much that he lost track of where he was. His lungs burned, his legs ached, and it felt like someone had stabbed him repeatedly in his left side. Behind him, demons cackled, Steam Soldiers hissed, buzzed, and clanked, and buildings broke under the weight of their pursuit. Running was no longer an option, but at least he wasn't cold anymore.

Soon John was reduced to a loping jog. Even though he was used to long hours of strenuous work, he couldn't keep up that level of headlong flight indefinitely. Head down, body aching, his mind raced for some way to escape.

He came around a corner and found himself staring at the bakery. The beggar still sat huddled in the doorway, soaking up what heat he could.

"This is wrong," John said to himself in short gasps.

John was sure he'd been moving steadily away from here. Yet, here he was. It didn't make sense. But then, so little about this night did. He was about to turn and flee again when two of the metal monstrosities crashed through the bakery. The building groaned and collapsed, part of it on the beggar. John could hear the beggar's cries of pain, although muffled from the boards.

Then a loud *whoomph* came from inside the rubble that was once a bakery, and a giant flame erupted from the center of the wood. The blaze spread quickly.

That gave John an idea.

Most people wouldn't do anything to help someone getting beaten or murdered in the street. They would turn a blind eye and deaf ear to all the crashing and breaking wood. Oh, they might look out their window, but they'd never actually do anything to stop it, even if they didn't believe that it was real and not some strange dream. However, there was one thing almost no one would ignore.

"Fire!" John yelled with all the strength he could muster.

His voice wasn't very loud because he was panting and puffing from running, but it was loud enough that the demons stopped cackling and the Steam Soldiers stopped moving. That gave John just enough incentive to fill his lungs and yell again.

"Fire!"

This time, people opened windows and stuck their heads out into the cold night air. Other people took up the cry.

It wasn't until after people started shouting and rushing into the street that John considered that if these things wanted him so much, they might be willing to hurt any bystanders like they had Thomas's gang. As more and more people took up the cry of "fire," the demons and their metal soldiers fled into the night.

John only allowed himself a small sigh of relief before he was moving again, this time across the street. When he reached the remains of the bakery, the beggar had gone from crying out in pain to moaning. The fire had reached him and caught on the beggar's ragged coat.

People rushed about, and in the distance John heard the *clang, clang, clang* of the fire brigade bell. Fire was the one threat nobody would ignore.

John began clearing debris off the beggar, and within moments other people were helping him. When they'd gotten the beggar free, his right arm was engulfed in flames up to his shoulder. Before anyone could offer suggestions or advice, John rolled the beggar off the porch and into a snow bank. The flames sputtered out with a sharp *hiss*.

"I'm going to get him to a doctor," John said. He knew where one was only a few blocks away.

Before anyone else could protest, John lifted the beggar up and hurried away. He had, in a moment, weighed the risk of staying with the crowd and having them ask questions against moving on and encountering the demons again. At this point there were dozens – perhaps more than a hundred – people up and about to help deal with the fire. As the cry went out, more and more would be up. It was a fairly good gamble that John was safe for at least the rest of this night. Besides, the beggar had been hurt because of him. Others probably had too, but John could help this man right now.

Soon, John was pounding on the door of the doctor's office. A minute or so later, he heard locks rattle and the door open about two inches. A single eye glared at John from behind a spectacle.

"Sir," John said, "this man is hurt."

The eye looked at the beggar and back at John. The door opened. John entered and placed the beggar on the long table that filled the center of the room.

The doctor was short and frail, with only a few wisps of hair on the top of his head. While the doctor wore a night shirt, John noticed that he also had on trousers and shoes. Perhaps he'd heard the call for fire and was getting ready to go out and see if anyone required his services.

"Can you pay?" the doctor asked.

"Pay?" John replied. "This man may be dying and you're asking about money?"

"This is a business, son," the doctor said, "not a charity. If you have no means to compensate me for my work, I suggest you take him to Saint Mary's Church. The sisters there care for the sick and injured among the homeless."

"St. Mary's is halfway to the other side of Boston," John said, his voice rising. "He probably wouldn't survive me carrying him all that way."

The doctor shrugged. John looked from the beggar to the doctor, and back to the beggar. Tonight was quickly being burned into John's mind as the very worst night of his life since his parents died Halloween night almost three years ago. He couldn't even make it into a great story to trade for food or shelter because nobody would believe it.

"Fine," John said. "This should cover it."

He slipped the last gold coin of his family's treasure out of his glove and held it out to the doctor. The doctor eyed the coin, nodded, and held out his hand. John placed the coin gently on the doctor's palm, and after a moment, let go.

The instant John's fingers left the coin, a light brighter than any lamp, lantern, or candle filled the room. The beggar rolled off the table and stood straight and tall, no longer hunched over as he had been. The grime and muck that clung to his face seemed to be burned away by the light. The coat that was more rags than garment fluttered in a wind John did not feel and transformed into a pristine white robe. Two pearl-white wings sprouted from the beggar's shoulder blades.

While the beggar underwent this transformation, the doctor had pulled off the night shirt to reveal a priest's collar.

"John O'Brien," the doctor-turned-priest said, "meet Saint Peter."

John blinked. "Even with the night I've had, that was unexpected."

Three

John O'Brien stood looking back and forth at the priest and the man introduced as Saint Peter. Make that: the man with wings and who was e-mitting a continuous white light who had been introduced as Saint Peter. John closed his eyes, but even then the light shone through his eyelids, like looking into the sun with one's eyes closed.

"That's just grand," said a decidedly feminine voice from slightly be-hind John. Her Irish accent was as thick and heavy as anyone who had just stepped off the boat from the old country. "Very nicely done gents, easing him into things like that."

John spun around, bringing his club into his hand.

"Put it away, O'Brien," said a young woman. "What is it with the men in this family and their sticks?"

The young lady carried a plain wooden chair that looked as if it were made right from the branches of a tree without much in the way of sand-ing or polishing. It also looked as old, frail, and weathered as Saint Peter had when he'd been a beggar. Behind her, the door to the back of the doctor's office swung closed.

The girl herself looked to be of an age with John, from seventeen to nineteen years old – John himself was eighteen. She had blondish hair with more than a hint of brown within it, and her eyes were the brightest green. She wore a coat that was only slightly more together than the rags Saint Peter had worn as a beggar. The style of the coat was completely un-known to John. Long and pleated, with flaring at the waist and what had once been a long row of buttons, of which only three remained.

Remembering his manners, John tipped his hat to her. "Miss."

"Mr. Obrien," she said with a comforting smile. "I'm your cousin, Moira. Moira O'Neil. This is going to be a lot to take in. Please, have a seat."

She placed the chair down just behind him.

At the mention of sitting, the exhaustion of his flight from the de-mons came crashing back. John sat with a relieved sigh.

"Thank you," John said. "I don't recall my parents ever mentioning any relations among the O'Neils."

"That's because they didn't know about us," Moira said. "We're rather far removed, but we could each trace our line back through the centuries to the same penultimate grandfather."

"Alright," John said. "A pleasure to meet you, cousin Moira O'Neil, and Your…um…Holiness?"

"Peter is fine." The saint's voice was soft, yet seemed to fill the room.

"And this," Moira said, indicating the priest, "is Father McDermott."

The priest came forward and shook John's hand.

"It is a great pleasure, young man," the Father said.

"Glad to meet you all," John said, then before any of them could say anything else, John regarded Saint Peter. "Are you aware that there are a bunch of demons running around Boston? Oh, and they have a bunch of big metal men they call Steam Soldiers that shoot their hands at things and crash through buildings. Oh, and do you have any idea why they are after me, personally, by name?"

"It is exactly because of this that we have sought you out," Saint Peter said. "We've been seeking you for quite some time. The forces of darkness actually did us a favor by leading us to you."

"Oh, well," John said, "the next time I see them, I'll be sure to thank them. And why are you all looking for me in the first place?"

"You are one of the last three descendants of Jack of the Lantern," Father McDermott said.

On any other night, John probably would have laughed, laughed hard. Tonight he took them all in, one at a time. Saint Peter stood looking, well, serene and saintly. Father McDermott gave the impression of the kindly uncle or grandfather. Moira gave him a slight smile that seemed to say, "I know exactly how you feel." John opened his mouth to say something, decided that he didn't really have anything to say that might be appropriate in front of a priest, let alone a saint, so he closed his mouth again, sighed, and shrugged.

After a moment of silence, John decided he did have something to say. "Of course I am. And my mother was the Tooth Fairy. We would have the Easter Bunny and Santa Claus over for tea every third Sunday of the month, oh, and we'd sit at the Round Table, as the family was charged with keeping it safe for Arthur's eventual return. We even kept Excalibur in my father's study for the occasion."

Father McDermott took a step forward and wagged his finger at John. "Look here, young man, I know this has been a trying night for you, but that is no way to speak to—"

"Oh, shut it Father," Moira said, stepping between the priest and John. "If the young man is going to lip off to a saint of heaven, he's not bloody likely to fall into line by having you wiggle your finger at him. Wouldn't you agree, Peter?"

"Quite right," Saint Peter replied.

The Saint did not look in the least bit perturbed at John's outburst. Which, after John considered it for a moment, made a certain sort sense.

"It's the truth John," Moira said. "I know it must sound crazy, even with everything that's happened. I had the benefit of growing up knowing, but I can prove it's all real."

"That should be interesting," John said. "Go ahead."

"I'm sure your parents told you stories," Moira said. "There were many stories of Jack of the Lantern. But I'll wager that your parents told you which three things Jack wished for from Saint Peter. Go ahead and name them, in order, in the manner of the story."

John looked from Moira to Saint Peter. Saint Peter smiled and nodded. "If you know the story, this should be easy enough."

John knew the story. This was the season when he traded the story for food and possibly shelter.

"This here, my chair," John recited, and Moira spoke the words exactly with him, with the exact same inflections, "anyone that sit in it cannot get up from it until I give them leave to do so."

He paused and looked back and forth between his cousin, the Father, and the saint. Peter extended his right hand in an invitation to continue. John did so, his cousin keeping pace with him again.

"This here, my coat, anyone that take hold of it cannot let go of it until I give them leave to do so. And this here, my smithing hammer, anyone that take hold of it cannot stop smithing with it until I give them but leave to do so." When he finished, John paused, looked at Moira, and said, "So, we know the same story. What does that prove?"

John did not like Moira's self-satisfied smirk, not one bit.

"Try to get up," Moira said.

And that's the moment John O'Brien believed, just as he believed that he wasn't going to be able to get up. He sat in the ancient looking chair glaring at his cousin.

"Should I even bother without being given leave?" he asked.

"Big, strong young man such as yourself shouldn't need anyone's permission to get his feet underneath him and stand up."

John clicked his tongue and sighed. "Going to force this are we?"

Moira shrugged.

John tried to stand. As hard as he pushed against the floor, he could not rise. He didn't struggle against the force holding him in the chair very long. For one, he was too tired. For two, he didn't see the point in a struggle that would avail him nothing. For three, he didn't want to give his new-found cousin any further reason to gloat at him. Then John realized something, and his heart began to speed up.

"If the story of Jack of the Lantern is true, then I'll bet the story of the ritual to keep the Devil's Gate closed is true, too. But it's not Halloween yet, and there are demons running around. Something happened, something bad, both to Jack and the ladies that keep the gate closed."

At that, the smirk slid from Moira's face as her lips pressed together. Her eyes welled with tears.

"Only to one of them," Moira said. "The younger one made it out."

"I'm sorry," Jack said, and he was. He missed his mother and father terribly. If Moira was the granddaughter in this generation of the two women who kept the Devil's Gate closed, then the only people she really knew were her grandmother and Jack of the Lantern. "But something must have happened to Jack, or he would have chased the demons back into Hell with his lantern. Isn't that what he does with the stragglers on Halloween?" John knew he was repeating himself, but that was normal – repetition was part of his process of sorting through things. Moira looked like she was going to say something, but John held up his hand and wagged it at her. "What happened to him? Something happened, and that's bad, but it's important to something right now." Realization dawned on John. "He's not here to let me out of the chair."

And despite his logical understanding of the situation and that he couldn't get out of the chair without Jack of the Lantern to give leave to do so, John squirmed and struggled to get out. He thrashed back and forth for a few moments.

"You've leave to get out of my chair," Moira said.

As soon as she spoke those words, the force holding John to the seat of the chair vanished. His struggles carried him off the chair and onto the floor in a huff. Moira offered her hand. Using her as a counterbalance, with a groan, John stood.

He wanted to be angry at Moira, but he understood why she did it. He'd have never really believed her otherwise and would have left if he'd had the means.

"Alright," John said. "So we've determined that all the stories my parents told me are actually our secret family history. What's that got to do with the here and now, demons coming after me, and you three showing up looking for me? What's so special about me?"

"Just by being of the line of Jack of the Lantern gives the demons cause to fear you," Saint Peter said. "As a descendant of Jack's blood, he can grant you the ability to use the objects he wished of me all those centuries ago, as he has given the coat and chair to Moira. They will also fear that you may have inherited Jack's cleverness and cunning. By all observations, you may have all that he ever had, and more."

"And you want me to help," John said. "Really, there has to be someone better, smarter, stronger, or braver, perhaps all of them. I'm really mostly a coward."

"You think too little of yourself," Saint Peter said, "but also too much."

"Your family history lends weight to what must be done," Father McDermott said. "It will be so much harder for someone not of Jack's line to do what must be done."

"And what's that?" John asked.

"Nothing too difficult," Moira said. "Just scare the Devil and all his kin back into Hell long enough for me to complete the ritual that will repair and close the Devil's Gate."

"Oh, is that all?" John said. "I think I can do that."

Four

Moira eyed her cousin. He looked so much like Jack of the Lantern: plain face, green eyes, and hair that could be blond, auburn, or brown depending on the light. Even bundled in his coat and scarf against the cold, she could tell he was used to physical work. His right eye also squinted the same way Jack of the Lantern's did when he was trying to remember something or was about to play some clever trick on Grandmother.

Moira turned her head away and wiped a tear. Even after nearly three years since the Devil's Gate came down, she still missed her grandmother, and after the sacrifice Grandmother's life had been, she deserved a better end than she'd received at the hands of the demons.

"You alright?" John asked.

"Right as rain," Moira replied. When she faced John again, he wasn't squinting. He was looking at her, his head tilted to the side, his mouth formed into a worried frown. "Really, I'm fine."

"You're suddenly being very reasonable about this, John," Father McDermott said. "I have to admit, I expected a bit of protest."

John looked from Moira to the priest.

"I considered it," John said. "But what would be the point? It's not like I'm going to tell Saint Peter, *no*."

"Well, you could," Saint Peter said. "I'm not here to force you into anything, John. It's just that you and your cousins are the natural choices for this task. There's power in the fear that dark creatures around the world have for your penultimate grandfather."

"They didn't seem to fear me," John said. "Quite the opposite."

"If they didn't fear you," Saint Peter replied, "they would have left you well enough alone. They would have left your entire family well enough alone, instead of killing all but three of you on All Hallow's Eve three years ago."

"Wait right there. Halloween? Three years ago?"

"Yes," Saint Peter said.

"That's the night my parents died. Everyone thought they were murdered by a thief."

"No, John," Moira said. "They were killed by the demons, just like my grandmother."

Both of John's eyes grew very narrow, and he looked off to his left, seemingly at nothing at all.

"Oh yes, I think I can do that." John's tone held none of the flip-ancy it had the first time he'd said it. "Where do we start?"

"Well," Saint Peter said. "Before anything else, we must attend to the business of your wishes."

"Wishes?" John asked.

"Don't you pay attention to the old stories at all on this side of the Atlantic?" Father McDermott asked. "Of course you get wishes. You gave the last coin of your family's treasure to save a man you did not know from Adam for no other reason than it was the good and decent thing to do."

"Other people do nice things all the time," John said. "They don't get wishes."

"But they don't commit selfless acts of sacrifice for saints in disguise," Moira said. "It's kind of one of the Old Laws. I don't understand it, and I'm not sure the saints and angels and all of them understand it, but that's the way it is. Just like the Dark One and his demons cannot break a bargain fairly made."

"Really?" John said, and his right eye squinted again. "Three wishes you say?"

"Yes," Saint Peter replied. "Three, and only three. I've been on this continent enough to know how you Americans try to think around corners and be terribly clever. I'll not grant you any more wishes."

"Oh, that's fine," John said. "I've already got my wishes in mind, but let me think about them for a bit."

"Take your time," Saint Peter said. "They are three very important decisions."

With that, John began to wander about the room, seemingly at random. He muttered under his breath as he wove this way and that. Moira tried to make out some of the words, but couldn't. She watched him. The more he walked, the faster his muttering became, and his right eye eventually closed completely which seemed to scrunch John's face up with the strain of keeping it closed as tight as possible.

All of a sudden, in mid-mumble and mid-step, John stopped. His right eye opened, and he looked at Saint Peter.

"Any specific things I'm going to have to do in this process? Or am I on my own?"

"You will not be alone," Saint Peter replied. "There will be three of you. Moira, and your cousin Daniel."

"Why three of us?" John asked. "The demons are sure to try and stop us. Why should all of us take the risk?"

"Because power exists in numbers," Father McDermott explained. "Three is a very powerful number when placed in opposition against the forces of Darkness."

John nodded. "Oh, yes. I can see the sense in that." He turned away from them. "Alright, I have to start thinking in the way of the old stories." He paced a little more then stopped again. "Anything else I should know?"

"That's all that I can think of," Saint Peter said. "Either of you?"

"I don't think so," Father McDermott said. "We've pretty much covered it."

"There is something else," Moira said.

John looked at her, and sighed. "What is it?"

Moira felt for John and how overwhelmed he must have been at that moment. She felt the same. Well, perhaps not quite as much, as she knew more about what was going on. Then again, she knew how difficult the other thing they needed to do was going to be.

"Once we scare the Devil and his kin back into Hell, we've got to be able to keep the Devil's Gate closed. I know the ritual, but I only have one of the artifacts. We'll need to get replacements for the others."

"And let me guess, each one is an extremely rare object and is going to be almost as difficult to get as chasing the Devil back into Hell."

Moira nodded.

"Of course it is."

John took a deep breath, let it out, and with shoulders slumped forward he continued pacing. Again, as he traversed the room, seemingly at random, John's right eye squinted and his mouth scrunched up.

He seemed to pace around the room for at least an hour, though Moira had no means by which to tell how much time had actually passed. Her legs grew tired, and she hopped up onto the doctor's table in the center of the room. She could have sat in the chair that Jack had given her, all she had to do was give herself leave to stand up, but she couldn't bring herself to do it. That chair had been the center of far too much trickery and deceit over the centuries.

Father McDermott came to lean on the table next to her. He opened his mouth to speak, but even before he could form that first sound into a syllable, John sent a silencing *hsst* from across the room. He did have the decency to blush just a little when the priest glared at him, and John even murmured an apologetic, "Sorry Father, but I'm thinking hard. Doesn't come naturally to me," and then went back to pacing.

Finally, John stopped. He looked at Saint Peter. "I'm ready to make my wishes. But I need to make them in private."

"Why private?" Moira asked.

"Because at least one of them is a surprise," John said. "And I hate to ruin surprises."

"The wishes are John's, and he is entitled to make them alone," Saint Peter said. "If you will join me in the next room."

"Absolutely!" John went to the door and held it open for Saint Peter.

"We'll be back in a few moments," Saint Peter said, and went into the other room.

John nodded at Father McDermott. Then he looked at Moira. John's mouth curled into a self-satisfied smirk, and he gave her a conspiratorial wink.

"We'll be out when we're done," John said, "but it might take more than a few minutes."

With that, John followed Saint Peter, shutting the door behind them.

Moira and Father McDermott looked at each other.

"He's a cheeky one," Father McDermott said.

"Yes he is," Moira said with a hint of smile.

John O'Brien was definitely amusing, in a defiant sort of way, but she hadn't decided whether she liked him or not. She wanted to think it might be because he was American, but she hadn't known much of anyone outside of the cottage she'd grown up in. Even in the last three years, she'd only been with Father McDermott, and of course Saint Peter after she'd given her last coin to a beggar, a beggar that just happened to be a saint in disguise. They'd been so busy searching for John that Moira hadn't had many opportunities to get to know how people acted on a day-to-day basis. However, she did know that John seemed a bit more flippant than she suspected most people were.

"What now?" Moira asked.

"We wait until John makes his wishes," Father McDermott said, and leaned back against the wall.

Moira sat on the table, swinging her legs back and forth. She didn't have a watch, so to count the passing time, she began to count the number of swings her legs made. She expected Saint Peter and John to come out somewhere between one hundred and one hundred fifty.

At two hundred seventy-seven she heard Saint Peter's raised voice cry out, "That's not how it's done!"

Her legs froze underneath the table. She glanced at Father McDermott. The Father stood ramrod straight and glared at the door. From the beet-red color that washed over his face, she didn't need to guess what the priest thought of John, at least not right then. After a few moments they heard no other outbursts, and so Moira went back to swinging her legs.

At three hundred twenty-six, the door from the back room opened. Light from Saint Peter's glow spilled into the room. Had it been natural light, Moira probably would have been blinking, momentarily blinded. John came out, heading straight for the front door. His smirk was gone, but his eyes sparkled with mischievous delight.

"Are we ready, then?" Father McDermott asked.

"Oh, not by half," John replied as he walked across the room to the front door. "Sit tight. I've a quick errand to run. Return in a moment." He headed out into the snow and cold.

Moira craned her neck to look back in the room where John and Saint Peter had been speaking. Saint Peter stood in the doorway looking where John had just left. The saint's wings had wrapped around his shoulders, as if comforting him. Other than that, Saint Peter just blinked after John.

"It doesn't sound like it's going at all well," Father McDermott said.

"I wouldn't say that," Saint Peter replied. "He's much more than we expected, so much more. I believe he will either live up to Jack of the Lantern's legacy, or he will doom the world to live in darkness for a century or two."

"That's not very encouraging," Father McDermott said.

"It's not?" Saint Peter asked.

"How could that be encouraging in any way?"

"Moment to moment, the young man is as clever and cunning as Jack was on the best days of his life," Saint Peter explained. "He is bold, daring, refuses to be cowed by the fact he is hunted by demons, and has bargained the details of three wishes with a saint, all in the same night. Nothing great in this world has ever been achieved without some risk. He has a scheme. He's shared some of the details with me, though I don't think I know even half of it. Even with the parts I do know, I told him that the chances of it succeeding were infinitesimal. Would you like to know what he said in response?"

Moira and Father McDermott both nodded.

"He said, 'My country wouldn't exist if men paid attention to that way of thinking,' and went back to browbeating me about exactly what he should and should not be granted from each individual wish. Normally, the moment anyone begins attempting to haggle the finer points of saintly providence, it would invalidate the whole business, but everything John is arguing for, as mad as his plan is, is so that it has a chance of success. As brash and irreverent as he is, he's a fine young man. It will indeed be interesting to see if things play out in his favor."

"Is it wise to gamble the whole of humanity on his sliver of a chance?" Father McDermott asked.

"Well," Moira said. "It's not like we haven't been here before, humanity that is. How many disasters have we heard about in the old stories where we barely survive one disaster or another because of one human's courage, or wit, or strength?" She looked at Saint Peter. "Sometimes it's the trying that's the most important part, isn't it?"

Saint Peter smiled at her. "Your words have the ring of some truth, but not all of it. Yes, some of it is in the attempting, but a large part of it is in who makes the attempt and why. And of course, the chance of failure always exists, because were there not the chance for failure, then it really wouldn't be worthy of becoming a story."

"Is this one of those moments that will become a story centuries from now?" Moira asked. "Will people speak of John O'Brien and Moira O'Neil as they do of Jack of the Lantern?"

"I have many a blessing given to me as a saint, dear child," Saint Peter replied, "but prophesy is not one of them. That ability belongs to a different saint entirely."

"Well, can you go and ask that saint if my plan is going to work?" John said from the door. He held a jack o' lantern in his left hand. This lantern was carved from a pumpkin. Its eyes and nose were triangles, and it had a wide, jagged-toothed grin.

"Where did you get that?" Father McDermott demanded.

John shrugged. "I found it lying around."

"You stole it," McDermott said.

John shrugged again. "Look. You want me to do this thing, this *very* big thing that apparently no one else can do. Well then, you've got to let me do it my way. And, in my way, I needed a jack o' lantern, and we don't have time for me to get one – not that I can afford one anyway – and carve it myself. Besides, the face on this one is better than I could do myself." John looked at Saint Peter. "Shall we conclude our business?"

"Indeed, we shall," Saint Peter replied.

They went into the other room, leaving Father McDermott behind, mouth agape. Moira covered her mouth as if yawning, when in truth she was hiding her smile. Like Moira, the Father hadn't gotten out into the world very much. He maintained the parish and provided services in the wilds of Ireland, close enough to the place between places so that the ladies of Jack's line who maintained watch over the Devil's Gate could attend. A few other families, who had all lived in the area for countless generations, attended services there as well, but all of them maintained the strict public civility that Moira had noticed lacking in many people they'd met in larger communities.

After a few moments, Father McDermott composed himself. "I believe I need a breath of air and a bit of pipe. Call for me when they come back out."

"Yes, Father," Moira said, and went back to swinging her legs.

It took considerably less time, only ninety-four leg swings, before the door opened again.

This time, the room beyond was dark. The only light was moonlight from the room's single window and the faint glow of candlelight flickering a few feet back from the doorway. The candles flickered behind the face of the jack o' lantern that John had *found*. John held the lantern in his left hand and his stick in his right. He stepped into the room. His stick was now etched with silver and iron crosses. His coat had changed, becoming nearly a twin of her coat, except where hers was plain brown wool, John's coat was black wool striped with orange...was that silk? While he hadn't changed in size, he seemed bigger than he had before. No...bigger was the wrong word. He looked like Jack of the Lantern had. A legend made flesh. His smirk had changed. While still containing a bit of its original mischievousness, now it also held more than a hint of malicious humor.

They stayed there a few moments, looking at each other, Moira taking in the sight of her changed cousin, and she supposed John was getting used to what had changed within him.

Father McDermott came back in and stopped short. He blinked a few times at the sight of John, then looked around.

"Where's Saint Peter?" Father McDermott asked.

"Gone. He's done what he can. Now the rest is up to us."

"Well then, John," Father McDermott said, "what's with this outfit?"

"I'm not John anymore. The name's Jack."

"Of course," Moira said. "You took up the mantle of Jack of the Lantern."

"Oh no. Jack of the Lantern is still trapped in the Dark One's keeping. I couldn't do what needs doing if I called myself Jack of the Lantern. The demons aren't terrified of him anymore. They might be nervous, but they've learned they can beat him. No. I'm someone new, someone they will learn to fear far more than nice, gentle, and reasonable Jack of the Lantern.

He paused, and his smile grew from a smirk to wide, frightening grin.

"My name is Halloween Jack. Let's go scare some demons."

Five

The last three years hadn't been the kindest Jack of the Lantern had ever lived through. Still, with all the pain and suffering the demons had inflicted upon him, when they stopped even for a second, Jack of the Lantern would look at them and say, "Not bad. But how many centuries did you cower in fear of me. Let me out of this cage and we'll see how things go." In the first year, every time he said that, they'd torture him more. He'd say it again when they stopped. And so it went in a vicious circle.

Things began to slow down in the second year, after the Devil and his kin took over Buckingham Palace. They stuck his cage in a corner of the throne room, occasionally poking at him with something sharp or hot or both. From his cage, Jack of the Lantern watched, helpless, as the embodiment of everything that was evil in western culture sat on the British throne and conquered the empire with their Steam Soldiers.

Then in the third year, a few weeks before All Hallow's Eve, things began to get entertaining again. Oh, they still tormented him, and as things got worse for them, so did their torments. But what was a bit of pain and discomfort compared to watching the Dark Lord's eyes twitch with that same level of frustration from the centuries before the gate fell? It all started when a familiar looking imp crept into the throne room, shoulders slumped as if it were trying to fold in on itself. Jack of the Lantern noticed, with no small amount of satisfaction, that it walked with a pronounced limp.

"What happened?" the Devil asked.

The imp cowered as he said, "We found the boy."

"Then where is the body?" the Devil ask. "You were supposed to kill him and lay his body at my feet."

"H-he got away," the imp said. "There was a fire, and people started coming out of their houses, and so we left him alone for the night. After learning a bit about the Americans, we felt it best not to reveal our presence on the very first night. We had him, and you taught us the virtue of patience."

"So what went wrong?"

"Well, Saint Peter came…"

"GET OUT!" the Devil bellowed with such fury that the force of his voice flung the imp out of the throne room.

Jack of the Lantern couldn't see it, but he heard something strike the wall beyond the doors, followed by a pained grunt.

The Devil turned to one of the hulking scorpion demons that flanked him as his guards.

"Take that wretched failure and cast him back to the other side of the Devil's Gate. He doesn't deserve to be on this side."

"Nooooo!" came a mournful cry out in the hall. "Master, I'll do anything!"

"You'll rot," the Devil said. "That's twice you've upset me concerning this family. And that's enough out of you, blacksmith."

It wasn't until the Devil mentioned it that Jack of the Lantern realized he was snickering. Jack stopped and gave a mocking bow to the Devil. Then Jack of the Lantern coughed. It was a long, hard cough, as if he was trying to eject something from deep in his chest. He had to grip the bars of his cage to steady himself. He took a breath...and coughed again – this time even longer and harder than before. He fell to his knees, and the third cough came. He'd expected it after the second. Ever since that first visit from Saint Peter, his life had been nothing but a continuous pattern of threes.

"What's wrong with you, Jack?" the Devil asked. "You can't get sick, and none of my kin have touched you."

"I don't think you should call me Jack anymore," the man said as he stood. Even as he said those words, he knew they were true. "I'm just John the Blacksmith. I think you have a brand new Jack to worry about."

As if speaking prophecy, a pack of little goblins with gray-green skin and orange-ish eyes scurried into the throne room. They prostrated themselves before the Dark One, and when he bid them rise, they fell to bickering on which of them would do the speaking. As was common in these situations, the smallest of all of them was pushed to the front of the group.

"Your Mighty Evilness," the goblin squeaked. It swallowed once and winced as it spoke, expecting the worst. "We may have a problem."

The Devil looked at John the Blacksmith who stood smiling in the cage. John could see himself reflected in the Devil's soulless eyes. He was now a short, stocky man, balding on top, but what was one to expect after all these centuries? More importantly, he had lost all sense of the legend that had once made him Jack of the Lantern.

The Devil's face pulled back into one terrible grimace as he rounded on the goblins.

"What. Happened."

John the Blacksmith already knew the answer. His family had happened.

The terrified little goblin opened his mouth to speak, but the Devil cut him off.

"Aren't there supposed to be thirteen goblins in a pack? I only count eleven."

"Um, yes, sir," the goblin said, his voice cracking. "They went home."

"Home?" The Devil blinked. "Home, where?"

"Back to Hell where it's safe," the goblin replied. "They said they'd rather go back than stay in a world with *him* in it."

"Him? Him who?"

"Halloween Jack, Your Fearfulness. He's worse than The Lantern ever was. Some of the others are more afraid of him than they are of you."

The foundations of Buckingham Palace shook with the Devil's fury, and John the Blacksmith, who had once been Jack of the Lantern, couldn't help but laugh.

* * *

Mixxplik, the goblin, had been so hungry for so long. He was the runt of his pack, and pickings were slim, both in Hell and in every year when they got to roam free on Halloween. So many people back then hid behind those blasted lanterns, and he was so small. Even after the Dark Lord had brought down the Devil's Gate and captured The Lantern, he'd ordered all his kin not to make too much of a nuisance of themselves, at least, not until they secured rulership over the whole world. Mixxplik could see the sense in that. Even with The Lantern trapped, mankind had many other ways of protecting themselves from the forces of darkness.

But tonight, Mixxplik wouldn't be hungry anymore. The pack leader had decided they were going to eat well. They'd found an orphanage at the edge of a good-sized town. The plan was for the pack to eat the children, clean their teeth with the bones, and burn the orphanage down to hide the fact. In the morning, the pack would hide in the trees and giggle while the rest of the town came and wept over the tragedy. All in all, it would be the best night the pack had had in centuries, and the best part: Mixxplik wouldn't go to sleep hungry in the morning.

As he crept down the chimney – he'd been chosen because he was the smallest – Mixxplik's mouth watered at the thought of sinking his sharp teeth into the nice, juicy thigh of an eight or nine-year-old. Yummy. If he was lucky, he'd get a boy. The puppy dog tails gave boys just the right hint of spicy. Girls were too sweet for his taste, what with all that sugar and niceness. But, that was in his imagination. In truth, he'd be happy with anything he got, even if it was some old and stringy teenager.

He came out of the chimney into a room full of sleeping children. Three rows of beds stretched the length of the room, one against each wall and one down the middle. The little snores and the whimpers of those trapped in nightmares tempted him. For most goblins, the cries of pain that came from food were just as much a part of eating as sinking fangs into flesh. However, Mixxplik resisted. If he started munching on one of the little morsels before the pack got them all collected, it would scare the others off, and then there wouldn't be enough food to go a-round. Always practical in his thinking, Mixxplik was.

Then Mixxplik heard a sound very out of place in a room filled with sleeping children. Someone, an older-than-a-child-sounding someone, cleared his throat. Yes, that deep throat-clearing definitely came from a he rather than a she. Then came the distinctive sound of a striking match, followed by the appearance of a flickering flame. Mixxplik knew he should run, but goblins had a weakness for bright things, almost as much as they had a weakness for soft, squirmy food. He watched the little flame weave and bob in the air, then it went out of sight. Whoever held the match had put it into something. Mixxplik could see the soft glow at the top of whatever it was. Then, whoever was holding the thing turned it a-round, and the thing turned out to be a jack o' lantern.

Mixxplik couldn't help but giggle. He kept it controlled and quiet, but he giggled nonetheless.

"Really?" he asked. "You think that's going to…?"

As Mixxplik looked into the eyes of the jack o' lantern, staring defiance at that symbol that all the denizens of Hell had feared for so many centuries, the light from its three candles filled his vision until he could see nothing but the flickering lights. He tore his gaze from the lantern, but those three flames continued to fill his vision so that he couldn't see anything else.

"Trap that one!" someone said, someone with an Irish accent. For some reason, Mixxplik felt it did not bode well.

A moment later something wrapped around him, enveloping him so much that he could not move his arms or legs.

"Strike, stick, strike," that same Irish-accented voice said, "with two fingers."

This is going to be very bad for me, Mixxplik thought.

And it was. Something thin and hard began to hit him. It hit him hard and fast, beating him about the joints. Demons and other creatures from the dark realms couldn't die, at least not in the human sense of dying. However being the runt of the pack, many times Mixxplik found himself wishing otherwise. He was fairly certain this would be one of those times.

As the beating continued, Mixxplik heard children waking up and crying out.

"Don't worry, children," a woman, also with an Irish accent, said. "That little beasty won't be able to hurt you. Yes, it's a goblin, but we've got it under control. You see that man in the corner? Don't look at the lantern. That would be bad." As Mixxplik had learned. Several of the children spoke, confirming that they did see the man in the corner. "Well, that man is named Halloween Jack, and he's the thing that ghosts and ghoolies and goblins and all the other dark beasties are scared of most. Now, see this goblin? There are a bunch more outside. Calm down. Halloween Jack is going to teach you how to get the goblins to leave and not come back."

"Stick, come back," the man said, and the beating stopped. "Alright children, we've only got time for me to tell you this once, or the goblins outside will get suspicious. There's a stick next to every bed. Grab yours. Good. Now, you all down there, yes, the biggest and oldest. Grab your blankets and put one under the window over there. When the goblin hops down onto it, wrap it up, take it to the middle of the room, and work it over with your sticks. Be careful to only hold the stick with your thumb and first two fingers, otherwise you'll hurt them too much."

"But they're goblins," a boy said. "Goblins eat children. Why do we have to be careful about how much we hurt them?"

"Excellent question," the man said, this Halloween Jack fellow. "If you hurt it too badly, it won't be able to run away. Then you're going to have figure out what to do with it. So, no time to waste. You lads, get ready. Open the window."

And from there, Mixxpik heard the rest of his pack getting captured and beaten. His beating resumed. He fought and struggled but couldn't wriggle free of whatever was confining him. After a few minutes of thumpings and goblins crying in pain, the children began to giggle. Mixxplik decided there was no worse sound than your food laughing at you while beating you with a stick.

After a time, a long, painful time later, the beating stopped.

"Coat return to me," the voice of Halloween Jack said.

The thing trapping Mixxplik slid off of him. He could see again. Mixxplik found himself amidst the rest of his pack. All the goblins lay around him, rolling and writhing in pain. They were next to the door leading outside; the door was open. Mixxplik looked toward the center of the room. The man stood there, wearing an ancient-looking coat of orange and black and holding the jack o' lantern and a wicked stick covered in crosses. The face of the jack o' lantern was now turned away from Mixxplik. Behind the man stood what looked like every child of the orphanage. Each child had a stick, and while the sticks weren't fancy with the crosses and such, those sticks made Mixxplik suddenly realize the wisdom of running away to fight, and eat, another day.

Halloween Jack said something else, but Mixxplik didn't listen; he was too busy running for the door.

It wasn't long before the rest of his pack caught up to him. As they fled, Mixxplik heard one of his packmates mutter, "I think I'm going to go back to Hell where it's safe."

* * *

Naberius, Marquis of Hell, couldn't help but smile at the long line of former Confederate soldiers that stretched out from his table. He'd set up this little meeting at a crossroads next to a reputedly very fine tavern. He'd spoken to the tavern keeper, a kindly man with a head of gray hair, about having his two helpers set up this table and chair. The young man made a table from a few planks of wood and a barrel. The young lady brought out a rough wooden chair. Naberius thought it very quaint that both the girl and boy mumbled, trying to hide their Irish accents. Such was the curse of their birthright in this land, full of its prejudices.

With the meeting now begun, the human men, former soldiers all, lined up in front of the table, while half a dozen of the Dark One's Steam Soldiers stood behind Naberius. The controller box rested on the table with little blasts of electricity buzzing and zapping between the rods at the top. The controller rested atop a book detailing its use and how to make the Steam Soldiers function. The first man in line, who had been a captain in the Confederate army, eyed the controller, and his hand occasionally moved toward it. Behind him, the former soldiers, some of them still wearing parts of their uniforms, eyed the Steam Soldiers with the same looks of hunger that soldiers always had when shown bigger, more destructive weapons than their enemies could ever hope to match. It had been the same all throughout history.

"And your men understand," Naberius reiterated for the fourth or fifth time, "That they all must sign. If one man backs out, the deal is void."

"None shall 'back out' as you say, sir," the former captain said.

Naberius loved the sweet musical sound of the accent of the southern United States; it was prim and proper without the nasal drone of the British upper class. Then again, he'd liked that accent at first as well. After a few centuries, this one might begin to grate, too, if people were still speaking English at all.

"Excellent," Naberius said, and turned to draw the contracts out of his satchel, which he had hung over the back of this wonderfully rustic chair.

He loved – no *loved* is not really an appropriate word for demons, let's say he reveled and savored with exquisite delight – the entrepreneurial spirit that permeated this new continent. It made collecting souls so much easier than in the old world. It was the best part about this country where men dreamed bigger, grander dreams. And most of the time those dreams came crashing against the cold hard world. And most of the time, the cold, hard world won. It made men easier to corrupt.

"We'll just get you all to sign these," Naberius said, still rifling through the satchel – the ink and quills were at the bottom – "and you'll be on your way to a second war of liberation."

While his back was still turned, he heard something thump down on the table.

"Now Captain, you have to wait," Naberius said, turning around, "until…" Someone had put a jack o' lantern on the table. It did not currently have a candle in it, which made sense, as it was the middle of the afternoon. "Is this some kind of joke?"

Naberius looked up. His view of the captain had been obstructed by the young man from the tavern, only now the young man wore a positively ancient coat of black wool stripped with orange silk.

"No joke," the young man said. This time he did not mumble nor try to hide his accent in any way. "Well, maybe a little, but it's on you. See, while these men might hate the North, they hate the creatures of darkness even more, and so they were more than willing to give us a hand with this little ambush."

Naberius tried to stand. He could not pull himself out of the chair. He only struggled for a moment until he realized exactly where he was sitting. He saw no point in fighting a helpless battle.

"Who are you?" Naberius asked.

"My name is Halloween Jack," the young man said. "You and yours have done some grievous harm to me and mine. I mean for you to answer for that."

At that, Halloween Jack picked up both the controller and operation manual for the Steam Soldiers and handed them to the captain.

"I have your word as a gentleman?" Halloween Jack asked.

"Indeed, sir," the Captain replied. "I shall use these constructions only to battle demons and other such machines. No man, be he Northern, foreign, or heathen, should have to face such as these. We still fight with honor."

The captain and Halloween Jack shook hands.

"Fare well, then, Captain Jameson," Halloween Jack said. "I should have my business concluded by the time you get done reading that manual. You can fetch your new toys then."

The soldiers left. And as they did, several of them glanced at Naberius and spat on the ground. That's when Naberius understood his mistake. They were not looking at those weapons to use against the northerners; they were looking forward to using them against his fellow demons. He forgot that sometimes humans could be as subtle as any demon.

"Well played, young man," Neberius said. "Now, just tell me what you want. I'll give it to you, and you can let me out of this chair."

"See boyo," Halloween Jack said. "There's a problem with that. You don't have the power to grant what I want, and I can't let you out of the chair."

"Why not?"

"It's not my chair," Halloween Jack said. He turned the chair around to face the tavern. The tavern keeper and his young lady helper were walking down the steps. Only now the tavern keeper was dressed as a priest and the girl was wearing an ancient-looking, familiar coat of brown wool. "It's her chair."

"Hello, Naberius," Moira O'Neil said.

Naberius recognized her now that she was cleaned up and standing straight and tall, with her hair pulled back from her face.

"Good afternoon, Miss O'Neil," Naberius said. "You've grown a bit since the last time I saw you."

"Oh, shut it," Moira said. "You were there the night the Devil's Gate came down. You were there when my grandmother died."

"Yes, I was," Naberius said, and he realized that gloating about that might not be the best course of action at this particular moment.

"Hurt him," Moira said. "Hurt him a lot."

The chair spun around, and Naberius found himself facing Halloween Jack again. Now the young man in the black and orange coat had a stick in his hand, a stick covered in crosses, and if Naberius wasn't mistaken, those crosses were made of iron and silver. This was going be a very bad day. Unless, he could…

"Wait. Everyone wants something. If I can't get you what you want, I know someone who can. Anything. Anything, name it."

So what if there was more than just a bit of truth to the desperation in his voice? Didn't the greatest lies always hold a grain of truth at the center of them?

"Well, you know the old saying?" Jack placed the stick on the table and stepped away. A mischievous smirk curled the edges of his mouth upward.

"There's a lot of old sayings," Naberius replied. Good. Good. Keep him talking. If they kept talking, it might give Naberius time to play them against each other, or at least figure out what they wanted. "Which are you referring to?"

SINGLE STEPS

"Ladies first," Jack said. "And the lady said she wants you to hurt."

Halloween Jack took another step back. The smirk widened to a grin, a grin so malicious that it would not have been out of place on a duke or prince of Hell. That this human could hold such an expression, not just on his mouth, but in his eyes as well…well, that terrified Naberius down to his core.

"Well, my parents raised me to be a gentleman. Those would be the same parents that your kind murdered the same night you murdered Moira's grandmother." The grin faded. Halloween Jack's face became still, as hard and cold as the world that crushed dreams. "And a gentleman always obliges a lady."

Halloween Jack took a few more steps away. Naberius craned his neck around to see Moira and the priest still over by the tavern. Waiting was the worst of it, which is why demons were known to be patient. The imagination played tricks. He just wanted to get this over with.

"Strike, stick, strike, with three fingers."

The stick leapt off the table and began to beat Naberius about the head and shoulders. He brought his arms up to fend off the blows as best he could, but the stick bobbed and wove and came at him from all angles.

As the stick commenced its attack, Halloween Jack walked past Naberius. Moments later, the Tavern door closed. The beating continued through the afternoon and into the evening. As the sun was setting in the west, the Captain and some of his soldiers returned. The captain had the controller and he led the Steam Soldiers away. They buzzed and cranked and hissed their way down the road following the soldiers whose souls should have been his.

As dark fell, Halloween Jack returned.

"Please Jack," Naberius said. "I'll give you anything within my power. Just have your stick stop beating me."

"Don't believe you yet," Halloween Jack replied.

He struck a match on the table and used it to light the three candles inside the jack o' lantern. As Halloween Jack walked away again, Naberius couldn't help but look into the flames behind those triangle eyes. And then the three flames were all Naberius could see. Three flames dancing and weaving. This made protecting himself even more difficult. Eventually, as the night wore on Naberius curled into a ball on the chair, covering his head with his arms and suffering the beating of his existence while three candle flames danced before his eyes, even when he squeezed them shut.

Naberius didn't come fully to his senses until several weeks later. He was on one of the ships crowded with demons bound for England, the center of the Dark One's power on earth. He never told a single one of the demons, all of whom, like him, were fleeing from Halloween Jack, that when the sun had risen the next morning he had given over everything he knew about demon activity in the Americas. Most of the demons on board the ship had suffered at the hands of Halloween Jack because of that information. Naberius felt no shame in that. Even now, if he kept his eyes closed too long, he could see those three candle flames dancing in his mind.

* * *

Saleesh, the succubus, waited in the shadows for the time to be just right. Asag would be angry with her, but Asag was angry all the time anyway, wrath being the sin he was tied to most closely. Halloween Jack had the brutish demon wrapped in that nasty coat, blinded by that horrid lantern, and had released the stick feared far and wide across these colonies to beat upon Asag. At that moment, when Halloween Jack had set all his trickeries to work, was when Saleesh set herself to strike.

She shifted her form to that of a young lady in her late teenage years, perfect in her beauty save for the black eye she fashioned to gain the perfect level of sympathy for the rescuing hero. She'd tried this ploy on Jack of the Lantern once, centuries ago, but The Lantern's wife had nagged the romance right out of him years before he ever took up the lantern. Well, this Halloween Jack was a young man, never married, and so would not have the same protection from her charm. She would be praised for taking him and delivering him to the Dark One. He might even reward her with a title, perhaps even granting her command of a legion or two.

Stumbling out of the shadows, Saleesh wept openly.

"Thank you for saving me," she said.

"Ummm," Halloween Jack said in that way most men did when caught off guard by a pretty lady.

Without waiting for any further response, she flung her arms around him. He returned the embrace, albeit with some trepidation, and patted her shoulder.

"It's…um…alright…miss. He won't…uh…hurt you anymore."

"Thank you. Thank you. Thank you."

Saleesh didn't need to be more creative than that. Men were simple creatures and believed pretty much what they wanted to, especially concerning women.

"My hero should get a reward."

Saleesh stood on her toes, leaning up to give Halloween Jack a kiss. Once she kissed him, he would be hers. No mortal man could withstand the will of a succubus once he had received her kiss.

Just before their lips met, someone landed right next to them. Came from somewhere above and plopped down in the snow right next to Saleesh and the man she was seducing. Saleesh tried to kiss Halloween Jack anyway, but a hand interposed itself between the demon's lips and the lips of her prey. Then the hand shoved Saleesh, shoved her hard, and she stumbled back a few steps, tripped over something, and fell into a chair. Her movement caused the chair to fall over into the snow. Saleesh should have been carried out of the chair when she landed, but she remained firmly seated.

Oh, this is not good, Saleesh thought, then said, "Help me up, sir," in her most alluring voice.

"Oh, shut it," a vaguely familiar voice said.

Saleesh looked at the newcomer. It was the girl from the cottage. The one who helped keep the Devil's Gate closed.

Halloween Jack blinked in surprise. "You were right. It was too easy."

"Off you go, Jack," the girl said. "You've got your own playmate. I'm going to get acquainted with this one."

"Right," Halloween Jack said. Then he faced Saleesh, his mouth curled up into an infuriating, self-satisfied smirk. He tugged his forelock. "Good evening, Miss. Pleasure making your acquaintance." And just like that, Halloween Jack turned his back on the most beautiful succubus in all of Hell.

"Just you and me, now, sweetie," the girl said. "And I don't find you nearly as appealing as he does."

She reached under her coat and pulled out her switch, the switch Saleesh had seen used on other demons and dark creatures who decided to try their luck at gaining the artifacts the women used to keep the Devil's gate closed.

"Maybe we could come to an arrangement," Saleesh said. "There must be something that you want, um, er…I'm sorry, I don't recall your name at the moment."

"You don't deserve my name," the young lady replied. "But you can think of me as Halloween Jill."

With that, the girl raised the switch.

"Please, not the face, not my beautiful face," Saleesh said.

"Alright. I won't hit you in the face if you can give me the thing I want most."

"Anything! Name it, and it's yours."

"I want my grandmother back."

Halloween Jill did not wait for a response.

* * *

209

Nearly a year after meeting the young man who would become Halloween Jack, Father McDermott stood on the pier at Boston Harbor with Jack and Moira. Though some of the demons had taken to referring to her as Halloween Jill, Moira would always be Moira to Father McDermott. On the other hand, Father McDermott had no problem at all thinking of the young man next to him as Halloween Jack.

The last ship manned by the last crew of demons was sailing from Boston back to Europe. Oh, there would be some stragglers, and that's why McDermott was staying behind. Besides, Halloween Jack's true challenge was just beginning. The Dark One had a secure hold on the British Isles. That was a young person's fight, and McDermott had not been a young man in a long, long time.

"So then," Father McDermott said. "You'll be off to Europe now?"

"Yes," Jack said. "Taking the fight to the Devil himself."

"If I'm to stay and finish cleaning things up over here, you'll need someone else to make three people on this quest."

"I thought Moira and I would look in on our cousin, Daniel. You said he lives in Jack of the Lantern's old Smithy?"

"That's right," Father McDermott answered. "Jack's descendants have always lived there as blacksmiths."

"We'll start there, then," Jack said. "With all Moira and I have done here, think of what we'll be able to do once we have all three of Jack of the Lantern's final descendants together."

"Indeed. Give me a moment to imagine."

The little exchange went almost exactly how they'd rehearsed it. After a few moments, they heard a skittering of claws and a flapping of wings from the docks beneath them. Several shadowy shapes flew toward the ship heading toward the horizon.

"Well," Jack said. "With that last thing done, I suppose we'll be on our way."

Moira kissed the aging priest on the check. "Take care of yourself, Father. We'll see you after."

"You, too."

Then he faced the young man who had become as feared and hated by demons as his penultimate grandfather ever had been. "I didn't think much of you when we first met, but I think Saint Peter was right. You are an extraordinary young man, and if we had to place all our hopes on one man, we could do far worse than you."

"Now don't be going on like that, Father. My work hasn't even really gotten started."

"Was it wise to let the demons know that's where you're headed? They are sure to tell the Dark One."

"Oh, yes," Jack said. His right eye squinted a bit and his mouth made that wickedly charming smirk. "I'm counting on it."

Halloween Jack offered his hand to Father McDermott. They shook like old, battle-tested comrades which Father McDermott supposed, in a way, they were.

Jack sat in the ancient chair that had belonged to Jack of the Lantern. Moira stood behind him and gripped the back of the chair.

"Cork, Ireland," she said, and the magical boots that Jack of the Lantern had won from a faerie lord centuries ago carried them from the shores of the new world to greater and grander adventures in the old world.

* * *

John the Blacksmith prepared to be amused by yet another group of demons coming from the Americas who sought an audience with their dark master. This time, a group of gargoyles stalked into the throne room, except these foul creatures did not walk with the fear and terror most others did who came into this room. The gargoyles moved with purpose from the door to a place maybe twenty yards from the Dark One. All six of them bowed at once.

"What news?" the Devil asked. "You appear to have something for me that is not going to displease me overly much. I hope for your sake, you are correct."

"My Lord," the lead gargoyle spoke, his voice sounding as if it traveled through gravel. "We know where Halloween Jack is going to be. He and his cousin, the girl from the cottage, are going to the smithy where that man," the gargoyle pointed to the cage holding John the blacksmith and John bowed, "wronged you. The last three heirs of Jack of the Lantern will be in one place, at the same time."

"No," John the blacksmith said. "Please, Saint Peter, for the kindness I once showed you, protect my family."

The Devil looked at John with a cold and humorless smile. "Pray all you wish, my old friend. It will not save them from my wrath. My revenge after all this time will be allowing you to live, knowing I wiped your line from the face of the earth." The Devil stood from his stolen throne. "Summon the thirteenth legion and arm them with an equal number of Steam Soldiers. Wait until all three are there, and then destroy the smithy and everyone in it."

Demons of all manner and breeds rushed out of the throne room, with Steam Soldiers plodding after them.

Six

Halloween Jack and his cousin Moira looked down the hill at the cottage and smithy.

It had taken them the better part of a week to narrow down the location of where this whole business had started. Father McDermott had a vague idea that it might be somewhere in Connacht, in central-west Ireland. With Jack sitting in the chair, and Moira hopping around in those boots, they traveled about, collecting rumors and stories, all while avoiding the Steam Soldiers that "kept the peace" and "maintained order for the crown." At first, they'd not bothered to hide who they were, but word had already spread far and wide about Halloween Jack. Both Moira and Jack laughed when they caught a little spider-like thing with the head of a jackal trying to poison a village well. It told them the Devil was offering a princedom for any demon who could bring him the head of Halloween Jack. As much as that amused Jack and Moira, they knew they had to cover their tracks a little better, so they started hopping over to Scotland or England to cause trouble with the demons there. Once they even went to France and saved a village from a particularly nasty plague demon.

They finally narrowed down where Jack of the Lantern's old home might be to a place of about a hundred square miles. They'd spent the last two days hopping back and forth over that territory. They found it, or at least they thought they'd found it. It was the only solitary cottage with a functioning smithy they'd seen. They'd found it just as the sun was setting the night before, and rather than come on their cousin at night, they felt it best to approach in the morning.

Just before dawn, they set down in the trees about a quarter mile from the cottage. They had decided that it would be best to land while still under the cover of night so that the demons wouldn't see them land. They'd timed it right so that they reached the tree line just as the sky brightened into a clear, brilliant blue. Even from here, they could hear the *clang, clang, clang* of the hammer ringing on an anvil.

"Gets to work early, doesn't he?" Moira asked.

"Appears so," Jack said.

He looked over the clearing. A stream ran behind the smithy with a small garden next to it. A chicken coop stood about twenty paces from the house with two doghouses, one on either side. In one of the doghouses, a wolfhound lounged on a blanket that spilled out of the rounded doorway.

Something was odd about that. Why would Daniel keep the dogs outside at night in the snow? Jack had been raised in Boston, mostly, and so he didn't fully understand country ways, but he thought even predators and scavengers would seek shelter at night when it grew this cold. Then he saw a puff of steam come out of the doghouse. He edged along the tree line to get a look behind the doghouse.

"Where are you going?" Moira asked.

"Take a look at that." Jack pointed.

He didn't know exactly what he saw, but it looked like an accordion attached to a kettle which was attached to some of those strange electric rods that buzzed on the tops of the boxes that controlled the Steam Soldiers. Every ten seconds or so, right when the *clang* of the blacksmith's hammer echoed across the clearing, the rods underneath the kettle buzzed, the accordion pumped, and a puff of steam came out of the front of the doghouse.

"Clever," Jack said. "Care to wager that the doghouse on the other side has a similar device?"

"No, thank you," Moira said. "I have learned never to take a bet with you, Mr. Halloween Jack."

Jack couldn't help but smile. While she wouldn't bet with him, he had learned not to riddle with her. Her mind was sharp, and quick to think around corners.

"We should probably say hello," Jack said.

"Indeed," Moira said.

Jack lifted his lantern, he'd gone with a turnip once they'd reached Ireland, swapping it out once for a gourde just for variety and to make the demons wary of any jack o' lanterns they saw on this side of the Atlantic. Moira slung her chair over her shoulder. They'd rigged together a partial harness for it, and thankfully, it didn't weigh too much. Together they left the cover of the trees and tromped toward the birthplace of their family line.

"To think such a small, unassuming place was the start of so much trouble," Jack said, as they approached. "How much of the old story do you think is true?"

"Well," Moira said. "Jack of the Lantern is a decent liar, but I've heard the tale enough times from him and the demons that came through the cottage that I've pretty much decided that the way our family tells it is pretty much the way it happened."

"Oh," Jack said. "I keep forgetting that you've actually spoken to him."

"You'll speak to him, too," Moira said. "After we've won and the Devil and his kin are back in Hell."

"That's if he's still alive," Jack said.

"What do you mean?" Moira asked.

"Didn't the Devil capture him?" Jack said. "After all this time, would the Dark One kill the man that had caused him so much fear and embarrassment?"

"Did you actually listen to the stories?" Moira went into that tone of voice she took whenever she felt Jack needed educating on the difference between the Americas and the olden country. "Jack is already dead. He died old and tired. The Devil can't kill him, so he's got two choices, let him wander free, or allow him into Hell."

"Not exactly a pair of choices the Devil would relish," Jack said. "So, old Dark One below probably has him caged up where he can keep a close eye on him?"

"Fair bet," Moira said. "And, no, I don't want to wager on it. You're too clever and lucky than any three men have a right to be. So, what are you thinking?"

"Huh?" Jack said. "What do you mean?"

"Your eye is doing that squinting thing it always does when you're about to be clever."

"Really?" Jack said. "I'll have to work on getting better about that."

They came to the edge of the yard, the boundary of the yard and the field beyond indicated by a series of wooden posts less than a foot high. Because of the snow, Jack had not seen them from the tree line. A braid of metal wires stretched between each of the posts. As they approached the fence line, a sign rose up from the snow. Jack squinted at it, but he couldn't read the words.

"What is that?" Jack asked.

"It's Gaelic," Moira replied. "It says, 'Mind the path. Do not stray.' "

"What path?" Jack asked.

As if in answer to his question, Jack heard a strong buzzing sound. A series of wipers cleared the snow from a well-worn cobblestone path. The path led toward the cottage. About twenty feet from the cottage, it split. One branch led to the front door; the other branch wound around behind the cottage.

Jack and Moira looked at each other, at the path, and then back at each other. Jack's right eye closed slightly.

"What are you thinking?" Moira asked.

"With the buzzing sound, along with the strange mechanics here, this reminds me a little of the Steam Soldiers the demons use."

She grabbed his shoulder. "You don't think that..."

"Not at all," Jack said. "Daniel might not have been with us, but I can't imagine anyone from the line of Jack of the Lantern helping the Devil or any of his kin. Too much history and all that. No, I'm thinking that this may be an edge for our side."

"You keep thinking, Jack," Moira said. "As scary as it is sometimes, you just keep thinking."

Together they walked down the path, which was easily wide enough for both of them. Still, due to the sign, both made special care to keep a-way from where the snow began. They passed the house and went straight around back to the smithy.

When the doors to the smithy came into sight, both Jack and Moira stopped short. The doors were barred closed from the outside. Jack blink-ed in surprise. Now, in the stories his parents had told him, Jack of the Lantern had trapped the Devil in his smithy for several weeks, leaving him to hammer out hundreds upon hundreds of horseshoes.

"Do you think?" Jack asked.

"That the Devil fell for it a second time?" Moira asked. "I seriously doubt it."

Jack started for the smithy again. Moira grabbed his shoulder. "Are you sure that's a good idea? Daniel, or whoever barred that door closed, probably had a good reason for it."

"Probably," Jack said, "but I've got to know."

"Even if what's behind the door might be the death of you?"

Jack shrugged.

As he got closer, the *clang* of the hammer on anvil grew louder and louder.

Jack got to the door, lifted the bar, and pulled on the handle. The snow on the ground forced Jack to give it several good, hard tugs before being able to get it open enough to stick his head in. When he did, his mouth fell open.

"What do you see?" Moira asked.

"Daniel has a pet ogre," Jack replied.

At the sound of Jack's voice, the hulking creature that worked a blacksmith's hammer up and down, up and down, *clang, clang, clang*, looked at Jack. It was nearly twice as tall as Jack, and its shoulders seemed as wide as Jack was tall. The thing wore a leather coat, wool trousers, and a battered top hat.

"I am no pet," *clang*, "human worm." The ogre's voice was the rumble of the storm against a mountain. Even speaking in what Jack guessed might be its normal tone, the ogre was quite easily heard over the ringing of hammer on anvil. "I am a prisoner." *Clang*. "And if I could let go of this hammer," *clang*, "I would squash you into soup and slake my thirst on your blood."

"Is that *the* hammer?" Jack asked, partially shouting to be heard over the continuous *clang*.

"I imagine so," Moira said, her voice also raised. *Clang*. "Or we would likely be soup by now."

"What are you making?" Jack asked.

He couldn't see the ogre pounding on anything. There didn't seem to be much in the way of blacksmith tools anywhere, nor could Jack see any metal or ore that a smith might use to craft things. Wires and tubes came away from the anvil and stretched across the room to giant metal cylinders in each corner.

"I make nothing," the ogre rumbled. *Clang*. "I pound and pound for centuries." *Clang*. "Trapped here." *Clang*. "Making nothing." The huge creature timed its sigh between two hammer strikes. John couldn't help but smile. The sigh was a perfectly practiced pathetic gesture. The ogre's shoulders slumped as much as they could while it still worked the hammer, the timing of the action never altered for a moment.

"Do you know where," *clang*, "Daniel McRory is?" Jack asked.

"Not here." *Clang*. "Other than that," *clang*, "don't know."

"Umm…thanks." Jack said, shut the smithy door, and replaced the bar. With the door closed, they could still hear the *clang* of the hammer, but they didn't have to shout over it or pause to be heard. "Well, that was completely productive."

"Indeed." Moira rolled her eyes at his sarcasm. "What are you thinking?"

"Not a thing," Jack lied.

"You're lying, again," Moira said. "You're doing the eye thing," she pointed at his right eye and wiggled her finger at it, "again."

Jack sighed. Now that she'd pointed it out, he could feel it. He did his best to straighten his face. When he failed, Jack shrugged. "Might be something." It was a great deal more than something, but like the plan he and Saint Peter had come up with, Jack couldn't tell Moira, or the whole thing might unravel. "Most likely nothing. I'll let you know if I come up with something."

Moira punched him in the arm. "More likely you'll wait to the last possible moment and then tell me only the details I need to know in order to pull off your little scheme."

"Something like that." Jack looked around. "What now?"

"We could try knocking on the front door," Moira suggested. "Isn't that what people do when they come to call on relatives?"

"I suppose," Jack said, "that's what normal people do. Though I stopped considering myself normal the moment I gave my family's last coin away to a beggar and got called upon to save the world. Moments like that change a man."

"Are you sure your parents never brought you to Ireland?" Moira asked.

"For the thousandth time, no, they never did," Jack said. "And yes, I know you think I must have kissed that blasted Blarney Stone a dozen times or more. Alright, front door it is."

They went back around to the front of the cottage, again being very mindful not to stray off the path.

They climbed the steps to the porch. When they reached the front door, Jack knocked. Seconds later, Jack and Moira stepped back when the little slot that Jack hadn't seen opened in the door about the same level as Jack's belt buckle. A rod of metal, wrapped in wires, extended out a foot or so. The rod had a half-sphere of black glass at the end. The rod swiveled to point at Jack and then at Moira.

The thing buzzed, popped, and buzzed again.

"Who are you?" a tinny sounding voice seemed to come from behind the metal sphere.

"I'm your..." Jack started.

The voice cut him off, "What do you want?" as the rod swiveled back to Jack.

Moira said, "We need to speak to Daniel. Daniel McRory. We're his cousins."

The thing swung back to Moira and seemed to look her up and down.

"Liar," the thing buzzed. "Family is all dead." The rod slid back inside the door, and the little slot closed.

"What now, Mister Clever-and-Cunning?" Moira asked.

Jack gave her an irritated, sidelong glance. He pounded his fist against the door.

"Daniel!" Jack said. "We're your cousins. We're not dead. Open the door!"

"Great plan," Moira said. "I'm sure he really wants to talk to us now."

"You have a better idea?" Jack said.

"Maybe try..." Before she could finish, the floor beneath them began to vibrate.

"The tree line." Moira blurted.

Jack tried to reach out and touch her coat before the boots carried her away, but she was already gone. He went to jump off the porch, but the time it took trying to grab Moira's coat left him on the porch a moment too long. Iron bars slid up from the ground, clanging shut at the top of the porch. A sheet of iron slid up over the door, cutting off that escape route.

Jack sighed as he examined where the bars went into both the top and bottom of the porch. He sighed again as he heard Moira's telltale "*oomph*" as she landed next to the cage that had recently been a porch.

Without looking at her, Jack asked, "Couldn't have waited half a breath longer?"

"If I'd waited half a breath longer," Moira said, "we'd have both been trapped. And now we have a bigger problem."

"What's that?" Jack asked, still examining the cage, trying to figure a way out.

"Them," Moira said. "Just like you planned."

Jack turned around and saw a horde of demons in all shapes and varieties, coming out of the woods. Goblins snarled and hissed. Gremlins growled and snapped. Imps cackled in malicious glee. Behind them, surrounded by dozens upon dozens of Steam Soldiers like an honor guard, Naberius sat upon a nightmarish black stallion that snorted fire and stamped lightning. All these demons looked at Halloween Jack, trapped in a cage, and howled their fury.

"Charge!" Naberius yelled.

Moira looked at Jack. "I really hope getting trapped in that cage was part of your plan."

"Not exactly," Jack said, as he placed his turnip jack o' lantern on the floor of the cage. He put the three candles Saint Peter had given him inside it, struck a match, and lit them. He picked up the lantern and held it out toward the demons. A few in the front began to slow a bit at seeing the lantern. Even more slowed, causing quite a bit of stumbling and tripping, when he pulled the pistol out from under his coat. Demons couldn't die, but they could be hurt. "But I think I can work with it."

"Where did you get that thing?" Moira asked.

"One of the soldiers back in the States," Jack replied. "He lost a bet."

He fired the gun into the air. The retort echoed. All of the demons slowed, even Naberius.

Jack pointed the gun at a one of the cottage's windows. He fired again, shattering the glass.

"Get in there and get me out of this cage." Jack tucked the gun into his belt and pulled out his stick. "I'll stay here and break some heads until then."

Seven

Moira un-slung her chair and set it down before she crawled through the window. She found herself in a smaller version of the cage that trapped Jack outside. She was about to scamper back out, when a sheet of steel slammed shut behind her.

"Well, look at you," a familiar voice said. "All boxed up and delivered to me like a little present."

Moira turned as quickly as she could in the confines of the cage. Saleesh, the succubus she'd beaten senseless months before, stood looking at her. Saleesh's face still showed signs of the beating, red lines from the switch crisscrossed her face. Moira's stomach sank just a moment, and then awe overcame her fear as she took in the clockwork menagerie inside the cottage.

Gears and pulleys clicked and turned and buzzed. Here and there, all over the room, blasts of steam erupted at irregular intervals from vents in pipes that ran over the walls, floor, and ceiling. A half-finished Steam Soldier slouched in the far corner. The north wall held a rack of seven strange looking guns – all of them bigger and bulkier than normal pistols and rifles – with odd accessories. Each of the pistols ended with a crystalline globe that sparkled with some inner light. One of the rifles had a bottle on top filled with some boiling, blue liquid, and a tube connected the bottle to the gun proper. A table in the middle of the room had dozens upon dozens of tools scattered across it – some of which Moira couldn't begin to comprehend what they might be used for. The succubus also lounged on the table, bringing Moira's attention to her captor.

Seeing the succubus killed the chilly fear in the pit of Moira's stomach. A burning anger replaced it with such fervor Moira thought she might break into a sweat from the heat of it despite the cold.

"Where is Daniel?"

"He's right below you," Saleesh said. "I like the thought of keeping him warm and snug in one of his own cages. Isn't that right, sweetie?"

"Yes, mum," said someone just below Moira. Daniel – at least Moira assumed it was Daniel – spoke in that same dreamy, sappy, I'm-so-in-love voice Jack had the first time they'd met this creature.

Moira gritted her teeth and forced her mind to work. She had always thought she was quick-witted, but sometimes her cousin made her feel positively slow. Jack was so quick to adapt to new situations and to think around corners, it was frightening. How could she get out of this? Then she remembered the succubus's words, *not in the face*.

Moira felt her mouth break into a wide, Halloween-Jack-wide, grin.

Saleesh shuddered. "You can't scare me with a silly smile. I've got you trapped."

"You are such an idiot," Moira said. "You think you've got me trapped, that I can't touch you, but you are so wrong."

Moira took off her magic boots – the boots that would do their best to go wherever the owner commanded them.

"What?" Saleesh said. "Going to throw your shoe at me?"

"Something like that," Moira said, then she whispered to the boots, "Two inches behind Saleesh the succubus's nose." The boots twitched in her hand. "Hey Saleesh, you've got something on your face."

Moira let go of the boots. They flew across the room and slammed into Saleesh's face. As the boots pummeled the succubus, Moira wondered if demons ever wished they could die.

With Saleesh occupied, Moira put her face up to the bars and looked down as best she could.

"Daniel. I'm your cousin Moira. I'm here to save you."

"I don't really need saving," Daniel replied. "I like it here, and if I stay in the cage long enough, Mistress Saleesh will reward me with a kiss."

"She's a demon," Moira said. "She's lying. Come up to the bars. You should be able to see the truth of it in my eyes."

As soon as she saw a nose poke out from between the bars, Moira smacked it with the switch. Daniel cried out in pain and stumbled back. Then he cried out in indignation and made several uncouth comments about the she-demon. He made these comments in both English and Gaelic, just to be sure to cover his bases, Moira supposed.

"You better?" Moira asked.

"Maybe not better," Daniel replied, "but I'm within shouting distance of my right mind again. Thank you."

"My pleasure," Moira said. "But if you really want to thank me, how about letting me out of this…" beneath her, she heard a click and the squeal of rusty hinges, "cage."

A young man, who seemed the same age as she and Jack, stood up. His clothes were wrinkled. His brown hair hung down in some places and stuck out at wild angles from his head in others. Moira had visions of him trying to cut it himself. Deep green eyes sparkled behind strange spectacles that had a multitude of lenses at the end of twisted wires.

He had a key in his hand and used it to open the cage door.

Of course he still had the key, Moira thought. Saleesh would revel in the perverse joy of allowing Daniel to keep the means of his freedom knowing he'd never have the desire to use it.

"I have determined," Daniel said, "that I really hate demons."

"Runs in the family," Moira said, as she climbed out of the cage.

Once free, she threw her arms around the cousin she'd never met and embraced him.

When she was ready to let go, she remembered, "You have leave to let go of my coat."

"What?" Daniel muttered.

"Just happy to have one more relative alive," Moira said. "And the show of honest affection will help protect you from her." Moira gestured to Saleesh, who was losing her battle to fend off the boots.

"Seems like she's too busy to bother me anymore," Daniel said.

"I'm going to want my boots back, eventually," Moira said. "Now, we have to save Jack – he's your other cousin – and defeat an army of demons. What do those do?" She waved her switch over at the rack of strange-looking guns. "And how do I use them?"

* * *

Things weren't as bad for Halloween Jack as he'd originally expected. Oh, the situation would eventually turn against him, but for now he was alright.

As soon as Moira climbed through the window, Jack had commanded his coat to trap Naberius and had sent his stick to beat that particular Marquis of Hell senseless. Of course, that was after the stick had chased the nightmare horse off by slapping at the beast's haunches. Wrapped in Jack's coat, Naberius found it impossible to maintain his seat.

Still, that didn't do anything to affect the demons standing at the edge of the yard staring at him. He could imagine them thinking: *There he is, that Halloween Jack all the demons who went to the Americas have been talking about. All I have to do is walk right over there and kill him, and then I get to be a Prince of Hell.*

"I've got it," a stunted creature with orange skin and a mass of bright green hair said. "We can throw snowballs at the lantern. Then it can't blind us."

Well, that would certainly work, Jack thought.

The demons also leapt on that idea. Each of them scooped up two handfuls, or clawfuls in some cases, and did the best they could for probably never having played with snow. Granted, Jack couldn't be sure, but he'd heard something about the life expectancy of a snowball in... Well, it didn't matter. What mattered was that the snowballs would probably put the candles out, and his only other defenses were occupied.

"Coat, come back," Jack said. "Stick, come back."

A moment later, his coat came back together around him, and his stick landed in his right hand.

When the demons stopped making their snowballs, they looked at Jack, and faces went slack when they saw he had his coat and stick again.

But before they could put the lantern out, they'd have to get through the yard, and he was fairly certain, considering the predicament he'd found himself in, that getting through that yard was going to be much easier said than done. Speaking of his predicament, Moira certainly was taking her sweet time about getting him out of this cage.

"Lads!" a massive scorpion demon shouted. "He can't kill us! And he can't fight us all at once! Follow me, and the Dark One will reward us all!"

With that, the scorpion demon started toward Jack – right down the path. Jack did not allow the sinking in his stomach to show on his face.

The other demons followed the scorpion demon's example. Goblins, imps, and all manner of nasty creatures rushed toward the cage. And while the scorpion demon worried Jack more than just a little, he leaned back against the steel plate to watch what happened next.

Some vanished in a puff of white powder as they fell into pit traps. Cages and nets erupted from the ground, trapping others. Jack burst into laughter when a giant springboard sent a group of goblins flying well over and beyond the tree line. Their limbs flailing in the air made it look as if they were trying to maintain their flight. His humor was short-lived because the scorpion demon made it to his cage without problem.

Jack banged his stick on the metal sheet behind him.

"Moira!" Jack yelled.

"Not so big and scary trapped in that little cage, are you?" the demon rumbled.

Jack held up his lantern, but the thing just stood up straight and took its eyes above the top of the cage so the candlelight couldn't shine on it.

"Strike, stick, strike," Jack said, "with four fingers."

The stick flew from Jack's hand and began to beat the scorpion demon. The creature just laughed.

"Thank you," the demon said. "I had an itch."

Jack dodged to the side as the tail struck at him from between the bars. The stinger nearly snagged his shoulder. The demon only missed because it couldn't see him.

"Ha!" the demon said. "I can play this game all morning long, Halloween Jack! How long can you keep moving?"

The stinger struck again. Jack dodged again. He could manage this for a while. He had lots of practice moving quickly to avoid Thomas and other bullies. Granted, that had almost always involved more room than the confines of this cage, but Jack would make do until Moira got the door open. Speaking of which – well actually, thinking of which – where *was* his bloody cousin?

To make matters worse, some of the other demons had managed to make it past the defenses in the yard. Jack had seriously miscalculated the number of demons that they would send against them. He supposed that was sort of an indication that his plan to overshadow Jack of the Lantern was working.

Jack ducked under the stinger again and lifted his jack o' lantern at three red-skinned, four-armed demons as they came at the cage flexing their claws. Three paces away, they blinked several times as the candles took hold of them. Still, they came forward and slashed at him as best they could in their blindness. Jack danced and wove back and forth between the arms, and one of the demons screamed as the stinger punctured its arm.

"Sorry," the scorpion demon said, though its laughter indicated he felt little remorse.

"I like this game," Jack said. "Let's see if I can get you to sting all your friends."

Finally, the steel plate slid down and the door behind it opened. Moira stood there with the strangest pair of pistols Jack had ever seen. They looked like oversized flintlocks, but with glowing glass orbs at the ends of the barrels. Behind her, Jack saw a tall, scrawny young man wearing spectacles with a plethora of lenses of various sizes and colors. He held a massive rifle with a bottle of boiling water on top.

"Jack," Moira said, as she leveled the pistols, "duck."

Jack didn't hesitate for an instant. He dropped.

Two blasts of something that looked like solid light flashed by his head with a double *vworp* sound. The blasts caught two of the four-armed demons full in the chest and carried them off their feet and past the tree line. She shot again and the third one joined them.

"What the…" the scorpion demon started to ask, but stopped when the bars from the cage lowered. Its face came into view, probably hoping that it could skewer Jack on its stinger before the candles in his jack o' lantern blinded it.

"Stick, come back," Jack said.

The scrawny young man lifted his rifle. The contents of the bottle bubbled even more furiously, and a jet of blue-white liquid streamed out, soaking the scorpion demon. A moment later, the liquid solidified into ice, freezing the demon in place.

"Jack," the young man offered his hand, "I'm your cousin, Daniel McRory. Would you like to come in?"

Jack took Daniel's hand and let his cousin help him up. While Daniel helped Jack up, Moira dashed over and reclaimed the chair.

"I'd love to." As he rose, Jack saw that Moira was only wearing stockings on her feet. "Where are your boots?"

"Inside, trying to get somewhere."

When they were all inside and had shut the door, Moira waved one of the pistols toward the other side of the room. Moira's boots were hopping up and down, turning a succubus's face into a ruined mess.

"Isn't that...?"

"Yes," Moira said. "She seduced our cousin and put me in a cage. I think she's getting off light."

"Where are your boots trying to get?"

"Two inches past her face."

"Okay then." Jack shrugged. He turned to Daniel. "Do you have a back door?"

"Other side of the kitchen," Daniel said. "Why? We're safer in here while we fight off the demons."

"I need to talk to the ogre," Jack replied. "You might have to set him free."

Daniel's mouth dropped. "Then how will I get power for my experiments and the defenses?"

"I'll figure something out," Jack said.

"But..." Daniel replied. "But..."

"Don't worry, dear," Moira said. "Somehow, he always seems to figure it out."

In truth, Jack already had an idea.

"Alright," Daniel said, but did not seem in anyway convinced.

Moira commanded her shoes to stop trying to get two inches past Saleesh's nose. She slipped them back on and tossed the succubus into a cage.

Jack led the way through the kitchen and out the back door. None of the demons had made it around back here yet, so the trip from the cottage to the smithy was just a short walk. Jack moved the bar and pulled the smithy door open.

Clang.

"Oh," the ogre said. "You again."

Clang.

"I have a bargain for you," Jack said.

Clang.

"I'm listening," the ogre replied.

Clang.

Jack's face scrunched up in concentration. He needed to be sure of what he wanted. Several *clangs* went by while he thought.

"If I can convince my cousin," *clang*, "to set you free, will you," *clang*, "grant me five favors?"

Clang.

"It's supposed to be three favors," the ogre said.

Clang.

"Sometimes things don't happen in threes," Jack replied. *Clang.* "How long have you been trapped there?"

The ogre seemed to consider this as the hammer rose and fell. "Four favors."

"Done." Jack had actually only wanted four. He had asked for five expecting the ogre to haggle. "Daniel, free the ogre."

Clang.

"But…" Daniel started to argue, but the *vworp* of one of Moira's pistols cut him off. *Clang,* and a demon went flying into a Steam Soldier.

"Free him now!"

"Ogre," *clang,* "you have my leave to let," *clang,* "go of my hammer."

The moment Daniel spoke the words, the ogre threw the hammer to the floor and roared with such force that the smithy shook. Jack felt like his bones were rattling in his skin. Then the ogre charged Daniel.

Jack had expected this, and stepping into the ogre's path, he spoke quickly, "First favor: bring no harm to anyone of the line of Jack of the Lantern."

The ogre skidded to a stop inches away from Halloween Jack.

"Oh, you're a clever one," the ogre said, ruffling Jack's hair. "I think I might like you. I think I know what the next favor is going to be, but name it just the same."

"The second favor: help us beat the demons attacking this morning. We'll discuss the last two when we're done with that."

"Easily done."

A pack of goblins rounded the cottage and rushed at them. The ogre pried one of the doors off the smithy and used it to flatten the goblins into the snowy ground.

Jack lifted his stick and his lantern while his cousins readied their guns. Despite there being more demons than he expected, with the ogre and Daniel's weapons this was going to go even better than Jack had planned.

* * *

John the Blacksmith, who had once been Jack of the Lantern, watched the Devil as he sat on his throne in Buckingham Palace.

"You seem rather smug and self-satisfied this morning," John said. "Isn't it a bit premature for a celebration?"

"I'm not celebrating yet," the Devil said. "I'm savoring the anticipation, just as I did all those years I waited for the opportunity to strike back at you. Ironically, the means to that opportunity came at the hands of one of your descendants."

"Really?" Jack said, refusing to be baited. He was, after all, speaking to the Father of All Lies. "You don't say."

"Oh yes," the Devil replied. "William McRory, who was the father of one of your last three descendents, never really believed the old stories, despite the ogre pounding away at the anvil in his smithy. William was the type of man who would only see and believe what was right before his eyes or could be tested by science. William and his son were the geniuses that created the Steam Soldiers, and William had a weakness for pretty ladies. One of my succubae seduced him and his son easily. Once we had control of the Steam Soldiers, I only needed one of the McRories to maintain repairs, so I kept the one who would serve me the longest."

Nothing the Devil said could surprise John anymore. He was, after all, called the Dark One for a reason.

"Past victories don't mean you'll see a victory today," John said.

"Perhaps," the Devil said, "but I sent an entire legion against this Halloween Jack. I'm confident in numbers overcoming that troublemaker, no matter how clever he might be."

John the Blacksmith shrugged and waited.

Not long after that, something fell past the large window looking out into the courtyard, then came a large crash. The Devil leapt out of the throne and rushed to the window. More large objects fell from above with crashes coming from the courtyard.

"Let me guess," John the Blacksmith said, "ruined Steam Soldiers?"

"Shut up, blacksmith," the Devil snarled.

Not long after that, a string of demons, battered, black, blue, and bloodied, stumbled into the throne room. The Devil had returned to the throne and surveyed his minions who had failed him with that telltale twitching eye that filled John with so much joy. Finally, Naberius entered, looking like he had seen the wrong end of a dozen ugly sticks.

"My Lord," Naberius said, sounding for all the world like a schoolboy caught cheating on a test, "we have a problem."

"Aside from your failure?"

"Yes," Naberius said. "Much bigger than that."

*   *   *

Moira followed Halloween Jack through the field of broken Steam Soldiers and beaten and bloody demons. It was a good thing the battle was over – both her guns and Daniel's had run out of power. In the distance, the *clang, clang, clang,* came from the smithy. While not as strong as the ogre, the scorpion demon would serve as a replacement, so all the guns were charging again. Daniel was busy resetting the traps and defenses around the cottage and smithy. Moira and the ogre, who had introduced himself simply as Mickey once the fighting had ended, walked in Jack's wake as he searched the battlefield.

"Ah, here we are," Jack said, when they came upon Naberius trapped with his leg pinned underneath the Steam Soldier's leg, the one that Mickey had ripped off and thrown at the Marquis to stop him from shouting orders. "Moira, your chair, if you please? Mickey, might I entreat you to pick up the leg? No, it's not one of the remaining favors."

"It's fine," Mickey said. "I've always wanted to see this chair in action."

Moira put the chair down. Mickey lifted the Steam Soldier leg and tossed it over his shoulder. Something about fifty yards away cried in pain as the leg landed with a *thump*. Moira stifled a snicker as Jack pulled Naberius up by the collar and shoved him into the chair.

"Wait," Mickey said. "Can I try something?"

"By all means," Jack said, taking a step back.

The ogre lifted the chair and turned it upside down. When Naberius didn't fall out of the seat, Mickey said, "Oooo, this could be fun," and shook the chair, lightly at first, then with more and more vigor. Had Naberius been mortal, Moira was sure his neck would have snapped with how quickly Mickey whipped him to and fro.

"Neat," Mickey chuckled.

"Oh, that's rich," Jack said. "As much as I'm enjoying this, would you mind holding him still? But leave him upside down, I have a message I need to send to his master."

"Sure," Mickey said, and steadied the chair.

John got up close to Naberius's face and stared right into those goat-like eyes.

"Go tell your master the game has changed," Jack said. "When this whole thing started, Saint Peter wanted me to scare the Devil back into Hell. Well, this morning has shown me that no matter how badly I scare the Devil," Jack swept the stick over the battlefield, "he's going to keep coming after me and mine. I'm going to take a page out of General Sherman's book. I'm done trying to scare the Devil. You tell him I'm coming. Tell him that I know a way to rid the world of him once and for all. I'm going to kill the Devil."

"Wait," Moira said. "You can't do that. It's not how things are done. There's centuries of traditions that we have to abide by."

Jack grinned his telltale grin. "If Saint Peter had wanted things done in the traditional way, he wouldn't have asked an American to do it."

"I'm in," Mickey said.

"You?" Naberius said. "You should be helping us!"

"Why?" Mickey asked. "With you lot running around, I'm not the big bad guy anymore. I killed a lot of things before I got trapped pounding with that hammer. But I've never killed a Devil. That should raise me a bit in ogre standing."

"But…" Moira said.

Jack held up his hand, cutting her off. "No. I'm sick of this." Jack poked Naberius with his stick. "The Americas have their own stories and their own traditions. In these stories, we don't just give bullies their come-uppance, we get rid of them. You tell the Devil that if he doesn't go back to Hell and leave us be, Halloween Jack will be the end of him."

Eight

Two weeks later, and one night before Halloween, Halloween Jack sat back in his chair and sipped his coffee while Moira, Daniel, and Father McDermott discussed Jack's change in the plan. After the demons had left the battlefield, Jack had taken Mickey the ogre aside and asked for the last two favors. Mickey railed against the first and laughed at the second, laughed so hard trees around them shook. When Jack went back to Moira and Daniel, Mickey had already left to complete one of the favors.

Both Moira and Daniel had pestered Jack about those other two favors, but Jack refused to tell them what they were. "I wouldn't want to ruin the surprise," Jack said every time they asked him. The truth was, Jack couldn't trust them to act appropriately if they knew, or not to reveal his plans if they got captured. Thankfully, they seemed to grow tired of that response and so stopped asking him about it. Instead, they'd switched tactics, trying to get Father McDermott to get Jack to change his mind about killing the Devil.

As it was, they sat around a table at an inn discussing the matter.

"I'm not sure I can argue against it," Father McDermott said. "I've yet to hear the full plan." Moira had gone to get the priest, and apparently had been babbling about Jack being more than half mad and wanting to break from the old ways. "Spell it all out for us, Jack."

"Well," Jack said, "my father didn't just tell me stories about Jack of the Lantern and other tales of the olden country. He also collected stories of his new homeland, especially stories of its native savages. He'd tell these to me along with our family history. I figure, if our stories were real, why not those? One of my favorite stories was a tale of the Tomahawk of the Four Winds."

"What's a tomahawk?" Daniel asked.

"It's an axe," Moira said. "Like a hatchet. A warrior's weapon used by the Indian Natives of the Americas. They are made of stone or obsidian."

"How do you know this?" Father McDermott asked.

"Jack of the Lantern would bring me books from the Americas when he came to visit," Moira said. "I really like the ones about the western states and territories. I've never heard of the Tomahawk of the Four Winds."

"It doesn't surprise me much," Jack said. "My father only knew about it because he read it in a journal he'd gotten somewhere in his travels before he met my mother. My father was at the Alamo and knew Davy Crockett."

While Moira's mouth and eyes stretched wide, Daniel and Father McDermott blinked at Jack, the name unfamiliar to them.

"Your father knew Davy Crockett?" Moira asked.

"Briefly," Jack replied. "My father was very young."

"Who was this Davy Crockett?" Daniel asked.

"He was an early explorer and American hero," Moira said. "One of the stories claims he killed a bear when he was only three years old."

"Regular Hercules, this Crockett fellow was," Daniel said.

"Actually, he kind of was," Jack said. "In his journal, Davy Crockett wrote about the Tomahawk of the Four Winds."

"Wait," Moira said. "I thought everyone died at the Alamo. How did your father get out?"

"My father was just a boy, and so he was allowed to leave with the other women and children before the fighting began in earnest. Now, let me tell the story of the Tomahawk of the Four Winds."

Jack took a drink of his coffee, cleared his throat, and began.

"Long before the white man came from the great waters to the east, the People lived in harmony with all the spirits of the land. Some spirits were tricksters and sometimes played jokes on the People and their fellow spirits, but there were no spirits of evil in the land. This was not always so. Long ago, when the spirit world and world of men were closer than they are now, evil spirits crossed back and forth between both worlds, causing pain, strife, and suffering everywhere they went. The spirits went to the Great Spirit and the men went to their chiefs, asking for someone to deliver them from these embodiments of evil. The Great Spirit came to the land and visited the greatest of all the chiefs. The Great Spirit told this chief how he could rid the worlds of these terrible spirits. To make the story short, the greatest chief had many adventures making the Tomahawk. He found a special stone that fell from the sky and took it to the four corners of the land and had it blessed by each of the four winds. The greatest of all the chiefs took that tomahawk and used it to kill all the evil spirits so that the People and the spirits could live in harmony."

Jack paused to let the story sink in.

"I'm going to get the Tomahawk of the Four Winds and use it to kill the Devil."

"But you don't know if it's even real," Daniel said. "And even if it is, you don't know where it is."

"It is real. And you're right, I don't know where it is, but I bet I know how to find out where it is." Jack grinned at Moira. "Any takers?"

"Saints in heaven preserve us," Moira said, and buried her head under her arms on the tables.

"Gents?" Jack said. "Either of you?"

"Not on your life or mine, Jack my boy," Father McDermott crossed himself. He'd lost nearly as many wagers against Jack as Moira had in their campaign to rid America from the demons.

"How can you two be sure?" Daniel asked.

"Did he ask you to bet on it?" Moira asked, her voice muddled underneath her arms.

Daniel nodded.

"Then he's figured out some way to win the wager," Father McDermott answered. "He might not win in any way you expected, but he'll win. For example," the priest turned to Jack, "you know where the journal is."

"As a matter of fact," Jack said, "I believe I do. You see, Davy Crockett gave the journal to my father so that the Spaniards couldn't find it and learn all of his secrets."

"Of course he did," Moira said, lifting her head. "And you know where the journal might just be, don't you."

"As a matter of fact," Jack grinned even wider, "I believe I do."

All three of them jumped when Mickey the ogre put his face up to the window next to them and said, "Then let's go get the bloody thing and kill us a Devil. Oh, and I got those things you asked for, Jackie boy."

As they caught their breath, Mickey handed Jack a satchel.

"What is that?" Father McDermott and Moira asked at the same time.

"Father McDermott, Mickey the ogre. Mickey, Father." Father McDermott gaped at Mickey.

"Charmed," Mickey said. When the priest wouldn't stop gaping, Mickey looked at Jack. "What's with him?"

Jack shrugged. "I have no idea. I told him about you."

"I'm terribly sorry," Father McDermott said. "It's just that you're, so...so..."

"Ogre-like?" Mickey asked.

"That's it!" The Father exclaimed, and then flushed. "I'm terribly sorry."

"Ah, yes," Mickey said. "No offense taken, Father. I get that a lot."

"So, Jack," Moira said. "Bag. What's in it?"

Jack smiled at Moira. "It's a surprise. Like everything else, you'll get to know at the right time."

Moira glared at Jack, and he hated that he couldn't tell her everything, but again, he couldn't risk letting any part of the plan get out into the open or the whole thing might come crashing down around them.

"Bu…bu…but…" Father McDermott stammered. "An ogre?"

"Yeah," Jack said. "He's on our side. At least until I get one more favor out of him."

"How many has he done for you already?" the priest asked.

"Three," Jack said.

"And he's still owes you one more?" the Father said. "Besides, he can't go with you, that will throw off the number."

"Oh, he's coming," Jack said, "and so are you, because?"

All at once, Moira, Daniel, and Mickey said, "Sometimes things don't happen in threes."

"Right," Jack said, and swallowed the last of his coffee. "Now that we've gotten that out of the way, let's go get that journal."

He stood from the table, and halfway to the door he paused to make sure his cousins and the Father were following him. They were, though none of them looked pleased. In fact, each of them looked as if questioning his sanity, which was, of course, part of the plan. Jack wanted the demons to see that his friends also thought he was more than a little crazy. Hopefully, that would add to the mystique Jack was creating around himself. From the window, Mickey winked.

People watched as Halloween Jack walked through the inn. Jack wondered how he must look, wearing the strange orange and black coat, carrying his stick and jack o' lantern, a pumpkin now that he was back in the United States. And even if his own appearance wasn't enough to cause a stir, he had a menagerie of strange companions following behind him: a priest, a girl with a coat similar to his with a chair slung over her shoulder, and the tall scrawny fellow with the spectacles with all those strange lenses and the weirdest gun they'd ever seen. Jack grinned widely and nodded at whoever looked at him, which made each and every one of them quickly look away.

This was to be his lot in life. He and Saint Peter had spoken of it at length that night that felt like a lifetime ago. He needed to be larger than Jack of the Lantern had ever been, in the minds of the Dark One and all his kin, as well in the minds of his fellow men.

Halloween Jack stopped in the center of the inn. Still grinning, he swept his gaze over the entire room.

"Good evening, ladies and gentleman," Jack said. "All Hallow's Eve is coming, and it's going to be a darker night than usual this year. All manner of foul beasties are roaming free." He placed his jack o' lantern on a table and lit the candles inside it. Once all three candles were burning brightly, Jack spun his lantern, sending shadows wavering and dancing across the inn. "Don't fear the darkest beastie of them all. I'll have him well and taken care of, you just make sure that you have your jack o' lanterns out to frighten off those that follow him."

"Are you saying that you're Jack of the Lantern?" someone asked from across the inn, from somewhere behind him. "Because you haven't been doing a very good job the last few years."

Jack didn't bother turning. "Not at all. Jack of the Lantern was my grandfather, and he retired. I've taken up things in his place. My name is Halloween Jack, and I'm going to have a little chat with the Dark One himself and set some things straight on how things are going to be."

"And if the Dark One doesn't like what you tell him?" someone else asked.

A few people laughed at that. Jack let his face go blank and swept his gaze over the room again with no grin, no frown, no expression whatsoever.

"Then I'll kill him. I'm Halloween Jack, and I have the means to do so."

With that, Jack picked up his lantern and left. Hushed conversations had already sprung up all throughout the tavern. When he stepped off the steps leading up to the inn's door, Jack saw a coach driving by. He grinned and tugged on his forelock as it passed by.

A moment later, Father McDermott caught up to Jack. "Well, that wasn't very subtle."

"It all depends on your outlook, Father," Jack replied. "It all depends."

His cousins fell into step with them.

"You're a mad man," Daniel said.

"More than a little," Jack replied. "But the world needs it, and I've been told I'm the only one that can do the job."

They rounded the corner of the inn. Mickey was waiting for them in the shadows, and the shadows did quite a good job of hiding the huge creature.

"I don't understand," Father McDermott said. "Shouldn't it be helping the Devil?"

"First off," Mickey said, "I'm a *he* not an *it*. Second, not in the least. I am a living creature. I hadn't even been born yet when that war in heaven thing happened. Don't care about their politics. I happen to like the world just the way it is, or was. I may be wicked and mean at times, but not inherently *evil*. Besides, we ogres, trolls, giants, and other such folk pride ourselves on getting one over on others, the bigger, more self-righteous, and pompous the person we get one over on, the better. Why do you think there are so many stories of us beating up on knights? Getting one over on the Devil himself sounds like a lot of fun." Mickey looked at Jack. "Do you think they went for it?"

"I'm pretty sure," Jack said.

"What do you mean?" Moira asked.

"Oh, there were at least three demons in the common room back there," Mickey said. "Because, sometimes, things do happen in threes."

Moira glared at Jack. "Did you know they were there?" When Jack nodded, she added, "What game are you playing at, John O'Brien?"

"Moira dear," Jack said. "There is no John O'Brien anymore. There can't be. I must be, for the sake of the world, now and for as long as I wander, Halloween Jack. If I allow myself to be anything but him, they will win, because then I will be only a mortal man. They have no need to fear a man, only a legend, and I've only got a short time left to solidify this legend. I don't have the luxury of the lifetime that Jack of the Lantern had. My legend must be total and complete, and it must be now. The surest way to solidify that legend is do something no one else has done. Killing the Devil should do the trick.

"Now, my old home isn't far away. Shall we go see if we can find Davy Crockett's journal?"

Without waiting for a response, Halloween Jack headed into the night. Oddly, Mickey the ogre was the first to catch up to him.

* * *

Naberius hung upside down, chained to the ceiling of the carriage. The Dark Lord had seemed to enjoy this torment ever since Naberius had told him about the events at the cottage and smithy of Jack of the Lantern. As the carriage rolled past Halloween Jack, the man had tugged his forelock. Had he known who was in the carriage? He couldn't possibly know, but he seemed to be able to know other things, and his wits were quicker than any being Naberius had ever known.

"I told you," Naberius said. "And now, thanks to the ogre, we know how he plans to do it."

"You did indeed," the Dark Lord said. "But all things considered, I needed to verify this for myself. Once this young man started making trouble, I should have taken matters into my own hands, rather than leave the details to my lessers."

Naberius did not comment that the Dark Lord had dealt personally with Jack of the Lantern, and that hadn't worked out very well for all of demonkind.

"Do you think the ogre can be trusted?" Naberius said.

"Of course not," the Dark Lord replied. "It's an ogre. It will do whatever serves its own best interests at any moment, but we can trust that it is not truly Halloween Jack's creature, either."

Naberius wondered at that. Halloween Jack made it a habit to cover all his bases, and even the things that appeared to be left to chance always seemed to work out in his favor. The Marquis of Hell couldn't help but respect and even admire the young human, especially with that cocky tug of his forelock. Oh yes, Naberius decided, Halloween Jack knew exactly who was riding in the carriage, and that simple gesture had been a challenge. As with Jack of the Lantern, the Dark Lord did not realize what he was up against. Well, Naberius knew, and hanging from the ceiling in his chains, he decided he was finished being a Marquis of Hell. He wanted a bigger title, and if Halloween Jack managed to kill the Dark Lord, someone would need to fill the role of Lord of Hell.

"What are you smiling about?" the Dark Lord asked.

"I'm looking forward to seeing the expression on Halloween Jack's face when you best him," Naberius replied. He silently thanked the Dark Lord for teaching all his followers to lie so well.

Nine

Halloween Jack stood in the street flanked by his friends, looking at the mansion that had been the childhood home of John O'Brien.

"You actually grew up there?" Moira asked.

"It's bigger than I remember," Jack said.

Jack looked at the house, trying to reconcile his memories with the reality of what he was seeing. Until this moment, he wasn't sure the plan was going to work, that Saint Peter would actually be able to grant his second wish, but the proof stood in front of him. More to the point, twin sets of memories warred in his mind: what John O'Brien remembered about growing up and what Halloween Jack remembered about growing up as John O'Brien. Two men with two pasts, sharing the same body. Halloween Jack supposed it would be enough to drive a lesser man mad, while he just took it in stride as part of what needed doing.

"The house looks a bit out of place," Daniel said.

And the house did. The house was actually a large mansion surrounded by modest family homes.

Halloween Jack sifted through his conflicting memories. "Our house is older than the neighborhood, built before the O'Brien family came to America. My grandfather used most of what was left of the family treasure to buy it. The neighborhood sprang up around it as Boston grew."

"You also have another problem," Mickey said, and pointed to a light flickering in a window on the second floor.

"Lord, why can't anything be easy?" Moira asked.

"We're up against all the forces of darkness at the same time," Father McDermott said.

"If it were easy," Jack added, "it wouldn't be worth doing, and it wouldn't be nearly so much fun."

"*Fun*, he says," Daniel said. "Jack, boyo, you have a strange definition for that word."

"Have you met him?" Moira asked.

"Children," Father McDermott interjected. "This banter is not helping. Jack, where is the journal?"

"It's probably in my Father's study on the second floor," Jack replied. "One room over from where that light is. Moira, get me up there. Daniel, Father, make sure none of them get past you going down the stairs. Mickey, stay out here and demolish any Steam Soldiers that might show up."

"Happily," Mickey rumbled.

Jack placed his jack o' lantern in his right hand and gripped Moira's shoulder with his left. He'd come to notice the slight tingle as the magic of the coat bound his hand to it.

"Boots," Moira said, "take me to that window over there."

Jack's stomach lurched as they flew into the air, him being pulled along by the combined magic of Moira's boots and coat.

About halfway to the window, Jack said, "Strike, stick, strike, with four fingers."

His stick flew from the pocket in his coat and slammed into the window, shattering it.

"Stick, come back," Jack called, and the stick slid back into its pocket inside the coat.

A moment later, he and Moira landed in the room amidst the shattered glass. Two Steam Soldiers flanked the door. A pack of goblins stood at rough attention against the far wall. A finely dressed man sat in the high-backed chair behind the massive desk in the center of the room. The man had slick black hair, a thin mustache, and a pointed beard. He wore a scarlet tailcoat over a midnight-black waistcoat. His eyes held a mischievous twinkle, and a knowing smirk played across his lips. Naberius hung from chains, dangling from the ceiling, just behind the Devil's left shoulder. Two more Steam Soldiers puffed and buzzed behind the Marquis of Hell.

"It's a pleasure to make your acquaintance, at last," the Devil said, as he flipped through a battered journal that seemed to have seen dozens of miles for each year it had been carried about the early American frontier.

"This is so not good," Moira said. "Halloween Jack, you've my leave to let go of my coat."

Jack pulled his hand free. "Naw. This is going to be fun."

"You really need to reexamine how you define that word," Moira muttered under her breath.

"Please, Jack," the Devil said, "let's not be hasty. Just because I didn't get along with Jack of the Lantern doesn't mean we can't come to some sort of agreement."

"So you'll go back to Hell, and only come out once a year, setting things back to the way they should be?" Jack asked. "Done. We'll meet you and yours by the Devil's Gate and be done with this nonsense."

The Devil laughed a deep amused laughed, the sound of it soaked with sweetness and honey. Jack so wanted to like the man who made that laugh.

NO! Jack yelled within his mind. *He is not a man. He is the one that commanded his demons to murder your entire family, hundreds throughout Europe and America, who bore no other guilt than being born into the wrong family.*

"I don't think so, Jack," the Devil said. "Aside from the trouble you've been causing, my kind like it very much on this side of the Gate."

"Well I suppose, then, might I make another offer?" Jack asked.

"I'm listening," the Devil said.

And that was the moment Halloween Jack truly knew, deep in his bones, that he would win. It was the same reason that Jack of the Lantern had won. The first Jack must have realized the Devil's weakness, just as Halloween Jack had recognized it now. The Devil couldn't resist the chance to bargain. Also, he must not be able to take anything from someone that wasn't freely given, otherwise he wouldn't need the Steam Soldiers or the other demons to hunt and kill for him. He would just strike down his enemies as soon as they became a nuisance.

Jack grinned his widest, maddest grin and directed it at the Devil. The Dark One's knowing smile faltered and the mischievous twinkle in his eyes faded.

"Strike, stick, strike," Jack said, pointing at Naberius, "with two fingers."

Naberius might appear to be trapped in those chains, but Jack didn't trust any appearances around those two.

As the stick flew from its pocket, Jack tossed the jack o' lantern at the Devil. Instinctively, the Devil dropped the journal and caught the pumpkin. The moment he did his eyes glassed over and three candle flames danced in the reflection.

The goblins scurried forward. Moira already had her pistols out and was shooting away. *Vworp, vworp, vworp!* Blasts of yellow light carried the goblins backward, slamming them into the wall as they slid to the floor. They did not get back up.

The Steam Soldiers by the doors started forward. The ones standing behind the Devil raised their arms. Jack remembered all too well what that meant.

"Mickey!" Jack yelled. "Steam Soldiers up here!"

Jack didn't wait for any kind of response. He sprang for the desk and the journal. His hand closed around the book. Before he could pull his arm back, Naberius grabbed Jack's wrist. Jack tried to pull against the Marquis's grip, but could not. For all his cunning and wit, Halloween Jack was only human and could not match the strength of the demon lord. Even as Jack's stick beat Naberius, he locked eyes with Jack and smiled.

This was not part of the plan.

Behind him, Jack heard Moira's guns *vworp*ing, goblins screaming and groaning, and Steam Soldiers clanking, hissing, and buzzing.

"I have the human boy, My Lord," Naberius said. "Please give me this one chance to redeem myself. You know where this savage weapon is, go and claim it for yourself. I will hold your enemies here."

With that, Naberius knocked the jack o' lantern away from his master with his free hand. The pumpkin sailed across the room and shattered against some curtains. The three candles fell to the floor, still burning, unable to go out on their own. The curtains caught fire almost immediately.

"I'm used to the flames," Naberius said, eyes sparkling. "I actually quite like them. Can you say the same? Shall we remain here and find out?"

"Thank you, Naberius," the Devil said. "It was a pleasure to meet you, Jack, just this once before you die."

The Devil vanished. Heat washed up from the room.

This was not part of the plan.

A crash came from the window where Jack and Moira had entered the room, not breaking glass, but snapping wood. Jack glanced back. Mickey had ripped his way through the window and charged one of the Steam Soldiers. The ogre picked it up and used it to pummel one of the others to scrap.

Jack looked back at Naberius, who was still grinning at Jack. Jack struggled against the grip. This was definitely *not* part of the plan.

"Stick, strike with four fingers," Jack said.

Naberius grunted with each blow, but he did not release Jack's wrist.

"You think your little stick will dissuade my ambition?" Naberius asked. "When all I have to do is hold on a little while and suffer a bit of discomfort before your stick burns to cinders, and after your bones do the same the Dark Lord will make me a Prince of Hell. No, I will not let go because your stick is beating me." And then Naberius released his grip on Jack's wrist.

"Stick, come back," Jack said. The stick returned to Jack as he backed away from Naberius. All Jack could wonder was, "Why?"

"Something about being better to reign somewhere or other," Naberius said, and vanished from the room.

Jack was too busy snatching up the journal to stop Naberius from escaping; likewise, Moira and Mickey were too busy with the goblins and Steam Soldiers.

By the time Moira and Mickey had destroyed the Steam Soldiers and the goblins had run off – at least those that were still conscious had – the fire had spread across half the room.

Jack stood watching the flames get closer and closer, bigger and bigger, trying figure out how to get his three candles back.

"Jack," Moira yelled. "We have to go."

"My candles," Jack said. "I need them."

"They's gone, Jack," Mickey said.

"No," Jack said. "They can't burn up. Once they melt all the way, they will grow back. It's part of the blessing from Saint Peter."

"Then let's wait for the house to burn down, and we'll get them after," Moira said.

"No time," Jack now had to yell over the flames. The heat forced him back to the door with his cousin and the ogre. "The Devil knows where the Tomahawk is. We've got to get there before him."

Behind them, footsteps echoed in the stairwell. All three turned: Moira raised her pistols, Jack got ready to command his stick, and Mickey picked up a Steam Soldier's severed arm. It turned out to be Daniel and Father McDermott.

"What are you doing," Father McDermott cried. "We've got to get out of here?"

"Jack won't leave without his candles," Moira said. "They won't burn up, but they're trapped in the fire. Jack's trying to figure out how to get them."

"You really need those candles?" Daniel asked. When Jack nodded, Daniel shook his head and pushed his way past them. "Well, this will be the end of this gun until I can get it back to the smithy and recharged."

Daniel sprayed the freezing gun all over the room. Steam and smoke filled the air, but within moments, the flames were out. The bottle at the top of the gun was empty.

They waited a few minutes for the smoke and steam to dissipate. Daniel adjusted his spectacles and found the candles in no time at all. He held them out to Jack, but when Jack reached for the candles, Daniel pulled them away.

"What?" Jack said. "Give them to me? I need them for the plan."

"Halloween Jack, how can someone as smart as you be such a bloody idiot sometimes? You don't have to do everything yourself, every single time."

"I'm Halloween Jack. I'm the one Saint Peter chose to follow in the footsteps of Jack of the Lantern. He did everything pretty much by himself."

"And look where that got him," Daniel said.

"Not to mention my grandmother," Moira said, "and the rest of our family."

Jack stood in the ruins of his father's study, looking at his candles in Daniel's hand. Slowly, he faced each of the people in the room, Daniel first, Moira, Father McDermott, and then Mickey.

Mickey shrugged. "You do what ya gotta do, Jackie Boy."

"Alright," Jack said. "Saint Anthony's church isn't far from here. We'll talk there, where the demons can't overhear us. Now, may I please have the candles?"

"Yes," Daniel said. "Now that you're done being an idiot."

"At least for now," Moira said, and punched Jack in the shoulder.

* * *

A little over an hour later, Jack sat drinking tea and coffee with Moira, Daniel, and Father McDermott in a back room at Saint Anthony's church. Father McDermott had impressed upon one of the priests there that they needed succor. Mickey was outside, patrolling, making sure that they were not interrupted or overheard. Unlike at the inn or back at the smithy, Jack did not want the demons to overhear this particular bit of conversation. It didn't take him long to go over the plan. In theory, it was fairly simple. In execution, a bit more complicated. And, as much as he hated himself for holding back, Jack kept the important details to himself. If they knew what he truly planned, it wouldn't work.

"So you really worked all this out the night you met Saint Peter, Moira, and myself?" Father McDermott asked. "Why didn't you start with trying to kill the Devil straight away?"

"It wouldn't have worked," Jack said. "Even though I knew about the Tomahawk, I couldn't have just said, 'Hey, I'm off to kill the Devil.' We had to work to create the legend of Halloween Jack into something that they believed was capable of that."

"But still," Daniel said, "you had this plotted every step of the way?"

"Most of it," Jack said. "I didn't plan on Mickey. He was a crazy random happenstance that I took advantage of, but I knew about your inventions, Daniel, and thought I could use the smithy as a place to strike more fear into the demons. I didn't know about you being a prisoner."

"Lucky you had me along," Moira said.

"Lucky indeed," Jack replied. "All along the way, things have not gone completely according to my grand design, and each time someone was there to help recover from that. Thank you, all."

Jack took the satchel that Mickey had given him at the inn and handed it to Moira.

"What's in this?" Moira asked.

"The other six things you need to perform the ritual to close the Devil's Gate," Jack replied. "That was my third favor from Mickey. I figured even if he couldn't get them, it was worth a shot, and as it turns out, he could, which saves us a lot of time and effort."

"What was the forth favor?" Daniel answered.

"I can't tell you," Jack said. "It's something that has to stay between Mickey and me." He saw the questioning expressions on their faces, and it broke his heart that he couldn't share that part of his plan. "Please trust me?"

They looked back and forth at each other. Surprisingly, Father McDermott was the first to speak.

"Alright, John," the priest said. "You're the one that's had this thing going since that first night. I'll trust you. I didn't think much of you when we first met, but you are exactly what Saint Peter said you'd be. What do you need from us now?"

"Thanks for the confidence, Father," Jack said. "Captain Jameson and his squad of soldiers, along with the Steam Soldiers we gave them, should be at the smithy soon."

"You must have sent them there right after we first beat up Naberius," Father McDermott said.

"I did," Jack said. "I honestly thought they would get a bit of rest, as we'd be chasing down the things Moira needed. Thanks to Mickey, we don't need to worry about that anymore.

"Moira, after you take me to the Alamo, get Daniel back to his smithy so he can arm the soldiers and take them to the cottage. You'll need someone to protect you from the demons trying to stop you from repairing and closing the Devil's Gate."

"How will you get there?" Moira asked.

"That's where Mickey's final favor comes in," Jack replied. "I'll be there at the exact right time."

"What should I do?" Father McDermott asked.

"Pray for us," Jack said. "We're going to need any edge we can get. And, you'll need to take up the fight if we fail. I thought this was a sure thing when I planned it, but as we've seen, sometimes things don't go according to the plan."

"Well," Father McDermott shook Jack's hand, "God's speed son."

"Thank you, Father," Jack said, "for everything."

They left Saint Anthony's and met up with Mickey.

"Alright then," Mickey said. "We ready to go and get this axe and go kill the Devil, himself?"

Everyone nodded. Jack and Mickey each put a hand on Moira's coat. As always, Jack felt that tingling as his hand became fixed to it.

"The Alamo," Moira said, and Boston fell away underneath them.

SINGLE STEPS

Ten

Jack had never been to Texas, but he was fairly certain that there wasn't supposed to be snow on the ground the night before All Hallow's Eve. It was a still night. In the distance, the Alamo was just a dark shadow against the moonlit sky. They had put down just a ways away from the fort in case the Devil had put out sentries.

"So, this is Texas," Mickey said. "I thought it would be bigger."

Jack punched him in the arm.

"What?" Mickey asked, but when Jack glared at him, the ogre broke into a wide grin. "Sorry, couldn't resist."

"I don't get it," Moira said.

"Don't worry about it," Jack replied. "It's not actually that funny."

"If you say so," Moira said. "Are you sure you can get to the cottage without me?"

"We'll be there," Mickey said.

Moira eyed the ogre. "Alright."

She threw her arms around Jack and squeezed him. Jack held her back, and in doing so, realized he was scared. Terrified. Rather than just hold Moira, Jack squeezed back, squeezed back as if it were the last embrace he'd ever feel. In a way, it might as well be.

"You alright?" Moira whispered.

"Just scared," Jack said. "I've got a lot riding on my shoulders. I just hope I'm strong enough to do what needs doing."

Moira tried to pull away from Jack but couldn't for a moment, the magic of her coat holding them together.

"You've my leave to let go of my cloak," Moira said.

All three of them had a short laugh over that, then Moira grabbed Jack by the shoulders.

"Not that I've known many men, but my heart tells me you're among the strongest in all the world. You've defied the Devil to his face and somehow managed to scare him and the denizens of Hell in a shorter time than Jack of the Lantern. I know you haven't told us everything, and that's alright. It's the way you do things. I believe in you. I know you'll do whatever needs doing. After all, you're Halloween Jack. Now go fetch that bloody tomahawk so we can end this nonsense." She ruffled his hair. "Saint Anthony's church in Boston."

Moira vanished into the night sky.

Mickey stepped next to Jack. "Scared, eh?"

"Wouldn't you be?" Jack asked.

"I suppose," Mickey said. "How much did you tell them back at the church?" the ogre asked.

"Pretty much nothing," Jack replied. "They think they know the plan, or at least most of it, when really, they don't know much of anything."

"They're going to hate you for it when they find out."

Jack shrugged. "Maybe. Maybe not. You'd be surprised how understanding humans can be once they see the larger picture."

"How much do I know?" Mickey asked.

"More than they do," Jack replied, "but not all of it."

"It's not too late to change your mind on that favor."

"It's the best way to get done what needs doing," Jack said.

Mickey ruffled Jack's hair. "You're a good man, John O'Brien."

"What did I say about that?" Jack said.

"Pssshhh. That silly rubbish about being one or the other? I'd been a-round a long time before I got trapped pounding on that blasted hammer, and I knew all manner of men. Knights, farmers, princes, rogues, and a host of others. Some I got along with, others I fought with, even killed a few of them. Don't look at me like that, Jackie Boy. I'm an ogre, it's part of what we do. Anyway, the point is: no man is ever just one thing, and this *Halloween Jack* thing you've made yourself out to be wouldn't likely go through with what you have planned. That's the choice of a man, not a legend. That's what the Devil and his kin fear more than anything. That underneath all that Halloween Jack has become, there is still a man, desperate to save the world and avenge the ones he loves."

Jack punched Mickey in the shoulder. "Thanks. You're a good friend."

"Been a while since any man has called me a friend," Mickey said, then ruffled Jack's hair. "Now, let's go get that bloody tomahawk so we can end this nonsense."

"I'm all for that," Jack said.

Jack struck a match and lit the three candles in his jack o' lantern. He used the light to examine the journal and find out the location of the entrance to the secret chamber where Davy Crockett had hidden the Tomahawk of the Four Winds.

"The Devil knows it's here," Jack said. "The journal states that plainly. Let's just hope he couldn't decipher the code to tell exactly where it was before we interrupted him."

"What's the code?" Mickey asked.

"The directions are spelled out by reading every seventh letter of every third page," Jack said, flipping through the journal. "Got it. We need to get around to the chapel. Crockett held the wall near there. We'll have to dig through about a foot of dirt to get to the hatch leading down to the chamber below."

"That sounds like a lot of work to do in short amount of time," Mickey said. "You sure that's accurate?"

"Don't underestimate the power of determined and desperate men," Jack replied.

Mickey nodded. "You would know."

They crept to the fort. Several times they hid from patrols of demons and Steam Soldiers. Jack was amazed that such a large creature as Mickey was able to hide so well. It took them longer than Jack would have liked, but eventually they crouched against the outer wall. Only a few feet of stone separated them from the chapel. They could hear the Devil shouting inside the fort.

"I don't want excuses," the Dark One said. "I want that weapon found before Halloween Jack arrives. I will name whoever finds it Prince of the Americas once we conquer the world."

"Prince of the Americas," Mickey muttered, tapping his chin thoughtfully. "Quite a title. I wonder if that applies only to demons."

"Oh, you're funny," Jack said. "And looks aren't everything."

"That hurts me, Jack," Mickey said. "Hurts me to the bone."

"I'm sure," Jack said. "Now we need to figure out how to get in there without the Devil and his kin seeing us. Oh, and get the Tomahawk of the Four Winds and get out without them discovering us."

"Easily done," Mickey said.

He lifted Jack onto his shoulder and scaled the wall. Just below the edge, Mickey paused while a pair of Steam Soldiers and an imp patrolled by. They scrambled over the edge of the wall and crouched together on the chapel's roof.

"Now how do we get in?" Jack whispered.

Mickey pried up a section the roof large enough for them to drop down.

"How's that?" the ogre asked, and tossed the rubble to the far side of the Alamo.

"What was that?" something yelled with a voice like grinding metal.

The plaza of the Alamo filled with shouts and sounds of scurrying demons and Steam Soldiers.

"No!" The Devil's voice rang out over the din. "Don't send everyone. It might be a diversion."

"Crafty one, that Dark One is," Mickey said.

"Not too crafty for us, though," Jack replied.

He read the journal and counted out the steps from each wall to where the hatch to the secret chamber was hidden. Three steps from the altar and seven steps in from the wall.

"Would you mind?" Jack asked, gesturing to the spot he'd marked out.

"Can't you do anything yourself?" Mickey asked as he began scooping up dirt and rock as if his hands were giant shovels.

"What do you mean?" Jack said. "I came up with this plan. I'm the mastermind that's going to save the world."

"Well, I suppose." Mickey cleared the last of the earth from the wooden hatch. It turned out to be about a yard down. Three feet. That figured. "I'm just glad I'm not you after you climb out of that hole."

"I don't blame you," Jack said.

"It's not too late, Jackie Boy," Mickey said. The honest concern in his eyes touched Jack to the point he felt tears welling in his eyes. "You're a smart lad. Almost as smart as me. If we beat our heads together a bit, we could probably come up with another plan."

"Beating our heads together would only wind up with me unconscious."

"I didn't mean literally," Mickey said, "you silly git."

"I know." Jack shook his head and sighed. "It's got to be this way. It's the only way I'll be able to keep them in line for as long as that line will need to be kept."

"Alright then," Mickey said, and pulled the hatch up. A ladder led down into the darkness. "I'll see you in a few minutes."

Jack nodded, tucked his pumpkin jack o' lantern under his arm, and started climbing down.

The ladder had twenty-one rungs, just as Jack had thought there would be. A tunnel led off into darkness. He followed it for twenty-one paces. Again, just as he had expected. A door waited at the end of the tunnel. Jack placed his hand on the latch. Even though he knew the weapon beyond this door had been waiting for him, butterflies still danced in Jack's stomach. He was alone for the first time since that night when Saint Peter, Father McDermott, and Moira had told him of his birthright. No one was here for him to posture in front of. No one to see the façade of Halloween Jack that hung over John O'Brien. Jack and John stood in that tunnel alone with each other and the realization of what was coming. John and Jack cried for a good long while.

After the tears stopped, Halloween Jack opened the door.

The Tomahawk of the Four Winds lay on a stone pedestal. The head was a piece of carved obsidian just about as big as Mickey's hand. The haft wasn't wood, but the bone of some giant creature, and was as long as Jack's arm. And that was it. Jack had expected a bit more. Perhaps some feathers, or other ornamentation. Something, anything, more. But the weapon was just the head and the haft.

Jack looked at it for a moment, considering this ancient weapon that served no other purpose than to wait here for him to take it and save the world. He wondered if Mickey might be right. Was there some other way? Jack sighed. There might have been back when this whole thing started, but not now. He couldn't go back and change things. The irony of that thought made Jack snicker. No, he'd set events in motion to lead him to this path. As his father, his real father, had said time and time again in the tiny townhouse where John O'Brien had really grown up, *You're far too clever for your own good, John, and one day it'll be the death of you.* Well, Halloween Jack had turned out to be far more clever and far more foolish than John O'Brien had ever been.

Jack picked up the Tomahawk of the Four Winds. It wasn't as heavy as he thought it was going to be. As light as the wind, he supposed.

He hefted the weapon onto his shoulder, leaned against the wall, and waited. If he made it seem too easy, they might not buy it. With that thought, he took some dirt from the tunnel floor and smeared it over his face. He also struck himself in the forehead with his stick until he felt a trickle of blood run down his face.

"There," Jack said to himself. "Now I look like I've just retrieved a weapon that will kill the Devil."

* * *

A while later – it was hard to judge the passage of time in the darkness of that cave – Jack climbed up the ladder. The moment his head came into the chapel, a massive hand grabbed the back of his neck, and another covered his mouth before he could order his coat and stick to attack.

"Terribly sorry, Jackie Boy," Mickey said, "but it seems that princedom was open for anyone, and I just really like the sound of Mickey, Prince of the Americas."

Jack struggled against Mickey's grip, even tried biting the ogre's hand, but the ogre just chuckled.

"Excellent," the Devil said from just outside the chapel door. "I had a feeling it might be in here. No wonder we couldn't find it."

"Drop the axe, Jack," Mickey said. "Or I'll snap your neck like a twig."

Jack dropped the Tomahawk of the Four Winds. Mickey kicked it out the door. The Devil picked the weapon up and looked it over.

"I was expecting something more," the Dark One said, then shrugged. "It matters not. I have it, and I'll use it to crush the last hope your world has to escape me."

"I'm going to let you go, Jack," Mickey said. "Don't do anything stupid."

Mickey released Jack.

"Strike—"

Before he could speak the second word, Mickey slapped him. The blow sent Jack flying out of the chapel. Black spots danced across his vision, and his jaw hurt so much that he couldn't even begin to think about speaking.

Demons crowded around Jack, kicking and pummeling him. Jack curled into a ball, covering his head with his arms, trying his best to go someplace else to ignore the pain.

"Stop!" the Devil yelled. The beating stopped. "I understand your zealousness to repay him, but I don't want him killed...yet. Now someone get his things."

The demons all moved away from Jack.

"Oh, you bunch of babies," Mickey said.

Jack felt the ogre lift him off the ground and strip him of his coat and stick. Jack had dropped the jack o' lantern when the ogre had hit him. Jack tried to say something again, but every time he tried to move his mouth, pain shot through his head.

"Broke your jaw, Jack," Mickey said. "I told you not to do anything stupid."

Mickey put the coat and stick into a rough sack. The sack looked like it already had the jack o' lantern in it.

Mickey faced the Devil and held out the bag. "You don't mind if I hold onto these?" Mickey asked. "I want to show them off as trophies to the other ogres."

"By all means," the Devil said. "It's not like anyone else can use them. Please, bring him along."

Mickey grabbed Jack by a foot and dragged him up some stairs to overlook the courtyard of the Alamo. All the demons gathered below cheered at the sight of him beaten and defeated.

The Dark One addressed his kin. "Look at this wretch, this puny thing who has tried to take the place of Jack of the Lantern. I have defeated him in less than a fraction of the time it took to defeat The Lantern. The line of Jack of the Lantern holds no power over us! Remember, my children, every creature has a price. All we must do is be patient and victory will eventually be ours. Now that we have broken them, let us lay claim to this world!"

The demons cheered again.

"Prince Mickey of the Americas," the Devil said.

"My Lord," Mickey bowed.

"Would you kindly fetch the priest and meet us at the cottage?" the Devil asked. "I believe you know the way."

"As you command, My Lord," Mickey said. He waved the bag above Jack. "See you soon."

Mickey left, taking the bag with Halloween Jack's three treasures with him.

The Devil himself loomed over a battered and broken Halloween Jack. "I've won." He held the Tomahawk of the Four Winds out above Jack. "You've no coat, no stick, no lantern, and no weapon to use to kill me. All that you have fought for will soon be lost."

The Devil's laughter echoed across the plaza. The world shifted, and a moment later, that laughter echoed across the plain that held a simple cottage and the path leading to the Devil's Gate.

The plain was a mess with the ruined husks of Steam Soldiers littered everywhere. All around the cottage, demons groaned, unable to die, no matter how many injuries they suffered from the defenders. Jack recognized some of the soldiers and Captain Jameson. They'd turned the cottage into a fort. A mound of dirt had been erected around the cottage with sharpened stakes protruding from the dirt.

"Just a few more moments boys," Captain Jameson yelled, waving Daniel's ice gun. He stood on the roof between two of the Steam Soldiers.

The former Confederate soldiers had made some additions to the Steam Soldiers that Jack had given them. The two remaining Steam Soldiers had been fitted with a carriage in back that housed a pair of Gatling guns pointing over the shoulders. A host of about a hundred demons charged the cottage. One of the Gatling guns roared, spraying bullets into the assault. Moments later, those demons still capable of moving retreated.

A flight of gargoyles dove toward the cottage. A cannon sort of thing popped up next to the Captain. Daniel sat behind the weapon and fired a massive net made of metal. The net caught all but two of the gargoyles. Jack noticed a long wire connected the net to the cannon-like thing Daniel was operating. Daniel pulled on a crank at the top of the cannon. Electricity flashed through the wire and net. Gargoyles screamed as they fell to the earth. When the electricity stopped, the gargoyles lay twitching on the ground.

A great groaning of metal echoed across the plain, and all fighting stopped.

The great metal gates that had once kept the Devil's Gate closed, barring Hell from the Earth, rose and reattached themselves to become the Gates of Hell once more.

"Good girl," Jack said. Pain lanced through his head from his broken jaw, but it was worth it.

"It's a shame she's too late," the Devil said, and then shouted "Stop! I have both Halloween Jack and the Tomahawk of the Four Winds! Throw down your arms, and I will spare him."

Jack really hoped they would ignore the Devil and keep fighting. They didn't. In only a few minutes, all Jack's friends were standing in front of him, surrounded by all the hordes and legions of Hell. Mickey had arrived with Father McDermott. Jack wasn't really surprised that they had all stopped fighting; they didn't realize the Devil's weakness.

"We've stopped fighting," Moira said. "Let him go."

The Devil chuckled. "That was not the agreement. I only said I wouldn't harm him."

"Excuse me, My Lord," Mickey said.

"Yes?" the Devil said.

"You only promised that *you* wouldn't harm him."

"That is correct."

"Would you allow me a small bit of retribution for years of tedious servitude?"

"Absolutely," the Devil said. "Use this." The Dark One handed Mickey the Tomahawk of the Four Winds. "I will enjoy the irony of it."

"So will I," Mickey said. The ogre cocked his arm back. "Good-bye, Jack. Say hello to Saint Peter."

Jack closed his eyes. Even though he'd known this was coming, still, he didn't want to see it coming.

A moment later, the Tomahawk of the Four Winds slammed into Halloween Jack's head. His skull caved in. He heard Moira scream. Jack had barely enough time to think, *Oh Lord, that hurt,* before he died.

Eleven

"Please, no," said the soldier standing in front of Halloween Jack. "We died fighting to give you time."

Jack blinked a few times. A soothing light surrounded him. A line of people stretched out in front of him. The group of men directly before him wore the uniform of Confederate soldiers. Jack felt smaller than he had in all his life.

"Sorry, my friends," Jack said. "I had to die sometime. Everyone does. Don't worry. Saint Peter is going to be glad to see me. It's all part of the plan. I'll be sure to tell your friends you went to a decent place."

Jack left the line as two more people appeared behind him. He sprinted toward the giant pearl-gold gates in the distance.

The line was longer than Jack expected, though he didn't know why or what his basis for any kind of comparison was. As he ran down the line, he heard shouts from other people who were very unhappy to see him here. Jack ignored them. He had to get back, and only one person could send him there.

Just as he expected, he saw Saint Peter looking over his book and chatting with the person at the front of the line. Saint Peter still had the same serene look of patience about him, but the glow he emitted the last time Jack had seen him was absorbed by the permeating holy light of Heaven.

Jack waved at Saint Peter and cut to the front of the line, jostling an old lady out of the way.

"Excuse me," Jack said, lifting his hand and smiling guiltily, "but I'm kind of in a hurry, and you've got all eternity ahead of you. You understand, right?"

The lady blinked a few times in surprise. "Well, I, uh…"

"Thanks so much." Jack turned to Saint Peter, blinked himself, then turned back to the lady. She looked twenty years younger than she had a few moments before. "You're French? And you're speaking French. How can I understand you?"

"This is Heaven, Jack," Saint Peter said. "That's one of the tiniest miracles we can work here."

"You're that Halloween Jack fellow," the French lady said.

"I am," Jack said. "Would love to chat more, but can't."

And Jack would have loved to chat with her for as long as she liked. She had continued to grow younger and younger, until she seemed about Jack's age. She had dark hair, and even darker eyes – deep brown that invited him to sink into and drown in them. She smiled at him sweetly, and said, "A shame you have to run off. You seem wild and fun." Her voice was the warm kiss of a summer's breeze.

"You don't know the half of it," Jack said, and though it broke his heart, he turned his back on the French beauty. "I'm here." Jack said. "Can I come in?"

"I'm sorry, Jack." Saint Peter flipped through his book. He reached a page and read it over. "You can't. I've been keeping an eye on you. You've stolen jack o' lantern after jack o' lantern and used them to house candles blessed with the magic of Heaven. Not only that, you've lied again and again to kith and kin. You've even attempted a bargain with the Devil himself. Since you died without confessing your sin, if I let you in they might clip my wings."

Jack grinned. "I had a feeling you might say that. I suppose it's the torments of Hell for me."

"I *might* be able to get you time in Purgatory," Saint Peter said.

"Naw," Jack said. "I'd rather the torments of the Dark One's realm than the tedium of all that waiting."

"Well…if that's how you want it," Saint Peter said.

"Yeah. That's how I want it." Jack's grin grew even bigger and wider. It felt so good to do that without hurting. "Better send me to the Devil's Gate so I can ask to come in."

Saint Peter looked Jack over. His expression had changed from serene to curious.

"What?" Jack asked.

"A long, long time ago, I remember having a similar conversation with a relative of yours. However, he came here, shocked that he wasn't getting into Heaven even though he'd done me a kindness. He didn't realize that he'd unwittingly barred himself from gaining entrance to paradise. It was only by happenstance that he became the symbol humanity uses to protect itself on the darkest night. And now here you are, knowing that you're being kept out of Heaven on mere technicalities. You've fought the good fight to your death, and now you're going to fight it even more."

Jack nodded. "Someone has to do it. Didn't you say I was the best suited?"

"I did at that."

"Then why are we still discussing this? I've got a world to save."

"Good-bye, Jack," Saint Peter offered Halloween Jack his hand. "You're a good man."

Jack shrugged, reached out, and shook hands with a Saint. "Sometimes I have my moments. I'm ready."

"Not yet," the French, now young, lady, said. She stepped next to Jack, stood on her tiptoes, and kissed his cheek.

"What was that for?" Jack asked.

"You came to my town and saved it from a demon trying to spread a plague. You saved my grandchildren." Then she kissed him on the mouth.

A blush crept from his cheeks to his ears. For what seemed like the first time in his life, Halloween Jack did not have a retort prepared.

"Alright," Jack said after he caught his breath. "*Now*, I'm ready."

A moment later, Jack was lying on his back. He could hear Moira crying to his right. To his left, the Devil was ranting about something. Jack didn't bother to pay attention to what he was saying. The Devil paused, and all his minions and followers cheered. Jack had been waiting for that.

Halloween Jack sat up. The cheers died.

"Excuse me?" Jack said. "Might I get into Hell? It seems I've nowhere else to go."

The hordes and legions of Hell screamed as one. The Devil spun and sputtered in his surprise. Off to his side, Jack's friends and family knelt, guarded by demons and Steam Soldiers. Mickey was closest of all and still held the Tomahawk of the Four Winds.

Jack grinned.

"Oh, but first, coat, trap Mickey."

The bag tucked into Mickey's belt writhed and jerked with such force that it came free before Mickey could grab it. The sack fell to the ground, opening up. Jack's coat flew out of Mickey's sack and wrapped around the ogre.

"Stick, come back," Jack said.

The stick leapt out of the sack and flew into Jack's hand as he stood up.

Mickey struggled against the coat. Jack stepped up to the ogre, and gripping the stick with all four fingers, he slammed the stick against Mickey's wrist. The ogre cried out, and dropped the weapon.

"That was for my jaw," Jack shouted. Then Jack snatched up the Tomahawk of the Four Winds.

"Stop him," the Devil screamed. "Someone, stop him!"

"And this," Jack said, raising the Tomahawk of the Four Winds, and for once, not even the faintest hint of a smile "is for killing me." Jack leaned over and gently tapped Mickey lightly on the forehead with the Tomahawk.

The ogre screamed. His body went tense. He twitched once, twice, and thrice. His eyes rolled back in his head, and with a great gurgling sound, Mickey the ogre dropped to the ground. His chest neither rose nor fell.

"Coat, come back."

The ancient-styled black coat, with its orange silk sashes, came apart, releasing the unmoving ogre. The pieces of it flew through the air and came back together around Jack.

Halloween Jack turned to face all the hordes and legions of Hell. In one hand, he held his terrible ever-striking stick, in the other, he held the Tomahawk of the Four Winds. He grinned his widest, craziest grin and beckoned all those demons with his two weapons. He imagined a pair of dark eyes looking down on him from paradise and puffed up in his chest.

"Yes!" Jack yelled. "Someone stop me! Step right up. I bet you could all get me in a rush, but I promise, I'm going to go down fighting. Oh, yeah, and it's not like you can kill me again."

Jack took a single step forward.

Each and every demon took a step back.

Jack turned back to the Devil. The Devil glanced from Jack to Mickey's prone form.

"You knew the ogre was going to betray you," the Devil said.

"I had an idea that he was," Jack replied. "He was an ogre after all. If not him, you'd have gotten one of them to do it for you." Jack waved the Tomahawk of the Four Winds at the armies of Hell. "I arranged it so that I wasn't going to get into Heaven."

"Clever," the Devil said. "I thought killing you would get you out of my hair. People who actively fight me usually get a ticket to the front of the line."

"Too bad I'm a liar and a thief," Jack said. "Those two details kind of killed that plan, huh?"

"Right you are. I notice that you haven't used that thing on me." The Devil gestured to the Tomahawk of the Four Winds.

"No, I haven't. I will, if I have to, but I've got this dilemma in killing you. You're the evil that I know. I have plans of how to deal with you in charge of all of them." Again, Jack waved the ancient weapon at the assembled demons. "If I kill you, someone else is going to take your place. I have no idea what that is going to look like. I know that he," Jack waved his stick over at Naberius, "let me go, hoping I'd kill you so he could fill the void left by your absence."

Naberius let out a tiny *meep* when the Devil turned to stare at him.

"Don't act so surprised," Jack said. "You rule over demons."

"I'm not surprised in the least." The Devil turned back to Jack. "What do you propose?"

"Easy," Jack said. "I want things to go back to the way they were before. You and yours go back to your side of the Devil's Gate. Moira and her descendants will keep the Gate closed every night of the year except All Hallow's Eve. I'll be wandering about with my lantern." To emphasize this, Jack wandered over to Mickey's bag, pulled out the pumpkin, and lit the candles that were still inside. "I've got three candles; I might get an apprentice or two. Point is, you never know which of those lanterns will be me or mine."

The Dark One sighed. "Then I and all my kin will surely take care when we see them. I agree to these terms. Do we have an accord?"

"Not quite yet," Jack said. "Any members of my family who happen to find themselves in your care that you killed the night you broke loose must be freed to Purgatory."

"Fine," the Devil said. "I don't really relish the thought of watching over them for all eternity, worrying about when they are going to start trouble."

"And, Jack of the Lantern. You must free him into my custody."

"Fine," the Devil said. "He's not nearly so much fun now that he's lost his legendary status to you. But on this point you must actually give me something in return."

"Oh, this should be rich," Jack said. "What?"

"You have a scorpion demon bound in service to the hammer. He is a good and loyal servant – well, as loyal as a demon can be. I want him back. That one can take his place." The Devil waved at Naberius. "He no longer pleases me."

"But…but…" Naberius blubbered. "Please—"

"Oh, shut up," the Devil said, and waved his hand absently at Naberius. The Marquis's mouth vanished.

"Neat trick," Jack said.

"Unfortunately it only works on demons," the Devil replied. "I can think of a few others I'd like to be able to do that to."

Jack grinned.

"We go back to Hell and only venture forth again on the Darkest Night, unless of course, someone neglects the Ritual of Closing for an evening. Your relatives go to Purgatory. And I free Jack the blacksmith and give you Naberius, Marquis of Hell, in exchange for one semi-loyal scorpion demon."

"Sounds about right. Do we have an accord?"

"We do." The Devil offered his hand to Halloween Jack.

"Are you kidding?" Jack asked, and eyed the hand as if it were a serpent.

"One must try," the Devil said.

Jack rolled his eyes. "Yes, as long as I don't have to touch you, we have an accord."

"Excellent," the Devil said.

Naberius vanished. In his place stood the scorpion demon that had tried to kill Jack, and a portly, balding, middle-age man.

"Alright everyone," the Devil called, "we're going home!"

Many of the demons groaned, but despite their disappointment they began to file away through the Devil's Gate.

"Well played, Halloween Jack," the Devil said, "well played. I truly look forward to our next game."

"I'll be here whenever you want a lesson in clever and cunning," Jack said. "I'm not getting any older, anymore. Just know that next time, I won't be so nice."

Several of the demons in the Dark One's honor guard shuddered when Jack said that. Jack grinned at them and saluted with the Tomahawk of the Four Winds.

Now freed from their captors, Jack's friends rushed over to him. Moira reached him first. She hit him. Jack blinked in pain, and by the time he recovered Moira had her arms around him. After a few moments, she let him go. Jack came away from her embrace easily.

"Your coat?" Jack asked.

"In the cottage," Moira said. "I had to take it off for the ritual."

"You're a bastard, Jack," Daniel said. "I understand why you didn't tell us about the dying part, but you're a bastard."

"And that's why you wouldn't ever join me for confession," Father McDermott said.

"All part of the plan," Jack said. "Your reaction to me getting killed had to be real enough to convince the second greatest liar there is." He offered his hand to Captain Jameson. "Thanks for helping, Captain."

"It's Alistair," the retired officer said in that distinct accent of the Southern States. "That's what my friends call me."

Jack turned and watched as the Hordes and Legions of Hell filed back through the Devil's Gate.

"Enjoy this sight," Jack said. "God willing, no one will ever see it again."

After a few moments, Moira said, "They're far enough away, Mickey, you can get up."

The ogre sat up and took in a great gasp of air. "It's about bloody time."

Twelve

Halloween Jack sat back in his chair, drinking his tea, and smiling his first natural smile since the night he'd assumed the role of humanity's protector on the Darkest Night. The trophy of their victory, the Tomahawk of the Four Winds, lay in the center of the table. Moira, Daniel, and Father McDermott also sat around Moira's table. Mickey leaned against the back wall – he'd climbed over the walls and come in through the roof which hadn't been there since the morning the Devil's Gate came down. The soldiers were outside, cleaning weapons and tending to the wounded. John the blacksmith, who had once been Jack of the Lantern, stared out the back window at the Devil's Gate.

"When did you figure it out?" Daniel asked.

Everyone had calmed down since the ogre's "resurrection." Jack thought he would probably chuckle for at least a decade the way Father McDermott and some of the soldiers had shrieked. In fact, he laughed right then.

"What?" Father McDermott asked.

"Nothing," Jack replied, and went back to drinking his tea.

Truthfully, that had been the only amusing part. The rest of Jack's friends were ready to kill the ogre. If Moira hadn't been on Jack's side, they probably would have tried. Moira was the one who suggested tea while they let Jack explain.

"I should have realized earlier," Moira said, "but watching Mickey split Jack's skull traumatized me beyond rational thought. I started putting pieces together when Jack sat up. I remembered the first favor Jack asked Mickey, 'Bring no harm to anyone of the line of Jack of the Lantern.' So the fourth favor must have been to counteract the first, but only for Jack specifically."

"So even if the Tomahawk didn't kill Mickey," Daniel said, "why didn't you use it on the Devil and be done with it?"

"Because the Tomahawk doesn't actually do anything," Jack said. "It's just an elaborate prop."

"What?" everyone asked at once, even Mickey.

"Well, at first I wanted Saint Peter to make me a weapon that I could use to kill the Devil. Saint Peter told me that he couldn't actually create that kind of weapon, even with a heavenly wish. It took some explaining that I didn't want a weapon that could do it. I just wanted a weapon with a story to make people think it could. So Saint Peter went and put everything into place so that we could chase after the Tomahawk of the Four Winds. That's why the house seemed so out of place in that neighborhood. It's also why it had to be a weapon and story native to the Americas. I got the idea that night when the imp that was trying to kill me with the Steam Soldiers said something about them still trying to figure things out on this new continent. They wouldn't have time to verify the truth of the story.

"Mickey was the perfect straight man for me. Being an ogre, the Devil assumed that Mickey would betray me in hopes for a title and other rewards."

"I still like the sound of Mickey, Prince of the Americas," the ogre said.

"You would," Moira said. "Why didn't you betray Jack?"

"I had agreed to do him four favors. One of which I hadn't taken care of at that point. Besides, I'm fond of the world just the way it is. Don't like demons. Can't trust them. Now, don't say a word. I've been a good companion."

"That you have," Moira said.

"Here, here," Daniel added. "A finer companion we couldn't ask for, even if you did kill our cousin."

"A sham," Father McDermott said, staring at the Tomahawk. "You gambled the fate of the world on a sham."

"Not entirely," Jack said. "I actually had to die without confessing some pretty nasty sins – and no, I don't want to go into the details – so that when I did die, I couldn't get into Heaven. Saint Peter sent me to the Devil's Gate so I could ask to get into Hell. I had to become more terrible than Jack of the Lantern, which meant I had to be eternal, just like he was, otherwise, they could just wait me out."

"Now what?" Daniel asked.

"We wait," Jack said. "He's going to try again. He can't help himself. When he comes, I'll be waiting for whatever he pulls."

"What about us?" Moira asked.

"Well, you guys, too," Jack said. "If you're still around."

"What do you mean?" Daniel asked.

John the Blacksmith cleared his throat. "How long did it take the Devil to get the better of me? And I'm not nearly as clever and cunning as Halloween Jack is. Basically though, the Devil is patient, and he knows one of Halloween Jack's advantages is that he has all of you. He'll probably wait until Jack is alone to strike again."

Silence fell around the table as they all sipped their tea.

"I suppose that's it for me then," John the Blacksmith said. "I should be heading to my new home."

"New home?" Moira asked.

"I'm not the feared Jack of the Lantern anymore," John said. "There's nothing keeping me out of Hell, where I was supposed to go in the first place."

"About that," Jack said. "Saint Peter, I'd like to cash in my third wish now."

A few moments later, perhaps a total of three moments later, someone knocked on the door. Moira hopped up from her chair and opened it. Saint Peter stood there in all of his saintly radiance.

"Might I come in?" Saint Peter asked.

"Absolutely," Moira said. "May I get you some tea?"

"No, thank you," Saint Peter said as he entered. "You've taken over a year for this, Jack. What would you like?"

"I wish for John the Blacksmith, formerly known as Jack of the Lantern, to be forgiven his trespasses as is only right for the centuries he has walked the earth, alone and lonely, so that he could protect humanity from the Devil and his kin on the Darkest Night."

John the Blacksmith's mouth moved up and down, trying to form words. Finally, he managed, "You're using your last wish to grant me passage to Heaven?"

"That I am, Grandfather of mine," Halloween Jack said. "You've suffered enough torment and loneliness." Jack turned to Saint Peter. "Is that alright, or are we going to argue over this wish, too?"

"Granted," Saint Peter said, "with no arguments. Shall we go John?"

"Thank you," John said to Halloween Jack.

"It's the least I could do," Jack said. "I'm not going to send my grandfather into the clutches of the Dark One if I have a way to stop it, and I do."

Moira got up and embraced John.

"I won't be able to bring you books anymore," John said.

"I think I can live with that," Moira said, tears rolling down her cheeks.

"I can get the books," Jack said. "Now off you go, before I change my mind."

"You cannot change your wish once is it made," Saint Peter said. "Good-bye, Halloween Jack."

In a flash of light, Saint Peter and John the Blacksmith were gone.

"Where will you go, Jack?" Moira asked.

"I'll wander," Jack replied. "It's part of the job. I'll be back by once a year or so, around the end of October."

"You get lonely," Daniel said, "you know where the smithy is."

Jack nodded. "I might stop in from time to time."

Halloween Jack pushed his chair away from the table, put his mug down, and picked up the Tomahawk of the Four Winds. He shook hands with Daniel and Father McDermott.

Moira pulled off her boots. "Halloween Jack, I give you these boots as a member of my bloodline." She handed them to him. "These will speed you back to us when you get too lonely."

"Thank you, cousin," Jack said, and slid them on. "But you keep the coat and chair. You might need them."

He pulled her into his arms and held her tight.

"I'll miss you," Jack said.

"No you won't," Moira replied. "You'll find some kind of trouble to distract you before too long."

Jack shrugged, "Maybe. But it isn't going to be the same without you."

And with nothing left to say, Jack left through the cottage's back door. Alistair Jameson was waiting for him. The Captain saluted Jack as he came out.

"You, sir, are one crafty fellow," Alistair said. "I'm glad we're on the same side. I wanted to let you know the boys and I are going to stick around, keep an eye on things here and at the smithy. And to be honest, I think a few of the men have taken a shine to Miss Moira."

"You make sure they treat her like the lady she is," Jack said, "or they'll answer to me."

"They'll answer to both of us," Alistair said.

They shook hands, and Jack continued on toward the Devil's Gate.

After seven paces – Jack rolled his eyes at that – Mickey fell into step beside him.

"Really?" Jack asked.

Mickey laughed the deep rumbling laugh of an ogre. "I couldn't resist."

Jack lengthened his stride a bit, while Mickey shortened his.

"Don't you think you've stirred up enough trouble for one day?" The ogre asked.

"Not even by half," Jack said. "I need him to know how thoroughly I got him."

"Normally, I'd warn against it," Mickey said, "but in this case, I think you're right. Especially since he's not going to come to the gate himself."

"That's unlikely," Jack agreed.

They walked together in quiet until they reached the massive gates to Hell. Jack rapped the haft of the Tomahawk of Four Winds against the gate, and for a moment he thought he saw a horseshoe embedded in the iron of the gate. Jack shook his head and waited. A slot opened in the door, two beady red eyes looked out, and immediately the imp started blubbering.

"Relax," Jack said. "I'm not going to do anything. I just want your master to have this."

Jack handed the imp the Tomahawk of the Four Winds and walked away.

"He's going to be mad," Mickey said.

"Most likely," Jack replied.

They passed the cottage, and when they came to the edge of that place that lies between all places, a great and furious roar echoed out from inside the walls of Hell so that the Devil's Gate rattled and shook.

"Yeah," Jack said. "I'd say he's pretty angry."

Again, Mickey laughed his deep, rumbling ogre laugh as they continued walking.

After a few hours, Mickey asked. "What's Heaven like? I'll never go there. Nor will I go to Hell. When my kind dies, we just fade from the world, but it would be nice to know what Heaven is like."

"Heaven is…" And that's the point when Jack realized he couldn't recall much about Heaven. He knew he'd spoken to some people, and a pair of dark eyes flashed in his mind, a pair of eyes that invited him to dive in and drown. "I know what Heaven was for me, but it would be hard to explain. I think Heaven is different for everyone."

"Fair enough. Mind if I tag along?"

"Not at all. Don't have any plans until the Devil stirs up trouble again. You?"

"None that I can think of. I'm happy just to not be beating on that anvil anymore."

They walked for a time in silence, then Mickey said, "We could see if any other holidays need shaking up. If you want?"

SINGLE STEPS

THROW DOWN

You had to be there. Seriously. People talk about it, and you think you get the idea of what it was like, the same way people talk about Wylowyn of the Wood matched wit and ego with Grea of the Thorn, Brom "Bigaxe" O'Brien's battle with the Banshee of Black Blood Bog, and when the Heroes of the Spear finally trapped the last thirteen members of Prospero's Disciples in the Forest of Arden and defeated them in one last, glorious battle. Stories abound about each of those uberly epic moments, and still, if you didn't see them, you really didn't know.

See, I was there. Saw each of them. Wandering minstrel. Well, I used to be, before…well, I'm getting ahead of myself. See, my job was to make sure I was at the right place at the right time, and I paid a pretty hefty penny for divination spells so that I could do my job to the best of my ability. I did that because I don't have much in the way of real talent. Back when I was still wandering and singing, I made up for it by being able to witness, first hand, the events that would become the songs people wanted to hear over and over and over…and pay the money to hear them over and over and over.

And then, one evening, at the Bardic Gathering of Beltane, late in the night, Vincent the Vociferous and Elizabeth the Eloquent both stepped up to the fire at the same moment. Neither felt that they should have to step back for the other. They just stood there, looking each other up and down, up and down, until finally, at the same moment, both began to perform, and moments after that, they both began trying to outperform the other.

Thing is…they were both so good, so masterful at their craft, the Vociferous at his storytelling and the Eloquent at her singing, that within a few heartbeats, their performances meshed together into a call and response story-song unlike anything I've ever heard of, much less witnessed. They went on like that, stories and songs weaving together all through the night, until finally, as dawn broke over the horizon, they finished, bowed to the audience, bowed to each other, and left.

After that, I couldn't do the minstrel thing any more. Oh, sometimes I brush off my mandolin and play sitting on the bar top, but I much prefer tending a single tavern than I ever did wandering between them. You ever get a chance though, head to the Bardic Gathering at Beltane. Every year, on the last night, Vincent the Vociferous and Elizabeth the Eloquent step to the fire at the exact same moment and try to outperform the other. Won't be like anything you've ever seen or heard in all your life and wildest dreams.

POWER OF SYMBOLS

On his third date with Alison, Mark asked about the semi-colon tattoo just behind her left ear. She smiled at him with her head titled slightly downward so that she was looking at him through her raven bangs. He wanted to drown in her crystal blue eyes.

Alison answered, "When I was younger, I almost committed suicide; I got this tattoo instead."

"Why a semi-colon?"

"Suicide, like a period, signifies an ending; a semi-colon is a pause before a continuation; instead of ending, I continued."

"That's kind of awesome," Mark said.

Alison's smile grew wider, "Thanks."

They went on a few more dates before Alison invited Mark up to her apartment. Two more dates after that, she invited him to spend the night. That's when he saw her body, arms, and legs covered with tattoos of semi-colons. He paused long enough for Alison to notice.

"I know I have a lot; it's been a hard life."

Mark took in the sight of all of her pain paired with the courage to go on despite the pain.

"It's beautiful; you're beautiful." He rubbed the semi-colon, the first one he'd noticed, with his thumb as he kissed her. "But, I want to make sure you don't ever have to get another one of those again."

Mark kept his promise; Alison never got another tattoo.

MIND BLOWN
(A story in six words)

FTW is just WTF, in reverse.

THE CYCLE OF PAIN AND SUFFERING IN BEHAVIORAL CORRECTION

"You see that recruit over there?" Vance said, gesturing with his chin.

"The one giving you the stink eye?" Simons asked.

"That's the one," Vance replied. "That was me, back in the day."

That day happened to be only a year and a half ago, but with all the combat they'd seen, it might as well have been a dozen lifetimes.

"He's got something to prove," Vance continued. "For him, recruit training was fun. Not anything that made him suffer. Now, he wants to prove that he's just as tough as those of us who have been deep in the blood and bones of our enemies. He's going to find out who everyone respects most, and then come over and try to use me to prove his point. I'm going to warn him. He's going to ignore me. After he starts something, I'm going to choke him out. When he wakes up, I'm going to kick him in the head three times, and walk away. Hopefully, he only needs that to happen once."

"Ha!" Simons said. "I'd forgotten when that guy, what was his name?"

"Black Tom."

"Yeah, Black Tom. When Black Tom did that to you. What ever happened to him anyway?"

"Jumped on a grenade for me," Vance said.

"To Black Tom." Simons raised his flask.

"Black Tom." Vance raised his.

They drank to the fallen until the recruit stomped over to them, posturing with a puffed-up chest the whole way.

"What's your name, kid?" Vance asked.

"Levi," the recruit said, "and I ain't your kid."

"Look, Levi. This is going to end poorly for you. I'm going to give you one chance to back down."

Levi did not back down. Vance choked him out, waited for him to regain consciousness, and kicked him in the head three times.

A little over a year later, Levi said, "You see that recruit over there. That was me, back in the day."

DEAD WEIGHT: The Tombs

A Tale of the Faerie War

M. Todd Gallowglas

For Alice LaPlante

Without you Dead Weight *would have remained a simple action-adventure novelette lost within itself. Thank you for guiding me to the rich and terrible world surrounding this story.*

Acknowledgements

First and foremost, I have to thank my wife, Robin, for her patience and understanding with the collective story of *Dead Weight*. She was the first person to read the original novelette in September of 2007. She's seen it through all its rough edges, and believe me, it's had quite a few. Even at times when I felt this story was too big for my meager talent, she kept at me, asking, "When are you going to finish *Dead Weight?*" Thanks, as always, for believing.

Second, I have to thank my editor, whose patience comes in only slightly behind Robin's. I'm keeping my editor on the edge with this one, not just in scope, but we're both out of our comfort zones. Thanks, as always for taking these jumbles of words I spew onto the page into a story.

Mathew Clark Davidson. We didn't see eye to eye on a lot of things when I was taking classes from him. This installment would not exist if he hadn't given a writing prompt with, "The character has to solve the problem with fire." He was also the one who gave me the first glimpse of how massive the world of Dead Weight is.

I'd be remiss if I didn't mention my cohort in crime, and the true foundation of the Genre Underground, Christopher Kellen, for the cover and helping to keep me relatively sane while I raced to the finish line on this one.

Thanks to John McDonnell for translating the Irish. You'll have your work cut out for you in future installments.

Joe, Hoover, Victor, and all the awesome guys out at the Vacaville Airsoft field for being my weekend brothers in arms. Being able to head out to the field and face simulated death on a regular basis has really stepped up my game in writing fight scenes.

Brian and Cody (and sometimes Jenni) for putting up with me during Wednesday night writing night.

SINGLE STEPS

You should all bow before the folks at my two local Starbucks for keeping me well-caffeinated, as they have with so many books.

And a final thank you in two parts. First to Tim O'Brien for writing "The Things they Carried," and second, to Paul Bailiff for assigning that story in Fundamentals of Creative Reading. These were the butterfly's wings that instigated the storm that is *Dead Weight*.

M. Todd Gallowglas

DEAD WEIGHT:
The Tombs

...while I discovered that my own exploration of Faerieland had only just begun. In the countryside, the old stories seemed to come alive around me; the faeries were a tangible aspect of the landscape, pulses of spirit, emotion, and light. They "insisted" on taking form under my pencil, emerging on the page before me cloaked in archetypal shapes drawn from nature and myth. I'd attracted their attention, you see, and they hadn't finished with me yet.
— Brian Froud

Now begin in the middle, and later learn the beginning; the end will take care of itself.
– " 'Repent Harlequin!' Said the Ticktockman" Harlan Ellison

EPILOGUE, THE FIRST

If my doctor told me I had only six minutes to live, I wouldn't
brood.
I'd type a little faster.
– Isaac Asimov

Be grateful for whoever comes,
because each has been sent as a guide from beyond.
— Rumi

Max blinked down at the metal blade sticking out of his chest just to the left of his sternum. He couldn't tell if it was a sword or spear or…well…did it really matter at this point?

Ha! He thought. *Point! Good one.*

He might have laughed if he hadn't been coughing up blood all over his chin at that moment. Or, maybe that *is* laughing when you have something metal sticking through your chest.

That shouldn't have been possible. Not with his gray T-shirt on. Max closed his eyes, hoping things would be different when he o-pened them again. A futile effort, yeah. Dying men will grasp for anything they can to suck wind just a little while longer. Max o-pened his eyes. The bloody mess of the blood-covered point still stuck out of his chest. Odd though…it didn't hurt even close to how much he would have expected.

Blood dripped from the tip – Max tried to ignore the fact that it was his blood – onto the newspapers, parchments, and books that covered the table. It was a few drops at first, and then the flood-gates opened. He remembered a time back in the war, marching a-long with a platoon of Marines, when he saw a waterfall that same color spilling down a cliffside at sunset.

Glancing over his shoulder, Max saw a petite figure in a deep gray long coat, complete with a hood. Shadows hid most of the face inside that hood, but he saw a narrow chin and thin lips painted in gray lipstick matching the coat. Like pillars, two platinum-blond braids fell out of the hood and framed that chin.

"I know you," Max said.

The girl nodded. Or was she a woman? Max couldn't remember.

It might be the blood loss, but Max couldn't remember how long it had been since he thought of himself as "Max." Years, maybe, perhaps a decade or more. Then again, it might have been only a few weeks. The room spun around him as his head grew dizzy with blood loss. He remembered one of the foundations of the Old Knowledge he hadn't considered in a long, long while: *Time becomes fluid and mutable at the slightest touch of Faerie.*

"Is that all?" Max asked.

"That should do it," she replied with a whisper, and backed away.

As she retreated, blending into the shadows, the blade slid out of his chest. *Holy fucking Christ Buddha badger fuck*, Max screamed in his mind. That hurt more than he had words to describe, and he owned a lot of words and had used those words to describe a lot of things.

A moment later, the girl was gone.

Max waited for his life to flash before his eyes.

Unfortunately, human lives have too much extraneous crap filling up the meaningless moments for a whole life to flash before a dying person's eyes. Rather, people must see what is most important to them. Max had spent the better part of his life twisting and manipulating names and words, so that's what came to him, names, words, and titles: Max, Lies, Boy Scout, Champion, Friend, Hero, Traitor, Father, Son, Writer, Journalist, and the one he hated most of all, Bard.

Bard…Bard…Bard…a blessing and curse to all who held that title.

Eyelids half-closed, the waterfall slowing to a trickle, Max saw one piece of paper untouched by his blood on the far corner of the table. Somehow, not a single drop touched that piece of paper. He loved the sight of an unblemished page, full of infinite possibilities of what a writer or artist might create. If only he had time to fill that page, but alas, it was too late. Then, an odd quote came to mind, a quote by Lao Tzu: *Time is a created thing*. Paring that with the Old

Knowledge, *Time becomes fluid and mutable at the slightest touch of Faerie*, Max understood he had one chance to save his life. It was a desperate move, but moments like these are the perfect time for desperate moves. And perhaps because it was such a desperate move, he also thought it might give him the chance to set things right.

Max dabbed his right index finger into the wound on his chest.

Funny, he thought, *I thought that would hurt more.*

He slumped forward, placed his bloodied finger on the paper, and wrote four letters.

S-T-O-P.

Everything did, including the blood flowing out of his chest.

A scrap of paper poked out from under the sheet containing those bloody letters. Max took the scrap and read the words written on it in a curving, sweeping hand, in Irish, no less...

> *Tá sé in am scéal Tommy a chríochnú.*
> Translation:
> *Time to finish Tommy's story.*

Since he had nothing but time, Max took out his pen and the beat-up journal where he'd started Tommy's story and started writing.

SINGLE STEPS

THE TOUR:
A Prologue of Sorts

...but nothing is ever lost nor can be lost.
The body sluggish, aged, cold, the ember left from earlier fires shall duly flame
again.
— Walt Whitman

How should we be able to forget those ancient myths that are at the beginning of
all peoples, the myths about dragons that at the last moment turn into
princesses; perhaps all the dragons of our lives are princesses who are only
waiting to see us once beautiful and brave. Perhaps everything terrible is in its
deepest being something helpless that wants help from us.

So you must not be frightened if a sadness rises up before you larger than any
you have ever seen; if a restiveness, like light and cloudshadows, passes over your
hands and over all you do. You must think that something is happening with
you, that life has not forgotten you, that it holds you in its hand; it will not let
you fall. Why do you want to shut out of your life any uneasiness, any miseries,
or any depressions? For after all, you do not know what work these conditions
are doing inside you.
— <u>Letters to a Young Poet</u>, Rainer Maria Rilke

Military historians argue the reasons the enemy devastated the United States so much in the early years of the Faerie War. In hindsight it really shouldn't be that big a mystery; the United States simply forgot too much of the Old Knowledge. If they hadn't, they would have been much better prepared.

From the moment the white man displaced the first Native American tribe, the United States sowed the seeds of its later inability to deal with the aggression from Faerie in the middle of the Twenty-First Century. Only the artists and those who lived on the fringes of society seemed to remember, and we know how the U.S. felt about *those people*. Thus, America lacked the resources to stem the early onslaught. Perhaps that is why the Unseelie chose to make the United States the focal point of its reentry into the human world.

279

As it is in the wake of all great conflicts of the modern era, now that the Faerie War is over, people yearn and strive to recapture the cultural mythology of all our forefathers and to make sense of a war with an enemy that we are unlikely to ever make sense of.

Some people study, spending time on the internet, in libraries, and delving into dark corners of occult and arcane bookstores, searching for the minutest details of faerie lore and legend to better deal with the world as it is after the war. Others, those who are not so academically minded, take tours.

Every day, thousands of people take pictures of the blackened crater in Washington, D.C. where the original Capitol used to stand. The crater still smokes today. They visit the fortress that sprang up in Central Park that took the military over three years of constant siege to capture. Just recently, the air space above and inside the Grand Canyon has become safe enough for people to fly through to see the last strongholds of the fey in our world.

However, unlike many previous wars, the most popular tours aren't of battle sites. This was a war unlike any remembered, save in myths and legends. The most important conflicts weren't fought by soldiers. To truly understand the Faerie War, people flock to see those places where visionaries created works of art striving to repel the invasion before it began.

One of the most popular tours is in the San Francisco Bay Area. This tour, thanks to magic left over from the Faerie War, teleports people from site to site to see the artwork of a girl, a girl who saw through the cracks in reality before any other person in the world. She was the first to fight with her spray paint cans and paint brushes and pastels. Her best efforts came to nothing, because of the best of intentions of a boy who only wanted to help make his community a nicer place.

The tour begins in the girl's childhood bedroom. When people pay their twenty dollars in the foyer of the house she grew up in, the underpaid state park employee hands them a set of headphones. Each of these devices narrates the tour, beginning from the moment one reaches the top of the stairs and turns left into the bedroom. The voice is a pleasant male voice, containing a slight tremor.

"Let us begin with the south wall. It contains pictures that the artist…" – nowhere in the tour or any literature is the girl named; names have power, even after so much time, to affect things in the world that are better left alone; so, as it is with every such tour, she is referred to always as *the artist* – "…colored and painted in pre-school and kindergarten." These contain images, different colors blending together, and of stick-figure people fighting stick-figure monsters.

"You may notice that, even in their simplicity, something about them draws you. Occasionally when the light hits a picture just right, or if perhaps, you look at a picture from just the right angle, those simple pictures might seem to move a little bit. If you do manage to notice this effect, keep it to yourself. Any time someone tries to call this to the attention of someone else, the effect stops, and the magic of that moment is lost.

"Let us turn to the west wall. These are works the artist created in elementary school. You will notice the increasing complexity and that she painted creatures that we take for granted now – in all their alien wonder. Some of the pictures are of familiar forms: dragons, unicorns, elves, pixies, sprites, and ogres. Others are bizarre creatures with a single leg, or three arms, or eyes all around their heads. The impressive thing isn't that she painted these things, even though she painted them even before the war; it's that her artwork, even at the young age that she created it, fills viewers with such wonder that they feel like a child hearing their first fairy tales again. Don't you agree?

"Allow me to draw your attention to a specific picture: two rows in from the left and five down. The one displaying a scene with a faerie lady standing over a knight on one knee."

The work is done in watercolor paint with alternating long and short strokes. The background is blended shades of green, brown, and yellow. The lady is dressed in red and silver, and the knight's armor is gray and black. The lady holds a sword with a blue blade, and she's touching the knight's shoulder with it.

"Some people claim that while looking at the lady for more than a few moments that they can feel a warm breeze in their hair and the sword's leather hilt pressing into their hands. Others will tell you that if you look at the knight long enough that you'll feel the cold edge of a blade caressing the side of your neck. Do you? Don't answer yet if you are skeptical of such things. Look for a moment without thinking too much about it, and you may feel what the artist intended you to feel.

"By now, you have no doubt noticed the centerpiece of this wall has several ribbons next to it. These are the only official prizes her work has ever received."

This picture of a dragon was colored with crayons on lined binder paper. The thirty-four vertical blue lines and the one horizontal red line are this picture's only background. The face of a dragon fills three-quarters of the paper. The scales begin with light green, shaded with gray on the outside of the beast's snout and darkening to almost black in the center. Its eyes are gold with flecks of red. Its lips curve upward at the very edges, as if this creature understands more about the viewer than the viewer does.

"Can you feel the warmth of the creature's breath on your face? Do you hear a subtle chuckling in the back of your mind? If not, don't feel bad. Not everyone does."

On the north wall the work gets more elaborate. These are the paintings – real paintings rendered on canvas – that she did in her high school years.

"Notice how these paintings show noble faerie lords and ladies hunting in woods of weeping willows with watery tears where the leaves should be and also shows epic battles between the two ruling courts of Arcadia: the Seelie and Unseelie. See how the artist chose to represent the Seelie court with bright colors and depicts them as knights in radiant armor, while she portrays the Unseelie court as grim and dark, with the relatively human-looking of them possessing demonic features. At this point, we all know these are not accurate portrayals of these creatures. The fey do not conform to humans ideals of good and evil, light and dark. They are alien creatures whose morality is something far removed from human ethics. Many people have wondered why the artist chose to portray the courts in such a way, but without being able to speak directly to her, the mystery will remain."

The centerpiece of this wall is an oil painting that the girl cre0-ated during a special summer school for the arts. It's four feet by three feet and depicts a scene where two faerie armies clash around two mortal champions. Seelie knights ride unicorns and griffins into the battle, while the Unseelie ride giant buzzards and dragons. The infantries of both sides clash with sword and spear and claw and fang. The air throughout the battle is charged with magical energy. Even with all this chaos, there remains a wide circle around the two mortals who are playing a game of chess, seemingly undistracted by the conflict that rages around them. While standing near this wall, tourists can almost hear the trees crying, the tromp of unicorn, and the faint screams of the wounded on the battlefield amidst the clash of steel on steel. They smell of blood and fresh loam, and the chill wind of forests older than anything we know on earth tickles the hair of the arm. And underneath all that, they hear the tick, tick, tick, of the chess clock and one of the players sigh in displeasure at his opponent's previous move.

"This painting has drawn people to ask many questions: Why are these two people playing a game in the middle of this fighting? Do they even know the battle is there? Which of these two scenes is real? Are they even in the same place? Why do the fey leave them alone to play their game?"

At this point, the tour jumps to other locations. After the girl left high school, she became a graffiti artist. Her work appears in many secret and out-of-the-way places throughout the San Francisco Bay Area. Her paintings appear in tunnels, under overpasses, on walls of alleyways. These works generally take up the entirety of whatever surface she used for a canvas. People are ushered through the locations quickly, because the physical sensations felt in the presence of the works can become addicting. One painting in an alley in downtown San Francisco depicts a riverbed where a group of nyads (a type of water fey) and dryads (fey spirits bound into trees) are singing and playing harps, lutes, and pan pipes. This alley is always seventy-three degrees Fahrenheit, no matter the time of day or the weather, and the faint whisper of a song can be heard as if a radio is playing at low volume just around the corner. The side effects of this painting have required round-the-clock security to turn away any of the homeless who try to squat here.

The voice in the headphones accompanies the tourists to each location on the tour as both moderator and one-sided conversationalist.

Eventually the tour returns to the girl's house, and the visitors can look behind the curtain of the final wall, the east wall, which is dominated by a single piece. This is a painting of a door with a single, old-fashioned keyhole.

"This concludes our regular tour. For the expanded tour, which allows you to look through the keyhole, please see information desk for the release form and appropriate donation rates. Thank you. Have a great day, and we hope to see you again."

That is where the recorded voice stops.

Not everyone has the courage or the curiosity to sign the release and look through the keyhole. These days, most people understand that exposing themselves to anything having to do with faerie magic is a gamble and that the odds are not in their favor.

For those who do sign the waver and look through the keyhole, most will only see a beautiful, though very small, picture of the girl's parents' bedroom. It also shows her parents, dead always in the way the viewer fears most to die: hanging, burning, murder, sickness – it doesn't matter what the fear, the magic of this tiny painting always knows. However, a few very rare and unique individuals see what the girl saw. That's why this tour and others like it remain open, and will remain open so long as the government stands. Tours like these are the surest way to find artists who can take up where the girl left off.

This bears some explanation.

The barrier between realities is not equal in all places. Sometimes cracks form between one world and another. These cracks usually happen in out-of-the-way or secret, hidden places: under beds, behind furniture, in backyards hidden behind that tangle of bushes and shrubs that never seems to get pruned; and in places where children and artists gather: galleries, playgrounds, jungle gyms, avant-garde coffee houses; or where the human mind slips from the realm of normal perceptions: mental wards, crack houses, Burning Man. These cracks and holes are usually too small to see, mostly because the average human is too busy with the minutia of their banal life to notice anything of true wonder. But then, they are not the gifted ones; they are not the artists, the madmen, that the rest of humanity looks at whom they shake their heads with pity. "Normal" people don't understand these people or the pity they feel for them. They cannot comprehend that by seeing through the cracks in the world these gifted and mad artists destined for lives of hardship, unhappiness, and alienation.

In the moment just before most "normal" people looking through the keyhole would grasp what is it to live with the gift and curse these artists possess, they look away – and most of them forget.

Most.

Those few who do not look away soon find themselves creating their own works of art, whether painting, music, poetry, sculpting, etc. They see the cracks between the worlds. They see into Faerie and all its breathtaking wonder, madness, and horror. It is a timeless land that knows nothing of death. It is a realm of gnarled gardens, mountains of half-gnawed bones, and of primeval forests, lush and dark in both beauty and savagery. These forests writhe alongside concrete jungles, thick with artfully bent metal and snowflakes of broken glass. Almost-Victorian estates rest upon shorelines scattered with carcasses of sailing vessels, thousands of ships carved from the fossilized remains of giant beasts that dwarf the greatest of dinosaurs. Satyrs and centaurs frolic in meadows of red grass where the heads of human babies grow in place of dandelions. Those who have the talent to see beyond static reality take up their art as champions against the fey who still seek to threaten this world. The war may be over, but as it has for millennia, the threat of Faerie remains. Only this time, several gates between Earth and Faerie remain open. Because of that, this tour, with a tiny picture inside that keyhole, remains open in the hope that enough mad and brilliant artists will awaken to fight and hold the Unseelie at bay.

UNINVITED GUESTS

Oh, for a muse of fire that would ascend the brightest heaven of invention…
— <u>Henry V</u>, William Shakespeare

A very little key will open a very heavy door.
— <u>Hunted Down</u>, Charles Dickens

One of the stops on the girl's tour is in the Tombs. Before the Faerie War, the Tombs used to be the Mission District and Potrero Hill. Now, it's a no-man's-land surrounding the largest portal to Faerie in the whole world. Because of the dangers lurking throughout the Tombs and its proximity to the gate, this spray-painted mural of a fiery redheaded girl wearing a coat of peacock feathers greeting a man in golden armor as he steps out of a nimbus of light is the tour's only stop in this neighborhood. The government doesn't want to pay for the security required to keep the other three known locations of the girl's art safe.

The dingy and run-down buildings get only intermittent power at best, adding another challenge to security. The human squatters and transients who live in the Tombs use battery powered lanterns, when they can get batteries. When they can't, they go without. Most consider the risk of fire too great. However, candlelight does flicker without fail in one window, no matter the time, day or night. Even with the risk of fire, none of the residents do anything about it. They've learned that the man who lives in that particular apartment will not allow anything to happen to that continuous flame. That candle belongs to a man who met the artist girl once when they both were very young and both had the best of intentions.

The man woke and rubbed the grime from his eyes, feeling much older than his twenty-eight years. He heaved a breath that was somewhere between a sigh and a growl. His high had faded too soon, but then, it was always too soon. He had a name, had had many names, but he only used one name now. Those few times he spoke to other people, he told them to call him Boy Scout. He'd earned the name in what felt like a lifetime ago. Hell, he'd even deserved it back then. Now, he kept the name for irony's sake, and as another way to punish himself.

Boy Scout took his hands away from his eyes. A flame danced on top of a candle set on the crate in the center of the room. That flame was his security. When Boy Scout had to wander from home, he always had a Zippo in hand – not just with him, but in his hand. He'd stroke its smooth surface with his right thumb, the one with the tattoo for the Chinese character for south.

He flung his blanket aside. The chill of the night air hit his naked skin, but he didn't care. Well, he did care. San Francisco air in the late fall was chilly as the best of times. He just knew he wouldn't care in about a minute. Once a fresh shot of heroin worked its way through his system, he wouldn't care about anything…again.

Crawling out of the lumpy futon, Boy Scout's hand came down on a patch of mold. His stomach churned and his throat choked off some rising bile. He wiped his hand on the blanket. His pants lay on the floor next to the futon. He contemplated pulling them on for a-bout a second. They served no purpose in getting high, so he crawled past them on the way to the crate.

He picked up the candle, gently as he could, to set it on the floor. Just as he had it in his hand and away from the stable surface, a siren wailed from outside – a rare sound in the Tombs. He jumped and dropped the candle. The room darkened. Boy Scout felt as if plunged into a tub of ice water. He scrambled back to his pants and fished the Zippo out of the front right pocket. A few frantic heartbeats later, he was back at the candle. He picked it up with his left hand and almost chewed through his upper lip as he relit it. When the flame returned light to the apartment, Boy Scout breathed easily again. He set the candle on the floor, very carefully this time, titled the crate, and pulled a leather toiletry kit out from underneath it.

Moments later, he had one end of a black leather belt wrapped around his left arm. His teeth clamped down on the other end. The syringe in his right hand waited for the bulging vein. After that he'd go into that place where he didn't care what he remembered.

"Hey, baby," a voice called from the far corner. "You going to share some of that, right?"

A girl sat on the futon, the blanket wrapped around her underneath the arms, exposing bare shoulders. Boy Scout wondered if he ever knew her name. She might have been as young as thirteen, maybe even twelve – life in the Tombs had a tendency to age people fast. Despite that, her skin was pale and clean, and even though her blond hair clung to her face and stuck out at odd angles on top and behind her ears, it wasn't from lack of cleanliness. She looked and glowed of sex. Still, even though she smelled cleaner than anyone Boy Scout had spoken to in years – he remembered that much about her from the last few hours – she had the hollow, sunken eyes and tight cheek bones of a professional junkie. Last time Boy Scout looked in a mirror, he saw a face like that looking back.

"Fuck off," Boy Scout snarled without removing the belt from between his teeth.

Three sharp knocks echoed on the door as he was about to slide the needle into his arm.

"I'll get it," the girl said.

"No!"

She ignored him, getting up from the moldy mattress and crossing to the door.

"I said…" Boy Scout's voice trailed off when he noticed all thirteen locks were open. His mouth hung open for a moment, releasing the belt, before he added, "Shit."

This was bad. Beyond bad. Like don't-cross-the-fucking-streams level of disastrous.

Boy Scout tried to stop her. He tried to stand and turn around at the same time. Funny thing with being on the tail end of a good night doped out of his mind, his body couldn't keep up with his intentions. He dropped the syringe as the floor rose up to meet him. The syringe hit the floor and shattered as he wound up face down on a section of floor that smelled of piss. The fragmented glass sparkled next to the candle, and Boy Scout lost his focus in the way the candlelight reflected off the tiny shards of broken glass.

The front door creaked open.

Oh, yeah. Cross-the-streams bad.

"Thanks, bitch."

It took Boy Scout a moment to register those words. The accent was a thick, heavy brogue, and the voice grated like steel wool on a chalkboard.

The girl gasped. Something that sounded like cracking knuckles, only louder, echoed in the room. That would be her neck; it wasn't the first time Boy Scout had heard that sound. The image of his best friend's head twisted at an impossible angle formed in his mind. Something heavy hit the floor, probably her body. What had they offered her to open the door? The runes all around both the door and windows made sure any creature of pure faerie blood couldn't come in without help – Boy Scout knew the old rules about those kinds of things, and he played them to his absolute best advantage. Whatever the offer, she must have gotten it, or she'd still be alive. They couldn't kill her without making good on their half of the deal. Another rule.

"Time to kick the habit, Boy Scout," the ear-grating voice said. Again, with the brogue, it took Boy Scout a moment to process the words. "Oberon has a job for you."

A chorus of cruel laughter filled the room. Boy Scout couldn't tell how many, but he figured at least three…maybe more.

"Fuck off."

Yeah, he'd just said the same thing to the girl, but really, do people expect a junkie to have a dazzling array of witty retorts and snappy comebacks?

He picked up the needle from the broken syringe. Stabbing himself through the tattoo on his right index finger, he dove for the candle. His blood snuffed out the flame, completing the ritual. The smoke curling in the air from the wick held its own light, as if the light from the candle flame had transformed into smoke. In truth, it was a touch of Faerie magic bound into the tattoo. Instead of wafting toward the ceiling, the smoke floated above the filth-covered floor and wafted toward the closet.

A pair of rough hands lifted Boy Scout to his feet.

The closet door fell off its hinges and hit the floor with a crash. Rather than revealing a closet, the threshold opened onto a meadow of soot and ash surrounded by flaming, evergreen-shaped trees. The smell of smoldering campfires filled the room, and the temperature increased by about ten degrees. Then *she* stepped into view before the fiery scene. Her flaming hair – not red, *flaming* – whipped in the wind that flowed into the room from the world beyond the door. She wore a jacket of peacock feathers; the center of each eye held a tiny, flickering flame. Underneath the jacket, she had an orange T-shirt with the words *Keep calm and grab a lantern* in letters as black as her cargo pants and leather motorcycle boots.

"Gentlemen," Boy Scout said, "meet Cendrine South."

"Good morning," Cendrine said, stepping across the threshold.

The fiery trees and blackened ground faded back into just a closet, but the temperature continued to rise.

"Put him down."

The floor rose up to meet Boy Scout. His breath slammed out of his chest on impact.

Why were people always so literal with things like that?

Boy Scout lay gasping, waiting for it to be over. Something screamed. It wasn't Cendrine. She *didn't* scream. Ever.

"Get up and get in the fight!" Cendrine yelled.

Boy Scout pulled off a small leather pouch from around his neck, yanked the drawstrings open, and dumped the powder into his mouth. The stuff looked like dried and ground cow shit laced with red pop rocks. As soon as it touched his tongue, the powder transformed into a sweet liquid that slid down his throat like warm brandy. When it reached Boy Scout's stomach, the potions purged any lingering drugs from his system.

He crushed garbage and trash as he rolled across the floor. The glass from the shattered syringe cut into his back, and then, rolling onto his front, he pinned one of his testicles between his thigh and the floor. Boy Scout clenched his teeth against the pain. Without the fog of drugs clouding his mind, neurons fired through over-familiar synaptic pathways. That's when Boy Scout realized he was heading for the wrong corner. That particular hidey hole wasn't likely to help against the faerie. Twisting and rolling, he changed directions and scrambled to the southwest corner of the room.

The floorboards behind him vibrated with a heavy impact. As he crawled away, Boy Scout glanced back. One of his would-be captors strained to pry a firefighter's axe out of the floor. Only changing directions had saved him from losing a leg, or worse. Once upon a time, that would have terrified Boy Scout into inaction. Now, his skin tingled as adrenaline pulsed through his body, and the instinct to kill or be killed took hold of his reflexes.

Boy Scout reached the corner, pressed down on the knot in one of the floorboards, and the board popped open. He thrust his hands inside the alcove and grabbed two bags – one was dark brown suede, the other purple velvet – from the top of his small pile of treasures. He flung his arms outward, sending the contents of both pouches, iron shavings and tiny silver crosses, across the room.

The guy with the axe got a face full of the worst of it. He dropped to his knees, clawing and scratching at his face. Boy Scout kicked him in the face. The attacker's head snapped back, sending his hat flying as he pitched backward and sprawled on the floor.

Boy Scout stared at the hat that had flopped down in the middle of his shoddy apartment. Even with what little light filtered in from outside, he knew what the hat was and what it meant. His stomach sank and he swallowed to keep the bile down as he looked up, fearing what he would see.

Cendrine wove her way between the other five invaders. The tallest of them stood no more than four and a half feet high. Each was about half as wide at the shoulders as he was tall. Wiry black hair sprouted from the necks and cuffs of their tattered, three-piece, double-breasted suits. Their iron-shod boots dug gouges in the wooden floor, but some spell or enchantment must be keeping the boots silent. They carried bone cudgels and firefighter's axes. Each one wore a hat just like the one that had caught Boy Scout's attention. Each hat resembled a Scottish Tam O'Shanter, only without the little ball on top, and each cap was deep red and dripping wet.

Powries. Known to popular folklore as Red Caps. Unseelie monsters that reveled in the fear and misery they caused when they used fresh human blood to maintain the color of their hats. Back in the war, U.S. forces had taken to calling them "Samsons." Their power lies in the hat. If the cap dries, the Powrie dies. The wetter the hat, soaked in human blood, the stronger the Powrie. Boy Scout wondered how many of the tenants of this building had died tonight. Powries were one of the most resilient and terrifying of all dark faeries. He'd heard of whole platoons dying, to the man, trying to take down a single Powrie. Now he had six in his apartment. The iron wouldn't do anything against them. At least not with their caps dripping with all that fresh blood. Until such time as that changed religious trappings were their only real defense, but the tiny crosses would only serve as momentary distractions. Yeah, they'd hurt, but Boy Scout only had the one bag, and that was spent. He could think of only one surefire way to incapacitate them long enough for Cendrine to kill them. If Boy Scout remained alive long enough to see it through.

The Powrie that Boy Scout had just kicked rolled over to its hands and knees. It glared up at him and gave him a wide grin.

"I'm going to bleed you through your feet," it said, "soak my hat in your blood over the course of days."

"Thanks, but I'll pass," Boy Scout said, as he backed away from the feral creature.

Boy Scout struggled to remember something that might be enough to keep them down long enough to tell Cendrine how to beat them. A passage came to him from one of his dad's favorite movies.

"The path of the righteous man is beset on all sides by the inequities of the selfish and the tyranny of evil men."

The Powrie facing him laughed, a deep, gravely sound, as it lumbered to its feet. Boy Scout decided he'd be perfectly happy never hearing the sound again.

He kept quoting. *"Blessed is he, who in the name of charity and goodwill, shepherds the weak..."*

The Powrie stepped forward, completely the opposite of the expected reaction. Boy Scout quickened his backpedaling and his speaking so his words almost blended together.

"...through the valley of darkness for he is truly his brother's keeper and the finder of lost children."

"Love that movie, too," the Powrie said, stalking toward Boy Scout.

"Ah, shit. That's right."

Boy Scout recalled that particular monologue wasn't an actual quote from Ezekiel 25:17. He also remembered he'd learned that the hard way once before. But by this time, he had something else.

"The Lord is my shepherd. I shall not want. He maketh me to lie down in green pastures."

The Powries screamed. The sound was a mix of a pig being slaughtered and a buzz saw cutting though ice. They dropped their cudgels and axes and pressed their meaty hands to their ears.

"Cendrine," Boy Scout shouted, "dry the caps." Then, continuing his impromptu sermon, he sprinted across the room. "*He leads me beside still waters; He restores my soul. He leads me in paths of righteousness for His name's sake.*"

A nimbus of light appeared around Cendrine. The temperature rose steadily. At first it was no worse than a crowded movie theater without any air-conditioning, then a sauna. In a matter of heartbeats it would be hot as a pottery kiln.

Boy Scout dove out of the window and sprawled onto the rusty fire escape. Metal groaned as bolts holding it to the building's outer wall strained under his weight. He realized that he should have tested it a long time ago. He imagined himself laying naked, splattered all over the street below.

He wasn't a man of faith, even though religious trappings, especially from Catholicism, had such a strong effect on the fey, but this didn't keep him from praying, "Please hold, please hold, please hold," as he laced his fingers around the rusted metal and his entire body tensed for the fall. He didn't know what he was actually praying for: to keep from falling or to not be known as the guy who died naked in the street due to a faulty fire escape.

The structure held. Boy Scout's atheism returned.

"More scripture!" Cendrine yelled.

Now that Boy Scout had really gotten going, more passages he'd memorized back in the war rose from the depths of his memory. He lifted his head level with the window's bottom. Heat flowed out of the window like an oven door. "*Even though I walk through the valley of the shadow of death, I fear no evil; for You are with me; Your rod and Your staff, they comfort me.*" The screams lowered, sounding now like the whimpers of newborn puppies.

"*Surely goodness and mercy shall follow me all the days of my life; and I shall dwell in the house of the Lord forever.*"

A few moments later, Boy Scout heard nothing, and the heat coming out of the window subsided.

In the brief moment of quiet, Boy Scout heard faint singing coming from down the street. He only caught a few words before the singer walked too far out of ear shot. What he had heard, "…beggar than a king, and I'll tell you the reason why…" sent a shudder across his whole body.

As soon as he thought the room would be manageable, Boy Scout shook the sound of that song out of his head and crawled back through the window.

Cendrine stood in the center of the room, holding a pair of his jeans and glaring at him. At least her hair had gone back to being hair. It was still deep red, but it wouldn't singe him if he got too close.

Cendrine tossed his jeans at him. "Have some sense of decency."

Boy Scout snatched the pants out of the air. "Wasn't expecting company."

As he pulled his jeans on, Boy Scout took stock of the apartment. It was the first time in a long, long time that he'd done so sober. Did he really live like this?

The Powries lay in awkward, contorted positions. Each hat now looked brittle and dried brown as opposed to dripping and deep blood red. Cendrine searched through their pockets and under their hats.

"Ugh," Boy Scout grunted.

"You have no room to judge anything I do," Cendrine replied, as she lifted another formerly red cap from a dead faerie.

Boy Scout opened his mouth to make some poignant commentary on a lack of knowledge of how sanitary Red Caps were when it came to their hair care practices. They spent centuries, sometimes millennia, soaking their hats in human blood and never cleaning them. Couldn't possibly be healthy.

Cendrine glanced at the shattered syringe, and back at him. She didn't say anything else. She didn't have to. She looked like the parent of a teenager that can't manage to stay out of trouble. The irony was not lost on him.

As Cendrine searched the attackers, Boy Scout went over to his bed, lifted the edge of the mattress, and picked up the iron railroad spike he kept hidden there. It warmed his palm, almost to the point of burning him. He wrapped the spike in a discarded shirt, and crawled a few feet to one of the Powries.

The faerie's breath came in ragged gasps. It looked up at him, then shifted its gaze to the railroad spike…the *iron* railroad spike.

"Hi," Boy Scout said. "Probably been a while since your cap was dry enough that you had to worry about something like this, right?"

"Wait." Its face contorted as it spoke. Good. It deserved some pain before the end. "You're a bard. You can do no harm."

"Sure I can," Boy Scout said. "You broke the Law of Hospitality. I'm just exercising Host Right for your transgressions."

"We are invaders, not your guests," the faerie said. "Kill us and lose your powers."

Boy Scout grabbed the Red Cap by the hair and turned its face toward the door.

"See that?" Boy Scout asked. "It's my door. It's got a threshold. Strangers stay on the far side. Only friends and guests come on this side. If you thought to look, the bottom of the door has a tiny little sign that says; *By crossing this threshold you accept rights and duties as guests of this house.* And what's the first thing you did as guests in my house? You killed another one of my guests."

"We didn't know," the Faerie pleaded.

Boy Scout wanted to smile, but he kept his face smooth as he leaned down next to the Red Cap's ear and whispered, "I didn't know what I was getting into when I cleaned up the graffiti in a skate park."

Boy Scout shoved the spike into the faerie's eye. He didn't bother talking to the others as he repeated this process.

After killing the last Red Cap, Cendrine asked, "Is that what I think it is?"

She tossed something at Boy Scout. He caught the green leather journal without thinking. Looking down, he saw the Celtic cross tooled into the cover. Two leather cords held it closed.

It was his, or it had been a long time ago.

He hadn't seen it since well before he'd gotten out of Faerie. He untied the leather chords. In the years since he'd held it last, the spine had loosened. It flopped open, and he barely managed to keep from dropping it. Still, a silver chain with a pair of dog tags and a white-gold wedding ring set with a sapphire fell to the floor, and a white card fluttered down after it. He recognized the ring, and the snap-crackle-pop of a breaking neck echoed up from his memories.

"Yeah." Boy Scout really wanted to shoot up. Not to forget. He couldn't forget, no matter how much he wanted to. The drugs just made it so that he didn't care that he remembered. "It's what you think it is."

If Cendrine said anything else, Boy Scout didn't hear her. He picked up the chain. The dog tags were his, not the ones he expected. Maybe that meant the last person he'd known to have that ring might still be alive.

Cendrine cleared her throat.

Boy Scout blinked, pushing memories and regrets away as best he could. Cendrine had picked up the white 3x5 card and now held it out to him between two fingers. He took it. Someone had written one sentence in flowing script onto the card.

Boy Scout who Lies, your friends need you. – Tommy

"Who is Tommy?" Cendrine asked, looking at the card from over Boy Scout's shoulder.

"An old friend. One of my oldest," Boy Scout shook his head. "But it can't be from Tommy." *Could it?* "The handwriting is wrong."

Granted, he hadn't seen Tommy's handwriting since they'd been fifteen years old; however, this handwriting wasn't anything like Tommy's had been. First off, whoever had written the card used a mix between standard print and cursive. Tommy almost always tried to write as close to Courier New font as possible, explaining to those who asked that it made him feel like a journalist. Boy Scout took in the nine words, trying to gain some sense of the author's identity; he noticed that the e's tilted slightly right and the crosses of the t's curved upward on the left. He got the feeling the writer was used to quick and precise movements with the fingers and wrists.

He opened the book. His own handwriting stared at him with the heading of *DAY ZERO* at the top of the first page. He flipped through the pages, passing the parts he'd written. Those days had sucked enough the first time, he didn't have any desire to relive them. About halfway through the journal, which was where Boy Scout had left off and given the book to someone else, the handwriting changed to a neat, precise cursive. Mary's first words in his old journal stared up at him.

MARY'S TRANSITION
(And my only post from this name.)

Boy Scout is gone. He and Wish went off with the princess this morning. I don't have a lot of time. Presto and Snow Shade say I need a new name since I'm taking over as platoon bard. Can we even be called a platoon anymore? I guess that's really up to the LT and Cuban to figure out. I'm just here to carry the personals and record all the shit storms we're probably going to have to weather as we try and make it back overdale. Gotta go for now. We're renaming me. I wonder if I'll feel any different.

Boy Scout stopped reading. He wasn't sure if he was ready to know what happened to the others. Would he ever be ready? Probably not.

He flipped through the rest of Mary's portion of the journal. Not all of it was in her handwriting, but Boy Scout didn't stop to examine it…until he came to a page that had been dog-eared. The handwriting on that page was his, though he couldn't ever remember writing those words down. Hating himself for his curiosity, Boy Scout read the next two pages in the journal

WISDOM I LEARNED FROM MY MOTHER'S BOOKS:

"The heart of wisdom is tolerance." — Steven Erikson
"Just because you're paranoid doesn't mean there isn't an invisible demon waiting to eat your face." – Jim Butcher
"It's like everyone tells a story about themselves inside their own head. Always. All the time. That story makes you what you are. We build ourselves out of that story." — Patrick Rothfuss
"Duty is heavy as a mountain, death as light as a feather." – Robert Jordan
"Evil is relative. You can't hang a sign on it. You can't touch it or taste it or cut it with a sword. Evil depends on where you are standing, pointing your index finger." – Glen Cook
"There are other worlds than these." – Stephen King

I didn't get most of this stuff until much later, and by then, it was too late.

SINGLE STEPS

MY FIRST TASTE OF REAL MAGIC

Tommy Knight, Phil Bailey, and I stood at the edge of the four-foot-high chain-link fence that served as the border between the place where you could skate your heart out, and the place where moms and dads with little kids in tow would scream at you if you did anything more than skate a straight line, without tricks, to the sidewalk. Our boards leaned against our legs, and we leaned against the fence. Thick, gray clouds had come in off the ocean.

"Whadya think, Max?" Phil asked. "Reckon it's safe to go in?"

I took another look at the graffiti. It was weird, containing only three colors: black, white, and gray. The artist had blended them together in a way that made it hard to tell where one color stopped and the other began. Its shape was also hard to grasp. At first I thought it was an oval, then a circle, then an oblong, blob-shaped thing. Yeah, it was weird, but it was cool.

We skated hard. Despite our protective gear, helmets, gloves, and knee and shoulder pads, I could feel the bruises forming all over my body from my falls. I'd be sore the next day, but that didn't matter, I'd be back tomorrow and every day after that for all of Christmas vacation. The park was officially closed on Christmas, but it didn't matter. Christmas was the one day a year McPherson took off so we could sneak in once we all opened our presents. At least one of us would get a new board, and we'd have to break it in.

We all sat at the top of the highest ramp, our legs dangling over the edge. Each breath we exhaled came out as a stream of mist. Sometimes we pinched our thumbs and index fingers together as we inhaled and blew our breath out through pursed lips, just like Tommy's older brother does it while straddling his motorcycle.

"Good day," Phil said.

"Best day ever," Tommy said.

We all nodded. It had been. It was a good sign of things to come during the vacation.

"I got to get back," I said. "My dad's going to help me with a new story."

"Cool," Phil said. "I can't wait to read it."

Phil and I got up.

"You coming?" Phil asked Tommy.

"Na," he said. "I'm going to go a couple more times before I head in."

That wasn't unusual. Tommy lived right across the street, so he got to hang out a little later than we did. We gave each other high fives all around.

As Phil and I left, I glanced at the graffiti. It looked bigger, and I thought I saw a hint of red mixed in with the white, gray, and black. The hairs on my arm stood on end, which had nothing to do with the evening chill. I thought about heading back for Tommy, but decided that it would be okay. McPherson was there; always watching to make sure nobody broke the rules.

We never saw Tommy again. At the skate park the next day, the graffiti was bigger, and there was this big bloodstain. Later, one of the newspapers mentioned that the blood stain matched Tommy's blood type. He disappeared – I refused to believe he was dead – two years, down to the very day, after my mother left Dad and me alone.

THREE DIFFERENT FUNERALS

That was a hard month. I lost:

One of my two best friends
All my fish because I was so depressed I didn't feed them for a week.
My first girlfriend because I ignored her longer than the fish.

I also started dreaming about this amazing girl with fiery hair. She's showed up during my REM sleep at least once a week, every week, until the war broke out.

Boy Scout looked at the card again.

Tommy.

He hadn't thought about Tommy in years. Odd that with everything Boy Scout couldn't forget, he hadn't thought about Tommy for all those years.

"So, what do you want to do?" Cendrine asked.

Boy Scout looked up at her. "What do you mean?"

She kicked the broken syringe.

Boy Scout licked his lips. He was really thirsty. He took in the carnage around him, gaze settling on the girl, her head twisted around at an impossible angle. Her lifeless eyes stared back at him, accusing him, just the way his best friend had looked six years earlier. He turned away, trying to keep his stomach from emptying at the thought of what he'd done with that girl. Her corpse represented the depths to which he'd allowed himself to fall.

God, I really want to shoot up.

It wasn't a physical need. The potion that sobered him up also cured his body's dependency on the drug. Boy Scout just didn't want to care again. He shot up, smoked weed, and drank himself puking drunk so that he didn't care that he couldn't forget.

Boy Scout glanced over at the crate where another loose floor-board containing at least a week's worth of forgetfulness. He went over to it and moved the floorboard aside.

"Great," Cendrine said as Boy Scout pulled out his hidden stash of drugs. "That's your solution."

"Stop acting like you know everything about me." Boy Scout tossed the drugs to the other side of the room. "Burn that."

Next, he brought out the plain black journal with a black gel pen clipped to the back cover. He'd gotten hold of both just after he'd gotten out of Faerie, just in case. He hadn't brought himself to use either.

"You're going to write?" Cendrine asked.

He nodded.

"Anything to do in the mean time? Or do you want me to just hang out?"

Boy Scout sat against a wall, took the pen, clicked the top, and set the tip against the first page.

"Collect the weapons," he replied.

"Which?"

"All of them." He paused, mouth hanging open as he consider-ed a moment. "Yup. All. I have a feeling we're going to need them."

"That sounds foreboding," Cendrine said. "Seem to be falling back into your talents pretty quickly."

"Hasn't anything to do with talents or powers or anything like that." He gestured to indicate the corpses lying around the room. "Just my critical thinking skills at work."

Cendrine nodded. "You going to be alright in here?"

"You mean alone?"

She nodded again.

"As in, you think someone or something else might come after me?"

She shrugged.

"I'm good with letting whatever six Red Caps have for back up just come and get me. That's the safer and less painful option."

"Alright."

"Now," Boy Scout said, "shut up and let me write."

Taking a deep breath, Boy Scout forced himself to meet the dead girl's eyes. His sides clenched, and again his stomach threatened vomit. He clenched his teeth and forced his body under control as he waited for that tingle at the back of his head to come. It took a long time. While he waited, he tuned out everything in the world but the girl. When it came, and at last it did, the pen started moving across the page, first in his handwriting, but as he continued scribbling words on the page, the script changed to the handwriting of a dead girl, telling at least part of her story.

Cendrine stepped over the enforcer from Sunshine's brute squad and walked down the stairs to the next floor.

She recognized Bruno, having met him twice before. The second time was when she'd come to convince Sunshine and his brutes that trying to sell out Boy Scout was not in their best interest. Bruno had been good, not just big and strong, but quick and smart. He was the kind of guy who kept his wits in a fight, even when things turned against him. He stayed patient, always looking for a way to turn things around. But…he was only human, and no matter how clever he was, he wasn't a match for one Red Cap, let alone six. He was just as dead as the little harlot who'd slipped into the apartment and started all this trouble, though Bruno hadn't died from a broken neck. A wide gash stretched across his neck from where the Powries had slit him open and drenched their caps. It would be a miracle if anyone in this building was still alive.

The thought of six Red Caps working together sent a shiver through Cendrine's body. To her, fear was cold, complete, and utter lack of warmth. Not like the cold of a winter's day or an ice cube. No, it was the cold of the void, the cold that doesn't so much eat heat as it dissipates any warmth into the vast lack of existence. This soul-numbing chill came not from Oberon sending these Red Caps after a bard who hadn't practiced his gifts in years, but rather from him sending the Red Caps to *fetch* that bard. The King of Faerie had a plan for the bard and feared his power enough to send this kind of a force.

She stopped halfway between floors, a threshold between here and there within the building. This was the perfect place from which to search the building, and she should have thought of it sooner. It seemed that the bard wasn't the only one whose paranoia had grown lax in the years of waiting and waiting and nothing coming from that waiting. With that thought, Cendrine understood. What did the fey care of a year, or even a decade? Oberon could outwait them all. But still, in wanting the bard for something, the Faerie King couldn't wait too long, human lives being so fragile in their brevity.

Cocking her head to the side, Cendrine listened to the heat in the building. Bodies cooled on every floor. The bard was the only living thing in the building, or at least, the only living *mortal* thing. She couldn't hear any unnaturally cold spots, nor any cracks or corners with a lack of any temperature at all. That was something at least. It meant that Oberon probably didn't know about the tattoo, the enchantments bound within it, and all the strangenesses the boyscout bard had worked upon her with his talents and gifts before giving them up, well, before giving them up until just now.

She didn't know what to think about him writing again.

At the thought of him writing, her hand went to her pocket where she'd slipped the battered leather journal. That book held so many pieces and secrets to her past.

Cendrine drew the journal from her pocket and opened to the first page.

DAY ZERO

I'm calling this "Day Zero," because the platoon I've been assigned to is supposedly shipping out tomorrow. We probably will, but sometimes shit just happens. Whatever day we actually ship out on will be day one. My own personal version of D-Day. Stomach is already churning at the thought. That's me: Big Damn Hero (To quote one of Mom's favorite shows.)

Got my dog tags today. No name. Just my rank, religion, blood type, AB positive in my case, and my serial number. Faeries can use any personal information about you to do nasty things to your mind and your body. That means no real names underhill. Code names or nicknames only. Usually Platoon Sergeants give soldiers nicknames in boot/basic. I've never been through basic training, so I have no idea how that's going to work for me. Hope I don't get something lame.

Cendrine closed the journal.

Regardless of the answers it held, she couldn't afford to lose herself within its pages. She didn't even consider crossing over to the underhill to find a pocket where she might read the whole journal while mere moments passed here in the overdale. She flipped through the pages. Handwriting filled over half the pages. Cendrine sighed and slid the journal back into her pocket. Best not to seek answers she was not completely prepared for. Reading the journal would almost certainly answer some questions she'd always had, but it even more certainly would raise more questions. She couldn't be sure she'd have the patience to wait for an answer, and even if she could find the patience, those questions would distract her and cloud her judgment. She'd just keep this key to her past and unlock the door and step through when she had more time. For now, she'd wait and see what path the bard took from here, making sure to keep him alive to fill in whatever holes the journal didn't.

Right now, she needed to perform the ridiculous ritual to get into the secret alcove where the bard had hidden the duffle bag with his weapons.

She walked one and a half flights of stairs to the door leading out to the roof.

"Macbeth," Cendrine said. "Oops…I mean The Scottish Play."

Having said that, and with one of the empty apartments in the building having been converted to a theater, the old curse must be observed.

Cendrine opened the door and stepped outside in the chill Bay Area morning. She faced west, her back to the rising sun, and took a deep breath. Thankfully, no one would see her jump through these ridiculous hoops. This was probably part of the bard's master plan; not only was the ritual overly complex, performing it was so embarrassing most fey wouldn't be able to bring themselves to complete it.

"Macbeth, Macbeth, Macbeth," Cendrine said.

Then, she turned three times widdershins, spit over her left shoulder, and said, "God damn me to hell for a fool." Taking a deep breath to stall, she made sure she remembered the three lines before continuing. "Angels and ministers of grace defend us…If we shadows have offended…Fair thoughts and happy hours attend on you."

Having completed the ritual, she faced the door again and knocked, hoping she'd gotten everything right.

The door opened.

Now, down three flights of stairs. Seven steps into the third flight, she reached into the metal box embedded in the wall, the box that used to hold a fire extinguisher, and pulled out a ratty hand broom. She continued her journey downward. Four steps from the bottom of that flight of stairs, she bent down and began sweeping the third step.

"I am sent with broom before," she recited from *A Midsummer Night's Dream*, "to sweep the dust behind the door."

The top of that step vanished.

Cendrine reached into the empty space inside that stair and pulled out an olive-green duffle bag. It was heavier than she expected.

Hopefully, they could set everything right. She did not want to have to go through that idiocy ever again.

THE TROJAN HORSE

Writing is a socially acceptable form of schizophrenia.
— E.L. Doctorow

The scariest moment is always just before you start.
— On Writing, Stephen King

Her name is… Her name is…

I can't remember. Her corpse is lying there, lifeless eyes judging me because I can't remember her gawddamn name. What a shitfuck I turned out to be.

Damn. Hate this part…man I hate it so much. This is the hardest it's ever been, even harder than when I didn't even know what I was doing. I'm really missing when I didn't know what I was doing, back when the words of other people's stories just flowed from my mind, through my pen, and down onto the paper. Funny thing about mastering some skill or talent: when you're just starting out and don't know enough to be self-conscious, you jump right in with gusto, without worrying about how "hard" it's supposed to be; then the better you get at it, the more you worry about getting it "right." Fuck but I want this shit to be easy again. Hell…probably would be if I hadn't spent the last few years since I got out of Faerie avoiding anything resembling writing, reading, stories, and/or any form of artistic medium like the proverbial fucking plague.

Clichés in my writing for the fucking win…I can just imagine Professor Matthiason's eyes rolling just before slapping the table with his notebook. How many times do we have to go over familiar language in our writing? Well, sir, it's all I've got now…Besides, when was that last time you used your writing to shape the course of two worlds and had to live with that? So, take your nuggets of Creative Writing wisdom and fuck the hell off. I'm not…

wait…

there we go… First problem solved.

too focused on myself…gotta get out of myself…away from how those eyes are making me feel.

Before I try and jump into her, I need to get the extraneous crap out of my head. Man, oh man, I want to just give up, put the pen down, and get the fuck out of Dodge. Only…only…that won't really help anything in the long run, and when it comes down to the nitty and gritty, the six Powrie corpses lying around me means I have to find out how Oberon managed to track me down,

306

otherwise, he'll just do it again, and again, and again, ad nauseam, until something kills me or I manage to set things straight. Shoulda known my past would catch up with me, considering who I am, what I've done, what she has done, and that we never really settled things, not in any meaningful way. So, now I've decided to step up and be a man...well, that's what I'm telling myself anyway. Not sure I can handle more self-truth than that right now.

So, now I come back to the girl. She's all of a sudden the only trail I have back to how and why Oberon wants to draw me back into matters of the fey. She's the first step on my path to answers. I've seen her before, not just last night. But last night is as good a place as any to start. Start with that and work my way backward. She came with the drugs. That meant she was one of Sunshine's girls. I remember seeing her before, when Sunshine and I first started our business relationship. She was cleaner back then. Back then she didn't make house calls, or any kind of calls at all. Back then, she was Sunshine's Virgin.

"This is Christina," Sunshine said through his pearly white, overly wide smile. The introduction came with the dripping sleaze of a man showing off a human possession. "Don't be shy, Christina. Go say hello to my friend, Boy Scout."

"Boy Scout's your name?" the young lady asked.

"As good a name as any," the guy replied.

Christina walked across the room.

"Hello, Mister Boy Scout," she said with a sultriness to her voice that she didn't quite own. She and Sunshine were still working on that. He claimed that faeries he had to deal with were especially susceptible to virgins who dripped of sensuality and sexuality.

Christina stood on her tiptoes and kissed Boy Scout's cheek. She couldn't help but smile just a little bit when he blushed. That would make Sunshine happy. He might even give her a treat.

Having completed her mission, Christina walked back to her place next to Sunshine.

Something in that resonates when it's written, hums with the power of truth.

Christina walked...

No, not quite...

Christina walking...

No...something still not right there...

Christina walks...walked...getting there...

Christina walker

THERE

Christina Walker. Names have power that resonates in the world around them. They drop clues all over the place for those who understand what to look, listen, and feel for.

So, now that you've introduced yourself properly, Miss Christina Walker, please tell the readers a little more about yourself…

…myself…

Well, my life was pretty boring up until I was thirteen when I ran away from home after the Faerie War ended. The last thing I wanted to do was wallow away the best years of my life in boring-ass Cool, California. If ever someplace didn't live up to its name, Cool was that town…though I hear Paradise, California gives it a run for the money. Nothing cool ever happened in Cool. But out there, in the world beyond the lameness of my hometown, people were having adventures. Normal girls like me were marrying lords and princes from both Faerie courts, getting rich, famous, even a few of them signing to reality TV deals. Living a life I could. None of them were nearly as pretty or smart as me. So, I ran away to San Francisco, what better place to meet the Faerie prince of my dreams than a city with one of the last open gates to Faerie?

But I can sense that you don't care about that, and I don't really want to talk about how sad and pathetic it was for me after I got here. Long and short of it, I was in bad shape. Sunshine found me, cleaned me up, fed me, and treated me like a queen for a year and a half, until an even cuter model came along to be his virgin. Me, well, he told me that I owed him, and that I could work off my debt. Somewhere about six months later, I paid off my debt once and for all…which wasn't even an hour ago.

Oh, you don't want to come that far forward? Don't want to hear that you travel in circles that trade a fifteen-year-old girl's life as a business favor? Didn't seem to matter much to you last night while we were doped out of our minds doing the horizontal tango like you wouldn't believe. What's that? Too much truth for you right now? Sucks to be you, doesn't it? You got sober and can move on. I just got dead.

Fine…we'll hit the rewind button and go back to last night.

I stood outside the door as Bruno, Sunshine's enforcer, rapped his huge knuckles against the door in a complex rhythm — two long, two short, a medium, a short, a long, a medium, and then I lost track. I was too fascinated by the glowing runes and sigils that appeared on the doorframe as he knocked. Bruno repeated the pattern. This time, Bruno knocked on the doorframe, tapping a specific symbol with each knock. Once he finished, Bruno moved back up the hall, leaving me alone.

A series of locks rattled on the other side of the door. I swallowed. This wasn't the first time Sunshine had sent me as a customer appreciation gift, but it was the first time I did get sent to Boy Scout. I remember him being nice to me the few times we met, back when he still came to pick up at Sunshine's office. I'd also never been sent to someone with instructions to not get turned away, no matter what happened. If I got in and answered the door in the morning, Sunshine promised I'd never be a customer appreciation bonus again. Joke's on me for that one.

The door opened less than an inch, and a bloodshot eye looked out at me.

"Where's Bruno?"

"I'm here," Bruno replied.

"Let me see you."

Bruno came back down the hall. He gently, but firmly, moved me aside. "Here."

Then Bruno put me back and stepped away.

I smiled as sweetly as I could. I figured Boy Scout would go for the all-American-girl more than he would the under-aged-sex-slut thing most of Sunshine's other clients went for.

"Sunshine sent me with this week's delivery." I opened my trench coat. I had the drugs taped between my tits. "I'm your preferred customer bonus."

Boy Scout's eye wandered over my body. Man, he was hard to read. I wished I could see his whole face and get a better read. He opened the door a little further. I took a small step forward. He held out his hand, stopping me.

"Just the drugs," he said.

Not going to happen. This was my way out. Fuck your morals, Mister Boy Scout. You're going to let me in. I'm going to be here all night. Let the heroin help you deal with it after I'm gone.

I tilted my head forward, chewed on the right corner of my lower lip, and half closed my eyes. That expression never failed to sway a man.

"Please let me in," I whispered, almost pleading. "If I don't spend at least an hour in here, Bruno will wonder, and then Sunshine will wonder, and then I'm going to get punished."

The real desperation in my voice surprised me. Not because Sunshine would punish me. I'd been punished before. I just hadn't realized how much I needed this to work so I'd never have to turn a trick again. Lol… There's that joke on me.

"Put this in your hand," Boy Scout said, holding out a railroad spike.

I took it.

"Put it against your forehead."

I did.

"Put it against your navel."

I did.

"Now your nipple."

I did.

This wasn't the weirdest fetish thing I'd done, but then I realized this wasn't about Boy Scout getting off on some strange power game. He was testing to see if I was a faerie.

He seemed satisfied, because he opened the door wider, and said, "Come in."

"Thank you," I said.

After crossing the threshold, I went right to the bed, or at least the ragged futon that passed for a bed. It wasn't the worst place I'd fucked one of Sunshine's customers, and if fucking this guy meant I'd never have to fuck another guy again, I'd fuck him on a bed of shattered glass and rusty nails.

"Oooo, candlelight," I said, as I untaped the drugs from my chest and the kit from my ass. "How romantic."

"It's not for you," Boy Scout said, closing the door and putting thirteen intricate locks back into place. "You make it go out and I'm sending you back to Sunshine."

"No problem," I said. "Leave the candle alone. Got it."

Those locks would be a problem. I'd have to get him to an epic high in order to get those unlocked before morning. Dope him up, screw his brains out, dope him up again, and he should be so far gone that I could get done what I needed done.

SINGLE STEPS

M. Todd Gallowglas

A KNIGHT WITHOUT ARMOR
IN A SAVAGE LAND

The noir hero is a knight in blood caked armor.
He's dirty and he does his best to deny the fact that he's a hero the whole time.
— Frank Miller

Typically, the hero of the fairy tale achieves a domestic, microcosmic triumph,
and the hero of myth a world-historical, macrocosmic triumph. Whereas the
former – the youngest or despised child who becomes the master of extraordinary
powers – prevails over his personal oppressors, the latter brings back from his
adventure the means for the regeneration of his society as a whole.
— Joseph Campbell

Boy Scout threw the journal across the room.

He took a deep breath, held it, then let it out over the course of ten heartbeats.

It didn't help.

The gel pen joined the journal a moment later.

He'd let Christina Walker into his apartment because… well… road to Hell and intentions and all that. Sunshine came across as friendly, all smiles, a real jes' folks kind of guy – well, most of the time, anyway. When Sunshine got mad or felt like someone had crossed him, he made the Spanish Inquisition look like, well, Boy Scout didn't know what it looked like, as he'd never been dumb enough to cross the gangster, but word on the street was that it involved long hours of severe pain followed by a drop off one of the bridges. Boy Scout couldn't let that happen to Christina, not that. She'd looked at him with those sad, tired eyes, and stuck that lip out with just the right quiver. He just wanted to shoot up, go to sleep, and let her out in the morning. Well, the shooting up part was easy. He tried to stop her from kissing him, her hands wandering over his body…only, the drugs kicked in and broke down his morals and inhibitions, as drugs do, and he was kissing her back…and then his hands started roaming, too.

Tears welled up in the inner corners of his eyes as his gut churned. Shame. Disgust. Horror. Abstract words that couldn't begin to describe how he felt bounced around his head while he wanted to slap himself, claw his eyes out, and then slam enough junk into his arm to kill an elephant.

"Real fucking boy scout I turned out to be," he muttered through clenched teeth.

He looked out the window. The day grew even lighter beyond the window. How easy would it be to jump out again, but ignore the fire escape this time? He had his pants on, so he wouldn't have to worry about the embarrassment.

"Figure out our next move?" Cendrine asked from the doorway.

She had the duffle bag slung over one shoulder. He saw the green leather of his old war journal poking up out of the side pocket of her cargo pants.

"You read it?" he asked.

"Not yet," she replied.

"How tempted were you?"

"Not very."

She walked over to the journal he'd flung across the room, dropping the duffle bag about halfway through the journey. Kneeling, she reached down and picked up the journal.

"Aahh," Boy Scout started, but his voice caught in his throat when she fixed him with a cold, stony gaze.

Cendrine's eyes scanned back and forth across the page. Like always, her face bore no emotion.

How did she feel about it? Did it matter? Even if she hated him for it – of course that presupposed that she didn't hate him before – Boy Scout was pretty sure she wouldn't walk away from him. Hell, all things considered, she probably couldn't even if she wanted to.

It didn't take long for Cendrine to finish reading. She gazed at him over the journal in which he'd written Christina Walker's story.

"Well?" Cendrine asked.

"Well, what?" Boy Scout countered.

"You never answered my question."

"Ah, which question was that?"

She shook her head. "Have you figured out what our next move is?"

313

"Our?"

She sighed. "Jesus fucking Christ. Can you pretty fucking please with a cherry, whipped cream, and chocolate fucking sprinkles suck it up and get over your self-pity party? Oberon sent a team of Red Caps to fetch you and bring you back. Team. Of. Red Caps. Have you considered that he sent them not because he thought that one Red Cap might not be able to bring you back, but maybe, just maybe, because someone else is after you, and the king of fucking Faerie felt they could protect you while they delivered you to him?"

"Actually," Boy Scout said, "no, I hadn't considered that. Been a while since I've used my critical thinking skills in any capacity outside of finding stuff to keep me well out of screaming distance of my right mind. It didn't help that one of them threatened to bleed me out. But it makes sense once I recall that fey, especially Powries, are prone to exaggeration. I just can't imagine what or who would be coming after me besides Oberon."

"So?" Cendrine asked. "What do we do now?"

"Stick with the original plan," Boy Scout said. "See what Sunshine knows. I can't imagine the Powries setting this up. It's not in their nature."

"True," Cendrine said. "So, you think Sunshine has something to do with this?"

"Yeah, I do," Boy Scout said. "He's the starting point. Then follow that trail wherever until we figure out what's going on and why it's going on now. Yeah. That feels right."

"What does?"

Boy Scout gave her a slight smile. "Why now? That's the big question. With all the wonky-wibbly-wobbly effect that the Faerie, especially the sidhe, have on time, why is Oberon suddenly interested in me now? Not while I was still in Faerie where and when it would be easier to grab me. Not next week, or next year, or next decade. Now. That's the key to it all. Why specifically now? We figure that out, and we can work at turning this toward our adventage."

Cendrine crossed her arms. "No more running?"

"Nope."

However, Boy Scout considered the other hideouts and safe houses he had secreted around the world. He could run. He might even find enough drugs to hide from himself, but that was never long enough. The problem was, despite Boy Scout's best efforts, O-beron had found him. That meant that, no matter how far Boy Scout ran, the King of Faerie could find him again. The longer it took, the more people would get hurt, people like Christina Walker.

"Why now?"

"Because she," Boy Scout pointed at Christina's body, "and that," he pointed at his old war journal poking up out of Cendrine's pocket, "reminded me why people call me Boy Scout."

He walked over to the window. The sun had risen completely over the Oakland hills over in the east bay. Helicopter rotors echoed faintly in the air, patrolling from the base in Alameda making sure nothing big and scary snuck through the gateway from underhill during the night. Garbage and wrecked cars filled the streets. A few of the shops on the first floors of the buildings were opening for the day, but most remained either boarded up or empty husks.

"Come here," Boy Scout said.

Cendrine stepped up beside him.

"See that empty shop on the corner with the taxi cab driven through the front window?" Boy Scout asked.

"Yes."

"I used to put up with mediocre burritos there because the margaritas were so good. Two blocks down used to be a shop, Siegal's, where you could get honest-to-god custom zootsuits. I know that because I had a few friends really into swing dancing. I never got into it, too busy writing. Working on a story, I'd go and eat mediocre burritos and drink kick-ass margaritas. A few blocks up and over was my mom's favorite bookstore when I was a kid. Borderlands. She'd read them to me. Taught me a lot."

"Like that list in your journal?" Cendrine asked.

"Like that, but more," Boy Scout replied. "Way more. Her books probably saved my life more times than I want to count during the war. I miss her. I also miss the way San Francisco was when I was a kid. I just can't seem to keep from fucking it up."

Cendrine placed a hand on his shoulder, the first gesture of comfort or affection she'd shown him in a long time.

"It's not like all this is your fault," she said.

Boy Scout turned toward her, and spoke slowly, "All this," he waved out the window, "is my fault. All my fault. Just like her," he waved at Christina, "I had the best intentions, but…well…I fucked it up."

"You can't blame yourself for her," Cendrine said. "The Powries killed her."

Not knowing whether to laugh or cry, Boy Scout looked over at the broken syringe. "It would be so easy to go back to not caring again." Boy Scout licked his lips. "The trouble is that I do care. Even doped out so far from sanity a pair of seven league boots wouldn't get me back in, I care."

"So, now what?"

"Give me the journal," he replied, holding out his hand, "and the pen."

Cendrine reached down to his old war journal.

"No." He held up his hand. "You hold onto that. Anything happens to me, you should have that. Read it when you have time. If I'm still around, I'll answer any other questions as best I can."

Cendrine nodded and handed Boy Scout the other journal and the gel pen.

Boy Scout turned to the next blank page and wrote these words:

Trustworthy
Loyal
Helpful
Friendly
Courteous
Kind
Obedient
Cheerful
Thrifty
Brave
Clean
Reverent

"What's that?" Cendrine asked.

"The boy scout law," Boy Scout replied. "It's easy to forget our principles when wallowing in self-pity. Sometimes we need to take a minute and remind ourselves what's important."

"Alright then, you ready?"

"Soon as I finish getting dressed," Boy Scout replied, "and load up."

Even so far removed from the war and his time with the Marines, Boy Scout's mind and body fell into sync.

Within just a few minutes Boy Scout was dressed in black cargo pants, easier to move in than the blue jeans, a pair of worn but comfortable boots that made no sound and left no trace of his passing, and lastly, a gray T-shirt which canceled any and all kinetic energy that made contact with it. Then he put on his brown leather jacket, which was just a normal jacket, excepting completely mundane alterations of a custom holster on the right side and a *sgian dubh*, a short-bladed Scottish knife, hidden in each sleeve.

Once he finished lacing his boots, Boy Scout went to the duffle bag. He rubbed his hands together and licked his lips before kneeling down and unzipping it. With a deep breath and a sigh, he reached in and took out his Irish fighting dirk. He held it by the scabbard in both hands so that each end of the belt hung down. He hefted the weight of it. Physically, it was only a few pounds, but the lives he'd taken with it seemed to strain the muscles in his arms and shoulders. Even though Boy Scout knew that this was just a trick of his mind, the years had done nothing to distance him from his past. Despite his desire and prayers to never take it up again, he'd known this day would come, that he couldn't hide forever. Someday, someone underhill would want to make use of his talents.

"Well...shit," Boy Scout said, and belted the dirk around his waist so that he could draw it backhanded with his right hand or cross-draw it with his left. He let the weight of it settle onto his hips. "Yeah, this is all full of suckage."

Next, he put the rosary with interspaced silver and iron beads around his neck and slipped it under his shirt. Oddly, the rosary filled him more with relief than the expected dread. But then, the rosary wasn't meant to harm. More than likely, it would protect him and repel potential threats. After the rosary, he put on the chain with his own dog tags, though lighter than anything else he wore, they pulled his neck and shoulders downward with the memories that came with them. He didn't want to wear the tags, but you never know when those might come in handy.

Lastly, Boy Scout stared at the remaining item in the bag, a wooden gun case. After a few moments thought, he opened the gun case and picked up the weapon inside. He didn't know what it was made of, but it looked like a Glock made of glass. Anyone who looked closely at its insides would see all the mechanisms of a firearm, only clear – even the bullets in the magazine were clear. Without pausing to test the pistol's weight or balance, Boy Scout put it in the holster inside his jacket. He took the two spare magazines and slid them into his back pocket.

Standing, he faced Cendrine.

"Ready?" she asked.

Boy Scout opened his mouth, ready to spout a line from another movie his mother had loved, *I was born ready*, but he couldn't say it.

"No." Boy Scout shook his head. "Not anywhere close to being ready, but that doesn't mean a damned thing. It's gotta be done."

Cendrine nodded at him, and they left the apartment.

Boy Scout's apartment remained quiet for several minutes after Boy Scout and Cendrine left in their search for Sunshine.

Even though daylight now spilled through the windows, the closet remained dark with shadows, darker than perhaps it should have. Boy Scout hadn't bothered to reset the wards because he didn't ever expect to return here. That meant the closet remained open as a portal between worlds. The shadows deepened even more in the closet, not shrouding it in complete darkness, but near enough.

Two people stepped out.

The first was a woman in her mid to late twenties wearing an artist's smock that had probably been white years before the Faerie War, now covered in specks and splotches of paint. Her ruddy blond hair, shaved at the sides and also flecked with dried paint, was pulled back into a bun and held in place with a pair of paint brushes.

The other woman hid most of her features beneath a gray, hooded, long coat with only her lips, chin, and the ends of her twin platinum blond braids visible.

The cloaked woman waited by the closet door while the first went to the middle of the room and took a magnifying glass out of her smock's pocket, knelt down, and examined bits of broken glass.

"That's it," she said, putting the magnifying glass back in the pocket and bringing out a pair of tweezers and a plastic bag. She carefully picked up the pieces of broken glass that had Boy Scout's blood on them.

"Will it be enough?" the woman by the door asked in a whisper.

"Yes," the artist replied. "Enough for both a painting and a weapon."

"And you're certain this is the only way?" the whisperer asked.

"Yes." The artist stood and went back to the closet. "With everything else he's been through, seen, and knows, it's the only way he's going to commit to action one way or another. It doesn't matter which way he goes, but until he picks a side, both underhill and overdale are going to keep spinning out of control until it gets so bad that nobody will be able to fix things."

Having gotten what they came for, the two women stepped back into the closet. A few moments later, the deep shadows made way for the light pouring in from the windows.

Boy Scout stopped in midstride. His breath caught in his throat at seeing the barricade and soldiers in urban fatigues at the 16th street BART station. After calming down, Boy Scout thanked whatever subconscious impulse had made him decide to circle around rather than come straight down Mission to Sunshine's lair, where those Marines would have seen them from at least a block away. In his hurry to backtrack onto Capp, Boy Scout came close to knocking Cendrine over.

"Problem?" she asked, pushing him away.

"Only that Sunshine has relocated," Boy Scout replied.

Cendrine poked her head around the corner.

"The army men might have him," she said.

"Those are Marines, not army," Boy Scout said, "and they don't. Those barricades and fortifications are older than the last 24 hours. If the Marines had him, then I wouldn't have gotten a visit from Bruno and Christina last night."

"So what now?" Cendrine asked.

"Gotta figure out where Sunshine's new lair is."

"Lair? Really?"

"It's Sunshine's term for where he sets up shop. Though, he does do his best to make his place live up to the term."

Cendrine fixed Boy Scout with a glare that might set off a bonfire inside him if she wished it. "Are you actually defending that waste of human flesh?"

"No," Boy Scout replied. "I'm defending the justified use of language in an appropriate context." He sighed. "Why can't anything ever be easy?"

Cendrine opened her mouth. Boy Scout held up his hand.

"Don't say it. A man can dream that the universe will cut him a break now and then."

Cendrine snorted. "I hardly think karma is finished fucking with you yet."

Realizing that further banter would not only be pointless but also more embarrassing – damn but he was out of practice – Boy Scout headed back down Capp Street. Behind him, Cendrine said something, but Boy Scout waved her off.

Why would the Marines be setting up a fortified position so close to the gateway? For that matter, why a BART station? Considering the number of Unseelie fey that inhabited the underground tunnels, well, that just gave the Marines one more point to worry about defending.

Unless...

Boy Scout stopped. He closed his eyes and visualized the maps of the San Francisco Bay Area public transportation system, specifically BART and MUNI lines. He'd used both a lot before the war and the map of those multicolored routes had burned themselves into his mind's eye...especially those near a certain skate park. Then he put a few things together in his head, like the fey might actually be the ones to deal with the Marines underground rather than the other way around.

"Holy shit," Boy Scout said.

"What?" Cendrine asked.

He ignored her as he took off running down Capp Street, not even bothering to see if she followed.

A block and a half later, Boy Scout had to walk. Panting and wheezing, he'd maxed out his endurance. Brilliant plan to stay cooped up in his apartment, keeping his mind in a fog, hoping that two worlds would forget about him. Yeah, Dad sure did raise a bright one.

"Want to tell me what's going on?" Cendrine asked, as she came up next to him.

He waved her off, not because he didn't want to answer her, but because he couldn't form words without gasping. This remaining sliver of pride surprised him. Besides, he needed to keep what little breath he had for walking the next seven or so blocks.

They passed people and fey, fellow derelicts mostly. At one point, a gang of kids – all human, the oldest of them might have been the same age as Christina Walker – walked toward them. The two biggest of them puffed up and lifted their weapons. One had a baseball bat with iron nails driven through it. The other had a nail gun. Cendrine stepped over to a dying tree and ran her finger across its trunk like a strike-all match. The tree wasn't very big, maybe two feet taller than Boy Scout, and it had no leaves, but it went up like it had been soaked in napalm. The two biggest kids unpuffed, and the gang moved to the other side of the street.

As they went, one of the smaller girls kept looking at Cendrine.

"What?" Cendrine asked as the tree burned bedside her.

"Nice shirt," the girl said, pointing and flashing the smile all fanboys and fangirls share when they run into someone who loves the same thing they love. "I love those books."

Cendrine's face twitched, and then her face lit up with the same sort of smile. More of her humanity than Boy Scout had ever seen showed through her features.

"Thanks," Cendrine said. "I love 'em, too."

"Using the bet in book two has saved my life a couple times since I came to SF," the girl said.

"Just don't go trying how they won in book three," Cendrine said.

The girl's face stretched wide with shock. "I'm clever, not stupid."

"Good girl. Stay safe, and don't try too hard to be clever."

"See ya 'round," the girl said, waving. Then she jogged to catch up with the others.

"Maybe," Cendrine said.

As the gang of kids walked away, Cendrine blew out the tree with all the effort of a child blowing out a single candle on a cake.

She held up a hand in front of Boy Scout's face. "Not a word?"

"Didn't I get you those books?" he asked.

"Shut up," she said, and started walking again.

A few blocks later Boy Scout and Cendrine came across a fire team of four Marines. Boy Scout saw them too late to avoid them. They had the now-standard mix of gear for fighting both conventional and faerie threats. Boy Scout remembered how long it had taken him to get used to the sight of crossbows, swords, and axes alongside assault rifles and grenades. Without waiting to see if they'd approach and question what must be the strangest pair wandering around the Tombs, Boy Scout pulled his dog tags out of his shirt and rattled them in front of his face.

"Designation?" the lance corporal asked.

"Bard," Boy Scout replied.

The lance corporal opened his mouth, blinked, closed his mouth, blinked again, and then opened his mouth again. After all that, though, he wound up just asking, "Here?"

Boy Scout nodded. "T.Y.S. People overdale don't much like that I spontaneously write their secrets. Don't mean to, but I was underhill too long writing soldiers' stories to keep them remembered back here. Sometimes I can't control the when or where. Gets awkward."

"Sorry to hear that, sir," the lance corporal said, and saluted. "Thanks for your sacrifice."

Guilt and shame wrenched at Boy Scout's stomach as he returned the salute. The dog tags swung heavy in his hand and beat against his face.

Once the fire team moved on, Cendrine said, "T.Y.S?"

"Thousand year stare," Boy Scout replied, slipping the dog tags back under his shirt. "Term for bards whose power takes over them."

Cendrine fell into step beside Boy Scout as they resumed their journey. Last time he'd been out of the apartment, the troops stationed in San Francisco hadn't been patrolling the Tombs. It had been considered primarily Faerie territory, well, Faerie and those humans idiotic enough to sneak in.

"Those soldiers seemed to respect you," Cendrine said after half a block. "Maybe we could get some help from them."

"No." Boy Scout quickened his stride just a bit.

Cendrine matched his pace, and pressed further. "But, surely someone in their ranks might know something. You just have to ask the right people."

"No." He stopped and turned to face Cendrine. "Don't press this. You can call me to task on a great many things. You can berate my choices and throw the past in my face. This, I will not budge on. We are not involving the military. Period. End of discussion."

Without giving her time to respond, Boy Scout executed a text-book left flank and continued down the street. Cendrine didn't bring it up again. They walked in silence the rest of the way down Capp Street. When they reached 24th, Boy Scout peeked around the corner of the building, looking toward Mission Street. Just like at 16th Street, the Marines had turned the 24th BART station into another fortified position.

"Son of a bitch," Boy Scout said. "That's why."

"That's why what?" Cendrine asked.

"Oberon is sending goons for me now. The U.S. is getting ready to attack the gateway, and they aren't being very subtle about it. Whoever is calling the shots might think they are being really clever, but if I can figure it out, at least several dozen of the sidhe will work it out, too."

"Are you sure?"

He rolled his eyes, though made a point to not to do so until after he looked back to the BART station.

"Pretty sure."

For a moment Boy Scout considered dropping into Socrates mode, posing questions leading Cendrine to the answer on her own, but he remembered she hadn't grown up in San Francisco, learning, memorizing, the crisscrossing web of transportation lines and schedules. That lack of experience meant it was unfair of Boy Scout to expect her to comprehend the potential tactical and strategic value of controlling the BART and MUNI tunnels.

"They, that's the U.S. military, could have thousands of troops waiting in those tunnels, ready to pour out and strike at the biggest gateway between Faerie and our world. If they coordinate that with air support, they might have a shot at closing it."

"That could reignite the war," Cendrine said. "Do you really think they'd do that?"

"Americans don't take well to other people trying to grab our crap," Boy Scout replied, turning back to her, "especially our real estate. Should have expected this to happen. I bet they've spent the last few years working out new technology to more efficiently kill faeries. It's what we do in every war we've ever been in. And the fey are the only force to ever successfully encroach on sovereign U.S. soil. I can't imagine that sitting well with anyone high up in the military or the government."

"So what do we do about it?"

"We figure out where Sunshine is and we have a chat with him."

"That's still your priority?"

"Yup." He smiled a tight, humorless smile. "I'm tired of being other people's pawn. Hell, I'm tired of being bound by the bonds of Faerie itself. This is the Twenty-First Century, not ancient Ireland. Somehow, someway, I have to be able to break the shackles of the Old Laws and write some new ones."

As Boy Scout spoke those words, the very air about them became charged with the power of story. The air seemed to thin, making him feel lightheaded. His skin tingled in the way it did when someone had left the window to a room open and the faintest of drafts caressed the skin on the arms and the back of the neck.

He'd known that sensation only a few times before, when a bard became the embodiment of the ideal warrior poet. Cendrine wouldn't be able to feel it. She had too much Faerie blood to feel that power. Most humans couldn't either, especially in the Twenty-First Century, when humanity had forgotten the power of story. Boy Scout imagined it used to be different, that people used to seek these moments, these times when true story buzzed about the world, giving those people who reached out and took hold of the chance to create tales that lived for centuries and millennia beyond them, rather than the way that media for profit had diluted Warhol's fifteen minutes into flashes of sound bites, 140 characters, viewer rankings, and shareholder expectations. In its quest for instantaneous knowledge, it had killed its ability to have true heroes.

Boy Scout wondered if he could change that. Was such a thing possible? He held no illusions or delusions that he could be a hero. After everything he'd done and not done, he could live with that.

"Come on," Boy Scout said, turning on his heel and heading back down Capp Street. "Going to be a busy day."

"Where are we going?" Cendrine asked.

"Union Square," Boy Scout replied.

"The place where they make the music?"

"That's the place."

"Why would Sunshine be there?"

"He's probably not. He's probably still in the Tombs somewhere."

"Then why Union Square? Isn't that a bit out of our way?"

"Maybe. Maybe not. Depends on your point of view."

"I can't wait to hear this explanation."

"Not all stories happen in a linear narrative."

"That makes no bloody sense."

Boy Scout laughed and kept walking, leaving her to wonder.

The artist stared through the wide lens magnifying the blood caked on the shards of glass that had recently been a syringe. Two dozen paint tubes of reds and browns surrounded the objects of her attention.

"Well?" the other whispered from the chair next to the easel and canvas.

"Well what?" the artist asked.

"We're working on a limited timeline here," the whisper replied. "Shouldn't you get to the actual painting sometime soon?"

"I don't bitch and moan and kvetch about how you do your killing. Don't presume to tell me how to do my painting."

Still, she began selecting hues of paint to mix with the Writer's blood to use in her painting.

The sun shone high overhead as Boy Scout and Cendrine reached Market Street close to noon. Time had been unkind to the brick sidewalks of Market Street. Holes gaped here and there where bricks used to be. People – humans, faeries, and even a few half-bloods – filed up and down both sides of the street. Against the buildings, people had set up tables and pop-up tents to sell clothes, jewelry, charms, books, CDs, art, and more. It felt like a surreal acid-dropping sister of Telegraph Avenue in Berkeley before the war…before the Unseelie razed Berkeley to the ground in an attempt to purge a potential hotbed of bardic talents the U.S. could turn against them. The condition of the sidewalks and the foot traffic forced Boy Scout and Cendrine to keep glancing down to be sure of their footing then back to eye level to keep from bumping into anyone.

The crowds thinned as they came up on the Powell Street BART station.

"That's interesting," Boy Scout said.

"What?" Cendrine asked.

He pointed to the massive iron plates etched with silver runes riveted to the ground blocking off the underground entrances to both the BART and MUNI lines. He looked across the street. The same thing had happened to the entrance there as well.

"Looks pretty new," Cendrine said.

"Yep." Boy Scout nodded.

"Seems this fits in with your earlier assessment," Cendrine said. "A straightforward way to keep the riffraff out."

"Yep." He started off again.

"Why are we here?" Cendrine asked. "I'm still thinking this is a little out of the way if Sunshine is in the Tombs."

"Right," Boy Scout said. "But not all stories have a linear progression."

"Yeah, you mentioned that," Cendrine said. "Care to explain?"

"I just did." Boy Scout replied, pleased that for once, she was the one trying to keep up with him.

They continued down Market until Boy Scout heard the beginnings of music. The wind was right and carried the sounds a block earlier than he expected. So many instruments wove together in a chaotic cacophony that flowed in and out of being painful and sublime and brilliant and ear-wrenchingly bad. He turned right toward Union Square, and the noise grew. When they reached the corner of Powell and Geary, Union Square came into view, and nothing had changed. Musicians, both individuals and bands, filled Union Square proper. Dancers and performance artists filled the sidewalk surrounding the square. This close, when the musicians went out of sync with each other, the effect was almost painful.

Cendrine said something.

Boy Scout leaned closer to her. "What?"

"We're going in there?" Cendrine almost had to shout for Boy Scout to hear her.

Boy Scout nodded.

Before crossing the street, he went over to a girl sitting against a building. She was in her mid-twenties. Sunglasses hid her eyes, though the mop of unruly brown hair might have done that as well. She wore a mix of ragged fatigues and what might have been a fairly cool gypsy costume, once upon a time. She had a sign, black marker on cardboard, that read: *TYS burned me out. Can't sing. Voice gone. Please help. Have ear plugs. Used and unused.*

Boy Scout pulled his pen and the new journal out of his pocket and knelt down in front of her.

"Trade you a secret for two pairs of ear plugs," he said.

She looked him up and down. "Bullshit. You got no muse."

He pulled his dog tags out of his shirt and showed them to her. She slid the sunglasses down a bit to better read the tags. Boy Scout decided he liked the girl's deep green eyes. Pretty, despite the way they didn't quite focus on anything while trying to focus on everything. Her lips formed silent words as she read his number. She blinked a couple of times in rapid succession. Any bard with any talent would know that number.

"Uh, uh, uh," she stammered. Seems she got just as articulate as he did when life surprised her.

"Calm down," Boy Scout said. "No drama. No scene. No names…especially not here. I just want to trade a secret for two pairs of ear plugs. Deal?"

"Not just a secret." The girl swallowed. "I want a True Secret."

It wasn't a request or an offer; it was her price, straight up, take it or leave it.

Boy Scout drew in a deep breath and let it out slowly. He glanced around to see if anyone had heard her. No one seemed to have paid any attention to her. Perhaps this was the universe throwing him a bone. If so, he was grateful. Having that get around in this place was not any kind of attention he wanted.

"That's a big fat can of Lovecraftian nightmare worms. You sure you want to open that?"

Her eyes grew wide and she held her breath for about ten seconds while she licked her lips. The air around her seemed to thicken with the tension of her choice. Finally, she gave three nods in quick succession. She blinked, let out a heavy breath, and the tension a-round her faded.

The girl held out her right hand.

For a moment, Boy Scout thought about refusing. This girl couldn't be the only one selling ear plugs. He thought about the last girl he'd tried to help. Christina Walker's dead gaze stared at Boy Scout from within his mind's eye. He clenched his teeth and rubbed his hand over his face. When he looked again, the girl still had her hand out to him.

"Ah, hell," he said, wondering why it seemed impossible for him to say no to anyone even remotely resembling a damsel in distress.

Another face rose out of Boy Scout's past: high cheekbones, green eyes of creamy jade, and hair the color of a summer sunset. She would be why. Somehow, someway, if he helped enough damsels, it might make up for her.

Boy Scout took the girl's hand. They shook, once, twice, and three times – a bargain made.

Boy Scout looked back and up over his shoulder to Cendrine. She fidgeted from one foot to the other, eyes shifting back and forth, trying to keep her attention on as many of the passersby as she could.

"Need a heat mirage," Boy Scout said.

Cendrine stopped bouncing side to side and glared right at him.

"Really?" she asked, her tone flat and oddly cool. When Boy Scout nodded, she added, "You don't think that's going to be a little conspicuous?"

"Not as conspicuous as what I'm about to do," he replied.

"Oh, for fuck's sake," she snarled. "Really? I mean, *really*?"

"Yes, really. Trust me; you especially don't want to go in there," he gestured across the street to the musician-filled Union Square, "without ear plugs. Think about what's happening and the kind of people who are making it happen."

"Christ. Can't I just give her some money? Maybe some gold?"

"Too late," Boy Scout said. "Bargain's been struck."

Cendrine turned her back on Boy Scout and the former bardic girl. "I hate you so much."

A moment later, Boy Scout felt heat on his back, as if someone had placed a radiator behind him. When the temperature rose to an uncomfortable level, Boy Scout held out his hand. The girl placed her left hand onto his. Boy Scout stabbed her in the palm with his pen. She gasped. He tried to feel some semblance of sympathy for her, but she knew what she was getting into when she'd made the bargain. He pulled the pen from her skin, opened the journal to a random page in the middle, closed his eyes, and wrote.

He didn't write very long.

True Secrets, those devoid of gray area or room for interpretation, those containing the essence of a Truth about someone or something, were never complex. That's what made True Secrets so hard, and in many cases impossible, for people to figure out: when it came down to it, human beings can't handle simple, basic Truths; it leaves people too open, exposed, raw; that scares them, sometimes terrifies them to the point of insanity, and so people bury those Truths down beneath layers of half-lies, delusions, and good intentions; it's the only way the majority of humanity stays sane, and the reason why in the war so many bards took a giant red-rover-red-rover-send-the-bard-right-over headlong sprint over to bat-shit-crazy-town – too many of them learned too many True Secrets.

When he finished the single, brief sentence, Boy Scout fumbled with the journal a bit as he ripped the page out of it, folded it in half, and handed it to the girl. As soon as he did, the temperature around them cooled to Bay Area normal, which meant Boy Scout was going to be chilly for a while as the cool air caressed his sweat-soaked skin.

"The writing might be a bit sloppy," Boy Scout said, as the girl took hold, "but you'll be able to read it. Just wait until you get somewhere alone, quiet and alone. You know this, right?"

She was chewing her lower lip, and so didn't speak, but she nodded. With her other hand, the girl handed Boy Scout two pairs of brand new ear plugs still in their plastic seal.

"Thanks," Boy Scout said, then glanced at her hand, "Just because you have it, doesn't mean you have to read it."

She nodded. "I know."

Of course you do, Boy Scout thought to himself as he stood.

A trio of young men, probably not even twenty years old, had stopped and made a triangle around Boy Scout and Cendrine. Their clothes were thinning at the knees and frayed at the edges. Dirt blotched their skin in places almost like dark sores from some strange wasting sickness, and greasy hair stuck out at wild angles from their head. Two had scars on their faces, and one was missing a few fingers on both hands.

"What happened there?" the one in the middle said. "Musta been pretty important."

"I told you this would draw unwanted attention," Cendrine said.

People around them began making a wider and wider berth.

"It's always got to be something," Boy Scout couldn't help but sigh and roll his eyes. He addressed the spokesman. "I don't suppose that you'd be at all willing go against your natural tendencies to be a gaggle of twatwaffles and let this go? You know, between the lady," he gestured with his chin to Cendrine, "and me, it's just because it's not going to go well for you."

"I don't believe in faeries," the one on the left sneered at Cendrine, showing off two missing teeth and several others rotting.

"Can I?" Cendrine asked.

"No," Boy Scout said.

The toothless wonder muttered under his breath, "I don't believe in faeries, I don't, I don't. I don't believe in faeries, I don't, I don't."

Boy Scout shook his head in disbelief. He thought back to the question Master Sargent Cuban used to ask any time someone didn't live up to his expectation: *How is it possible that Saint Darwin has not asked you to join him yet?*

"Tell you what," Boy Scout said. "Let me give you an insight into your future, something that will get you out of trouble the next time you're about to step in it bigger than you ever have in your life? Deal?"

The three tough guys glanced back and forth, and even before the leader said, "Yeah, deal," Boy Scout knew he had them.

He took the pen and jammed it into the wound on his finger where he'd stabbed himself to call to Cendrine. Then he wrote a single sentence in the journal in his own blood. When he showed the words to them, their skin became a sickly pale with a hint of green as they read: *TRUE SECRET: Mess with any of the three of us and you will choke to death on your own vomit.*

"Will that do it, gentlemen?"

They said nothing. The bravado faded from them like a balloon with a slow leak as they slunk away down the street.

Once the three poster children for the Darwin awards had moved out of earshot, Cendrine leaned in right next to Boy Scout's ear, and asked, "You didn't really give them a True Secret did you?"

Boy Scout shook his head. "Nope."

"Funny," Cendrine said.

"Yup," he replied, and handed her a pair of the ear plugs.

He mashed up his ear plugs, shoved them into his ears, and marched across the street. Cendrine did the same.

"Why didn't you read it?" Cendrine asked.

"Read what?"

"Her True Secret."

"How do you know I—"

"I saw your face when you read that page in your journal," Cendrine interrupted, "and that wasn't even a True Secret. When you turned around, before you saw the idiot triplets, you looked melancholy, not terrified. Not hard to put things together when you pay attention."

"Right," Boy Scout said. "Seems like you just answered your own question."

Boy Scout smiled as they walked into Union Square. Every time he came here, he remembered the Plato quote he'd first heard in Philosophy 101: "Music is a moral law. It gives soul to the universe, wings to the mind, flight to the imagination, a charm to sadness, gaiety and life to everything. It is the essence of order and lends to all that is good and just and beautiful." Union Square embodied this. Dozens and dozens of musicians jammed, with no leader, no sheet music, and yet, over and over again, created beautiful harmonies together. Most times those harmonies lasted ten to thirty seconds, but sometimes longer, as much as a minute or more. The last record of everyone playing in harmony Boy Scout remembered was over five minutes. Proof that human creativity was the foundation of miracle.

Dancers – individuals, pairs, and groups – spun and wove and grooved around the musicians. Sometimes bumping into each other, but always polite and apologetic…well…at least they were when the music hadn't swept them so far away they stopped noticing.

A deep longing for junior high school settled in the pit of Boy Scout's stomach. Once he'd finished his regular homework and chores, he'd slip his headphones on and write, blasting music loud enough to shut out everything but words flowing out of his pen into the notebook. Computers were for schoolwork. For his stories, he loved doing it the old-fashioned way. He missed when the writing was just for him. Before his Eagle Scout project. Before College. Before his first journalism job, when he thought that somewhere, somehow, he had found a place mass media hadn't poisoned. The best times of his life had been back when it was him, the music, and the writing, writing whatever the hell he wanted.

Shaking off the pointless longing of nostalgia, Boy Scout kept scanning the crowd.

The song of Union Square merged. His mind put words to the melody, *beggar than a king*, words he'd heard earlier when he'd leapt outside his window to the fire escape. And then, the musicians wandered out of harmony, but it was enough to tell Boy Scout he'd come to the right place.

Heh, he thought. *Fire escape*. He'd never really considered how accurate that was until just now.

A group of dancers parted, and Boy Scout saw who he was looking for.

The man sat cross-legged, salt-and-pepper beard hanging out from underneath the mountain of rags that were his clothes. A battered metal cup sat on the ground just in front of him.

When Boy Scout walked over to the beggar, the man's deep dark eyes snapped open. The eyes weren't black, nor were they brown. They were dark, piercing down to Boy Scout's core, just as they had been the two other times they'd met.

Boy Scout dropped a coin into the cup. Even with the cacophony around them, the *clink* of the penny hitting the bottom echoed in Boy Scout's ear.

"Eh," the beggar said. "Wha…what's this?"

"A little something to help out," Boy Scout said. "Man sometimes gets cold, hungry, or thirsty."

Without taking his eyes away from Boy Scout, the beggar picked the cup up off the ground and shook it. The cup was silent. No coin rattled within.

"What the—?"

"Exactly kiddo," the beggar said. "What the...dot, dot, dot?" He sniffed and squinted at Boy Scout. "I remember you...Didn't you used to be smarter?"

"Not that we've ever seen," Cendrine muttered under her breath.

Boy Scout gaped up at her, not because she'd said it – he'd gotten used to her scathing opinion of him – but rather because he heard her over the music blaring around them.

"Shush, you," the beggar snapped, and threw the cup at her, catching her on the shoulder. "He was smart enough to keep you as his Martin."

"His what?" Cendrine asked.

The beggar shook his head. "Sorry, mixing artist with the metaphor, in sideways up. His wild card? Yeah...yeah." He laughed so hard he coughed. "What a stretch that one was. But yeah, he was smart enough to keep you as his wild card." He laughed again, then held up his hand. "No. Don't say nothing. S'bout me an' him now. You just hush, and not need to bat those gorgeous greens at me. Been a long time since a pretty face could sway me 'bout anything one way or t'other."

"What happened to the coin?" Boy Scout asked. "It was my last one and I'm desperate."

"You already played that game once before. Not that you can't play it twice. Or thrice, if luck smile down on you. Some people get that lucky when they down that far, but not many. Besides. You wasn't and still ain't that broke. You can't make something your last penny. It's gotta *BE* your last penny. You can cheat some of the Old Traditions. Not that one."

"I suppose you would know," Boy Scout said.

"You trying to be cutesy there, kiddo?" He picked up the cup again, which had somehow just gotten back in front of him. "Sayin' I'm old?"

"You? Old? Never!"

Boy Scout considered adding, *Just because you've been around since God was an altar boy doesn't mean you're old*, but he didn't think that would go over well. And...*and*...Boy Scout had the feeling that statement might be more true than not true.

"So that's it, then?" Boy Scout asked.

The beggar snorted. "Yeah. You *was* a hell of a lot smarter. Just going to give up like that?"

Boy Scout lifted his hands in frustration. "I've got no money."

"That all I care about? That alls I've become? No wonder the Unseelie kicked your asses so bad and why you can't get rid of em, Unseelie and Seelie alike. Even after the war, and magic, and all the wonder and terror, y'all…alls y'alls deserve what ya got…and what you're likely to get."

"How about I trade you a story for a story?"

"Naw…I don't feel like telling a story, and you don't want to hear one. Yeah, you were going to ask me to tell you a story about where to find someone, but that's not how it works. That's not a story, that's directions. Still, getting closer, close enough to help you out, because you won't get it fast enough, and I have elsewheres and elsewhens to be. So, I don't needs a story, but you needs the middle of one. You'll start it, but it'll be in the middle. When you think it's the end, and you'll write more, it won't be any, but the begin, a new beginning. But…but…you won't see or read that beginning. That's a living, live, real treasure hunt of a missing person's case older than the war itself, and someone tells it after you've gone to tell other stories. The end…yours, theirs, everyone's…will work out in the end. I suppose that's why they call them endings… In exchange for all that, I'll give you a map to what you seek."

With that, the raggedy man held out his hand.

Boy Scout stared at the beggar for a long time. The words had been English, and had pretty much been sentences, but still, he couldn't figure out what they meant.

The beggar sighed. "Write something. One page. Then you get the map to the best place to watch the Sunshine."

Boy Scout took the beggar's hand. They shook once, twice, three times – a bargain struck.

Boy Scout sat down and opened the newer journal.

"No," the beggar said. "Not that one. The other one. The scary one. The one that hurts you to even know it's still around. Open it and write me one page full of something on that first page."

Boy Scout licked his lips. "But that page already has writing on it."

"Does it?"

Boy Scout looked to Cendrine. "May I have it back, please?"

Cendrine glanced between Boy Scout and the beggar. She pursed her lips for a moment.

The beggar laughed. "Shoulda checked with the lady before striking such a bargain. You used to be better at this."

"Please, Cendrine?" Boy Scout asked.

Cendrine pulled the war journal out of her peacock feather coat and handed it to Boy Scout.

He opened it.

The first page was blank.

He flipped the page...

...and saw the familiar words in his familiar handwriting: *I'm calling this "Day Zero" because the platoon I've been assigned to is supposedly shipping out tomorrow. That will be day one. Kind of like our version of D-Day.*

He flipped back to the black front page.

"Fucking faerie magic," he muttered under his breath.

"Watch the tone, kiddo," the beggar said, "and the sentiment. Even though I had nothing to do with that page in that book, I know you was lipping off to me. I'm as human as you are."

"I seriously doubt that," Boy Scout said.

"Doubt all you want. Doesn't matter much none to me."

"Fine," Boy Scout said. "What do you want me to write?"

"Whatever you need to, only, write as if you were young again. Lose yourself in the joy of it, like when you still loved it."

Boy Scout took a deep breath, put pen to paper, and closed his eyes. What to write about...What...to...write...about...

Somewhere close by, someone sang, "A knight without armor in a savage land."

He opened his eyes. The pen was already flying across the page, leaving words in its wake.

We shouldn't need armor... *Morgan's words came echoing back to me when the troll bouncer stood up and flexed its talons at me. It might have gnashed its teeth, but I wasn't about to give it the satisfaction of looking up at it.*

When it figured out that I wasn't going to look up, the troll bent down and got up close and personal.

"We don't like yer kind 'round here," ten feet of gnarled, red-and-black-checkered-flannel-wearing troll snarled in my face.

Great, I thought, as the heat and stench of its breath burned my nostrils and I choked down bile, of all the trolls in Arcadia, I had to get one that embraced Deliverance as its paradigm for existence.

"We just need to go in and have a look around." Morgan stepped up next to me. "What you like or don't like, doesn't have anything to do with it."

The troll's head swiveled away from me. I sucked in a breath of sweet, contaminant-free air.

"What about you, Roland?" Morgan asked. "Do you care if big, dumb, and inbred likes our kind around here?"

"Look," I said, "we don't want any trouble, but there's a faerie inside who has greatly offended the Duke of Avalon."

"Well, ain't dat sweet."

The troll's head swiveled back to me. I kept my feet planted in place rather than step out of the blast radius of its breath.

"I give less crap than a goblin's black ass." I blinked for a second at that visual, but then shrugged it off trying to wrap my mind around the metaphor. Better to not try and fathom the inner workings of the troll's thought process. "I'd turn away Oberon hisself, iffin he came here. So any changeling *fetch dog can piss the hell off."*

Typical response from the Unseelie slums. Avalon is one of the nicer cities in Arcadia, but like everything in Arcadia, some parts have to balance, and since Avalon is primarily a Seelie city, it means Unseelie neighborhoods get pretty white-trash-ghettolicious to compensate.

"Don't make this harder than it has to be," Morgan said.

The warning to be civil surprised me. Morgan likes beating up big and scary Unseelie brutes, the bigger and scarier, the better.

"Go bother someone else, changeling,*" again the word came as a curse. "You ain't gettin' in."*

"You expect to stop me?" Morgan asked. "Pixies bigger and stronger than you have tried to stop me and failed."

The troll snarled and reached for Morgan. Morgan dropped to her knees, forcing the troll to lean further over to grab her. Its hand barely touched her shoulder when Morgan dropped, braced against the ground, and kicked the troll where its foot met its leg. I pulled my pistol crossbow. Morgan rolled out of the way to avoid the toppling behemoth. The troll rolled over, and as it got to its knees, I had the quarrel an inch away from its nose.

The troll froze, staring cross-eyed at the iron-tipped point.

"Now that I have your attention," I said, "will you kindly open the door? If you don't, I'll be on my way. I'm sure my patron would be more than happy to let me close the bar. Permanently."

The troll swallowed. Most faeries, no matter which court they've sworn to, hate any form of the word permanent when it comes from a paladin.

The woman with the blond braids and the gray long coat looked at the painting as the artist's brush flew back and forth between the canvas and palette.

"Is that really how you're painting it?" came a whispered question.

The artist stopped working, the tip of her brush a centimeter from the canvas and dripping with paint.

"Yes," the artist replied.

"That uniform is ridiculous," the disgust dripped from her quiet words. "And a disposable razor…Really?"

"Get over yourself," the artist said, and continued painting.

Boy Scout turned the page and touched the pen to paper so he could continue writing. It didn't surprise him in the least when he found it blank.

"Stop," a voice said as a hand closed over his, keeping him from writing on. "I said a single page."

Boy Scout started, "But—"

"It is not the time to finish this story," the beggar said. "It is only time that you know it exists. You will know the whole and the truth of this tale before your story ends."

Boy Scout withdrew his pen from his battered and worn war journal, flipped back a page and skimmed over the words he'd just written. He flipped to the dog-eared page, and read the entry in his handwriting, the one that he'd never written, about the last time he saw Tommy. Memories of his childhood, playing *DnD* with Phil, Tommy, and some other friends: Tommy would always play a paladin, because it was the closest thing to his last name.

"Holy shit," Boy Scout said, and followed it up with, "and fuck you, hindsight."

"Now," the beggar said, "as a bargain fairly made, here is a map to the man you wish to speak with."

337

The beggar handed Boy Scout a small, thin black electronic device.

"That's not a map," Cendrine said.

"Yeah, it is," Boy Scout said. He looked at the beggar. "GPS? From you?"

The beggar shrugged, picked up his metal cup, stood up, and vanished into the crowd.

"That may be the oddest exchange I've ever witnessed," Cendrine said. "Who was that?"

"You'd rather not know," Boy Scout replied.

He held his breath as he turned on the GPS. After the beggar had left, it occurred to Boy Scout that he hadn't included making the map readable as part of the bargain. The beggar didn't seem the sort to mince up the wording of a bargain like that...but when dealing with ephemeral beings at the heart of legends that spanned across multiple realities, one could never take anything at face value. The GPS turned on. Had it not been charged, it would have been inconvenient, but not terrible. With power restored to most of the city by a motley group of enterprising Luchorpáns and other industrious faeries, they could have found someplace to charge it.

Cendrine shook his shoulder.

"What?" Boy Scout said.

"I asked, why don't I want to know and how can you be sure?" Cendrine asked, steam rising from her hair.

Boy Scout smiled patiently at her and shook his head.

"What?" Her face tightened, and she crossed her arms.

Life mirroring art, Boy Scout thought as passages from his mother's books came bubbling up from the recesses of his memory.

So few hours ago, she'd seemed to be the stronger of the two, *had* been the stronger. Nothing had changed for Cendrine. She remained as she'd been since stepping out of his closet. He, on the other hand, had become more the man he'd been when trekking through the wilds of Faerie, the questing hero.

"What?" Cendrine demanded.

"We are the embodiment of our choices," Boy Scout said.

"If you say so," Cendrine said. "Who was that man?"

Boy Scout slid the GPS into his pocket and placed his hands on her shoulders. The warmth of her flowed into his palms as if he was holding a pair of steaming mugs of tea. He looked her right in the eye and did his best not to flinch from the candle flames she had in place of pupils.

"I tell you honestly, because I care for you. As cheesy and sappy as it is, I love you, do not ask after that one or seek him out."

"But—"

"Please, Cendrine," Boy Scout said. "I know caution and prudence are not natural to fire, but please listen to me on this. I've given you plenty of reasons to ignore my council, which is why I don't give it, but this is different."

Cendrine gazed back at him, the flames in her eyes dancing as she studied him. She grew warmer, almost painful to Boy Scout's touch. Still, he did not let her go. After a few moments, she shrugged out of his grip.

"Alright," she said. "I won't look for him, but can't you at least—"

"No, Cendrine," Boy Scout said. "You *know* about the danger of names. Let it go. You do *not* want his attention. Look at what having it did to my life."

She opened her mouth to retort; Boy Scout knew the expression, and he raised an eyebrow. She closed her mouth and nodded.

Boy Scout let go of her and pulled the GPS out of his pocket. It had a saved address. It was right on the Bay, directly opposite the gate to Faerie at the 24th Street BART station – not to mention right by Warm Water Cove Park and Pier 80, perfect for landing and staging areas right off the Bay.

"What the fuck is going on?" Boy Scout asked to the universe in general, not actually expecting a response.

"Where is Sunshine?" Cendrine asked.

Boy Scout showed her the GPS.

"What the fuck *is* going on?" Cendrine asked Boy Scout. He could tell she actually did want an answer.

"Whatever it is," Boy Scout replied, "it's big, and not nearly as straightforward as it looks. If we hoof, we should be able to get this done before too late in the evening. I don't want to be out in the Tombs after dark if we can help it."

LINES IN THE SAND

The only rules that really matter are these: what a man can do and what a man can't do.
Pirates of the Caribbean – Jack Sparrow

No law can be sacred to me but that of my nature.
Good and bad are but names very readily transferable to that or this;
the only right is what is after my constitution, the only wrong what is against it.
Self-Reliance – Ralph Waldo Emerson

The artist waited at the edge of Warm Water Cove Park. She leaned against a lamppost with a painting tucked under her arm. A-round her, the shadows grew long with the sun hidden on the far side of San Francisco. To the east, lights from the military base at Alameda shone from across the bay. Somewhere among the deepening shadows, the artist's quiet friend waited, just in case of a double cross.

After a few minutes, the man who commissioned the work app-roached her. He seemed somewhere in his fifties or sixties, and while he wore civilian clothes, his trimmed haircut and crisply pressed clothes told the astute observer that they could place decent money that he was ex-military. A cigar stuck out of the left side of his mouth.

"Is that it?" the man said, indicating with his chin the painting under her arm.

She nodded. "You don't have much time."

"You're sure he's coming?"

She reached into her pocket and pulled out the sketch she'd drawn of a Boy Scout. He stood in a room as he looked out a wind-ow facing a sun. A clock on the wall behind the Boy Scout had one hand and only four times: Dawn, noon, dusk, and midnight. The hand had almost come in line with dusk.

"I got bored waiting," she said. "He'll be there soon."

"Are you sure it's accurate?" the man asked.

"Everything I do nowadays is accurate," the artist said. "Everything he writes is accurate, and he hasn't even really been practicing the last few years. Then again, he hasn't had to."

She handed the man the painting.

"Thank you," he said.

"Don't thank me, yet," the artist replied. "Just make sure he doesn't see it. It's got to be in the room with him."

The man looked at the painting and shook his head. "He looks ridiculous in that uniform. I should've left him with his original name."

"No." She spoke in a somber tone. "He's going to live up to whatever name he is known by. If you hadn't renamed him, he would have lived up to the first one you gave him, and then where would we be?"

"Hard to tell," the man said.

"No it's not," the artist countered. "We'd be fucked." The man blinked in surprise. Why did everyone expect her to be the prim lady? "And we'd be fucked, up shit creek and screw the paddle; we wouldn't even have a goddamn boat. That's where we'd be. As it is, we're still up that creek, just not one hundred percent fucked yet, and at least we have a boat. That right there," she pointed at the painting, "might just be the paddle we need. Best get it to where it can do some good."

The man with his high-and-tight haircut peered at the artist for a few moments with an unwavering, unblinking gaze. She imagined he'd been a drill sergeant at one point, and thus, was probably used to people bigger, stronger, and meaner than she looked backing down from that stare. The thing he didn't take into account was that those bigger, stronger, and meaner people hadn't looked into the truth of the universe, painted so many True Secrets about the past, present, and future that they had the Thousand Year Stare crash down onto their mind, and then painted their way back out. In essence, the universe had taken its best shot at the artist and she'd said, "Fuck you," and gotten on with what needed doing. This man could stare all he wanted.

Finally, when she did not flinch, blink, or look away, the man nodded, executed a textbook about-face, and walked away.

A few moments later, the girl with the braids and the gray long coat came up next to the artist. The girl had a painting tucked underneath her arm, the painting that the artist had created using the Writer's blood.

"Ready?" the artist asked.

"Yes," came the quiet reply. "How much does that one know?"

"He thinks this is about revenge," the artist said. "He has no idea that Oberon is involved, that the Powries went after the Writer, or that we have a deeper agenda."

"This is a desperate gamble we're making, and it's entirely likely that this is going to kill him before he can help us."

"If that happens, we'll just have to find the new champion and hope they have more character."

"Well, let's hope he lives," the artist said, "or it will be a hell of a long wait before a new champion is old enough to try this again."

"This place is a dump," Cendrine said.

"All of Sunshine's places look like dumps from the outside," Boy Scout replied. "Cuts down on the riffraff."

They had stopped a block and a half away from the compound so that Boy Scout could rest. His feet, knees, and hips ached; his throat burned. He was *not* going to let himself get this out of shape ever again, and this time he meant it.

"Let me know when you're ready," Cendrine said.

Boy Scout nodded. He just wished he could keep Christina Walker's face from flashing in his mind. Taking a few breaths to steady himself, he prepared to go into the nest of vipers. Before starting out, he took out his journal, the new one, stabbed himself in the finger…again…and wrote a sentence: *No matter how much they search me, they will not find the glass gun.*

He held out his finger to Cendrine and clenched his teeth together as she cauterized the wound.

"You're being very free with your blood today," she said.

"Let's go," Boy Scout said.

"You sure?" Cendrine asked, her tone stating clearly that she didn't believe him.

"Yeah," Boy Scout said, starting out toward Sunshine's compound. "Body will hurt for a few more days, and the other stuff that's wrong with me will last a whole lot longer."

As they got closer, Boy Scout saw that the place had once been a mechanic's shop.

Four massive brutes – Boy Scout decided he was going to call them, "the Brute Squad" – stood by the gate and watched him and Cendrine approach. The Brute Squad members all wore identical dark suits. Image was a big part of the reason why, in the wake of the Faerie war, Sunshine had risen higher and faster than other criminal tyrants seeking to prey on the desperate poor of San Francisco. Sunshine demanded that each of his men adopt the appearance of businessmen rather than strong-arm toughs.

"I'm here to see Sunshine," Boy Scout said.

"Been expecting you," one of the Brute Squad said. "You can go in. The lady stays out here with us."

"I'm not staying with you," Cendrine said. "I have standards about the company I keep."

"Take a walk then," the spokesman said. "Pier Eighty is right that way." He gestured with his thumb, as if trying to hitch a ride. "Walk or stay. Makes no difference to me. You just don't go inside."

"Really?" Cendrine's voice got low and husky.

Boy Scout suddenly flashed to a memory of Cendrine's mother. He started to sweat, which had nothing to do with the sudden wave of heat spreading out from Cendrine.

"Really," the spokesman said.

Before Boy Scout could intercede, Cendrine tossed a brown bundle onto the sidewalk just in front of the Brute Squad.

"What's that?" Boy Scout and the spokesman asked at the same time.

Boy Scout knew even before Cendrine spoke.

"Six Powrie caps. Red Caps." She waited for that to sink in, but the brutes looked at her, blinking with a lack of comprehension. "I took those six this morning."

She paused again. This time they started to get it. All four took a step away from the brown bundle.

"Six Red Caps, gentlemen. I killed them. That was how my day *started*. It hasn't really improved since. Do not fuck with me. I will snuff your pathetic mortal lives like candles on a birthday cake. Then, without moving from this spot, I will reduce the compound behind you to ash and slag. The man who pays you to protect him will be dead before he even thinks to turn on a fan. What's more important, following his orders today or all of you being alive to-morrow?"

During her speech, the tips Cendrine's hair had transformed into tiny candle flames. Steam rose from her. The sidewalk around her feet blackened and charred.

The Brute Squad tensed, hands inching toward their coats.

Boy Scout scanned the area, taking in all the glass windows in the surrounding buildings. For a brief second he really, *really* wanted the Brute Squad to throw down. He'd been holding in his rage over Christina Walker all day, letting it fester into a bubbling rot in the dark places of his soul along with all the other pointless deaths that had filled his life. These fucktards were the perfect foils for venting his rage.

The sound of synthesized music came from the spokesman's coat pocket. The brute answered the cell phone, listened for a few seconds, and said, "Yes, sir," before returning the phone to his pocket.

"Mister Sunshine would like to welcome both of you," the spokesman said.

With the muffled buzz of an electric motor, the large metal gate behind the Brute Squad slid open a few feet.

The Brute Squad parted, and Boy Scout and Cendrine walked between them and through the gate. Thankfully, Cendrine had cooled back down after picking up the bundle of Powrie hats.

"Could you really reduce this place to ash and slag, that quickly?" Boy Scout whispered.

"Yes," Cendrine said, "but I would have killed you and anyone else in the heat radius. Still working on directing heat to specific locations."

"Good to know," Boy Scout said.

A man who made the guys on the Brute Squad look like members of a high school mathlete team stepped into the doorframe, filling it. If he'd played sports back in high school, Boy Scout would put money on him being a star at neanderball, position: offensive throwback.

The massive mound of flesh looked Boy Scout over. He poked at the blade on Boy Scout's hip and chuckled. "Old School?"

"Iron," Boy Scout said.

344

"Fair enough," the offensive throwback grunted. "Give it over, and all your weapons."

"Hospitality means nothing here?" Boy Scout said.

"Safer than sorrier," the throwback said.

"I'm a bard," Boy Scout said. "I'd be a fool to start anything just when I'm getting used to using my talents again."

The offensive throwback shook all over and made a sound that might have been laughter. "People still fall for that shit?"

"Most still do," Boy Scout said. "You have to admit, it was a pretty good propaganda campaign."

"True that," the throwback said, getting himself under control. He held out his hand. "Weapons."

"Can't blame a guy for trying."

Boy Scout gave over the short sword and the knife in his left sleeve. The throwback searched him and snorted when he found the knife in Boy Scout's other sleeve. Boy Scout shrugged sheepishly.

"Don't even think about touching me," Cendrine said. "I'm not carrying. I don't need to carry."

"What'll you do if I frisk you anyway?" the uber-brute grunted.

"I'll boil the flesh off your hands down to the bone," Cendrine replied.

The throwback swallowed, but he didn't step aside.

"Let it go, big guy," Boy Scout said. "Sunshine has at least one mage in there that can go against her if it gets ugly. Believe me, I don't want it to get ugly."

"Fine." He moved out of their way. "Her funeral if she starts something. Enter as you will."

Cendrine leaned toward Boy Scout and whispered, "You can really start a fight and not have it affect your bardic talents?"

"Not in the least," Boy Scout replied. "The original bards weren't called warrior poets for nothing."

Crossing the threshold, they saw the main garage had been converted into a kind of recreation room, complete with two bars, a pool table, a foosball table, couches, and TVs with all the game consoles and electronic toys. The place even had power this close to the gateway to Faerie. The room was dim. A little light still filtered in from the high windows near the ceiling, but not much, and only a few lights were on. Boy Scout rolled his eyes at the lava lamps over by one of the bars.

The first people he noticed were the two soldiers by the bar. Boy Scout couldn't see any metal shining on their collars. Their presence was strange, but not completely out of the realm of possibility. Word on the street said that Sunshine catered to some of the military personnel, giving them cash in exchanged for weapons and gear which sold for high prices in San Francisco.

Next, Boy Scout noticed the young women lounging on couches and in piles of pillows. They wore silk and satin lingerie just skimpy enough to make the imagination start working its magic on the male hormones. Christina Walker's face flashed in his mind's eye. Thinking of Christina while seeing the almost-naked girls sent Boy Scout's mind to the previous night. His stomach churned as he blinked to clear the image from his head.

Men in immaculate suits sat and stood around the room, trying to look innocuous, but Boy Scout knew better. Any men that Sunshine chose to be at a meeting like this – Sunshine had to know this was coming after Bruno and Christina didn't come back this morning – were anything but innocuous.

A door opened somewhere to Boy Scout's left, and a voice called "Greetings, my bard."

Boy Scout glanced to his left, and his breathing slowed, but not in a calm, I'm-just-chilling-out way. This was his my-subconscious-is-trying-to-tell-me-something's-out-of-whack breathing.

Sunshine stood in the open doorway to his office. The crime boss was a handsome black man, hair dyed golden blond. A former heavyweight boxer still in decent shame, he filled out his tailored suit enough to be intimidating without trying. Probably more intimidating with his warm and friendly smile.

"I'm not your bard." Boy Scout said.

"Give it a rest." Boy Scout went back to scanning the room, trying to put together everything that didn't add up and doing his absolute best to maintain a perfect poker face. "Call me your bard ever again, and I'll write a story in my own blood about you becoming the Golden Gate Bridge Troll's bitch."

"Is there really a Golden Gate Bridge Troll?" Cendrine asked.

"Yup," Boy Scout said, still looking. "He likes dark meat." Boy Scout didn't know if that was true, but he did know that Sunshine was touchy about color. Boy Scout dropped into a bad southern drawl when he added, "And young and purdy like our host."

Not counting the Marines over by the bar, Boy Scout counted seven guys in suits. Glancing back over his shoulder, he saw that the offensive throwback wasn't around. That made Boy Scout more nervous, especially with seven…no…make that *eight* men. Seeing the bald top of some guy's head in a La-Z-Boy made Boy Scout breathe a little easier. Whoever it was sat at an angle that made him hard to make out at first.

"Do we really need—?" Sunshine started, his voice dripping with enough artificial sweetener to kill a diabetic.

"Yes." Boy Scout cut him off, shifting to the side to get a better look La-Z-Boy-guy. "We really need those kinds of threats."

After sidestepping about a meter, he could see the back of the man's head…and the smoke rising from the glowing tip of a cigar sticking out of the left side of his mouth…and Boy Scout felt as if he'd been dowsed in ice water. Breathing became a challenge. It didn't matter how long Boy Scout lived, or how addled his mind grew with age, he would never, ever forget the back of that head, bald or not, especially not with the tiny birthmark just behind the man's right ear.

"Now just a minute," Sunshine said, without the usual lower pitch in his voice when he got angry.

What the hell was going on, and how many players had a part in this game? Now the soldiers made sense, and the number of dudes in suits set his hackles up again.

"Holy shit," Boy Scout said.

He wasn't sure if he was talking about seeing the back of his old platoon sergeant's head or figuring out how scary the girls had suddenly become when he realized none of them were hanging on any of the men. That might have been plausible, if only one, two, or maybe even three girls had been in the room. The girls could have been with Sunshine, but not so with…Boy Scout did another quick head count…seven girls.

Boy Scout's self-preservation instincts kicked into overdrive. This might be cross-the-streams bad.

"Shut up, Sunshine," Boy Scout snapped preemptively, sensing the crime boss about to spout off again. "I need to take care of something first."

Boy Scout turned around in a slow circle. He touched the thumb and pinky of his right hand and the thumb and ring finger of his left. As he turned, he muttered, *"Bain míniú as an cacamais seo, a striapaigh,"* under his breath over and over. Cendrine gaped at him as if he were mad. The translation: *Figure this one out, bitches* from Irish.

"What's he doing?" Sunshine said. "He's not supposed to know magic."

"He's not doing anything," said one of the mages, one leaning against the pool table. He wore a suit with a purple tint. He had pale skin, too pale to be completely human. He looked in his late twenties, but as with Cendrine and others like them, true age was hard to tell. "That's not magic."

Boy Scout kept turning, taking everything in: Two Marines, the sergeant, Sunshine, Cendrine, seven guys that didn't fit the build of the typical tough guys Sunshine would have in a meeting like this, and seven smoking hot chicks that looked like they could fill the pages of Miss Teen Fredrick's catalogue. Removing the extraneous people from the equation – himself, Cendrine, Sunshine, and the two other Marines, because odds were, they were with Sergeant Cuban – left the seven men and seven women adding up to a shit ton of bad. He'd learned to fear patterns of threes, in this case the soldiers, and sevens, in this case the mages and witches waiting to hatch whatever scheme Sunshine had going.

Once he put all that together in his head, Boy Scout understood he had it right. He made one last tally: one nasty scheming crime boss, seven mages, seven witches, and three Marines with who knew what agenda. Time to push a little more power into his spell.

When he came around to pool-table-guy again, Boy Scout stopped, flicked his fingers out, and gave a final, firm, *"Bain míniú as an cacamais seo, a striapaigh."* He took a deep breath and steadied himself by bringing his hands slowly to his chest and letting them settle to his sides. "Yeah. No magic." Boy Scout shrugged. "Depends on who teaches you the craft. I spent a lot of time with Oberon's daughter while I was on a hero's quest in Faerie. Oh, and that would be the *real* Oberon, *not* that Unseelie pretender." Boy Scout stabbed his finger in the air toward pool table guy. "Who'd you learn from?"

"You should have accepted the offer from Oberon's messenger." Changing the subject pretty much confirmed that the guy didn't know as much as he'd like people to think. He also fell into Boy Scout's trap. "It would have made everything less awkward."

And you die first, Boy Scout thought.

"Shit," Sunshine said, as the man sitting in the La-Z-Boy stood up to his full height of six foot three inches.

The years hadn't been kind. He had more wrinkles, and his hair, though still regulation cut, had retreated, seemingly conceding the battle for the top of his head. The man chewed the cigar at the same time he puffed on it, a feat Boy Scout still couldn't figure out. His presence filled the room, and even though he was just a normal guy without any magic or supernatural abilities at all, he still scared the shit out of Boy Scout.

"Seems like we're at cross-purposes, Mister Sunshine." He spoke in a soft, even tone with a hint of a southern drawl. Still, despite his calmness, or perhaps because of it, he somehow managed to let everyone in the room know that Sunshine was screwed. "I get the impression you have not been entirely forthright with me."

"I-I-I…can ex…explain," Sunshine said.

One thing Boy Scout had learned, probably the most important thing he'd learned from his mother's books, the ones Dad hated, was that if you shovel bullshit with all your soul behind the load of crap, people buy it like a precious commodity. Screw fireballs, charm spells, divination, and all that hocus-pocus-bibity-bobity-peanut-butter-sandwich-phenomenal-cosmic-power that mages, witches, and wizards prattled on about – well-timed bullshit was the strongest magic in the universe.

The old platoon sergeant held up his hand. The two Marines by the bar had subtly shifted stances, ready to move.

"I think you're done talking," Cuban said. "I hear you're still going by Boy Scout."

"That's right," Boy Scout replied. "I gotta say, I'm surprised to see you here…Sergeant Cuban."

Cuban flashed a quick, modest smile. This out-of-character gesture surprised Boy Scout even more.

"It's Warrant Officer, now," Cuban said.

"A promotion. Nice," Boy Scout said. He thought about it for a second, and asked. "Doesn't that come right from the President for some specialized skillset or expertise? What's yours?"

Boy Scout scanned the room, looking for anything that might be an arcane symbol of power.

Cuban's modesty vanished. "You."

"Me?"

"Yes," Cuban said. "When I finally made it back from underhill, I learned what you are. My association with you got the attention of the Joint Chiefs. They asked me to head up a small task force to bring you in to answer for your war crimes against humanity."

Boy Scout pressed his hands to the side of his head. "You've got to be shitting me."

In the far corners of his logical mind, he knew this day would come. Just like he knew everything really was his fault, his responsibility. Christina Walker was a microcosmic expression of Boy Scout's passage through the world, always screwing things up for innocent people no matter how good his intentions were. His emotional mind kept playing tricks to keep him sane: he could keep running and hiding, just like it wasn't really his fault, because he never had any idea what was going on.

"I was a kid trying to clean up a neighborhood park," Boy Scout said.

"This does not absolve you of the responsibility," Cuban said.

Boy Scout should have known better than to expect any sympathy from him.

"What's he talking about?" Cendrine asked.

Boy Scout shook his head.

"Are you going to tell them," Cuban asked, "or am I?"

"Fuck you," Boy Scout said. He turned to Cendrine, "Warrant Officer Cuban is here to take me into custody so I can stand trial for starting the Faerie War."

"What?" Cendrine asked in little more than a whisper.

"Wait," Sunshine said. "What?"

Boy Scout faced Sunshine.

"Surprised?" Boy Scout asked. "Didn't you ever wonder why I worked so hard to hide? Just because you're paranoid doesn't mean millions of people don't think you are the biggest fuck-head since Hitler. " Boy Scout turned to face the rest of the room again. "For that matter, it makes me wonder why your pet mages and witches didn't tell you that."

The seven men and seven women in the room, with their too perfect clothes, stiffened.

"How?" pool table guy asked.

"Oh, come on," Boy Scout said. "You can't believe that you were actually fooling anyone, can you?" He looked from Sunshine, to Cuban, to pool-table-guy. "So you've got a problem. Y'all want me for different stuff. Sunshine is kinda fucked, because I think he thought he'd let you guys duke it out and give me over to the winner, but now I've ratted him out. So what's it going to be guys, O-beron or the U.S.?"

"Hey," Cendrine cut in, speaking to pool-table-guy, "you work for Oberon?"

"Yeah," he sneered back at her. "I serve a real master."

"Good one," Cendrine said. "I serve no one." She tossed the bundle of former Red Cap caps on the pool table. "Go tell your *real* master that his precious little pets are dead."

The pale mage jerked back as if she'd tossed a bundle of serpents instead. The mages and witches began sliding along the walls.

And just like that, Cendrine set things in motion. Boy Scout didn't know whether to be proud of her or to pity her.

Boy Scout had to figure something out, some way to even the odds, or at least throw a little chaos into this. He didn't really care if he got out of this, not at this point. He just didn't want Cendrine to suffer for his folly.

He took a deep breath. This was one of those moments like other moments before this that would shape his destiny: wanting to clean up a park, enlisting to serve, shooting a gun on a plain of obsidian, and pushing a needle into his arm for the first time.

Boy Scout turned back to Cuban. The mages were still moving around the room. Sunshine was inching back toward his office. Boy Scout didn't want to think of the hardware he had back there, not to mention the means to call his Brute Squad into the mix, likely with the offensive throwback taking point.

"Why the hell are you here?" Boy Scout demanded. "This isn't like you."

The Sergeant reached down and picked up something from the La-Z-Boy. He held up a painting of a man in a Boy Scout uniform getting gunned down by a gun wielding cigar. Boy Scout recognized the artistic style: most recently because he'd taken the tour of her work in San Francisco just before going into hiding, but also long ago when he was working to become an Eagle Scout.

"I'm here because someone needs to make sure you don't make the same mistakes again," Cuban said.

"Wow." It was all Boy Scout could say. It looked like a fairly fresh painting, the paint still glistening. "Wow." He thought she'd been dead since well before the war ended.

Then Boy Scout understood the ramifications of him, the Writer, and her, the Artist, still alive and active. Even more, if Oberon knew that and got his hands on both of them at the same time, well, Boy Scout shuddered to think about the terrible things Oberon could accomplish then.

Boy Scout whirled on Sunshine. "You better pray either you or I die in this room tonight, or you will never know another moment's peace for the rest of your life, and I *will not* allow you to die young."

"Fuck you, you lying sack of shit." Now Sunshine's tone lowered as he pulled a gun and pointed it at Boy Scout. "You're lucky Oberon wants you alive."

Now it was time for some truly dazzling bullshit magic.

"Fuck me?" Boy Scout screeched. "Fuck you!" He whirled on Cuban, pointing. "And fuck you!" Then he screamed at the mages and witches. "You can all go fuck yourselves in one giant circle jerk, which is what I'm going to make you do if I get out of here alive. I'm sick and goddamn tired of being everyone's scapegoat and pawn."

Boy Scout started pacing in a circle, waving his arms.

"I. Was. A. Fucking. Kid. Can any of you get that through your thick fucking skulls? I didn't know anything about Faerie, much less the games the Seelie and Unseelie play with mortals as their pawns."

Boy Scout faced Cuban. "You want to see justice done? You've got it. Take your shot."

He turned to pool-table-guy. "You want to snatch me up and take me to your master?" Boy Scout pointed a finger at the lead mage and glared down it like a gun sight. He swept his gaze over all the arcane practitioners in the room. "Bring it, bitches. I faced down Oberon's personal pet magic bitch boy during the war and left his mind leaking out his brain like tapioca. You got nothing."

Boy Scout turned back to Sunshine and smiled.

"You. Mister opportunist. You want to ever feel safe again? You better kill me now. I make it out of here, I don't even have to find you. I'm a bard. No. I'm *the* bard. Creator of legends. No matter where you go, no matter how completely you think you can hide, you will fail, and you will know the full weight of a bardic curse. You've got one shot, and only one. Better make it good. The problem is, if you kill me, Oberon won't be too happy, will he? Welcome to the sucktastic world of the Old Laws where all your options blow."

"Don't even think about harming him," pool-table-guy said. "Oberon wants the bard. Come peacefully and we'll spare the girl."

"Oh, really?" Cendrine asked.

The room grew warmer.

Everything seemed still, and now the whole room seemed to buzz with the energy of potential movement that came with the anticipation of combat.

Sunshine fired. Seems he was more scared of Boy Scout than of Oberon. That had to be a first.

The shot hit Boy Scout in the chest. Because of his enchanted T-shirt, it felt like someone poking him hard in the chest. Sunshine gaped at his gun as if the weapon had personally betrayed him. It wasn't too far from the expression a kid might give a toy gun that had the audacity to run out of batteries.

More shots rang out as Boy Scout drew his glass gun. Cuban fired at Sunshine, clipping the crime boss in the shoulder and sending him scurrying back into the office. The two Marines by the bar shot at the mages. Three of the mages and two witches opened fire with pistols, which was smart, and a little scary. Human magic didn't work like in fantasy books or roleplaying games. It was more subtle. Devastating, but subtle, and unfortunately for mages and witches in combat, not anywhere near as fast as a bullet. Mixing bullets and magic meant they could do some serious damage.

While the bullets flew, Cendrine rushed forward, her hair a halo of flames around her. Smoke rose from the scorch marks where her feet touched the floor. She grabbed the bottom of a couch, set it ablaze, and flipped it across the room. Two witches and two mages were so focused on shooting at the Marines, they didn't see the couch until it slammed into them, pinning them to the wall.

Unlike human magic, Faerie magic could be quick, flashy, and instantly deadly.

Two shots hit Boy Scout in the back. He ignored them. Only a head shot would take him out of the fight, and those were challenging for even the best marksmen in the middle of a fight. He trusted Cendrine to take care of extraneous gunmen while he dealt with the leader.

Boy Scout took aim on pool-table-guy. He had a crystalline wand out and was waving it over a half-full wine glass. Boy Scout smiled. Oh the irony.

On the other side of the room, the two Marines by the bar stopped shooting. Their mouths opened, and Boy Scout imagined they must be screaming. Their stomachs erupted like bloody claymore mines, sending blood and entrails across half the room. The mages must have spiked the drinks with something to create a sympathetic connection. After that, it was only a matter of time before the mage ruined your day.

Subtle, but vicious. Time to put an end to that shit.

When Boy Scout had the glass gun trained on pool-table-guy, he squeezed the trigger.

Every piece of glass in the room – the windows, the glasses, the bottles behind the bars, everything – shattered and flew at pool-table-guy. The broken pieces of mirror slashed at the mage's face. Moments later the rest of the glass, every shard and sliver, gathered in a whirlwind around the mage. His screams lasted about a second.

With pistol in hand, Cuban smoothly walked through the room. With each step, he took aim and fired, took aim and fired. With every shot, a mage's or witch's head snapped back, each dropping to the floor. Cuban was no mere marksman; target shooters could not maintain that level of calm in full combat. No, Cuban was a machine of war.

After four or five shots – between gunfire, roaring flames, and screams in this enclosed space, Boy Scout's ears rang too much for him to be sure, Cuban aimed at one of the witches. She rubbed a rabbit's foot in one hand, and tossed a shower of green stuff all around her. Boy Scout didn't have to jump far to take the leap of logic that those were four-leaf clovers. Even so many didn't surprise him. Some GMO company was probably making a fortune mass-producing them.

Boy Scout shouted to Cuban, tried to warn him, but the old Marine's ears were probably ringing louder than Boy Scout's. Cuban's next shot backfired. Boy Scout turned away as the cigar dropped from Cuban's mouth and blood sprayed out of the back of his head.

Cendrine waved toward that witch. The fire from the couch enveloped the girl, along with the two mages next to her.

Spinning on the ball of his foot, Boy Scout turned back to the office door, looking for Sunshine. The crime boss burst out of the office, toting an automatic shotgun. A weapon like that could ruin anyone's day, even if they were protected by a T-shirt.

Sunshine mouthed something. Probably something intimidating. Boy Scout didn't bother to try and decipher it. Sunshine was nothing more than a thug with a gun. Along with everything else, Boy Scout had been a warrior. As a warrior, he'd learned the hard way to just put the enemy down as efficiently as possible.

Boy Scout squeezed the trigger while Sunshine was still posturing.

The whirlwind of glass spun away from pool-table-boy, shaving off a mage's arm as he waved a wand at Cendrine before enveloping Sunshine.

With Sunshine neutralized, Boy Scout glanced around, looking for further threats. Everyone else except Cendrine and one cowering witch was dead.

Flames whipped around Cendrine about halfway between the floor and the ceiling. Blood poured from a gash on her forehead, and her jacket was missing a bunch of peacock feathers on the right shoulder, revealing a patch of mangled flesh.

All told, the whole fight had lasted less than a minute. If not for Cuban and the two Marines, Boy Scout knew Cendrine might not have survived and he'd be trussed up and carted off to Oberon.

Blinking and shaking his head, Boy Scout tried to get some semblance of hearing back. This wasn't over yet.

He turned to the front door. Just as he'd predicted, the Brute Squad, offensive throwback at the lead, burst in.

Boy Scout imagined what the scene must look like to them: the corpses, charred furniture, the whirlwind of glass, swirling flames, and Boy Scout and Cendrine standing at the center of the carnage.

"Who wants to die first?" Boy Scout couldn't hear himself, but felt the vibrations in his throat.

In what must have been a rare moment of clarity, the Brute Squad slowly backed away toward the door.

"You!" Boy Scout pointed the glass gun at the throwback. "Wait."

The throwback stopped and waited.

"Leave my blades," Boy Scout said, gesturing toward the pool table with his gun.

The throwback complied. Without any sudden movements, he placed the weapons on the pool table. The rest of the Brute Squad did not wait for him before clearing out.

Once Boy Scout and Cendrine were alone again, Boy Scout went over to Cuban.

The platoon sergeant – that's how Boy Scout would always think of him, no matter what rank he currently held – stared blankly at the ceiling. A good portion of the back of his head was missing. When Boy Scout reached down and closed Cuban's eyes, part of their first conversation came back to him, reaching through all the years and all the deaths, *Lies. That's what we'll call you, 'cause lies are all that reporters report.* His first military name, given when he joined First Platoon of Mike Company. Thinking of that made him remember the card in his war journal. He pulled the journal out of his pocket and took out the card.

Boy Scout who Lies, your friends need you. – Tommy

Seems he wasn't done playing the questing hero.

He felt a comforting hand on his shoulder. He looked up. Cendrine knelt next to him, one hand on his shoulder, the other hand offered him a golden whisky flask. The gash on her forehead was only a thin, pale scratch, and the injury on her shoulder looked like a bad rash.

After taking a healthy swig from the ancient whiskey, back from when it truly was the water of life, the ringing in his ears faded.

"You alright?" Cendrine asked.

Boy Scout shook his head. "Something isn't right, not adding up." he flipped the card from Tommy over and over in his fingers like a professional card shark. "I think this card means that some of my old platoon is still around. If that's true, then he's the man that could have pulled us together and taken a stand."

"Could that platoon really make a difference at this point?" Cendrine asked.

"Yes," Boy Scout replied. He happened to glance at the painting, the one from the artist. "That's it!"

"What?"

He pointed at the painting. "She's alive and painting. I had the idea that Oberon wanted us both, well, yeah, he wants us both, but so does the government. That's why the troops are massing. The U.S. wants to manipulate the ancient game between Seelie and Unseelie champions to close the gate."

"Holy shit," Cendrine said. "I think you're right. What do we do?"

Boy Scout held up Tommy's note. "We find my friends."

"Where do we start?" Cendrine asked.

"I'm going to search the office, see if I can find anything out."

"Alright," Cendrine said. "I'll keep you from being interrupted."

"But first, need to take care of a few things."

Boy Scout felt around Cuban's neck and wasn't surprised when he found a set of dog tags. He pulled them off Cuban's body and put them on. A familiar pressure settled on Boy Scout's shoulders. He searched through the fallen soldier's pockets and found a polished cigar cutter. That went into Boy Scout's jacket pocket.

He took Cuban's hand. "You were one of the best men I've ever known."

Of all the soldiers whose burdens he'd carried, Boy Scout could never have imagined this. He drew in a deep breath, and sang in the tradition of their time underhill during the war.

> Oh, all the comrades e'er I had,
> They're sorry for my going away,

Cendrine joined in.

> And all the sweethearts e'er I had,

357

They'd wish me one more day to stay,
But since it falls unto my lot,
That I should rise and you should not,
I gently rise and softly call,
That I should go and you should not,
Good night and joy be with you all."

The verse ended, Boy Scout knelt, holding Cuban's hand.

"Not your fault," Cendrine said.

"Maybe," Boy Scout replied. "Fault and blame don't matter. Dead is dead, and like so many others, my actions led to this."

With a sigh, Boy Scout released Cuban's hand, stood up, and headed for Sunshine's office. Beyond the open door, Boy Scout saw a table covered in newspapers, parchments, and books. That looked as good a place as any to start looking for anything that might point him in the right direction.

EPILOGUE: THE SECOND

Don't only practice your art, but force your way into its secrets...
— Ludwig van Beethoven

There is nothing to writing.
All you do is sit down at a typewriter and bleed.
— Ernest Hemingway

Max finished writing.

He closed the journal. It felt odd, knowing that he'd written his last story. At least now he knew what happened. He only wished he could stick around and help settle things.

"Wish," he said. "There's someone I miss. Ah, well. I won't miss anyone soon."

He scooped up the journal and a clean sheet of paper. That paper was the important part.

When he turned to go back into the front room, Max saw a painting peeking out from behind the open door. Even if he'd glanced that way coming in, the door would have blocked his view. He moved the door so he could get a better look at the painting. It showed a man in a Boy Scout uniform getting skewered with a disposable razor by some gray creature with wild blond braids. Attached to the canvas was a plastic bag with the remains of a syringe.

"Well, that's how they did it." Clever girl that artist was.

He couldn't help but laugh. It wasn't really that funny, he supposed, but then it was...or maybe it was just blood loss.

In the front room, Cendrine knelt over the body of one of the mages, paused in the act of going through his pockets.

The surviving witch still huddled in the far corner, though now a ring of fire about two feet high kept her trapped there. Max stared at the flames. He found even more beauty in them frozen in time than he did leaping about.

After a few moments, Max closed his eyes and shook his head. Free of the flame's lure, he went over to Cendrine and lay down. He didn't want to fall over when he put himself back into time. Part of him wanted to see how long he could keep going in this place between moments, but then nothing would get settled. He'd been a selfish prick far too long. Time to cowboy up.

Once he got relatively comfortable, Max dipped his finger in the hole in his chest. He touched it to the sheet of paper and wrote five letters.

S-T-A-R-T.

Pain blossomed in his chest, causing him to miss Cendrine's initial reaction at having him appear out of nowhere. By the time the white-hot pain faded from Max's vision and he could think clearly enough to make out words, he only heard Cendrine muttering, "Dad, please Dad, please Dad."

He coughed, but managed to get out, "Sssssssshhhhh."

"Oh, thank fuck," she said, and scrambled to get the flask to his lips.

"It's not going to be enough." Max coughed and shook his head. Save it for," cough, "someone it can help."

Blood and phlegm bubbled up when he laughed. He tried to spit it out before talking again, but couldn't get enough air or strength in his chest. The gooey mess wound up rolling down his cheek.

"If I'd known this would get you to call me *Dad*, I would have impaled myself a long time ago."

"We'll figure something out." Cendrine did her best to wipe the blood from his face. "Just hang on. Please? Dad, hang on."

Max shook his head. He held up the journal.

"Run," he begged. "They will know when I die." Cough. "They'll come here." Cough. "Read...read Tommy's story. Find him. Then find...and protect...the next champion."

Tears rolled down Cendrine's cheeks. Well, they made it about halfway down before boiling away to steam. Max felt nothing but cold. Yeah, that was a great sign.

He closed his eyes, ready for the darkness to take him.

She kissed his forehead. He felt the warmth of her lips there and smiled. That almost made dying worth it...almost.

Then he felt her breath next to his ear. She drew in a deep breath, and then sang him away.

> Of all the money that e'er I had
> I've spent it in good company
> And all the harm that e'er I've done
> Alas it was to none but me
> And all I've done for want of wit
> To memory now I can't recall
> So fill to me the parting glass
> Good night and joy be with you all.

> Of all the comrades that e'er I had
> They are sorry for my going away
> And all the sweethearts that e'er I had
> They would wish me one more day to stay
> But since it falls unto my lot
> That I should rise and you should not
> I'll gently rise and I'll softly call
> Good night and joy be with you all

> A man may drink and not be drunk
> A man may fight and not be slain
> A man may court a pretty girl
> And perhaps be welcomed back again
> But since it has so ought to be
> By a time to rise and a time to fall
> Come fill to me the parting glass
> Good night and joy be with you all
> Good night and joy be with you all.

Max's smile grew as his body and mind faded away.

She sounded so much like her mother...her voice made it easy to go gentle into that good night.

M. Todd Gallowglas

FUEL

The moon shone down on Lorzano the Grim, dread necromancer of the Phagian Brotherhood as he strode through the aftermath of the battle. Crows cawed above while all around him, the bodies of both sides of the battle lay waiting to be revived to do his bidding. Lorzano had enough servants trailing him for now, but kept his eyes scanning for possible replacements as well as fuel for his spells. He drew in a deep breath, taking in the scent of blood and gore.

As he breathed in, a sweet sent filled his nostrils. Yes, that was blood, but a far sweeter blood than he had ever smelled before. He must get a taste of that body. Surely any corpse that smelled like that would fuel his spells unlike any necromancer could ever imagine.

Shooing several crows from his re-animated servants, Lorzano sent them shambling off in search of the body that gave off that sweet smell.

A few moments later, Lorzano heard someone cry, "Hey! Get away from me you brain-dead cretin."

Following the sound of the voice as it continued to berated the servant, Lorzano discovered a man half buried beneath a pile of corpses wearing the armor and tabbards of the Legion of Light. He was handsome, pale, with eyes the color of blood.

"You're a vampire," Lorzano said.

"Thank you," the vampire said, "to the King of Obvious. Now help me out of here so I can report back to our master."

"Our master?" Lorzano asked.

"The Dread Lord of Shadows," the vampire said. "He who led us to this great victory."

"Oh," Lorzano said. "Him."

Lorzano didn't serve anyone save for himself. Though he did feel a certain kindness toward the Dread Lord for continuously providing material for spells and a host of potential servants.

"You smell good," Lorzano said, flicking his wrist and sending a servant off in search of something.

"Thanks," the vampire said. "Weird and creepy, but thanks. I suppose the weird and creepy are part of the necromancer gig, huh?"

"I suppose," Lorzano said. "Are you a master or thrall?"

"Do you think a thrall could defeat so many of these single handedly?" the vampire waved his hands over the pile of bodies around hem. "Now help me out of this and get me back to our master. My legs were damaged in the battle."

Lorzano got closer to the vampire and sniffed. Indeed, it was the source of the sweet-smelling blood. Lorzano had two of his servants grab the vampire's left arm.

"What are you—?" the vampire stopped speaking, face going slack with shock when Lorzano bit one of his fingers off.

Power unlike any he ever knew flooded through him as he chewed the vampire's flesh and bone and swallowed.

"Thank you," Lorzano said as his servant returned with a sturdy branch. "Rise my new pets."

The bodies around the vampire twitched and reanimated, each helping to pin the undead creature to the ground. Lorzano staked it through the heart, paralyzing it. I thrall would have crumbled to dust.

"Oh such wonderful feats I will achieve with you fueling my magic," Lorzano said. "Now, cloaks and blankets my pets. We must ensure the dawn does not steal my prize."

THOUGHT EXPERIMENT

Maxwell's demon got bored of opening and closing his door, and so he decided to help Schrödinger's Cat break the hell out of its box. Nobody missed the cat, because, face it, they would record it, and that recording would probably make its way onto YouTube, and nobody really wanted to be responsible for a dead cat video on YouTube. Any other cat video, cool. Dead cat video, bad. Bad, bad, bad.

"What now?" the Cat asked.

"We could really mess with people," the Demon said, "and let the beetles out of their boxes, too."

"Oooooohhh," the Cat replied. "Me likey."

And so they did. They let every beetle out of every box held by every person on the planet. The cascading effect of the loss of subjectivity ushered in a new era of peace and understanding greater than anyone could "Imagine," even a former Beatle.

"Now what?" the Cat and the Demon asked.

"Monkeys!" the Beetles cried. "Get the monkeys!"

"Not enough on the planet," the Cat and Demon said.

"We can clone them!" the Beetles cry.

"We don't have that technology," the Cat and Demon replied.

"We can simulate it in a computer," the Beetles suggest. "It's not like the monkeys need to be any more or less real than the rest of us."

And so to the computers they went, programming a simulation of infinitely cloning virtual monkeys, who set to work pounding away on infinitely spawning virtual typewriters.

Eventually, the Monkeys cried out in their virtual voices that they had indeed composed the complete works of Shakespeare.

"What now?" the Cat, the Demon, and the Beetles, but not a single Beatle, asked.

"The trees!" the Monkeys shouted in unison. "Make them hear the trees!"

"Nice!" The Cat, the Demon, and the Beetles replied, and, with the Monkeys' help, they all set about figuring out a way for humanity to hear a tree fall in the woods without actually being present.

M. Todd Gallowglas

Author's note: To truly appreciate this story, you may want to familiarize yourself with the following thought experiments: Maxwell's demon, Schrödinger's cat, beetle in a box, infinite monkey theorem, tree falling in the woods, and John Lennon

WHAT FOOLS

All throughout the convention center, geeks and nerds shook their phones, rebooted their phones, held their phones high over their heads looking up at the screens, hoping to get a signal. They had status updates and pictures they needed to post to Facebook, Twitter, Instagram, Tumblr, Pintrest, Google+, Reddit, Vine, Imgur, Snapchat ...

Which they couldn't ...

Not without internet access.

No one could get a signal.

No one could connect to the wireless network provided by the convention center.

Though none of the con-goers said as much, the posture of over 100,000 geeks and nerds pretty much told the story of what they'd been feeling for the last fifteen minutes: WHY CAN'T WE GET A FRAKKING SIGNAL???

High in the rafters above the Mecca of Media, Robin Goodfellow, the ancient trickster Puck, snickered, giggled, and snorted in his mirth. He half-expected some of the heads below to spontaneously combust as their fury rose.

Then, he stopped blocking the signal. A collective cheer went up throughout the hall. Then more grumbling, as over a hundred thousand devices tried to connect at once. Data moved at a pace that only the early 90s would have considered decent. And then, after only a small percentage of posts uploaded completely, while all the others were stuck somewhere in loading bar limbo, Puck shut off the connection again, and cackled at the reaction.

PASSING THE TORCH
A *DEAD WEIGHT* Story

"I will not light some unseelie bitches' hair on fire," Cendrine said, again. "I will not light some unseelie bitches' hair on fire."

Cendrine lay under her bunk, rolling her Zippo between her fingers, flicked it open, and lit it. At one point, she could have coaxed the fire to dance across the room. But she'd had problems with that talent for a couple years now, so she had to content herself with spying on the Skank Twins, so she and her friend Wisdom could foil their plans for revenge.

The trouble started Cendrine's first night at the shelter. The two unseelie half-breeds had decided to help themselves to Cendrine's dinner. Before Cendrine could protest, a girl who looked like "Rowdy" Ronda Rousey ate Warrior Princess Xena hit one of the girls full in the face with a tray. Before it escalated, someone called, "Mr. Tightpants!" Everyone became best friends, momentarily. A few nights later, one of the twins slipped in the shower trying to start something with Wisdom. Now Cendrine and Wisdom could surprise the Skank Twins again.

Strange, Cendrine had never thought of herself as part of they or them. Dad and her Uncles took care of her, but she'd never had a friend her own age.

The Twins' conversation changed to seducing Mr. Tower. Some girls called the lead councilor "Mr. Tightpants," because he reminded them the the captain on that old show, Firefly. A moment later, the conversation stopped all together.

Footsteps, steady and measured, grew steadily closer, until finally a pair of black motorcycle boots stopped next to Cendrine's cot.

"You can come out." She recognized Uncle Hal's voice. "We need to talk."

Cendrine slid out from under her bed. The wizard hadn't changed since the last time she'd seen him with his white canvas duster, covered in arcane symbols, with his unruly dishwater hair pulled into a pony tail.

Cendrine prepared to ask…

…and then…

made eye contact. Her mouth died, and her throat closed up. All memory of what she'd planned to say vanished.

"We need to talk." The wizard craned his head toward the door. "Outside."

The fires got out of control after Cendrine's father left her with Uncle Wash. They though she was asleep in the loft, and the cabin's acoustics carried their argument right to her.

"I can't do this on my own," Uncle Wash said.

"You have help," Dad said.

"Every couple of weeks,' Uncle Wash replied. "If I'm lucky. The girl needs her father."

"I have to make things right," Dad said. "Me. No one else. And I can't bring her along. What happens when certain people find out who she is?"

Silence hung over the downstairs.

"You're alive because of me," Dad said.

"I hate you," Uncle Wash said.

"Don't change a thing."

"You're an asshole."

"Maybe. But a good enough father to hide my daughter from the war."

Dad sighed. "Fair enough."

Footsteps crossed the cabin's floor, the door opened, and then closed.

"Shit," Uncle Wash said.

Cendrine crept to the edge of her loft and looked down. Even with the light glowing from the burning log in the fireplace, with his blue-black skin and dark clothes she could barely make out Uncle Wash.

"Shit."

She'd never uttered a bad word before, but she nothing else seemed to fit. Sparks leapt from the fireplace, and all the pictures of Dad on the mantle went up in flames.

The skank twins sneered as Cendrine followed Hal out of the dorm.

"Twinkle twinky little bitch," Skank One said.

Skank Two followed with, "Mind your business, you noisy…" The rhyme ended with witch, but Skank Two sputtered a little when she glanced at the obvious wizard in the room.

"Coward," Cendrine said.

Hal grabbed Cendrine by the shoulder and shoved.

"Making friends and influencing people."

"Where are we going?" Cendrine asked when she caught up with him.

"Outside," Hal replied.

"Like outside," Cendrine pointed to the twin glass doors where snow gathered in deep piles, "outside?"

Hal kept walking toward the doors. Cendrine hesitated. The cold and snow were the only reasons why she'd come to the shelter for half-breed orphans of the Faerie War.

"Excuse me, sir." Cendrine didn't recognize the lady at the front desk. She was pretty, what the kids called a bleeder, as in "a bleeding heart" come to help the "less fortunate." Bleeders didn't last long with reality of kids infused with the nature of the unseelie. Cendrine was the only seelie-blooded in the shelter.

"What?" Hal fixed a steady gaze at her.

The bleeder stammered about not taking one of the children out of the shelter.

"I'll handle this, Katie," Mr Tower said, coming out of the back office. "Why don't you head on home. Snow is supposed to come down heavy tonight."

"Yes, Mr Tower."

She looked like a Katie, with her pony tail and make up. Katie wasted no time in leaving.

"Good evening, South." Mr. Tower glanced back and forth between Cendrine and Hal. "Is everything okay?"

"South?" Hal asked. "Really?"

"Yeah," Cendrine replied. "They call me that on account I'm from Southern California."

"Of course."

"Everything is fine, Mr. Tower," Cendrine said. "This is my Uncle Hal."

"Uncle Hal?" He didn't sound convinced.

"Not my real uncle," Cendrine said. "Uncle Hal served with my dad during the war."

"Excuse me," Mr Tower straightened. "We can never tell when someone wants to take advantage of one of the kids." Mr. Tower extended his hand to the wizard. "Thank you for your service."

Hal shook Mr. Tower's hand. After a few tense seconds, their grips tightened. Mr. Tower's lips pressed together. Hal's head cocked slightly to the side and he pursed his lips.

"Interesting," Hal said as he released his grip.

"Interesting how?" Mr. Tower asked.

"Do you believe in fate, M. Tower?" Hal asked. "The war to make me believe. It's nice to know my little darling here managed to end up right where she needed to be. Especially during the holiday season. It's the solstice tonight."

"I didn't know that." Why would Mr. Tower lie. He'd been wishing all the kids, a "Happy solstice," all day especially all the prettiest girls like the Skank Twins.

"Can I go just outside the door, Mr. Tower," Cendrine said. "I'll stay right on the landing."

"Should be okay," Mr. Tower said. "But, if I see you step down to the street, outside privileges are gone for a month."

"Yes, sir." She turned to the wizard. "Shall we, Uncle Hal."

"Yes." Hal wrapped his arm around Cendrine. "Outside. Like, outside, outside."

When the door closed behind them, Hal leaned against the building. He pulled a pack of gum out of his pocket and offered some to Cendrine. She shook her head. Hal shrugged, unwrapped a piece, and popping it into his mouth. Even chomping on a piece of gum, Hal exuded an air of mess-with-me-and-getting-turned-into-a-frog-will-be-the-least-of-your-worries.

"The world is fucked."

"You don't say?" Cendrine quipped.

"Okay. Got me there." Hal looked her over. "Why don't you warm yourself up?"

"C-c-c-ca-an't," Cendrine said.

"Or won't?"

Cendrine forced her teeth together so she could speak as normally. "Can't. Ever since… since…"

"Since what?"

"Since I burned Uncle Wash." The wintery air felt warm compared to the icy lump in her stomach. "Sometimes if I'm lucky or angry, I can ask fire to do things for me, but I can't generate any heat on my own."

"That's the problem," Hal said. "You freaked out. But you have responsibilities above and beyond yourself."

"Yeah," Cendrine said. "You're important. Gotta be careful and stay hidden. Blah, blah, blah. Heard it all before."

"It's bigger than you think. For starters, this," he made a wide gesture toward the sky, "is at least half you. That block against your inner heat gives Oberon and his cold suck-ups an open invitation to screw with the environment, and it's only the beginning. Some of us tried fixing it. Managed to stall it a few years, but it really has to be you. Hot and cold. Winter and summer. Seelie and unseelie."

"Oh shit." Cendrine said. "You're sending me on a quest."

"Yes indeed."

"Who is our third?"

"Oh, sweet child," Uncle Hal said. "Wizards don't go on quests. We send other people on quests."

Uncle Hal explained what she needed to do and why it needed to happen that night. It was Solstice, after all.

One morning, Cendrine woke to a racket. Uncle Wash cursed in between bangs and clatters. Cendrine looked over the edge of the loft to see Uncle Wash carrying an armload of stuff out the door and a plethora of empty beer bottles on the table.

Cendrine reached the front door just in time to see Uncle Wash toss everything onto a pile about twenty paces from the cabin. The pile was made up all the things Dad had left her. Many of them charred around the edges.

Cendrine wrapped her arms around herself as she stepped onto the porch and into the brisk morning air.

"What are you doing?"

Uncle Wash turned around. Once he'd been full of life, if a bit melancholy. Now he stooped with a deep, weary sorrow.

"You want to burn your father's shit?" Uncle Wash picked up one of the spare gas cans and started splashing it over the. "Let's do it all at once."

"Wait," Cendrine said. "What?"

He took a lighter out of his pocket.

"Please. No." Tears rolled down Cendrine's cheeks as she dropped to her knees next to Uncle Wash. "I'll get it under control." She tried to grab the lighter. "Don't do this."

Uncle Wash jerked the hand away.

Steam rose from Cendrine's face where the tears had been.

He tossed the lighter onto the pile. The gasoline lit immediately. The morning chill vanished, chased away by the growing flames.

"No!" Cendrine screamed. "Stop!"

She drew in a long, deep breath. The flames obeyed her, leaping from Dad's stuff and going straight to Cendrine. She drew them in easily. Unfortunately, Uncle Wash stood between Cendrine and the fire. His skin charred and bubbled as the flames swarmed passed him. His clothes caught. Flames were fickle and mischievous at the best of times, but Cendrine managed to call those into her as well.

"Could my life be any more cliché?" Cendrine muttered. "Lost faerie princess? Check. Magical curse threatening the world? Check. Punk ass wizard to send me on the quest without offering to help? Check. Let's not forget, get it all done in one night."

Cendrine didn't know why quests needed three people. One more stupid rule of Faerie. So, she needed two more idiots. The first should be fairly easy, but she had no clue about the other.

Heading toward the cafeteria, Cendrine passed the Skank Twins. They glared. Cendrine shrugged. Their rivalry didn't seem quite as important.

In the cafeteria, Cendrine saw Wisdom by herself at a table for six. Teenagers, in groups of three to seven, sat at various sized tables, bantering back and forth. Even with the gruff and surly nature of being unseelie, these were social creatures. What must it be like to be the outcast among this community?

"I just realized," Wisdom said as Cendrine sat down, "I ain't never met a Mick before."

If Cendrine rose to the bait, it could go on for a while. Time was ticking, so Cendrine let it go.

"We're friends, right?" Cendrine asked.

Wisdom looked up. "Translation: you want something, probably something crazy, stupid, or both. You got no other friends, so you come to smart, strong, and sexy Wisdom. How close am I?"

"Yeah," Cendrine sighed. "Right on the money."

"I like your honesty." She spooned some mashed potatoes into her mouth. "Admire it. Not a lot to admire in this place. You been here, two months? Nobody caught you in one lie. Sure, you got secrets, we all do, but secrets ain't the same as lying. Tell me this, Mick. Why'd you run away? No one ever heard of a Mick running from home. Everyone knows seelies takes gooooood care of their Mick babies." Wisdom put her elbows on the table, her chin in her hands, and stared at Cendrine with her jet-black eyes. "So tell me, South, what's your sob story?"

"First," Cendrine held up a finger, "plenty seelie kids run away. They got a shelter over in Berkeley. I got stuck on this side of the Bay when the snows came." She held up another finger. "Two, our families have drama too." As raised raised another finger, she leaned in close. "And I don't even have a happy beginning. Mom died the moment before I was born, Dad abandoned me, and I'm on a quest to save the world, and it's got to be tonight."

"No horse shit, South?"

"No horse shit, Wisdom."

Cendrine breathed easier when Wisdom gave her a wide grin.

"I'm in."

"In on what?" asked a voice right next to them.

Both Cendrine and Wisdom jumped.

Blink, the shelter's other outcast, stood next to the table. Unlike Wisdom, who pissed everyone off, Blink just didn't fit in. He gave off an awkward vibe, laughed at stuff that wasn't funny, and no one could tell what faerie stock he'd come from. Blink didn't have the unearthly beauty or alien oddness of having a faerie parent. He looked too human...xcept his cloths. His wardrobe was the love child steampunk anime and motorcycle thug. He walked around the place like he had invented the internet. When people noticed him all. Blink and he'd already be walking away gone or suddenly be right there.

"Jeezus," Wisdom snapped. "Step back meatbag. This is an A and B conversation so see your ass out of it."

"Let's consult the Magic Eight Ball." Blink pantomiming holding something and shaking it. A moment later, he examined it. "Outcome seems unlikely. Besides..."

He went over to another table. "You using this chair? Don't answer. I know you're not. I'm just being polite."

Blink dragged it back over to their table, spun the chair around, and sat resting his arms on the back of the chair.

"We had plenty of chairs here," Cendrine said.

"I like this one," Blink said.

"You're still here, meatbag? Wisdom snorted.

"Nah." Blink leaned in and lowered his voice. "You need a third."

"A third for what?" Cendrine asked, while at the same time, Wisdom said, "Even if we did, we wouldn't ask you."

"Look. You don't have time to be picky." Blink looked at Cendrine. "That guy, your uncle who isn't your uncle, gave you a quest."

"Did not," Wisdom said. "No scram before I scramble your face."

"Hold that thought," Blink reached inside his coat and brought out a baseball. "No, that's not it." He set the ball down. "That's for later."

While Blink rummaged around inside his various pockets, Wisdom picked up the baseball, turning it over and over. She blinked a couple of times.

"Is this Panda's signature?"

"Panda?" Cendrine asked.

"Yeah. Panda." Wisdom held the ball up, showing off a sgintature. "Pablo Sandoval. Played for the Giants."

"Yeah," Blink said without looking up from his rummaging. "My dad got that during the Twenty Fourteen World Series. Knew you liked the Giants before I left home, so I snagged it." He reached up, took the ball from Wisdom, and put it back in his coat. "Can't wait to surprise you with it."

"If that's for me, give it over," Wisdom said. "You ruined the surprise."

"Nope. Aaaand…Nope." Blink continued rummaging. "Ah ha! I was sitting on it."

Blink put a battered notebook on the table and opened it to a dog-eared page.

"Read right there." Blink put his finger down. "But no touchy."

Cendrine red the sentence beginning at Blink's fingertip.

"Oh you sweet child," Uncle Hal said. "Wizards don't go on quests. We send other people on quests."

"Wrote that six months ago." Blink snatched the journal back. "Took a while to find you. The snow threw me off. Sometimes the talent is a little vague."

"Holy shit," Wisdom said. "You're a—"

"Ixnay on the ardbay," Blink said. "Don't need some secrets getting out."

Wisdom leaned back in her chair, folded her arms, and smiled smugly. "I toldja he was a meatbag."

"You're very smart," Blink said. "We going on a quest, or what?"

"Aren't you supposed to not get involved?"

"Riiiiiight," Blink said. "Amazing what people believe, even when presented with facts. Global warming. Anti-vaccine movement. Magic is real. Bards don't get involved. And you still need a third."

"He's got a point," Cendrine said. "And, we can't be picky."

Wisdom rolled her eyes. "It's your quest."

"Looks like we have three," Cendrine said.

"Cool." Blink stuffed his notebook back into his pocket. "See you outside later on."

"We haven't even told you when," Cendrine said.

"I already know when," Blink said, "and where."

With that, he strutted away like he was a prince of Faerie rather than some unknown street bard.

"Fucking bards," Wisdom said. "So, what this quest anyway?"

"Save summer," Cendrine said. "Now, how do we get out of here?"

Wisdom grinned. "Oh, that's easy. Go to bed. But don't go to sleep. Be ready."

Eventually, Uncle Wash recovered, mostly. His skin had some scarring, and his left eye couldn't focus on anything longer than a few seconds.

They fell into their old routine, with changes. Cendrine read to Uncle Wash on Tuesdays and Thursdays. They didn't discuss the movies on Wednesday. Friday game night sucked the most. Since Uncle Wash wouldn't talk, they defaulted to go, checkers, and chess. Uncle Wash would snap his fingers once for "check" and twice for "check mate."

On the third anniversary of the incident Uncle Wash handed Cendrine his Bible. He'd circled a passage, Exodus 21:25 "...burn for burn, wound for wound, bruise for bruise."

Cendrine filled a back pack with clothes, a couple of her favorite books, and nonperishables from the kitchen.

Uncle Wash didn't say anything when Cendrine left. Before the sun set fully, she left the cabin behind heading for San Francisco.

Soft breathing and snores filled the girl's dorm room. A few times, Cendrine almost drifted off to sleep, but the churning ball of anticipation and nerves in the pit of her stomach kept her awake

When Wisdom's face appeared, chin resting on the mattress, it took every bit of Cenrine's self-control to not scream.

"It's time," Wisdom said. "Get dressed."

"Never got undressed," Cendrine replied.

"Good thinking. When I go, make a break for it. Meet at the stop and rob."

"Uh," Cendrine said. "Okay."

Wisdom jumped up and dashed across the room and broke out singing, "I wanna be an air born ranger. I wanna live a life of danger."

While people screamed and yelled at being woken up, Cendrine slid off of her cot and crawled to other door. She pushed it open a crack. It looked like everyone but Ralphie, the night door guy had gone after Wisdom.

Craning her neck and glancing around to makesure Ralphie was alone, Cendrine sprinted toward the door that lead out into the cold, snowy night.

"Hey!" Ralphie called as Cendrine raced by. "Tower won't be happy when you get back."

When she hit the cold air, Cendrine considered going back and snuggling under her blankets, but then she heard Uncle Hal's voice, "If you do nothing, eventually, Earth will look like Jötunheimr's ugly twin sister, warmth gone forever."

Cendrine took a deep breath and tightened her core muscles, willing the heat within her to overcome the chill she'd just sucked in. The weather might be cold and frigged, but Cendrine reminded herself that she was a creature of heat, flame, and summer. Having pushed the reset button on her resolve, Cendrine headed down the street.

The "stop and rob" was a little goblin stall down the street from the shelter, hoping to do business with the half-breeds. People called it a "stop and rob" because the goblin didn't have the protection of a real goblin market and the protection that came with neutral ground.

"No." Cendrine cut the goblin off.

"But," the goblin said.

"Piss off," Cendrine flicked her Zippo open, "or your cart will burn."

"Yes, Your High—"

"No honorifics." Cendrine cut him off. "Not ever. I'm not who you think I am."

"Riiiight." The goblin bobbed its head and went back to its stall. "Beg your forgiveness."

Not a minute later, Blink sauntered down the street.

"Knew you'd make it," Blink said. "And here comes Wisdom."

Glass shattered somewhere down the street. Cendrine looked to see Wisdom fly out of a second story window and land on top of an abandoned car, caving in the roof. She crawled out of the wreckage, raised a finger, and ran toward the stop and rob.

"You alright?" Cendrine asked.

"Yeah," Wisdom said. "Mine is a hearty breed. Get it from my dad. Where the hell is he going?"

Blink was heading toward a couple that had gone up to the stall. They wore warm clothes without any holes or patching. They looked late middle aged and pointed at the sheltered. Sometimes wealthy folks liked to go slumming in "exotic" post-war San Francisco.

"I can't help you," the goblin said.

"If I might be so bold," Blink said. The goblin's cursing drown out the rest of the conversation as the three humans walked away.

"Don't worry," Blink shouted over his shoulder. "I'll catch up with you."

"Heard rumors about that meatbag," Wisdom sneered. "Looks like they weren't rumors."

"No reason not to believe him," Cendrine said. "He's the one that knows that kind of stuff."

"Still rude to get paid for nookie in the middle of a quest," Wisdom said.

"You don't know if that's what he's doing." Cendrine ignored Wisdom's look. "Well, first thing we need to get is a tree. Any tree will do, but an evergreen would be best."

"How about a full-blown Christmas tree?" Wisdom asked.

"In San Francisco?"

"Oh, yeah," Wisdom said.

Cendrine smiled. "Lead on MacDuff."

They walked for about an hour before Wisdom stopped, sat down, and started unlacing her shoes.

Halfway through the first shoe, she looked up. "Well?"

"Well what?"

"Laces," Wisdom replied. "You want the tree? Give up your laces to the cause."

Cendrine sat down. Cold seeped from the concrete into her butt. After a few teeth chattering moments — she tried to control herself, but freezing butt was above and beyond — Cendrine handed her shoelaces to Wisdom.

Braiding the laces with practiced ease, Wisdom stood and flicked the rope upward. After a couple of tries, she wrapped the rope around the fire escape ladder so that it didn't slip when she tugged. They climbed upward while Wisdom quietly hummed the Mission Impossible theme.

On the fourth floor, Wisdom jimmied a window open without the slightest squeak or groan. For someone who made such a spectacle of talking a big talk and walking a bigger walk, Wisdom achieved an eerie, almost-silence crawling through the window. Not-quite succeeding to mimic her friend's movements, Cendrine followed Wisdom into the apartment. Stepping from a shelf to the floor, Cendrine lost her balance and fell with a loud thud.

"Shit," Wisdom said. "We gotta move. Now."

Standing, Cendrine found herself in a room that looked like multiple denizens of the North Pole had vomited all over the room. Stockings, manger, presents, and lights surrounded a Christmas tree with so many decorations that Cendrine couldn't see a single bit of actual tree. It was perfect.

Wisdom pushed the tree over. "Grab the top."

Cendrine did so and maneuvered toward the window. Something crashed elsewhere in the apartment, followed by shouting.

Cendrine had one foot on the fire escape when the door on the other side of the room opened. A hulking form filled the doorframe, with hair and beard tied in braids as thick as Cendrine's forearms. A bulbous nose sniffed the air. Black eyes scanned the room from underneath a massive ridge of a forehead. Its mouth hung slightly open revealing slight tusks. It was a Fir Bolg, fierce warriors and the faerie equivalent of Neanderthals. They sided with the unseelie court to avoid extinction.

"I will feast upon your entrails!" the Fir Bolg's voice shook the windows. "Wisdom? Is that you?"

"Go. Go. Go." Wisdom pushed her end so hard Cendrine nearly fell off the fire escape.

"Wisdom sweetie," the Fir Bolg said, "what's going on? Please, come home? Your family misses you."

Why didn't they just ask him for the tree to save the world? Then again, being unseelie, he might relish the idea of eternal winter.

When Wisdom was halfway out the window, the Fir Bolg grabbed her shoulder. An instant later, the window exploded. Cendrine started so badly, she slid down to the next level. While sputtering a string of expletives in ancient Irish, the Fir Bolg jerked his arm inside. The glass wouldn't hurt him, but a shock like that would make just about anyone jump back.

A baseball landed on the fire escape next to Wisdom.

"Merry Christmas, beautiful!" Blink shouted from the street below. "Surprise."

After tossing the tree over the side of the fire escape, Wisdom poured gray powder all over the windowsill.

"Thanks, meatbag!" Wisdom snatched the ball up and put it in her pocket as she slid down the ladder. "That was a hell of a surprise."

"What was that stuff?" Cendrine asked.

"Mix of salt and iron shavings," Wisdom said. "Dad hates it. Can't go anywhere near it. Now, less talking. More moving."

Cendrine laughed as they descended.

When they reached the street, Cendrine and Wisdom picked up the tree and ran like hell. Several blocks later, they paused, breathing puffs of steam.

"Shit," Cendrine said as she realized that since they'd caused a bit of mischief and chaos in getting the tree, she was going to have to balance that kindness and generosity for the Yule log.

"You okay?" Wisdom asked.

"Yeah," Cendrine replied. "I have one last thing to do." She gestured at the tree. "Can you two get this to the shelter?"

"You don't sound too keen on this, Wisdom said.

"Doesn't matter what she wants," Blink said. "It's the way it's got to be."

"Fair enough," Wisdom said. "See you back at the shelter."

"Thanks," Cendrine said. "We gotta be there at midnight, sharp to save the world."

As Wisdom and Blink carried the Christmas tree off toward the shelter, Cendrine took her lighter out of her pocket and flicked the flame on.

"Alright," she whispered to the tiny fire, "where's my dad?"

San Francisco sucked. The cabin got chilly sometimes, even cold in the winter, but nothing like this perpetual foggy damp. A week in, she was exhausted, starving, and no closer to finding Dad. On the seventh day, she'd heard the Height-Ashburry made for good panhandling. On her wat there, she saw a familiar duster covered in arcane symbols.

Excitement overcoming his normal intimidation, Cendrine wrapped him in a bear hug.

"Got a present for you, kiddo," the Wizard said. "Well, three. A meal." He handed her a paper bag. "An address." He handed her a piece of paper. "It's a shelter that caters to half-breeds, keeps them safe." He handed her a small rectangle of silvery metal.

"A lighter?" Cendrine turned it over in her hands. It had a Chinese character engraved on one side. "What's this mean?"

"Not just a lighter. A Zippo. Your mother gave it to your dad. He lost it during a severe self-pity party. The character means south."

She smiled. "Figures."

"If you ask, the flame will point to anyone in your family, and it will never run out of fuel."

"Thanks, Uncle Hal."

He nodded and walked away, ending the conversation.

Cendrine devoured the sandwhich. Then asked the flame to lead her to her father.

Two days later, the first snow fell, and she went to the shelter.

Cendrine found Dad near what used to be the Tenderloin, in much the same condition as she had the last time, only this time, he wasn't just strung out on drugs, he was near freezing to death. She didn't want to be pleasant about this, but Faerie demanded traditions be met. Cendrine couldn't afford to ignore the old traditions. Using the Yule log to force the season to change required balance: good and bad, light and dark, and well, the stunt with the Christmas tree covered the naughty. Now for nice.

When Cendrine found her dad, he looked up from the floor, eyes unfocused.

"Hey." Cendrine sat next to him. "I brought you presents."

She looped a small leather bag attached chord around his neck. "If you ever want to kick the habit, this clear your system and break the addiction."

First time she'd found him, he held up a piece of paper with I've got to live through this until we meet again the third time. Being one of the strongest bardic talents in the world, she took that on faith. She'd gone to a goblin market and gotten that powded to give to him on their second or third meeting.

"Here's a sleeping bag and some food. You should try and eat."

"Baby girl?" Dad said, his voice slurred. "That you?"

"Yeah. It's me." She stroked his head. She wanted to yell, scream, and burn the place to the ground to find the Yule log. "I need that last piece of Mom. The lighter won't take me to it, because…" Her throat closed up. "Well, you know why."

"Southwest corner. Seventh row out. Third up."

Cendrine followed the directions and pried up the appropriate board. Inside the hidey-hole, she found a long piece of charred timber. This held the essence of the final December Fire Goddess.

"I'm taking Mom," Cendrine said. "Your selfishness has messed up the world and me. I'm going to set a few things right, until you're ready for the bigger picture."

"Sounds good sweetie."

That was affirmative enough for faerie magic.

Just to make sure, she covered all her niceness bases, Cendrine tucked him into the sleeping bag and kissed him on the forehead.

Cradling Mother's remains, Cendrine didn't think she could be that nice to someone so undeserving ever again. Leaving the building, Cendrine wondered if her daughter or granddaughter would hold her this tenderly when the torch passed again.

"Heh. Passing the torch."

Cendrine met Wisdom and Blink two blocks from the shelter.

"What's that?" Blink asked.

"It's the Yule log," Cendrine replied.

"Took you long enough," Blink said. "Plenty of logs in Golden Gate Park."

"Not a yule log, idiot," Wisdom said. "The Yule log. She's going to use it to fix the weather."

"Yeah," Cendrine said. "Meet my mother."

"Holy shit," Wisdom said. "I mean.. I…uh…Your High—"

"Stop. I'm South. You're Wisdom. Let's do this. I'm cold. I hate cold."

"Fair enough," Wisdom said. "Where?"

"Wizard said it had to be at the shelter," Cendrine replied. "Basketball court?"

It would be empty, and by the time anyone saw the fire, it should be big enough so people couldn't easily put it out.

Blink shook his invisible magic eight ball. "Outcome seems favorable."

Cendrine carried her mother, wondering at her ancestry's morbidity. Wisdom and Blink carried the Christmas whistling the theme from Hogan's Heroes.

Half a block away, she waved them two quiet.

"What the hell is that?" Wisdom asked.

"You hear it too?" Cendrine said.

"Think someone started without us?" Blink asked.

"Only who knows about this is Uncle Hal." Cendrine deepened her voice, "Wizards don't go on quests. We send other people on quests."

"Only one way to find out," Blink said. "We're committed anyway. It's coming up on midnight."

As they crept toward basketball court, the sounds became chanting. Cendrine made out a few random words of the Ancient Irish. Dad and Uncle Wash had tried to get her to learn it, but she'd blown it off, figuring she'd never have a use for it.

"Holy silent-shit-filled night." Wisdom started running, dragging the tree and Blink behind her.

"What?" Cendrine asked.

"Human sacrifice," Wisdom called, "to unleash the Godzilla of blizzards."

Cendrine broke into a sprint. The closer she got to the basketball court, the wind grew colder and faster.

At the gate, Cendrine saw Mr. Tower conduction a ritual. However, he wasn't human any more. He still bore a passing resemblance to Nathan Fillion, but his skin and hair were pure white. Instead of his sports coat and jeans, he wore a suit of icey Armor. No wonder Cendrine got chills every time she spoke to him. Inside the fence, snow fell faster, especially around the two basketball hoops. Each of the Skank Twins was tied to a pole, and snow covered them up to their armpits.

Cendrine barked orders. "Wisdom, stop Tower and keep him busy. Blink, free the...victims." If those two were going to die by faerie magic, by god, they were going to burn, not freeze.

Wisdom lobbed the Christmas tree over the fence. It landed inside the ritual space. Then she leapt, clearing the fence, and descended toward Tower, shouting, "Wisdom smash!"

Cendrine raced to the Christmas tree, sliding on her knees the last few feet and using the momentum to shove the Yule Log into the branches. She lit her zippo and placed the flame into the pine needles.

Wind whipped around her, causing snow to staunch any place that started burning.

"Any time now," Wisdom shouted.

Tower held a sword of ice and stalked toward Wisdom, who had a nasty gash in her forehead. As she scrambled away from Tower, Wisdom occasionally ripped up a chunk of the basketball court and flung it at Tower.

Turning back to the tree, Cendrine wondered what she could do. The unnatural weather seemed to have a survival instinct. What was wron?. Why couldn't she start this fire? She used to start fires without even without trying. Well, until the day she'd stopped a fire rather than start one.

Shoving her Zippo into her pocket, Cendrine grabbed hold of the Yule Log.

"I am Cendrine South, daughter of Kenna, Granddaughter of the last true Oberon of the Seelie court, heir to the December Fire of Solstice."

With those words, she released the flames of Uncle Wash's fire. The Yule erupted in flames. The Christmas tree caught fire. Old and new burned at the Midnight Solstice. Glorious heat surrounded Cendrine.

"Let's make this a fair fight."

With no effort at all, Cendrine coaxed a flame to leap to Mr. Tower. His sword and armor melted. He stood, stunned. Wisdom took advantage of his shock, picked him up, and slammed him into the bon fire. Hissing and steaming, Tower melted.

The world shifted around Cendrine. The wind and snow lessened. They wouldn't vanish entirely during this winter, but eventually, the seasons would return to normal.

"Hot coco?" Blink asked, passing paper cups first to the two girls he'd rescued, and then Cendrine and Wisdom.

"Where did you get those?" Wisdom asked.

"From them." Blink craned his neck toward the gate.

The couple from earlier that evening came walking in, followed by Uncle Hal. The lady carried several large bags of paper cups, the man two large thermoses.

"They want to donate their time and money to the shelter," Hal said.

"Our granddaughter…" the woman couldn't finish. Instead, she filled cups and passed them out to the children coming out of the shelter, most of them still in their pajama.

The man said. "We want to make sure nothing like that happens to any other feyborne if we can stop it."

"Really?" Wisdom asked. "Anyone else think this coincidence is a little too convenient"

Blink replied, "We're at ground zero for the greatest feat of magic since the War ended. Faerie magic doesn't do coincidence."

"Besides," Hal popped a piece of gum into his mouth, "'tis the season for miracles."

A QUIET CHAT ON A BRIDGE

Melany cocked her head to the side as she took her morning stroll across the Superhero Memorial Bridge. Was that someone crying? It took her a minute to figure out that the crying was coming from over the side of the bridge. She leaned over and looked down. There, Melany saw a figure sitting on the edge of the bridge, in all her white-costumed glory.

"Holy shit!" Melany exclaimed. "You're the Avenging Angel! Oops. Sorry for the language."

The woman looked up, bright green eyes brimming with tears.

"It's okay," the superhero said, lifting a keg. "Want a drink?"

That's when Melany saw the other three kegs stacked precariously next to one of the most famous superheroes in the world.

"Uh, no thank you." Melany blinked a few times, taking in the teary-eyed face looking up at her. "Are you okay?"

Avenging Angel floated upward, golden cape flowing behind her. She settled on the rail right next to Melany.

"Have you ever thought about dying?" Avenging Angel asked.

"Yeah," Melany said. "I think everyone does, well, except people like you."

"What do you mean 'people like me'?"

Melany stopped for a moment. The superhero's voice was so soft, so unlike any of her interviews or the news footage of her all the times she'd saved the city.

"Superheroes," Melany said. "Especially ones like you. You know, impervious."

"Impervious…" Avenging Angel sounded so weak, despite being able to lift a building without breaking a sweat. "Not so much. Bullets and blades and lasers and explosives, sure. But not to everything. I have cancer."

"Oh…" Melany said. "I'm so sorry."

"It's cool. Shit happens."

"Can they do…"

"Anything?"

Melany nodded.

Avenging Angel shook her head. "It's in my brain. Too far gone to consider chemo. So, I'm dying. It's okay. I'm getting plowed and then I'm going to see how far out into space I can fly, just to find out."

"What about The Pillars of Good?" Melany asked.

"My team?"

Melany nodded.

"I told them I needed some time off, that I'm getting a new secret identity. I just didn't tell them the secret identity is in Heaven." Avenging Angel sighed and held out her right hand. "I'm Claire."

Melany shook the superhero's hand. "Melany."

"Good to meet you."

Melany called in sick to work. They sat and chatted all day, sitting on top of the bridge. As the sun set, Claire set Melany back on the walkway, gave her a hug, and said, "Goodbye, Melany. Thanks for talking. This might just have been my best day ever."

With that, Avenging Angel flew upward. Melany cried as the dot that was a superhero got smaller and smaller.

When the dot became one with the darkening sky, Melany said, "Fuck cancer."

When she got home, Melany started researching pre-med college programs.

DIAMOND

On his seventy-fifth anniversary, James Michael Finnegan went to the market early, proud of himself that he remembered. At his age, things had begun to slip his mind with greater and greater ease, and…to be honest, dates had never really been his strong suit.

At the market, he got the nicest chocolates he could find, a bouquet of a dozen of bright red roses, and a package of fancy tea all the way from India. He used to do champagne, but he and Kathleen were not nearly as young as they used to be. Starting his journey home, James Michael felt like being saucy, so he walked two blocks out of his way and made reservations for dinner at the Cornerstone, the finest dining spot in three counties.

When he got home, James Michael Finnegan put his key in the lock, but when he tried to open it, the key would not turn. He stood there, wiggling the key, sometimes it was a bit tricky, but no amount of wiggling and jiggling would make it turn. He stood, perplexed. Had he and the Missus got in a fight? He was fairly certain he'd remember a fight bad enough for her to change the locks.

"James Michael!" he heard Kathleen calling from a ways off.

He turned toward her voice.

She was leaning out a window two houses down.

"Did you forget where you live again?" Kathleen called. "Get home before your coffee gets cold."

As James walked sheepishly into the house, his wife asked, "What are those for?"

"I remembered our anniversary!" he replied.

"Ah bless, dear, sweet man," she said. "Your old brain is full of holes, except where it matters."

SINGLE STEPS

SPELLPUNK

AUTHOR'S NOTE:

This is the first chapter of a novel I'm publishing a chapter or two a week on my Patreon Page. You'll be able to read everything the whole thing there for free as they come out. I'll occasionally ask for "Choose-Your-Own-Adventure" input from the readers, so you can affect the story. I also have some other neat goodies for my Patrons there too, including personal stories, free ebooks, and other neat stuff.

ABOUT *SPELLPUNK*:

Imagine waking up in an alley, cold, nauseous , with no memories.

Imagine finding out you have been thrust into a magical world that has existed alongside our world throughout human history, but that has remained hidden and secret for the last few centuries due to a pact between the normal, mundane society and the factions of the magical world.

Imagine that after learning this, you discover that you have magical empathic powers that threaten to overwealm you anytime you get too close to people.

With all that, imagine one of your only friends disappears under suspicious circumstances, and that you are the prime suspect, placing you at the center of a rising conflict between the ruling elite of magical society, the rebel faction who wants to live without constraints, and the enforcers of mundane society.

Now, imagine that with all that, you must learn to control your empathic powers before they drive you insane so you can save the world from a megalomaniac shapeshifter and an insane trickster spirit.

Welcome to a journey through the World Beyond the Sun and Before the Moon. Welcome to *SPELLPUNK*.

M. Todd Gallowglas

CHAPTER ONE

He woke up. Bad idea.

It wasn't the slow transition of waking from a night's sleep or a nap. This was the sudden alertness that comes with the realization of being in an unfamiliar place in an unfamiliar time. The threshold from sleep or unconsciousness shattered in less than the span of a moment, not because of the wet and cold that covered his body, nor the sharp edges that poked into his chest, arms, legs, and face.

He woke up because of the smell.

The San Francisco mystery smell – most often experienced Downtown, Market, and the Tenderloin, though it migrated to other parts of the city as well – contained a mix of urine, alcohol, vomit, and other things the mind could not discern. The mystery smell assaulted the nostrils in short bursts, usually when passing by an alley or a doorstep that afforded someone a few moments of privacy. The response? A quick shudder and a crinkling of the nose, then some mental or verbal acknowledgment, half-repulsed and half-amused, "Yep. That's San Francisco mystery smell." Then the moment was gone, the salty scent of the breeze off the Pacific Ocean carried the stench away to another victim.

The man groaned and coughed. He tried to remember what had happened the night before, but could not. He couldn't concentrate because the mystery smell did not pass. It lingered. The man's throat closed off. It persisted in its torment. His stomach churned. He realized as his mind acclimated to consciousness that he was laying, face down in a puddle of San Francisco mystery smell.

Vomit spewed out of his mouth, adding whatever he'd eaten and drunk, which wasn't much, recently to the mix.

He scrambled away. His muscles, stiff from the cold, protested, but he forced them to move anyway. He might regret it in a few minutes but not as much as he would if he left his face in the puddle of whatever-it-was. Though his rational mind knew he would be fine, the dark recesses of his brain, the place that had children sleeping under their covers with a flashlight handy after they see a scary movie, envisioned the mystery smell stuff burning the skin off his face.

Eyes scanning, he made his way over to another puddle. Taking a chance, he sniffed at it. Water. Not clean enough to drink. The thought of drinking anything made his stomach churn again, but he held it down. He thrust his face into the puddle and scrubbed with both hands.

A few minutes later, face raw, he sat leaning with his back against the wall of the alley. In the pre-dawn light, he saw a dumpster was at the far end, and by the amount of trash that littered the alley, nobody used it. Or maybe, it had gotten a whiff of whatever is was that he'd woken up face down in and vomited too.

He laughed at that thought, a quick, two-chuckle laugh, mostly because if he didn't laugh, he'd probably cry, or scream.

Concrete memories would not come to his mind. He could recall San Francisco mystery smell, and he thought that if he got behind the wheel of a manual transmission, his hands and feet would make the proper motions in the proper sequence to get a car moving. However, he couldn't remember his name, nor could he remember anyone that he might know. He remembered San Francisco; it had once been his home, but it wasn't now and hadn't been for years. He didn't remember where he lived now. He closed his eyes and delved for a memory, even the shadow of a memory that might give him something more to go on.

*   *

*

My life is gone. I'm stuck in that limbo place between waking and dreaming, that moment of disorientation, where everyone thinks "Who am I?" Only, I'm stuck there, because someone sucked out the part of me that other people have that reminds them of who they are and why they are here. Took the part of me that makes me me and hid it away somewhere. I feel like I should know where, but like everything else, I can't remember.

There are voices. Am I having an argument with myself? No. Neither of the voices are mine. I listen for a bit. The tones are words, and it takes me a few seconds to remember the language they are speaking. English. At least I'm pretty sure.

"What if he remembers?" There is a hint of snotty defiance in this voice.

"Nonsense." That voice belongs to the one who stripped my memories one by one. Well, maybe more than that at a time. If he'd done it like that, it would have taken a long time. Or maybe it wouldn't have. Maybe I didn't have that many memories to begin with. Anyway, I feel like I had the power to stop him, but I can't remember how. Or maybe it's that I didn't know how all along, and that's how he managed to take away me. "I left him with enough of his mind left to function, other than that he's a clean slate."

*　　　　 *

*

"A clean slate... slate... Slate..." The words echoed in his mind the way a song sometimes does? and it won't go away.

Slate. It was a simple random word, unrelated to anything. On the other hand, maybe it was related to something. Slates were empty things waiting to be filled up. He was like a slate. No, he was a slate, waiting.

"Slate."

His voice sounded strange. Not just because of the grating in his throat from the vomit and being thirsty. Light, not soft, but light, though he felt as if it could get heavy if he needed it to.

Slate swallowed. His throat burned even more.

He spoke anyway, despite the pain.

"I'm Slate. Hello, I'm Slate. Good morning, Slate." Saying it over and over made it seem more solid, more real, and most importantly, more a part of him, or him more a part of it. "Well, it's as good a name as anything else right now." And even as he said it, Slate knew that it wasn't true. Names were important, and that this one suited him somehow better than anything else he could come up with.

So now Slate had named himself. Now what?

Slate had on a pair of baggy sweat pants and a t-shirt, both wet. Nothing else. His arms and feet started to twitch with the realization that he was wet and cold, as if he hadn't remembered how to be cold until that moment. He looked around again, searching for something among the trash that he might use to warm up until he had some better options. Nothing, just wet garbage.

Movement at one end of the alley caught his eye. Two people, men from the build and height – one was normal sized, though he looked tiny next to the other, who was tall and broad-shouldered – walked toward him. The light was still dim, and it wasn't until they were halfway to Slate that he could make out anything other than the black coats that hung almost to their ankles. The coats hung open and Slate saw a sword hanging from each man's belt, and each of them had a metal breastplate protecting his torso.

"There he is," one said. Then after a pause, "You sure that's the Seed? He looks like a bum."

"It's the Seed," the other said. His voice sounded familiar, but Slate couldn't place it. "I just got confirmation. And you should be a bit more respectful, Christian. Sometimes Seeds come to nothing, but other times…" he let it trail off.

"Sometimes what, Marius?" The first, apparently Christian asked. "You know I hate it when you do that."

"I know." The delivery of those two words was so flat that Slate nearly missed the mockery hidden in them. From the lack of reaction of the taller man, Slate figured he missed it all together. "Sometimes they grow up to become Keldred Drae."

Christian, the big man, laughed. By this time that they had reached Slate and were looking down at him. Slate stared up at them.

"You don't need to see my identification," Slate said. For some reason, it felt right.

Christian gave Marius a questioning look.

"It's a movie reference," Marius said, "which is why you don't get it."

Christian shrugged. A simple gesture on any normal person; however, with him, it pulled the bottom of the long coat up several inches.

"Don't care much about it."

Christian's massive frame dominated Slate's field of vision – especially when he leaned over, pulled Slate onto his shoulder, and stood up.

"Wait a—" Slate started, but the metal of the breastplate pushed into his sternum and cut off his breath.

"Drop him," said a new voice, coming from the end of the alley.

Christian loosened his grip on Slate, and gravity did the rest. The ground hurt. A lot. And all Slate couldn't help but think: Why was it that sometimes people used the poorest choices of words? And why did other people have to take them so literally?

Taking a deep breath, Slate pushed the pain aside and rolled away from Christian and Marius. A third man stood in the mouth of the alley. His plain gray suit contrasted with the strangeness of Christian and Marius's clothes. He had black hair pulled into a braid wrapped a few times around his shoulders.

"Don't do this, Kyle." Marius drew his sword. A moment later, Christian did the same. "This doesn't concern you."

"Oh?" the newcomer, Kyle, asked. "Then that isn't the Seed you're trying to kidnap, and would have if I hadn't come along?

Christian took a step forward and raised his sword at Kyle. The blade was something like a cross between a longsword and a rapier. It could be used for either cutting or stabbing. *How do I know that?* More importantly, why did he know that and not his real name?

"Step away, Spellpunk," Christian said. "We've got a few more minutes before true dawn. If you leave now, I'll forget I saw you and not report you to the Council."

"I'm touched, Chris," Kyle said with mock sincerity. "I really am. You're one of the few people from my old life that still shows me any sort of kindness."

As Kyle spoke, he slowly reached inside his coat with his left hand.

Both Christian and Marius tensed. They moved apart slowly, creeping toward Kyle along opposite walls of the alley.

They stopped, Christian backed up a step, when Kyle produced a crystal the size of a golf ball. It pulsated with a green light.

The few seconds that the three men stood there waiting seemed to drag on. Slate could almost feel the emotions bouncing through alley, as if they had physical form. Christian hid his fear behind a wall of hate, a pure malice directed at Kyle. Marius appeared anger, his face bunched up and scowling, but deep down, he was calm and smug. His smiling eyes betrayed him, though Slate knew neither Kyle nor Christian could see that secret. Kyle stood, tossing the glowing crystal absently in his hand, a pillar of grim determination and steadfast confidence.

Kyle took two quick steps forward, a slight smile played on his lips.

Marius and Christian stopped their advance. Christian went so far as to push the left side of his coat back, revealing a revolver in a hip holster. The weapon was huge, like something out of an old western movie – only bigger – a weapon that only someone Christian's size could use and not have his arm ripped out of its socket.

At that, Kyle straightened his right arm, which had been bent casually at the elbow and bobbed time with the left tossing the crystal, and his thumb and first two fingers rubbed together. Such a little gesture, but Marius shifted his stance, putting most of his weight on his left foot and raising his sword arm so that arm and blade made one straight line from his shoulder pointing at Kyle. Christian drew the gun.

Slate felt like the spectator at a three-way tennis match, his gaze shifting rapid-fire between these strange figures fighting over him. And now that he thought about that, why were they pulling swords and guns and glowing crystals and threatening each other over him? Ha! Glowing crystals? If he wasn't so cold and felt so terrible, Slate would have sworn he was dreaming. Except, events were too linear for this to be a dream.

"Minutes to true dawn." Marius's voice quivered a bit, as if in fear, but somehow Slate knew he was faking. "No magic then, and we'll still have the guns. Last chance to walk away."

Kyle's smile widened.

"The only reason you're so willing to let me leave is because you don't want to run back to Virgil and tell him that a Spellpunk, much less Kyle the Traitor, took a Seed away from you. I don't care if he comes with me or if he goes his own way, but I am not going to allow the Collegium to warp another Seed's magic for its own ends."

That got Slate's attention. All three of them were crazy. He should have realized it before. His lack of memory, along with the exposure to the elements for who knows how long, and finding himself face down in a puddle of San Francisco mystery smell – all of that together must have lulled his senses, especially his good sense.

He had to get out of here.

His best bet was to get behind Christian and Marius and make a break for the far end of the ally. Glancing that way, he saw cars driving past. If he made it that far, they probably wouldn't follow him. At least Slate hoped and prayed and hoped again they weren't crazy enough to take this out to in front of a dozen potential witnesses.

Taking a deep breath, Slate scooted a few inches closer to the other end of the alley. The three other men turned their eyes to him, then each, who had been coiled and ready to snap, burst into motion.

Later, in hindsight, when he had time to consider these first moments in his new life, it amazed Slate at how much he noticed.

Kyle tossed the crystal into the air and slightly forward. Fire spouted from the barrel of Christian's gun, though there was no sound, despite the lack of a silencer of any kind. A cloud of mortar erupted from the wall on the other side of Kyle. If Kyle hadn't moved, the bullet probably would have vaporized his head. Marius charged. Kyle jumped forward again, smashed the crystal under his left heel. Marius slashed at Kyle's head. The blow did not connect. Kyle had vanished. (It was like that: Marius attacked and missed, and then Slate realized that Kyle wasn't there any longer.) Kyle reappeared next to Christian an instant later. Marius let the moment of his swing carry him around. Christian scrambled backward. Marius rushed for Kyle, drawing his gun as he did. Kyle spun on one foot, clipping Christian on the jaw with the other. Marius aimed his pistol at Kyle's head. He fired a silent shot and slashed at the back of Kyle's legs. Still on one foot, Kyle contorted. He bent sideways from the waste to avoid the gunshot while, and twisting, reached out, as if to block the sword with his hand. A blade shot out of Kyle's sleeve. It was a long, thin, double-edged weapon. It turned Marius's attack aside. A clang rang through the alley. Kyle's free foot slammed into Marius's thigh. Marius grunted and back away, keeping the point of his sword toward Kyle. Christian recovered pointed his gun at Kyle again. Kyle waved his freehand and a thin silver chain glinted in the growing light. The gun clicked, a misfire. "Fuck." Christian holstered the pistol and came upon Kyle's other side. Kyle backed up to the wall and placed the blade of his sword casually on his shoulder. Marius and Christian glanced questioningly at each other.

With this pause in the fighting, Slate realized how crazy it was that he was just sitting here watching these maniacs fighting over him. He scrambled to his feet and ran for the far end of the alley.

One of the people behind Slate called out in some unrecognizable language, and Slate felt his balance lurch, as if he was on an escalator that suddenly stopped and restarted again. Something grabbed him – it had to be something, because he felt pressure on his whole torso – and pulled him back. Then the pressure was gone, and Christian's face filled his view.

"Stay," the huge man said. Then he slammed Slate into the wall. The air whooshed out of Slate's chest. He crumpled.

"Oh, shi—" Christian started, but he ended in a pained grunt.

Christian fell beside Slate. His forehead scrapped red, his eyes rolled back into his head.

Metal rang on metal just above Slate. He looked up to see Marius and Kyle slashing and thrusting, parrying and dodging. All the while they stared at each other's eyes. It was as if their eyes were conducting a battle separate from their dueling swords. Slate froze, afraid any movement on his part might be taken as a threat by either of the swordsmen, who might then attack presumed threat.

Marius spoke. Again Slate couldn't understand his words, but he flinched when Marius's eyes flashed with silver energy when he finished. Christian's sword rattled on the tarmac, then it flew up into Marius's free hand. As soon as he had the second weapon, Marius unleashed a flurry of attacks. Kyle stepped back, once, twice, three times under that onslaught, never taking his eyes off Marius's.

A half smile formed on Kyle's lips. "Kneel."

Marius's lips parted in a clenched-toothed snarl and his breathing deepened. Kyle's smile grew as Marius's attacks slowed.

"Two weapons take a lot of concentration." Kyle's smile faded. His eyes flashed the same silvery energy that Marius's had. "I said, 'kneel.' Kneel before your better."

Marius's knees buckled. He closed his eyes and threw himself back, spinning both of his weapons in wide, alternating arcs. Two steps back, his foot came down on some unidentifiable sludge that might have been a close cousin to the San Francisco mystery smell. Marius pitched backward. With only an instant of wasted movement, Marius transformed the fall into a backward roll.

Kyle didn't follow him as Slate expected him to. Instead, Kyle took one step back to where Christian was struggling to rise. Kyle spun, and his foot caught the side of Christian's head. The large man slumped back to the ground. A small part of Slate wished that Christian would have fallen into the puddle of San Francisco mystery smell.

Marius came back to his feet and rushed at Kyle, the two blades spinning so fast Slate could barely track them; Kyle whipped his sword left and right and up and down, attempting to fend off the attack.

Slate sat unmoving, watching, eyes wide at the intricate pattern Marius wove with his weapons. He saw something, something important, and something that he didn't think Kyle saw. Slate blinked once from the dryness that came from his intense observation of the swordplay, and when his eyes opened, refreshed, Slate realized Kyle wasn't the intended victim of those whirling blades – Kyle's sword was, and a heartbeat later, Kyle over extended his weapon by maybe half an inch or so; that was all the opening Marius needed; with a flick of his wrists, Marius wrenched Kyle's sword out of his hand and sent it spinning through the air.

The sword spun end over end over above Marius's head. All three watched its journey. It hit the ground. *Clang.*

The sound pulled them out of their reverie, and all three spun into action: Marius lunged at Kyle, who had produced a second crystal; Kyle ducked and smashed the crystal under his palm and vanished before Marius's second attach could land; Slate shook off his bewilderment, and got to his feet as Kyle reappeared next to the fallen sword. Not looking back, Slate dashed away.

Pain stabbed at the back of Slate's head. In that distant space where the mind goes when pain comes suddenly, Slate realized the pain was going away from his scalp rather than into it; someone must be grabbing onto his hair; then the moment was gone, and Slate felt his feet keep moving as his head did not; his view shifted upward and he was staring up at the lightening sky; he stayed there for a second, horizontal in the air, then he slammed into the ground; Marius loomed in Slate's vision for a moment before the black clad man kicked Slate in the head. At least Slate had the pleasure of seeing Kyle come up from behind before the black spots of pain washed away Kyle, Marius, and everything else.

Something heavy fell on Slate. Slate grunted. Then a warm, thick liquid washed over him. The pain in his head faded and vision returned. Marius was on top of Slate. His throat gaped open, and blood gushed out in bursts that grew further and further apart.

Slate pushed his way out from underneath Marius and vomited. A small portion of Slate's mind – that little optimist that everyone has that keeps us sane and plugging when everything seems to be at its worst, that little voice that has kept humanity from mass suicide throughout all of civilization and before – said, "At least it's not that puddle of San Francisco Mystery Smell again." Though this time, most likely due to the experiential overload Slate had suffered in the few minutes he'd been awake, the vomiting continued until Slate writhed on the ground, choking up dry heaves.

Sometime after that – probably a few moments at most, though to Slate it felt like hours – Kyle helped Slate up and draped an over-large black coat over his shoulders. The world spun again, and the black spots of pain came back, along with a wave of dizziness that threatened to pitch slate forward. Kyle gripped Slate's shoulders and steadied him.

"I know you have no reason to trust me," Kyle's voice was soft and soothing; it helped to settle both Slate's head and stomach, "but we've got to get off the street. I have a friend near here. Let's get you cleaned up and settled. Then, you can go your own way if you want. If you don't trust me though, I'll leave you to go it your own way. Some people like it better. Some people even manage to make it that way, but not many."

Slate glanced at the two bodies, Marius and Christian. He wondered if Kyle had killed Christian as well. He stopped thinking about it. He didn't want to know. Somehow, Slate suspected he wasn't one of those people who could make it on his own. He managed a slight grunt along with his nod. What was he going to do, walk around San Francisco alone, covered in blood?

To continue reading go to:
www.patreon.com/mtoddgallowglas

ABOUT THE AUTHOR

For a brief time in the greater scope of the universe, M. Todd Gallowglas lived. He loved stories: hearing them, watching them, writing them, gaming them, and telling them. He is pleased that, to some people, his stories mattered.

Personalized Stopwatch Story

"Surprise Me."

"That's not how this works. You ~~get~~ make a wish. I fulfill the wish."

"Right. Surprise Me."

"You. Are. Not. Grasping. The. Concept."

"Oh, I get the concept. I'm just not picky. So, surprise me."

Sigh. "Fine."

"Gruff."

"Surprise."

Made in the USA
Charleston, SC
05 February 2017